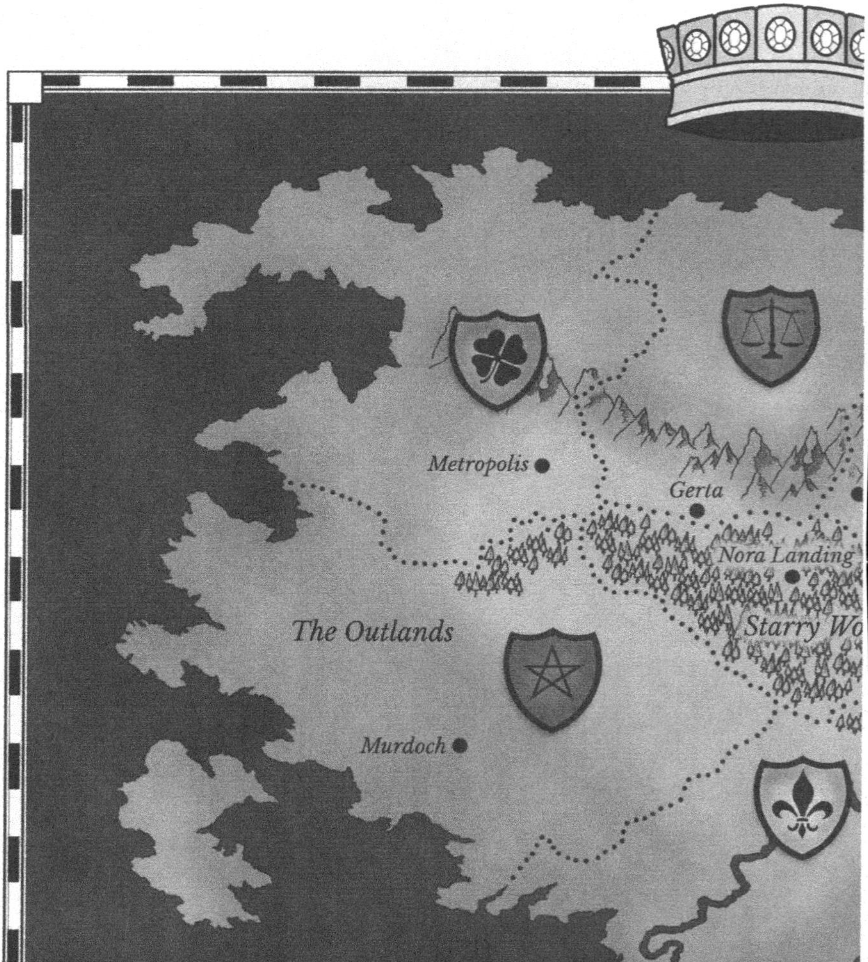

Metropolis
Gerta
Nora Landing
The Outlands
Starry Wo
Murdoch

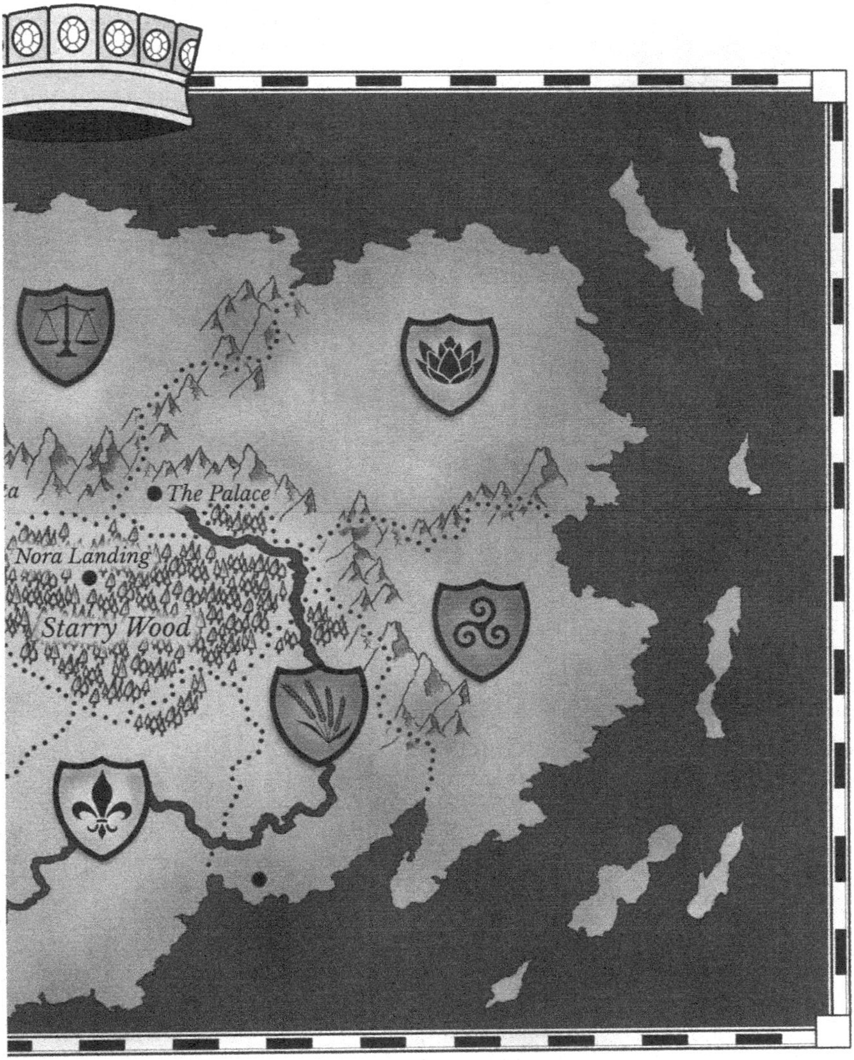

The Palace
Nora Landing
Starry Wood

# A SOUL FRACTURED

sands press
Brockville, Ontario

# A SOUL FRACTURED

By SHAYNA GRISSOM

sands press

**sands press**

A Division of 3244601 Canada Inc.
300 Central Avenue West
Brockville, Ontario
K6V 5V2

Toll Free 1-800-563-0911 or 613-345-2687
http://www.sandspress.com

ISBN 978-1-988281-98-8


**Publisher's Note**

This book is a work of fiction. References to real people, events, establishments, organizations, or locales, are intended only to provide as a sense of authenticity, and are used fictitiously. All other characters, and all incidents and dialogue, are drawn from the authors' imaginations and are not to be construed as real.



For information on bulk purchases of this book or any book published by Sands Press, please call 1-800-563-0911.

1ST Printing

To book an author for your live event, please call: 1-800-563-0911

Sands Press is a literary publisher interested in new and established authors wishing to develop and market their product. For more information please visit our website at www.sandspress.com.

# PART ONE

# Chapter One

Nora's crown never did fit quite right. On some days it was too loose, falling over her brow, cutting into the thin skin between her ears and head. Other days it was too tight. Squeezing at her scalp, it left indentations against her skin when she took it off. There were days where it was so small that she would pin it to her head like some stupid little hat. She was always worried people would notice, but if they did, it didn't matter.

There was a soft knock at the door. "Come in," she said.

It was Bosh, her manservant. He was a tall and stout man around her age. He had ginger hair that stuck out in every direction no matter how short it was, a pale face with freckles, and a great fat bottom lip that trembled when he stood with his mouth agape—which was often. Behind him were two new maids in black uniforms with white aprons.

"Morning, my queen!" Bosh waved the two new servants into the room. "We're training some new p-people," he stuttered. "I hope you don't mind."

"Not at all," she said.

She was the queen of Hell. It wasn't her job to look majestic in a crown that wobbled against the hairpins that held it—her job was to rule the seven regions of Hell. A vast forest and a canyon separated the seventh region and palace, but even that was too close for comfort.

If one of those rotten souls managed to pass the canyon, a dense forest filled with monsters separated her from them. An outlander's options would be to head north to the sixth region or south to the fourth. The fourth region was full of snobs who would never help any monster from the seventh, but the sixth region was one of gamblers and cheats.

Suppose an outlander scaled the canyon and made it to the sixth region undetected. They would need to amass a fortune through gambling and bribe their way east through the fifth region. They would then need to escape the fifth region's zealots without getting burned alive before reaching the first region.

Then it was a simple matter of getting around the castle fortifications and a barracks full of trained killers and trackers before reaching her royal bedroom where she stretched away the aches of another restless night.

It would be difficult indeed for an outlander to reach the queen, but it kept her up at night all the same. The former steward wasn't like other outlanders. He was smart and manipulative. Not for one moment did she think he wouldn't find a way back.

Her servants helped her out of the massive canopy bed and into the copper clawfoot tub where they helped bathe her. Bosh stood outside the bathroom door. "Is the new décor to your liking?" he asked.

"It's not red," Nora said. That was her only requirement. The royal chamber was covered from wall to wall in red. It made her nauseous just thinking about it. Red curtains gushed from the windows aside crimson brocade walls. Flush red pillows floated on a sea of scarlet velvet blankets. It was as if Vinicio wanted the reminder of everyone he and his descendants killed to sit on the black throne.

"Don't get me wrong," she said. "I like red, but it was a little much."

"It was quite garish."

The female servants said nothing as the queen stood, tiring of their clumsy hands fumbling around her. Wrapped in a towel and her fluffy white robe, she went to a great big wardrobe. The servants pulled the doors open, and several wooden hangers popped out, revealing all her clothes. She did this every day but never got used to it. She wore the same dress for months on the road with Aegis. Her heart hurt with how much she missed him.

Two great big wooden wings emerged from the wardrobe and a rainbow of satins and silks pressed tightly in the nooks. She hopped back when the wardrobe unfolded in her direction, revealing a series of drawers holding far too many shoes. She gave the maids an awkward smile. "Still not used to that. There are so many," Nora said, unsure of what to pick for the day. "Boshy, is anything special happening today?"

"The floor is yours today, my queen."

With a sense of destiny, the queen approached the wardrobe again. She pointed to a black satin and beaded gown. It reminded her of the crown, black steel laced around the various gems. The dark stones sparkled when the light hit them just right. When she twirled in this gown, the beading caught the sun and a dark spectrum of color lit the room.

Boshy's bottom lip was trembling as she smiled. "You like it?"

"I love it."

That morning she joined her council for breakfast. She took most of her meals with the group that consisted of Peter, her former tutor—now advisor; Hacia, the leader of the trackers; and Alfie, the leader of the hawk hunters. It was just the four of them. She sat at the head of the table, and they all gave a small bow before reseating. Peter was at her right and Alfie at her left, with Hacia beside him.

"Morning," she said as she ate a spoonful of oatmeal.

Peter's hawkish grey eyes flickered at her from behind bushy grey brows. "How are you feeling this morning?"

"Good," she said as she drank her orange juice, relishing the sour-sweet drink. "It's still weird, sleeping in that room."

It had been six months since Nora had staged a coup against the steward of Hell. His family was only intended to be a placeholder until the true king was born, but the stewards found the power too much to give up. Nora was the true ruler even if the crown didn't always fit quite right. She had the King's Soul and all the powers of Hell.

"I can only imagine," Peter said. "The gown is lovely. From the fourth region?"

Where else did people care more about gowns and finery than life itself? Her hands ran down her lap. The fabric had a satiny feel. "A gift from one of their diplomats."

"There are dressmakers here," Hacia said. "If you want something made, it can be done."

"I know," she said. "I like to wear gifts to court, though."

Alfie didn't care for the talk of dresses. He stabbed at his steak and sliced off a sizable rare hunk of meat. He chewed it slowly, savoring the tenderness of the cut. "It looks nice," he said at last.

She loved that Alfie didn't give a rat's ass about the dress. Peter approved of the strategic reasoning behind wearing gifts to court, but he didn't say it. It would have been nice if he could say as much. He would remind her that a queen shouldn't need approval from others.

"Any word?" Nora asked.

All three shook their heads. A queen shouldn't be spending valuable resources searching for a friend, either. She couldn't help that she missed him. The hole in her heart was so large she swore she could hear the wind whistling through it in a quiet room. Her whole world had changed the day Aegis found her on the edge of the Starry Wood. She understood why he needed to go, but he could have sent a letter. Vampires probably didn't send letters, though.

Peter interrupted her reflections with a nervous throat clearing. "Remember," he coached. "You must sit up straight on your throne. Don't forget your tone. You're young, and nothing is worse than a petulant young person. You want to appear wise beyond your years. Your reign must be accepted as rightful."

"My reign *is* rightful," she argued. There was only one King's Soul, and it was hers. If the stewards hadn't sought out and assassinated kings in their cribs, she wouldn't have had to fight to sit on her throne in the first place.

"Yes," Peter said. "But comfortable and known is easy to fall back on. You're the first female king. Most souls don't even know what to call you."

The crown was heavy today. She let out a quiet sigh before standing and throwing her napkin on the table and made her way to the courtroom. "I'll be making a decree today," she announced.

Peter turned to look at her. His fingers drummed on the wooden table in the most infuriating manner. "Care to share what that decree will be?"

"No."

She swallowed hard and scurried a bit faster from his gaze. She was the queen, and queens did not owe their advisors explanations. He needed to have faith in all the years he'd taught her as a child. She would prove to be a good queen and make him proud. He just needed to give her a chance.

The people of the court bowed and applauded as she stepped out the side door, making her way to the black throne. Acrobats and jugglers entertained the guests, and she couldn't help but glare at them. There was no purpose for these things in court. She had told Peter as much, but he insisted they make no dramatic changes to the court.

"It's just a show," she had said. "Nothing more."

Peter had nodded, "It is a frivolity, I agree. The stewards loved their performers. At this point, you need to be seen and heard. Word of how you intend to rule needs to spread. The court is the best form of propaganda for your reign."

It had been nearly six months since that conversation, and she was unsure of just how effective this was. The same people attended these court sessions. What if they decided to spread rumors of her undoing instead?

It was stupid to put her faith in the hands of a court jester and the social gala from the fourth province. A fire swallower on stilts blew fire so close to her that it nearly singed her dress. Did the farmers in the third region care about what gown she wore? Would the monks of the first find the jesters stimulating? Nora doubted it. The nomads certainly didn't care. Clothing was optional in the second region.

The crown was so weighty that her neck was beginning to ache. This would be her first decree as a queen without Peter's permission or coaching. It was time to prove to him and everyone else that she belonged here and not the murdering stewards.

She stood up and began to speak before she lost the nerve. Her dress had become more constricting than it had been at breakfast, and she was all hot and sweaty and her hands clammy.

"I have an announcement to make." Her voice was much louder than she had intended. The entire court went quiet. She glanced at the stained glass windows that told the story of the first king. They shared the same soul, the first king and her. She needed to be brave like him now.

"I will be opening the court to people outside of the social gala. My court will now be a place where people can make requests of the queen."

The onlookers only stood in confusion. Their painted faces were clown masks staring back at her. Rebus, the advisor to the former steward, stepped forward, his face was like a great big prune. She had half a mind to render the soul from his body right then and there. "Forgive me, your majesty, but how will we ascertain these people?"

Her mind went blank. Honestly, she hadn't considered that. She had only just come up with the idea moments before saying it out loud. It was only a warmup in case she lost her nerve to announce her real decree. She didn't have plans, only wishes. She was only seventeen, after all.

"I am sent letters by the thousands each day. I shall have the hawk hunters retrieve people on my behalf."

Rebus relented with a bow. His baggy robes draped across the floor as he showed her his bald, sun-spotted head. Just what color were his eyes under the folds of his eyelids?

*Brown, of course.*

The voice came unbidden and was not her own. It was infuriating. Nora imagined a cell door closing shut, locking the voice of the King's Soul away. She and the King's Soul were supposed to have merged in spirit when she learned the truth of who she was, but for some reason, the voice remained. She had no choice but to lock it away in her mind. It was the only way to get anything done.

"Is something wrong, my queen?" Rebus asked.

Her cheeks stung from embarrassment. Everyone was staring at her while she fought with the voices in her head. She gave Rebus a scathing glare before resuming. "Also, from this point on, I will not send souls directly to the seventh region. People are not born evil, they are made. Having been one of the few people on Hell who has witnessed the outlands firsthand and lived, I cannot with good conscience send children to that place. From this point on, black souls will be sent to other regions, and if they are proven evil, they will be sent to the outlands."

There was a paralyzing silence. She anticipated some reservations about this decree, but the people only stared with their mouths agape. Her breath quickened and she resisted the urge to run. The social gala was still watching the queen as if she were about to say something else, but she had nothing else to add.

A smile slipped across her lips then. The people in this room were unaffected by her decree. They wanted to witness a miracle. Closing her eyes, she imagined green, curling vines making their way up the palace's stone walls. The vines bloomed with crimson flowers with purple centers—a flower that only existed in her imagination.

It was the power of the King's Soul. She drew power from Hell itself and could make nearly anything happen. Her powers were dormant as the King's Soul sought to protect itself from the steward. It wasn't until the steward made his attempts on her life that the King's Soul surfaced and her powers came to life.

In the hallway, Peter stood eyeing her skeptically. "Giving them what they want?"

"Nothing new based on the accounts of the kings before," she said.

His drawn face posed a smile. His wiry grey hair was cut much shorter than before. She didn't like it. Despite all her gifts, he still insisted on the long, black, double-button coat with a red silk lining and fitted black pants.

"I'm not criticizing," Peter said.

Then why did it feel like he was? Ever since she took the throne, all Peter had done was question and criticize. For someone who faced treason and near-death to put her on the throne, he certainly griped a lot. She didn't want to hear it today. She walked past him and headed towards her chambers to take the monumental weight off her head.

"Your decree…" Peter called out. "I just wanted to say that I liked the idea."

She was not in the mood to hear his opinion today. It was bad enough that the voice had come back again. The last thing she needed was another man's voice in her head. The King's Soul wasn't supposed to be talking to her, was it? It wasn't like she could ask anyone.

The crown pillow rested on her dresser in front of the mirror. She couldn't lift the crown off her head. Instead, she bent over and it rolled onto the pillow. It wasn't the most majestic of actions, but it did the trick. Why couldn't she manage the crown the way she had in previous incarnations?

Alone in her bedroom, she still saw the room as it was before. No amount of redecorating washed the red away. It still reminded her of Vinicio and her mother. Now it was adorned with a cream linen canopy bed, dark wood that matched her wardrobe, dresser, table, and chairs. The sofas were crafted with the same wood and white linen fabric. Gold embossments decorated the room sparingly to give it a modern aesthetic, but she still expected it to be red at every turn. She just needed some air.

She opened the doors to the balcony where she once stood half a year ago. How young she'd was in that ugly yellow sack dress and chopped hair. Her fists had balled as she glared at her mother. She hadn't spoken to Bella since she sent her back to the fifth region with the rest of the zealots.

If all had gone well, she might have a baby sibling by now. Nora had always wanted a sibling, even if they were nearly eighteen years apart. She didn't know if she was ready to face her mother again, but Nora did want to learn if she had a baby brother or sister.

Pushing the balcony doors open, she gazed at the afternoon setting on the horizon. The weather was always nice in the first region, it was one of the perks of living there. She inhaled the light, dewy air of the morning before moving back into the bedroom. She wished Aegis were here, but he was off with his lover, Minerva. He was supposed to be her vampire—hers to command.

She shook herself free of that mentality. He didn't belong to her, and Aegis was her friend. The images she couldn't control disturbed her the most. Cruel and irrational inclinations to hurt and control others gripped her at the most random times, leaving her trembling like she was now.

Taking lunch in her room, she read some fictional work for several hours before spending several more signing papers. If provoked further, would she really have killed Rebus? He was old and annoying, but that didn't warrant death. She could force Aegis to her side, to be with her, but it wasn't right or fair. Did everyone get these urges? Aegis said she had to stay in the castle because the other regions influenced her too greatly. If what he said was true, then why was she struggling to contain such horrid desires?

In their brief tour of the regions, she did indeed take on attributes of each region, but what she was experiencing now reminded her of the way she was in the seventh. She wasn't evil, but in that place, she was forced to make evil decisions. Were the rest in the seventh doing the same?

Unfastening the silken black dress encrusted with dark gems, she was freed from the upper parts of the dress. She glanced down, releasing a cry of relief, and nearly wept. Her work was still not done. She had no idea how to take off the large bottom portion that to her resembled a cage. Wiggling through the center of the dress, she crawled out from the bottom.

She searched through the gathers with one hand and, holding the edge of the bustle, finally emerged, peering out from the bottom of the dress. Nora stood up and smiled, not noticing the dark figure in the corner of her bedroom.

"You have maids for that sort of thing," Hacia said, emerging from the shadows.

She jumped back like a cat and let out a threatening hiss before realizing who it was. "Oh," she said in relief. "It's just you."

Hacia stepped into the light.Her black locks were pulled back, exposing sharp cheekbones and deep brown eyes. Nora never realized just how flawless Hacia's skin was. She had to be nearly forty but she appeared half that age. Her sleeveless leather vest displayed her strong arms that, too, were bare of any scars.

"You don't have scars," Nora said.

Hacia frowned and tilted her head as if to question why such things would be relevant to a queen.

"You're the head tracker. You've spent most of your life in the wild, hunting outlaws, fighting, yet you have no scars," she explained.

"I have scars," Hacia said. "I don't try to hide them. I don't have any on my arms, I suppose. My queen, there are important matters to discuss."

The dress she had worn to court remained standing where she left it while she and Hacia moved to the balcony to talk. She didn't care if Hacia saw her in her underclothes, but she did pull a robe off its hanger and put it on to prevent a chill. It was a fluffy white bathrobe and, given the chance, she would never take it off. It was so comfortable.

Sitting at the little dinette table on the balcony, she crossed her arms and faced her advisor and general. "Would you sit with me?"

Hacia gave a bow. "It is not my place."

Nora shrugged. She wouldn't force the matter. Though it made her nervous when people stood around as she sat, but it was understandable. Hacia had spent her whole life on the edge of a fight and had long forgotten how to live any other way.

"So, what is it you want to talk about?"

"There are pockets of rebellion throughout the six regions," Hacia said.

Nora imagined there was rebellion in all seven regions, but no one went to the seventh region unless they wanted to be torn apart and eaten. There had been fewer accounts of outlanders reaching the other areas, and the issue of kidnapping and enslaving souls had been eradicated, but turmoil always bubbled. This was Hell, after all.

"They had been under stewardship for hundreds of years. It's only natural to fear change."

Hacia's eyes scanned the edge of the balcony out of habit. "That's not what has people so upset. The souls could care less about the steward, though there are rumors that he still lives."

Nora's jagged little fingernails pressed into her palms, cutting the flesh. Despite all attempts to keep them manicured, she still chewed her nails at night. Nora's dreams were often filled with fear of the steward returning. Vinicio was living, thriving in the seventh region. It put her on edge.

Her mother had once promised her the world as well as a father. Instead, she was almost assassinated by the steward in a desperate ploy to maintain his grip on power. It wouldn't have stung so bad if her mother had come to her defense, but Bella lived in denial.

"He should be dead," she said through gritted teeth. If no one else made it happen, she would march to the seventh region and do it herself. "What of my mother?" Nora asked.

"She is well," Hacia said. "The fifth region is her home. She belongs there."

"And the baby?" Nora asked. "Did she have it?"

Hacia gave her a curiously warm smile. "Bella has given all her love and dedication to the baby."

She sighed and leaned back into her chair. It was a relief to know that the baby was loved by their mother even if Bella couldn't love her. It didn't hurt the way she anticipated, just so long as her brother or sister was happy. She supposed it was because she was older and understood why her mother struggled to be a parent. Bella had been younger than Nora was now when she got pregnant. Her mother was older; her obsession with love was set in the right direction.

"That's not important," Hacia said as if she'd forgotten her purpose. "The rebellions are the concern."

"What are they so upset about?" Nora asked. Her voice was dripping with condescension. Everything she had been doing these last six months were for them. The food supply from the third region was able to make it to all six regions unhindered by raids. Souls were no longer kidnapped and sold to the seventh region. With the King's Soul on the throne, the borders between regions were returning.

People were safer, better fed, and that wasn't enough to keep them from rebelling?

"Someone is spreading rumors that you have died and that we're covering it up."

Oh, she supposed that would be a good reason. She shook her head, not understanding why someone would need to create such a rumor.

Hacia continued. "News of your new law has spread quickly. I fear it has people even more upset."

There was only one region that would be able to push out court news that fast—only one region that would genuinely be upset by the prospect of fostering a black soul. "You mean the fourth region is upset," Nora countered.

Hacia shook her head. "Between the fourth's outrage over today's news and the rumors of an illegitimate queen, our troops are having trouble keeping the peace."

"I haven't sent any souls yet." She laughed.

Black souls were rare for the most part. In the last six months, Nora had encountered just one. It had hovered around on the floor. The weight of its misdeeds forced it low. Evil didn't cling to clothes or spread like some disease. Bad choices were often choices between bad and even worse options.

"They're just afraid," Hacia said.

Nora placed her hands on the table and rooted her feet. No one understood because they had no idea what the seventh region was like. She did. Why couldn't they trust her? "Well, they will need to get used to it."

"Couldn't we just notify the region if you send a black soul their way?" Hacia asked.

She shook her head. "What am I?"

"The queen."

"No, what am I?"

Hacia's brow furrowed.

"Did no one tell you?" Nora asked. "My mother is of the fifth region but my father was an outlander. Growing up among the lawful is not easy when you're the result of a broken law."

The tracker's eyes went wide. "You don't want the children persecuted."

"Not just the children, the parents would suffer, too. In places like the fourth and fifth regions, they would encourage the parents to kill the babes or leave them for dead like they wanted to leave me. They all assumed I was born evil because my father was an outlander."

Hacia gave a deep bow of respect to the queen. Hacia might know tracking, hunting, and killing, but Nora had firsthand experience with how people operated. If they had even the slightest idea that a black soul was among them, they would resort to extreme measures.

People did this in the other world as well. When the babe was an unfavorable gender or had a deformity, parents would dispose of it. Hacia wouldn't have such knowledge and nor would anyone else in Hell. She only knew this because of the knowledge the King's Soul imparted to her despite her numerous requests for it to shut up.

"Why didn't you mention this to Peter?" Nora asked.

Her jaw set firm as if she were afraid something unseemly would escape. "We did. He told us not to worry you about it."

She wasn't the least bit surprised by that. What else was Peter doing behind the scenes that she wasn't aware of? The news of her decree spread far and fast. An open rebellion was enough of a threat that the general came to her personally. This wasn't the first time she had received secondhand news that Peter had been managing things without her consent.

"I will deal with this personally. Thank you, Hacia. You may go."

She sat on the balcony long after Hacia left. The maid brought in her tea set and a small pot of herbal tea designed to help her relax. While the drink did nothing to soothe her nerves or help her sleep, she did enjoy the ceremony of making it.

With a tiny copper sword, she broke off a piece of the tea from its brick and put it in a bowl. She poured the hot water from the kettle into her teapot before sealing the teapot with its lid and an outer coat of boiling water.

She watched the water pour over the tiny ceramic pot and onto the slotted tray. Ignoring the chunks of her brown hair that fell forward, she poured the water from the teapot into three teacups until they overflowed. With a small wooden stick, she carefully dropped just the right amount of the dried tea into the teapot before filling it with fresh hot water from the kettle.

Moving the kettle in gentle circles, she rotated pouring water around the outside of the teapot as well as filling the contents. People put so much emphasis on keeping everything inside the cups, but the monks of the first region had taught her better. Pouring the hot water along the outside as well as the inside kept the contents pure and evenly heated.

Once the tea leaves rehydrated and floated towards the top, Nora sealed the lid with more hot water before draining the pot into a small pitcher, not allowing the tea to steep, only to rinse. She discarded the water over the tiny stone figurines. Refilling the teapot one last time, she let the washed tea leaves steep while waiting for her company to arrive.

# Chapter Two

"You're dragging your feet. Why?" Minerva asked.

Aegis had indeed been slowing since the castle came into sight. He wasn't sure why. He could only pretend he didn't hear Minerva. She scoffed at him and laughed. It was a misty night, and he did not wish to startle any souls that might encounter the pair of vampires.

"Honestly, you can be such a child sometimes," she teased. "It's okay to be nervous. Even if you are an immortal, who is quite durable with the knowledge of several ages …"

"I'm not nervous." He was just enjoying the starless night.

Minerva's wild eyes bore into him. "You're not afraid of a teenage girl?"

"I'm not nervous," he repeated a bit more gruffly.

Minerva hadn't a clue. When the vampires woke several hundred years ago, he had woken with no knowledge of who he was or where he had been. The long sleep took away all his pain. When Nora used her powers to restore his memory, it changed everything. It didn't change his admiration for Minerva, but Nora's claim on him far surpassed anything the two of them shared. He had avoided that fact for the last six months, and now he was going to pay for it.

He was bound to the King's Soul. Not just by oath, but by love. He had a connection with it that surpassed any soulmate. He could feel Nora's fears, her anger, and when she had nightmares about the seventh region, he experienced her discomfort. Minerva didn't know that. He should have told her the moment he understood it all, but he didn't know how to tell her that she was technically the other woman.

It was a cruel necessity that Nora was born a female. It muddled and blurred their intimacy in ways he never imagined possible. It was part of the reason he ran off with Minerva at the first chance he got. With Nora safely on the throne, he could leave her and allow her to grow up without the confusion of his presence.

He beheld the high tower. The smooth grey stone appeared more seamless than the last time he'd been here. Was it Nora's doing? The fortification had grown stronger, more renewed by her occupation.

"It's like the borders between regions," Aegis said. "The walls are stronger and the canyons deeper. It's like everything in Hell is in better shape."

"Yes," Minerva said. "But it's still not quite right, is it?"

She was right. The canyon that separated the outlands from the rest of Hell was deeper, but in the time of Kings, it was filled with lava. He believed that with Nora's return, the world would resume in its natural order. Yet, with each passing day, a slow, twisting knife in his heart suggested otherwise.

"Perhaps we should go through the gates," Minerva suggested.

He shook his head. "No, she's waiting for us."

Minerva gave him a curious smile but didn't question his statement. Wrapping his arm around his mate's waist, Aegis leaped onto a lower balcony and proceeded to skip from windowsill to chimney until he landed squarely on the oval balcony where he found Nora at a small table pouring tea into three cups. Minerva went limp and allowed this gesture despite being able to scale the castle better than him. It reminded him of how he used to travel with Nora. Did Minerva know this, or did she assume it was a way to be closer to her?

Nora no longer resembled the little girl in the Starry Wood, wide-eyed and covered in sap. Her hair was now long and flowed freely around her dark face. She'd grown into those big brown eyes and her skin, once sallow, had softened into a dark olive tone. Her thick brows were shaped, and her cheekbones finely emerged from her once rounded cheeks. She was a woman now.

It made him sad to have missed it, but it was for the best. The lack of love in her upbringing leveled her self esteem, making it impossible for her to distinguish between a watchdog from a lover.

Nora tried her best to keep control of her smile, but when he smiled, she abandoned the notion of playing coy and ran to his outstretched arms. "I've missed you so much," she murmured against his chest.

Wholeness had returned to him at last. "And I've missed you."

Minerva stood beside them, smiling. Her beaming smile at the sight of them reunited was genuine. He loved her for that.

Nora peeked out from his coat at the unnaturally pale vampire. "Hi, Minerva."

"Hello, darling."

Nora greeted Minerva with a hug before motioning to the table. They sat, and his eyes fell to the tea ceremony. It was beautifully orchestrated, and he was impressed by Nora's sophistication. There was only one place where tea ceremony stood on such formality.

"You learned this from the monks?" he asked.

Nora blushed. "It was a coronation gift from the monks of the first region. I've used it every night since. Peter insists on it as well. Says it's good for my health."

"How is the old man?" Minerva asked.

He had nearly forgotten that Minerva and Peter had shared a cell in the steward's private dungeons while Nora was in exile. She never spoke of it, but they must have had many discussions throughout their incarceration.

"He's good," Nora said, a bit too sharply for Aegis's liking. What had come between them? He would speak with Peter later.

"What brings you two here?" Nora asked as she tested the tea against her lips.

Minerva glanced at him with a raised brow. She didn't ask him whether he wanted to skirt around the issue or outright tell the truth: they were concerned she was not living up to her full potential and wanted to find out why. He couldn't deny that his senses were telling him that something wasn't right, but what could it be?

The King's Soul was eternal. There would come a day when Nora would be too old and weak to hold its power. It would slowly leave her and inhabit a new child at birth just as it always had. As her abilities faded, she would die, but the new child would grow stronger. As far as Aegis could tell, Nora was safe and flourishing within the castle confines, but why did the scar on his palm buzz? Why was he compelled to this place with every fiber of his being?

"It's the forest," Aegis lied. "With the giants gone, other beasts are climbing out of the water caverns, threatening to wreak havoc."

A wide grin spread across her face and she sat upright in her chair. Danger and uncertainty. Of course she'd be thrilled. "What kind of creatures?"

Aegis told her of the massive winged lizards that would breathe fire or sometimes ice. Of the nasty wolf-beast he'd encountered. It had such intelligence it made him shudder. A boar with sharp tusks emerging from all points of his head. All these accounts were concerning to them, and they were the truth.

Minerva played along, but in the corner of her eye, a coy smile lingered. "I encountered an eight-legged horse," she added.

"Oh yeah," Aegis remembered. "That was odd. Not dangerous, just clumsy."

"Well," Nora said. "Now that you're here, I'll have rooms made up for you."

Aegis and Minerva exchanged glances. The plurality of the word was a point of contention with his mate. He gave her a gentle nod, and Minerva let it go. This was Nora's castle and she wanted them to sleep separately even if they did not actually sleep. The need to separate the pair was a sign of immaturity on Nora's part, something he'd speak to her about later.

"Bosh!" the queen barked.

A young man rushed into the room, stuttering noble titles along the way. "Y-Yes ma'am. My q-queen. Di-di-di …"

Nora rolled her eyes but her voice was gentle and calming despite the boy's stutter. "Bosh, I want you to prepare two guest rooms. The white room and green room."

His face was puckered, and his eyes lost until she gestured to the balcony, "These are the friends I told you about. This is Aegis, and this is Minerva."

He wasn't one for smiling, but Minerva beamed bright. Bosh's ruddy face went pale as he looked them up and down. "You don't have fangs."

"Bosh!" Nora chastised in a mocking tone.

A laugh erupted from Aegis. He had forgotten all about the odd rumors about vampires. Minerva only tilted her head. She had little interaction with souls; she was in for a treat.

"No, good lad. We don't have fangs. We don't drink blood—"

Minerva gasped at the idea, and he couldn't help but enjoy the silliness of it all.

"We don't die in sunlight, and we're not allergic to garlic. We're very old, strong, and nearly indestructible, but none of the other stuff is true."

He could practically see Minerva's thoughts as they whirled with the absurd ideas about her species. "Garlic?" she muttered under her breath. As if a rooted plant could take down his mate. He didn't know where the speculations came from, but he loved hearing them all the same.

"For a moment, I wondered if you weren't going to have a go at him. Poor Bosh, he's a sweet butler," Nora said. Aegis detected more than a hint of affection for the boy. Not that he was one to judge, but he would have thought a young lady as beautiful and clever as

Nora could do a little better than her servant. He would need to investigate the matter further.

"The white room was freshly made this morning, I'll check on the green room," Bosh said.

"I'll escort Minerva to the white room myself while you check," the queen informed both men.

Minerva didn't glance back at Aegis. Even if she wanted to, she didn't want to give off an air of suspicion. She walked beside the young queen out of the bedroom door and out of sight.

He remained on the balcony and sipped his tea. He didn't remember the last time he'd had tea. It wasn't something a vampire required. They needed no food nor drink, but he could still enjoy it if he so desired.

He noted the evidence of the elaborate tea ceremony. Nora said she did this every night. It made him sad, knowing she went to all this effort every night without anyone to share it with.

She could have maids make it, or perform this ceremony with guests, but no. She did it every night alone. He assumed that in the castle she wouldn't be so isolated, but here she was, lonelier than ever. The only difference was that, for whatever reason, Nora chose to be alone. The gargoyle stone on the tea set mocked him. One monster to another, he supposed.

Gentle footsteps came from a different wing of the castle. He had his suspicions, but his hearing was heightened to such a degree that he was often left in anticipation for several minutes before the person came through the door. It was a man's step. He could tell by the weight against the stone floors. Not a large man. His shoes were slightly worn, and the sole was dulled more so on the left than the right foot.

It was Peter who came around the corner, a slim, tightly tailored man who let his eyebrows and grey hair fray wildly. He had laugh lines, and frown lines, all sorts of lines in between, yet he moved as a younger man would. Aegis suspected he appeared older than he was due to hardship in his life. His eyes were bright and wild despite his rational nature. It reminded him of Minerva.

"So you've come," Peter greeted him.

He gave a deliberate nod. "How is she?"

Peter's skittish eyes flickered. "Where is she?" he whispered.

"She took Minerva to the white room," Aegis said. He found Peter's paranoia off-putting.

"Oh, she is having you stay in the farthest wing?" Peter asked. His expression must have given him away. Peter gave a knowing little smile and Aegis considered throwing him out the window. "Ah, she's having Minerva stay in the furthest wing. Where will you be staying?"

"The green room," Aegis said.

"The room next door."

He didn't like being toyed with, and that was most certainly what Peter was doing. Nora always spoke highly of the tutor; he was like a father to her. He always assumed that would be enough for him, but in their exchange, Aegis found that Peter was falling short of his expectations.

"She won't like us speaking. If I may, I'd like to visit your room tonight to discuss Nora."

Aegis put his hands in his pockets and reminded himself that this was his queen's advisor. Nora would probably forgive him if he chucked the man off the balcony. Still, Peter had insight that he needed. He could listen to what the man said, and if he didn't like it, he could snap his neck and say that Peter had fallen down the stairs. He shuddered at his hostile inclinations. The gargoyle taunted from its rocky perch.

"I await your visit," he said at last.

Peter bowed and shuffled out the door. By his approximation, Nora was still a long way off, but he enjoyed watching the old tutor flee from the room like the coward he was. Afraid of a child. He had just arrived and Peter was already attempting to sow discord.

Nora was the next to come through the bedroom door. Her fluffy white robe had fallen around her shoulders, exposing her delicate collarbones.

"It's getting too cold to stay out there. Shut the doors and come in."

He did as he was asked and sat beside her on the bed, but not before he gave an awkward nod to the dress standing in the room. Nora laughed. "You like my companion, eh?"

"How have you been?" he asked.

Nora's face went sullen and her eyes wandered as if they didn't know where to look. "It's hard to be queen."

Aegis nodded. He could only imagine.

"Everything I say and do is criticized. Every moment of my life feels scheduled. I can't even go to the bathroom without help." Nora's voice strained with frustration, and it made his heart sink. She wasn't sick; she was just miserable.

"Is that why the dress is just standing there in the middle of the room?" Aegis asked.

"Yeah," she said under her breath. "I didn't want to have a bunch of maids in here undressing me, so I got out on my own. The maid will probably come in and deal with it once they think I'm asleep."

"You don't sleep?" he asked. Sleep was something souls required, and judging by the dark circles around her eyes, she wasn't getting enough.

Nora's dark eyes met his. "Not since you left."

She slept that night. He laid across the edge of her bed and stared at the linen canopy. The whisper of Nora's breathing soothed his spirit. He understood now that he could never leave her again. This is where he belonged. What that meant for him and Minerva, he didn't know.

It wasn't just Nora who depended on him. The borders that separated the layers of Hell relied on the health of the King's Soul. If she weakened, so would the borders that locked the foulest of souls away from the rest of the populace. For whatever reason, she wasn't strong enough to do it on her own. She needed him by her side.

The bedroom door gently opened, and a young maid no older than Nora herself crept in. She was a blonde girl with a button nose. She leaned over to peer over the bed to check if Nora was asleep before squeezing through the cracked door and shutting it behind her. Aegis wasn't sure if she was aware of him or not, but he did not wish to startle her.

"Just so you know, I am here," he whispered.

"Is she asleep?"

"Yes."

Despite the darkness in the room, the maid was quite adept in her maneuvering. She did this often enough to have the room memorized, and she wasn't the least bit startled by his presence. Word must travel fast in a castle.

The maid went over to the door across from the bed and opened it just a crack. "The green room is straight through here. I'll be taking her dress. Is there anything you require?"

"Thank you, no."

The maid gave a bow before leaving. Her black and white uniform fluttered as the wind caught her skirts on her way out. Aegis slipped off the bed and into the green room. He would wait for Peter to speak his mind before returning to the end of Nora's bed.

The room held a soft glow from the candlelight, but even in the stark black, he recognized Peter leaning against the door. It wasn't an attempt to startle the vampire, though. If it was Nora who had come through the door, it gave the advisor some cover. One by one, he lit the candles in the room, revealing a brown room rather than a green one.

Perhaps the brown room didn't have the same appeal as a green room. The bedding was a rich brown with cream accents and the ivory rugs contrasted against the terra cotta tiles. The off-white wallpaper was textured and adorned with little brown flowers and large mirrors with ornate wooden frames that matched the furniture. It was a serene yet masculine décor.

"She had this done with you in mind."

"I can tell," Aegis admitted.

"She fretted over every detail," Peter said as he examined himself in a mirror. He poked at the bags under his eyes. Why did the advisor have such a lack of self-awareness? Maybe the man thought himself above the need for his approval.

"What is it you want to speak of?"

Peter turned to face him. "It's about Nora. Something isn't right."

Something was indeed wrong, but he would not confirm these suspicions with the advisor without knowing his true intentions. Too often, suspicious men went on to create conspiracies with disastrous results.

"In what way?" he asked.

Peter took a deep breath and began, "Ever since she claimed the throne, Nora has been different. She explained to me how the King's Soul merged with her own. I expected changes based on that alone, but there's more to it."

That much was true. When Nora and Aegis were on the run, the King's Soul finally surfaced. Nora had held it with her all along, but it remained dormant to protect itself. He didn't note any specific change to Nora's personality because she was constantly changing.

"She was a different version of herself in each region we traveled," Aegis said. "I had to pry her from a gambling table in the sixth region. She was snotty and arrogant in the fourth, she went near-catatonic in the first …"

"And the seventh?" Peter interrupted.

He didn't need to answer; his expression gave him away. The old man nodded. "It seems the King's Soul has had some effects on our girl."

*Our girl?* He slammed his teeth together so hard he could swear they were cracking. Who was this man to claim Nora as his girl? As far as he could tell, Nora was deeply at odds with him. Taking a deep breath, Aegis forced himself to relax. Peter was nervously jittering around the room, so much so that he didn't notice Aegis's reaction. He wanted to keep it that way.

"Do you know how to resolve it?" Aegis asked.

"No, but I'm trying to find out. That's why I need your help. Nora told me she restored your memories, back to the beginning. Do you have any ideas as to what's happening?"

He shook his head. That was like asking a man what he had for breakfast fifteen years ago. The memories were restored, but they were distant, as if he learned them secondhand.

"All the kings I served before were born with the abilities at birth. Whenever a king began to falter, it would only be a matter of time before the soul made its way to another. A steward or I would be sent to retrieve the child."

Peter's eyes narrowed. "What did it look like when a king faltered?"

Peter was searching for signs of Nora's demise. Was he genuinely trying to save her? None of this would've happened in the first place if he had kept to the king's side. By allowing the stewards to take up his duty, he allowed souls the opportunity to manipulate the situation as they always did.

"They begin to lose control of their powers. At first, it's too strong or too weak, followed by a slow decline in abilities. Sometimes the borders weaken …" He hated to admit that last part, even to himself.

"What of the black crown?" Peter asked.

He had no idea. It was a crown and kings wore it, wasn't that it? It did appear on Nora's head when she took the throne. There was a connection between it and the King's Soul. Just what was the advisor getting at?

Peter shoved his hands deep into his pants pockets and looked down. He was trying to find the words to explain. "There, eh, there is a reason why Nora won't let anyone help her dress. The crown doesn't fit."

"The crown fits the soul, not the head," he said.

"Well, that's just it. Sometimes it's too big, other days it's too small. Nora doesn't want anyone to know. I only know because I bribed the maids to spy on her."

"I imagine she enjoyed that," he said as evenly as he could manage. Nora would be enraged if she knew Peter was having her spied on. He reconsidered throwing Peter off the balcony, but the advisor was on to something. The crown could only be worn by the King's Soul, which is why the stewards kept it put away. It was a reminder of what they could never be. But if Nora couldn't wear it, what did that mean?

"She doesn't know about it. No, she's miffed at me because I challenge her," Peter explained. "She thinks I'm overbearing, and perhaps she's right. I want her to go down in history as the best ruler Hell has ever had."

The sincerity on Peter's face was genuine, yet it made him sad for some reason. "And you think she has the makings?"

Peter's response wavered. "Not really, to be honest. I don't think she wants to be queen. I don't think she knows what she wants."

He disliked sharing his suspicions with Peter. Having once begged Nora to live out her life with him in the third region, he wouldn't have picked this life for her. He had warned her that being queen would be miserable work, but he suspected Nora saw a certain measure of safety in being queen. Life at the castle was all she knew. It was well-guarded and as far away from Vinicio as she could get without killing him.

"She doesn't want spying or lies," Aegis said. "Don't let me catch you doing such things again."

In one sweep of the room, he extinguished the candlelight before leaving the tutor in the green bedroom in the dark.

He carefully laid on the edge of the bed. Nora slept on as if he'd never left. There he spent the rest of the night in the darkness, wondering what would come next.

# Chapter Three

Nora woke early that morning to find Aegis staring at the ceiling near the edge of her bed. It made her smile, knowing he was there to stay at last. She'd wanted him to come alone, but if she were patient, the third wheel would fall off. Minerva was nice, but she wanted Aegis to herself. Did that make her selfish? She didn't care.

She got up and got dressed on her own before any of the maids could rush in. Nora opted for a pale blue gown with pearl accents. It reminded her of the lavender dress she'd worn while traveling with Aegis. Her things were much more elegant these days, but she never lost her love for the dress that made her feel like a woman for the first time.

Wearing a corset took a little getting used to. She didn't usually wear them, but she wanted to look exceptionally beautiful for Aegis. Once dressed, she glanced back at him. He was still staring vacantly at the ceiling. There was a moment of panic just then—what if the crown gave her trouble today?

Nora went to great lengths to keep that secret hidden. She didn't know what it meant, but it couldn't be a good sign. No better than the borders of Hell being only half-restored. Her vampire, no doubt, had observed as much but said nothing. What would he do if there was some mistake and she wasn't the rightful queen? Would he leave her?

He appeared so peaceful and handsome laying there. Aegis usually didn't sleep, but when he did, he was hard to wake. Sometimes it was difficult to pull him out of it. Her secret was safe for the time being.

She tiptoed towards him and waved a hand over his eyes. Aegis didn't so much as blink. He was somewhere far, far from Hell. Nora let out a sigh of relief before turning a sullen face towards the crown resting on its pillow on her dresser. She gave herself a little pep-talk before attempting to pick it up. She was a good queen, one who would care about her people, and was changing the world for the better.

On this day, the crown was light, to her relief. As she placed it on her head, she realized it was not only light but somehow bendy. If she wiggled it back and forth, the tips that held the gems gave slightly. It fit on her head well enough, but in place of cold metal across the top of her forehead, it warmed to her face.

She rocked her head back and forth as the peaks of her crown waivered before bursting into giggles. Not wanting to alert Aegis, she clamped a hand over her mouth and checked to make sure he was still asleep. The absurdity of it was too funny to ignore or even be angry about. It was on her head, and that was the critical part. Just so long as Nora didn't swing her head around or encounter a strong gust of wind, things would be okay today.

She gave Aegis a gentle kiss on the forehead before skipping down the stairs to the great dining hall for breakfast. The table was broken down to seat only eight on this day, but it could be extended to seat as many as sixteen. It was a square, sturdy table with a lace tablecloth she'd found at the market a few months back.

She sat with her back to the grand fireplace, and servants came shooting out of the corridors to serve. It wasn't long until Rebus and Peter joined. Peter's eyes kept diverting from her own. It made him appear suspicious, probably because he was. After her private meeting with Hacia, she was deeply concerned about Peter's priorities.

"Good morning," Peter said in greeting.

"Good morning."

Peter did a double take as she skipped in but said nothing as he sat down to join her. It wasn't long until Hacia came into the room donned in her leather pants and vest and her braids pulled away from her face ornately.

Alfie sheepishly followed soon after. She should have told him that, from her angle, it was apparent that he was waiting in the hallway to make it appear as though he and Hacia hadn't come together. While the two military faction's relationship had improved, their coupling would have been a scandal for the military, but she deeply approved of it.

"It's good to have vampires around," Rebus said. "They make for good security."

"Not as good as us," Hacia challenged. "Our anti-vampire weapons are quite effective."

"That will never be necessary for a true king or queen. The late steward only developed those because he feared an uprising," Peter said.

Nora gave a polite smile before taking a bite of a current scone with a plum jam. The rest of her advisors took note and ate their breakfast in silence. When the black tea was served, she left the cup where it was. She watched the others. Alfie tried to sip and blow at the tea while Peter mixed sugar and cream in his.

Hacia watched the wisps of steam rise from her cup while Rebus sat muttering about the history of anti-vampire weapons to avoid the discomfort of silence. Hacia would test her tea every so often, but the more Rebus carried on, the more frequent her test sips became.

Minerva wandered her way into the room, seemingly by accident, but she knew better. The female vampire was searching for someone dear to them both.

"Morning, Minerva," Nora greeted. "Did you enjoy your room?"

"Yes," she said with a coy smile. "I thought Aegis would be here with you."

"No," she said, stroking the outside of her teacup with one finger. "He's still in my room."

"Your room?" Minerva asked.

Nora took a full sip of her tea. The temperature was perfect. Peter was staring at her while Alfie tried to hide his laughter at the awkward moment.

She nodded, perfect indeed. "In my bed."

Minerva vanished in an instant, but she went in the direction she'd come instead of the course that would've led her to Aegis.

Hacia drank her tea to keep from smirking while Rebus stared blankly at his plate. He was oblivious to what had transpired, but his hands trembled more than usual.

"You're not afraid of the vampires, are you, Rebus?" Nora asked.

The man stumbled over his words. It was treason to lie to the queen, but it was difficult for an older man to admit his fears to a young woman. She understood that and interrupted him rather than watch his quivering beard stew in his lukewarm tea.

"It's only natural to find them unsettling. It took me a while before I got over how quickly they move."

"Aegis does appear more … natural," Peter confessed.

"Minerva had been in that cell for a long time. Before then, she had little interaction with souls. Aegis has more experience is all. He had to walk with me for months in what I imagine would be like slow motion to him."

"The two of you spent some time in that cell together," Rebus said to Peter. "Did she not move like that before?"

Peter turned and glared at Rebus then. He hadn't forgotten that Rebus was complicit in their imprisonment. The grand advisor didn't have a say in who went into the cells and who didn't, but it still ruffled Peter's wiry feathers. She found those ruffled feathers quite amusing.

"I am curious as well," Nora said, resting her head on her fist.

Peter wiped his lips with a napkin. "She was in a death-like sleep most of the time."

"Their lives are lived in chunks between long periods of sleep. Sometimes they don't wake up for centuries. Memories are heavy for them."

"Immortality is a gift as much as it is a curse," Peter said.

They all sat in silent awe of the vampires for a moment before Rebus cleared his throat and laid the agenda for the afternoon. She struggled to pay attention to most of it, but she remembered there was another essential task she needed to do.

"Before the afternoon court, I need to clear the soul bank."

The others stood as she did. "Do you intend to continue putting black souls into the other regions?" Rebus asked.

"Of course," Nora scoffed. "Why wouldn't I?"

"Well, with all the controversy surrounding the decree—"

Peter began to object on her behalf, but the heat rushed across her face and the band of the crown pressed against the flesh of her forehead. "I am the queen! You and every other soul in this world will do as I say from here til the end of time."

Rebus tried to apologize but couldn't stop.

"If you try to go against any of my orders again, I'll throw you into the seventh region with that steward who you followed so obediently."

"Nora," Peter spoke softly as he tried to stand by her side.

She took another step back to keep Peter at a distance as she did with the military and the former advisor. "And you," the queen said to Peter. "I'll not have you constantly questioning everything I say and do."

"Think about what you're saying, Nora," Peter said as he stood. "You want to rule without question, second thought, or wisdom of others?"

Digging her heels into the stone floor beneath her feet, she refused to be lectured in front of everyone. Not by someone who was telling them not to bother her with important matters. She knew he was using the maids to spy on her but she didn't want to play all her cards just yet.

"I want to rule without your scheming and plotting behind my back!"

Peter's voice rose. "I thought you would be a good ruler, a better one than the steward. This is not how a good queen rules."

She was seething with a rage that had no end. How dare he talk about goodness and rules when he broke them all the time! Was she a bad ruler for not deferring to others? If anything, he was a bad advisor by hiding things from her and scolding her like a child in public.

She lifted her chin and said, "Put him back in that cell."

In an instant, Hacia was over the table and on Peter. He didn't attempt to run or resist. He only stared at her with disappointment. She lifted her chin and turned away. Alfie was behind Peter with a blade to his back, using the knife to guide Peter out of the dining hall.

"You know the way," Alfie said.

She waited until they were gone before she flew from the room. There were things to be done that only she could do. On her way to the soul safe her breath quickened and hurt. The stupid corset bit into her ribs and made her dizzy. How could Peter challenge her in front of everyone like that? If he believed she would allow him to mistreat and embarrass her, he was sorely mistaken.

Her chest fought against the corset and she found herself regretting ever putting it on. Peter was her tutor and now advisor, but he took far too many liberties.

Her lungs cried for air and she leaned against the tapestried wall. Aegis didn't even like corsets. She closed her eyes and called to Aegis. She envisioned him holding her, kissing her.

Warm arms held her then. It had worked—mostly. She opened

her eyes to find Aegis was indeed holding her. Nora's gaze held firmly on his lips, hoping he would follow through, but Aegis turned away. She could make him kiss her. Use her powers or even just order him to indulge her. Deep down, he felt the same as her. He just didn't know it yet.

She pushed those ideas from her mind, untangled herself from his arms. She couldn't demand he kiss her. That wasn't love and it was wrong.

Straightening her dress and her composure, she reached for the brass door that stood across from her bedroom. It was a small room, no larger than a closet, with a chair and a safe with iron bars across the front. Nothing adorned the walls apart from the map of Hell.

Aegis leaned against the wall as she opened the safe, hHis dark hair and linen tunic was disheveled from rushing to her call.

"You don't have to stay," Nora said.

"I love watching this."

That made her smile. It made her forget all about what had happened at breakfast. She imagined the bars spinning and the door opening. When she opened her eyes, small orbs of various colors filtered out of the opened safe. There was no back to the safe; it was an endless void that the souls traversed between Hell and the other worlds.

Lifting her arms outward, she began orchestrating the souls. They floated in full circles around her arms. She would use her fingers to pull and push them into their designated region on the map. Most of them went to the third, fourth, fifth, and sixth regions. Once those were sorted, there were only two souls left: one black and one white glowing orb.

"A pure soul," Nora said. It was pearlescent in its coloring yet nearly transparent. If she focused hard enough on the soul, the core of it sparkled and refracted light like a diamond.

"It's beautiful," Aegis said.

She used an expanding hand motion to enlarge the soul's size. From there, she peered inside the person's previous life as she had done with the others. She did this with the black soul to help her understand just what had darkened their spirits. Never until now had she thought to examine a pure soul's life to discover what they had done that made them so special. Once she saw it, she understood that this soul did not belong in the first region at all. Instead, she sent the soul to the third region.

"It was a pure soul," Aegis said. "Why didn't you put it in the first region?"

Nora stared down at the black soul hovering above the ground. The darkest ones moved the slowest in this form. They were sad, wounded things. "The pure soul's only memories were of bright lights followed by a mother's face, then nothing."

Aegis's eyes watered at the answer. "Are you sure it's healthy for you to be looking into souls like this?"

She cupped her hands underneath the black soul and lifted it upward before stretching her hands outward, expanding the soul. "If I'm to send a soul to a life of pain and evil, I should at least look at them first. From what I've seen, people don't wake up evil. They make choices, act on inclinations, turn the other way, but they didn't start that way."

"Nora, what was all the noise downstairs earlier?" Aegis asked with his arms crossed over his chest.

Inside the black soul, she saw what had turned it into the dense, dark ball that it was. It was like many other souls. People with white coats gave them pills, then the soul bought the substance on streets and inside houses. This drug changed their world and deteriorated the person until they died of it.

This soul had gone down a much darker path to maintain its drug use than most. She minimized the soul before she lost her breakfast. This person needed a world of rules and structure. She would put it in the fifth region and allow it to find a new drug.

She closed the safe, spun the lock, and gave Aegis a sad smile. She had seen enough today. Nora's crown wasn't nearly as heavy as her heart. Aegis didn't ask again about what had happened in the dining hall. He would find out eventually.

"I must attend court," she told him as they walked through the halls. "Please come with me. I'd like to have someone to talk to."

Aegis nodded. "Of course. I need to find Minerva as well."

"I'm sure she will turn up." She pursed her lips together and said nothing more on the subject.

She was not going to let the events of the morning ruin her day. On most days, the court was something she disdained, but today, she was going to find something to enjoy while in the company of others. Notably, a band of trapeze artists was scheduled to perform. It was a departure from the jugglers and clowns, and she wanted to see what these trapeze artists were all about.

The court had metal loops mounted into the ceilings and tall bars standing in each corner of the high ceiling. There were three women and three men in matching leotards. She didn't know what to make of the black and white striped design, but her eye was drawn to the tight, flashy material. The troop stood in a row and bowed before her. "We thank you for your invitation, your majesty. We are honored to perform before the true king of Hell."

Rebus interrupted, "The true word for the female king is queen."

The man who had spoken began to stutter. "My apologies—"

She smiled and waved it off. "I take no offense at those who do not know terminology from the other world."

"That's where the word comes from?" the smallest and plainest of the girl trapeze artists asked suddenly. The others shot her a warning look, but Nora couldn't understand why. She was genuinely curious and not at all offensive the way some people had been when corrected.

"Yes, in the other world, female rulers have all sorts of names."

Unlike the others, the girl didn't flinch when their eyes met. She supposed it was rude to look royalty in the eyes, but Nora hated that. She needed connection just as anyone else would. She realized that she had been staring too long at the girl. Tearing her gaze away, Nora clapped her hands together to indicate the performance should start.

She gasped as the troop climbed the tall ladders. It was so high! They dusted their hands with chalk before swinging on the swings mounted to the ceiling. She chewed at her lip as they took the rings. If they fell, they would surely die.

They swayed back and forth, gaining momentum with each swing until a man let go of his swing the same time a woman did. In an instant, they switched bars, and she cried out, but her voice was lost in the crowd.

From the opposite corners, another couple leaped off their platforms and started swinging. Soon, another couple was joining them, and people were flying around from all corners of the room. Nora's eyes darted all over the place, unsure of just who to watch. She gripped the arms of the black throne as her head followed the performance. Nora feared that if she stopped watching, they could plunge to their deaths. She held her breath when they started to let go. Some flipped in the air while others grabbed on to the ankles of those still on the bar.

So enthralled with the performance, she didn't notice that Aegis had entered the courtroom with Minerva until Rebus gave them a nod. She fixated on the dark, petite girl. Being the lightest, she was twirled from swing to swing. The performers caught her by the arms and feet before throwing her higher with each upswing.

One by one, the trapeze artists were caught by their awaiting handlers on their platforms. She took the first gasping breath she'd made since the performance began. The courtgoers applauded and cheered loudly. She stood up and applauded. The artists bowed and bowed again, but something was missing.

Closing her eyes, she imagined flowers were being thrown at their feet. When she opened her eyes, black roses were at the feet of five of the performers, and the petite girl had bunches of red roses. The crowd applauded and bowed to their queen. The girl scooped up her red roses and smiled at Nora.

# Chapter Four

Aegis had found Minerva laying on top of the crisp white linens of her bed, her grey hair fanned away from her face. The draped canopy moved gently with the wind from the open window. The walls were a silky white, allowing the pine furniture to warmly contrast. He noted the colors of the room were like the silk blouse and tan pants that Minerva was wearing.

"She had the rooms made up to our aesthetics," Minerva said.

"Mine is green and brown."

"Did you sleep there?"

"No." There was no point lying to her. Not that he had any intention in doing so. Withholding important information? Sure. But he was too old to lie outright.

Minerva didn't open her eyes, but she smiled a bitter smile. She was starting to understand, even if he didn't tell her. He was for the King's Soul. He had room for Minerva in his heart, but she would always be second to the king. Was that something she was willing or able to accept?

"There's a performing troop in the courtroom," he offered.

"It was just you and me for so long," she said. "I was a fool to think it would always remain that way."

"How could you be a fool?" he asked.

She was staring up at him then, her eyes steely despite the tears dripping from them. "What have you not told me?"

There it was at last. Time to confess. He sat down on the bed beside her. "You know how we defeated the titan …"

"How *you* defeated the titan," she tried to correct.

He shook his head. "No. That thing would've ripped me apart if she hadn't restored my memories from before the long sleep."

Minerva sat up on her palms. Curiosity stemmed from the heartache.

He told her about the memories he'd regained. He spent the better part of the morning giving her the shortened version. There was much that was still foggy to him. He got the crucial details of his life but faces and exact timing mostly eluded him.

"So, what you're saying is that you're effectively married to her," Minerva said at last.

"I made a vow to the first king of Hell. On behalf of all vampires. That's what this is from," he said, holding up his necklace with a dagger carved into it.

"And this?" Minerva asked, nodding at the scar on his palm. She had more of it put together in one afternoon than he'd had over several months.

"That's why you feel it, too, when she needs us. I've guarded many incarnations of the king, and I always will. When a king weakened, it was usually my job to bring the child with the King's Soul back to the castle. To protect the king in that vulnerable state. I got careless and ran off, and a greedy steward killed the incarnations to claim the throne for himself."

He took all the blame for the line of the stewards, for all the pain that Hell endured. If he had kept to his oath instead of chasing after his desires, things would have been different. Then again, if things were different, Nora wouldn't have been the queen of souls.

"It's not your fault," she started. "Well, it is your fault for not telling me everything several months ago, but it's not your fault that the kings were lost."

He remembered something then. Of all things, how could such a detail go amiss? "You weren't there," he said. "How come you were not present during the ages of kings?"

Minerva's moist eyes glistened, and she gave a mysterious smile. "You have your secrets, and I have mine."

"Then you won't tell me?" He supposed he deserved as much. She wasn't one of the nine sworn to the king. If there was one trait required for immortality, it was patience.

Minerva hopped off the bed, setting her sadness aside, or perhaps leaving it altogether. There was no telling with her. She offered a gloved hand to him, and together, they went to the courtroom to see what all the excitement was about.

The hallway from the white room to the courtroom was a narrow, winding one he was not all that familiar with. Perhaps it was an addition from when the stewards ruled. It was an ill feeling along its narrow hallways, which made him conclude that steward had built it. Not the last one, Vinicio, but one of his predecessors.

Minerva and Aegis emerged from the passageway and stood, mouths agape, at the ceiling. Souls were swinging from deadly heights and flinging themselves into the air without harnesses, depending only on another to catch them. Minerva let out an astonished laugh, and he resisted the urge to stand underneath the swings to save anyone that fell.

"You can't save them all," Minerva said.

"They're such amazing creatures."

"But they frighten you."

He lost his breath when a small girl was flung from a pair of ankles and caught by another's arms. "Does their mortality make them capable of such things, or do they risk it all in spite of it?" he asked.

"Which do you think?"

"Somewhere in between, I imagine."

The show finished with all the performers back on the ground where they belonged. Nora rose to her feet and gave a standing ovation. She beamed in a way he hadn't seen since he arrived. Roses fell at the artists' feet, and one of the girls was receiving red flowers.

Minerva observed the smile on his face and narrowed her brow, wondering why he was so amused.

"Nora is rather taken with one of the performers," he whispered in her ear.

Her eyes went to the black girl who was now holding two armfuls of red roses. The girl's eyes locked with Nora's, and Minerva gave him a knowing nod. He was delighted with the prospect of Nora having a companion. Hell knew she needed that intimacy with someone.

In a side entrance, Alfie appeared from the shadows. His angelic face was troubled. There was a knot between his eyebrows that threatened to remain there permanently. He had his hawk with him, too. Usually Alfie didn't bring the bird into the castle; most of the hawk hunters didn't. This was a formal appearance. Before Nora could engage the artists, Alfie interceded and whispered something in her ear. Her smile vanished, and the lonely queen returned.

"I apologize," she announced. "I have some business to deal with, but please, continue to enjoy yourselves. Rebus," she called.

The old man waddled after her, and she gave him instructions before turning and leaving the room with Alfie.

"We should go," Aegis said, pulling on Minerva's hand. There was a stony resistance in her gloved hand, and he turned to find her deliberately letting go of him.

"You mean you should go," she corrected. "I'll remain here."

It pained him to leave her behind, but he didn't have time to soothe her. If something was wrong, he needed to be with Nora. He caught up to them quickly enough. Both Alfie and Nora turned when sensing his presence. They said nothing until they were in the small dining room just off the queen's bedrooms.

"What is going on?" he asked.

"A riot broke out in the fifth region. The souls demand to behold the queen in person. They suspect foul play," Alfie explained.

"What? That's ridiculous," Aegis said. "All of the court can see her."

"Only a select few," Alfie corrected. "Each region is mostly isolated from the other. While courtgoers can see her, only the fourth region receives the news."

Nora plopped on a chair. "This is why I wanted to have people come to the castle from most of the regions."

"We put out most of the fires," Hacia said, but other regions are showing signs of unrest. The fourth is swarming with petitions to validate the queen, to unseat Peter. The third is threatening to withhold resources until it's proven that Nora isn't compromised."

He muttered curse words under his breath as he paced around the room. The third region was responsible for most of the food in Hell. Without their supplies, many people would starve. The fourth region was useless for the most part, but their claws held fast to the court.

"Hacia, is Tina still with you?" Nora asked.

Hacia caught what Nora was saying straightaway. "I'll have her write to her family. The people there will be eased by Tina's confirmation for now, at least."

Nora's eyes wandered the table as she considered what to do next. "As for the fifth and fourth, I will deal with them. Who's leading them?"

"Take a wild guess," Alfie said.

***

Aegis followed her to her bedroom, but she wasn't sure she wanted company, even his. To her relief, when they entered her room, Aegis went to the balcony and closed the doors behind him. She needed to work out her feelings privately.

She sat at her vanity to have a look at herself in the mirror, but when she did, the crown pillow blocked her reflection. All she could see was the crown before her. Tall, sharp barbs jutted from unseen edges, ensnaring the precious stones in their grasp. It wasn't as beautiful as it once had been. Her resentment toward the crown made it less attractive. Perhaps it resented her and that's why it didn't fit.

*It doesn't belong to you.*

"If not the queen, then who?" she argued.

It was a trap. The King's Soul never gave her clear cut answers, only bits and pieces to remind her that she was not in full control.

*It belongs to Hell.*

What did that mean? She repeated the question several times and received no reply. The King's Soul had given up for the day, or perhaps it had used up all its strength, escaping the place in her mind where she locked it away. She unclenched her fists and took a deep breath.

Why hadn't someone found a better place for the crown cushion by now? She had been queen for the last six bloody months. She had four rooms counting the one she had fashioned for Aegis. Couldn't any of her maids find a dresser or stool for the thing?

She swiped at the pillow, knocking it to the ground, then slammed both fists on the vanity tabletop and glared at herself in the mirror. She bore no resemblance to her mother. Perhaps she took after her father. Was that why her mother hated her as much as she did?

Bella had been sent back home, pregnant with the steward's baby. She thought that the next time she saw her mother it would be on her terms. She was the queen, after all. It didn't matter who she was. Bella always got what Bella wanted. Her mother wanted to see her, for whatever reason, and she would throw the whole region into chaos to get her way.

Fuming as she stared in the mirror, she hated feeling so helpless. What would she do? Of course, she had no choice. Bella was playing the frantic, concerned mother who just needed assurance her baby was alive. The people of the fifth region were zealots of one kind or another, and they were easy to whip into a frenzy. The last thing she needed was for them to charge the border that separated the first region with their own.

No, she would go. She would go to the fifth region and throw around a few parlor tricks to prove she was who she said. It would be a campaign of sorts. She would do the same in the other regions as well. Not the seventh region, of course, but all the others would see the queen and the truth would be confirmed. After that, she would demand Rebus send invitations to people *she* requested to see from all the regions.

She would put on a happy face and spin her magic. She smiled at her reflection, but what smiled back was mocking, like a caricature of an evil villain laughing after ripping someone's heart out. She couldn't look away as the face shook from side to side, only pausing for brief moments, each displaying an expression more horrifying than the last until it warped into a myriad of faces all posing in various horrific expressions simultaneously.

She must have been screaming. Aegis had her pressed to his chest. "It's all right," he promised.

Aegis could say those things, but he didn't know what she saw. Was she going mad? The crown was no longer on her head but the floor. It was such a trinket against the lush cream rug—thinner, more like a piece of wire than a crown.

"What happened just now?" he asked.

She couldn't say for sure. Her mother was forcing a reunion when she hoped never to see her again. There were rumors that she was dead and a puppet for the advisor had taken her place. Aegis's girlfriend was still wandering the castle. She had a kingdom on the verge of revolt. So, it was safe to say she was stressed and tired, but Aegis didn't always understand souls.

"Are you going to keep Peter in that cell forever?" he asked.

Did Aegis see what had happened? For a moment, she was

trapped in some sort of freak out. It was the most horrifying thing she'd ever done. Why would he bring up Peter at a time like this? Maybe he thought Peter would be able to help, but no one could help her. No one understood what it was like to have two souls constantly battling within them.

"You can let him out." She sniffed back the tears. "I just need him to stop questioning me in front of everyone all the time."

Aegis scooped her up and set her on the bed. "I'm sending someone in to help you dress and to bring you your tea."

The vampire opened the door and called for Bosh. He whispered instructions to her servant and waited until a maid came to help her undress. "I'll be back in a little while. You should try to get some rest."

She allowed the maid to undress her, saying nothing all the while. The pretty blonde maid was oh so careful.

"Rebus wanted me to tell you that the girl trapeze artist, Elise, is staying in the orange room with the other ladies in her troop. They will be staying for the next few days."

At this she brightened, and the scary ordeal faded slightly. "Maybe they will do another performance?"

The maid smiled and hung up her gown. "I imagine so."

Her mind swam with the possibilities, but of what, she wasn't sure. She wanted to see Elise again. She didn't need to be performing death-defying tricks. She just wanted to talk to her. "I have many things I'd like to ask her. Do you think she would come and speak to me?"

"I can ask." The maid opened the door, and Bosh came in with her tea set. "Bosh, go fetch the smallest girl from the trapeze show. The queen would like her to join her for tea."

The servant practically tripped over his own feet with various tasks. He uttered little "ohs" and "nos" and the occasional curse word in the utmost polite fashion. She couldn't help but giggle at the constant plight that was Boshy's life. It was while watching him that she discovered something was amiss with his shoes. They were far too big. Maybe four sizes bigger than what he normally wore. It reminded her of a clown.

"Bosh, are those your shoes?" she asked.

"No ma'am, they're not. I was in the stables and stepped in something unfortunate. I had to borrow a pair from the kitchens. This is all they had."

She closed her eyes and imagined the shoes shrinking, conforming to Bosh's feet perfectly. When she opened her eyes, one shoe was smaller, but the other remained the same.

Bosh reared up in surprise and said, "Oh, it's no trouble, ma'am. Mine are nearly dry."

"Sorry, I guess I'm just fatigued." Her powers had been consistent since she and the King's Soul had merged—until now. Panic and doubt nipped at her fragile sense of calm. What was happening to her?

The maid appeared impervious to what had just transpired, but she was smarter than that. Peter paid her for information. She could hear whispers every time she glanced at the maid. Her mind whirled with what Peter would do with the gossip and how far it would go.

"Should I tell Aegis not to disturb you and Elise?" the maid asked.

She shook her head. "No, he will know if he's wanted or not."

She closed her eyes and gave the shoe one more fitting. This time, when she opened her eyes, both fit. Relief washed over her, and she fell into the bed. The mirror episode had rattled her confidence, but it was probably nothing more than a dream. Sometimes her insomnia led her to fall asleep in inappropriate places.

"Oh, there it is," Bosh announced. "Two perfectly fitted shoes. Thank you, ma'am." The maid said nothing as she followed Bosh out the door.

Nora put on her fluffy white robe, opened the doors to the balcony, and brought her tea set with her. Before long, a knock came at the door, followed by the maid escorting the trapeze artist into the room. She was wearing a modern, sophisticated pale violet dress. Her brown hair was released from its ponytail and allowed to stand out in every direction, shaping her oval face.

"Please, sit down," Nora beckoned.

"My name is Elise, your majesty," she said with a curtsey.

"Just call me Nora."

Elise sat down, and she began performing the tea ceremony. She hoped Elise didn't notice how clumsy she suddenly became. Her fingers grew stubby and dumb under Elise's gaze.

"It's a beautiful set," the girl said.

She told her about how she got it and described each of the different components. Elise listened and watched until a cup of tea was sitting before her. "Such patience," she commented.

"Well, the ritual helps me sleep. I'm sure it's nothing compared with trying to learn how to fly through the air."

Elise laughed. "Well, it's not like I had a choice."

"Tell me about it."

***

Aegis stood before a thick, ancient door in the castle dungeon. It was still mostly a secret—only one key had been made. Nora gave the worn skeleton key to him, and it was clear she intended for him to stay. It made sense; he was the safest person to hold on to it. He was not only her friend and protector, but now, her prison guard.

The stairs behind the door were steep, and a lever on the side of the wall started up a series of pullies and cords that buzzed and hummed. There was a mix of awe and fear of the dungeon. Lamps flickered to life and the heat met his face, as did a lingering, musky rot.

He sped down the steps at a pace only a vampire could. At the base of the landing, he glanced around at the small room surrounded by cells. There was a bookshelf and a writing desk that went unused. Only one cell was occupied; the rest were open. Nothing but a bunk bed, a toilet, and a small barred window resided within the cells.

There was another set of steps that spiraled into a lower level in a far corner. Peter could wait a few more minutes. From the cooling air around him, Aegis understood that this was an underground level. It led to a wide cell door that was left open.

This cell was much larger than the others. There was no bed or toilet, only markings around the inside of the cell—scratches of an outline of a blade. It hit him like a blow from a giant. This was where the last titan had been kept all those years.

Before the stewards and kings, there were titans. They ruled Hell without order or mercy on the souls. Good and evil meant nothing to them. So many lost their lives to the titans, soul and vampire both. The titans treated them as playthings, the souls more so than the vampires.

His kind wasn't called vampires then. He couldn't remember what they were called. They tried to steer clear of the titans. Souls found themselves in trouble no matter what they did. He never intended to get into the fray, but when he met Tom, everything changed.

He had been standing on a grassy embankment when he first encountered the first king. Only he wasn't a king then. He was nothing more than a boy.

A heavy fog lined the glades, and a morning chill bit at his fingertips when he saw a boy standing in the distance. The boy's limbs were long and gangly, and he had wild ginger hair. The vampire watched with curiosity as the boy waded into the fog. Aegis couldn't recall if he were doing anything significant at that moment. He supposed no one is doing anything important the moment their life is forever altered.

A snake-like creature pooled upward until a head split from the skin. Arms grew and stretched into branch-like claws. It had black eyes and a pale moon of a face with a gaping hole for a mouth. Its sharpened teeth were stained red, no doubt from the souls it fed on. The vampire gasped. The creature was grotesque, even for a titan.

He grabbed the boy and dodged. A spindly hand snagged at their clothes. In mid-air, he had a better look at the titan. It was staring at them unblinking before splashing back into a murky puddle. They landed several feet away, but the boy's face scrunched up, and he pushed Aegis aside.

"What are you doing?" the boy asked.

The expression on his face must have been one of confusion because the boy laughed and said, "Just watch and see."

The snake titan charged at the boy who confidently strode at the horrifying creature. It lowered its head, intending to gobble the boy up whole, but the boy reached into a tan leather satchel, took out a fistful of white crystals, and threw them at the thing's face.

A piercing shriek came from the titan as its face went waxy, then melted. The fragments of its face fell into the hole that served as a mouth. It looked up to the sky in its last moment before the breach was all that remained. The mouth fell open, consuming the body until nothing was left. It was the strangest thing he had ever seen.

"The mouth ate everything?" Aegis asked.

The boy smiled and showed him what was in the satchel.

"Salt?" He couldn't believe it.

"That titan was nothing more than a giant slug," the boy explained. "Salt kills slugs."

His mind was blank with wonder. This boy dumbfounded him. He was just a soul, but he took down a titan in one throw. His kind had lost many a battle with the impervious titans. This boy was fearless but also rather peculiar. He had a sense of purpose that Aegis found tantalizing. Purpose was a vision to behold for the likes of a lone vagrant like him.

"What are you?" he asked.

The boy grinned. "No one yet." Without another word, he walked into the fog.

Aegis tried to hail him, but he didn't stop. Silently lecturing himself on getting involved with souls, the vampire followed. The boy, not much older than Nora was now, faded in the fog, and he had no choice but to follow if he wanted answers.

"How did you know that salt kills titans?"

"It only kills that titan," the boy explained. "It was that titan's fatal flaw."

"Fatal flaw?"

"The only way to defeat a titan is by discovering its fatal flaw and to use it. Each one is different. Some are harder than others. That was an easy one."

The boy's face was unreadable. He didn't know what to make of him. The boy's clothing was ragged and there were holes in his shoes, but he walked as though he were the wealthiest soul alive.

"I'm going to hunt them down. Every last one of them," the boy promised. Aegis didn't doubt that he would, but the vampire hadn't expected that such a thing could be possible.

"How are you going to do that?" he asked.

"There's a witch in the southeast mountains. I'm going to strike a deal with her."

He had heard of witches. They were souls that brought with them their magic to Hell. Some were born with the wisdom of their past lives. Others acted on instinct; some learned the magic here on Hell. He didn't know why one would live on the mountain, but he was curious. He was—after all— much younger then, and all this talk of fatal flaws, witches, and young men with resounding purpose had intrigued him.

"I'd like to accompany you," Aegis said.

"That is fine," the boy said.

"What's your name?"

"Tom. What's yours?" he asked.

"My kind doesn't have names."

Tom observed him with keen brown eyes and said, "You have one; you just don't know it yet."

A voice called to him in the distant fogs. One that knew his name. Aegis turned around for the caller as Tom walked away. The voice shouted with an older man's voice, one frayed with age and annoyance. He snapped into the current day to find Peter screaming in his ear.

"Aegis, you going to leave me here all day?" he called. "I know it's you."

He left the titan's cell and went up the spiral stone stairs. Peter waited for him to unlock the door. He was disheveled and the stench of human odors clung to his clothes.

"She's going to let me out, or is she going to have me killed?" Peter asked.

"Like she could ever kill you."

Nora was working through something; he had learned that much. She was hiding something dark and painful, and he wanted to help. He had his reservations about Peter, but the man cared enough to go back to a cell for her. "What do you think is wrong?"

Peter shrugged. "I don't know. Do you have any ideas?"

"Each incarnation is different," he explained. "Some are better than others, but this time is different. She's in trouble. Earlier today, she did something strange—something I've never seen before."

He told Peter about how Nora was staring into the mirror, how her head began shaking in every which direction. Her reflection laughed, cried, and screamed all at once. It wasn't something Nora could control. He had to pull her away from the mirror and calm her before he could leave.

"Does she know you saw?" Peter asked, eyes wild with fear.

"I'm not sure." He didn't see how it mattered.

Peter walked out of his cell and investigated the bookshelf. "Maybe there's something in here or the library. We need answers before she puts herself or anyone else in danger."

He helped Peter carry a stack of books up the stairs and to his room. The books landed with a dull thud on an uneven table. "In the meantime, try to stay out of sight."

"Yes, I'll research it. You stay with her. We'll keep each other in the loop?"

"Yes." He had agreed to keep Peter in the loop, but that didn't mean he was going to hide anything from his queen. He would talk to Nora about it. They would have an open and honest conversation where Nora would understand their concerns and feel safe enough to tell them more about what she was going through. He and Peter only wanted what was best for her. Nora had to have realized that.

He was just about to put his hand on the doorknob to Nora's room when a new voice chimed in. She was talking to someone, another girl from the sounds of it. He overheard some of the conversation. It certainly wasn't a maid; she was speaking too informally for it to be a maid.

It occurred to him that if Nora had a guest, it would be best to go to his room and wait until the guest left. The voices became giggles and then whispers. He could still hear them over his pacing feet, and he was too agitated to go into one of his sleeps. Despite all his efforts, it was hard for him not to listen to parts of their conversations.

He couldn't take it anymore and became flush with embarrassment as their conversation turned into other noises. He wasn't about to leave if the companion had ulterior motives, but still, he didn't want to listen to them. There was nothing for him to do.

He opened the window to his room and scaled the wall.

When he reached the rooftop, the fresh night air released his tensions. He breathed in deeply and stared at the night sky. This world, despite all its flaws, was worth fighting for. Nora was worth fighting for. She just needed to grow into her status.

With Nora's room just underfoot, he assumed it was at a safe enough distance to give his queen privacy and not suffer from embarrassment.

Moans echoed up the chimney and his mouth fell in horror. There was no escaping it.

# Chapter Five

Daylight warmed her face and Nora opened her eyes to bask in its gentle glow. Beside her was Elise, the beautiful trapeze artist. She was older than Nora by several years—made even older by her difficult life. She was from the sixth region. Her mother had lost her in a bet, and Elise was sold into the circus at the age of eleven.

At eleven, Nora had spent the bulk of her time with Peter and her maid Sarah. She was coddled and safe at that time. Vinicio was uncertain if she possessed the King's Soul. It had never been a female before, and she demonstrated none of the usual kingly gifts.

The steward married her mother to keep her close, just in case. Bella didn't think twice. She thought she found her happily ever after with Nora safely tucked away somewhere within the castle. Her mother's negligence aside, she lived a sheltered life until she was left in the Starry Wood for dead. Things could have been worse for her. In comparison, she was fortunate for the life her mother gave her, even if it was accidental.

Elise stirred in her sleep but gave in to the comfort of the blankets and pillows. Her cheekbones were piercing in the morning light. She was perfection.

Nora's mind turned from the lovely woman to her mother. She would have to deal with the racket her mother was causing. Why couldn't she just write a letter instead of inciting rebellion? If she didn't squash the rumors, souls could get hurt.

Slipping from the bed, she went to the bathroom and rang the copper bell mounted on the wall. Her stomach rumbled and she wanted a bath.

Elise woke gently from the noise and found her with her dark, sleepy eyes and smiled. Ignoring the pang of guilt for what she was about to do, she reminded herself it was for the best.

"I called for breakfast. You can eat with me before leaving if you like," she said as she slipped on her robe.

Elise frowned, taken aback by her sudden coldness. She sat up, pressing the sheets to her chest as if the exposure was shameful. It couldn't be helped.

She understood Elise's motives now. It wasn't like she expected the girl to love her at first sight, and Elise was indeed infatuated with the queen, but deep down, Elise wanted a way out of the life she had.

The girl didn't tell Nora this—she didn't need to. Elise's subconscious had mingled with her own when they slept. They all had motives that were not entirely pure. Much of Elise wanted love just as much as she did, but if things didn't work out, she would only remain for the luxury, and Nora would feel that lie night after night.

The maid came bustling in with a cart, and several others followed behind with buckets of hot water. They fussed over her and shook out the bed, ignoring Elise entirely. Nora also ignored her as she stumbled from the bed and rushed to her clothing while she glowered at the queen.

"Is that it then?" Elise asked. Her nostrils flared as she tried to contain her anger. She didn't blame her.

Nora swallowed hard and turned away. "That will be all."

The girl left, and she turned to her maid, "See that she is well compensated before they return to the sixth region."

The water was scalding hot as she stepped in. Her skin cried out in protest as she submerged up to her chest. She'd had this bronze bathtub made for her as she didn't want to bathe in the same tub as her mother and stepfather once had. She needed to focus herself for the day ahead, but she couldn't do that when the day would bring her back to the place of her childhood, of her sour grandparents and her mother.

She didn't have time for lovers or fanciful things. She had to perform her magic—and prove that she indeed still lived—to quiet the rumors that she had somehow died. The plan was to leave Peter and Minerva here to handle things while she and Aegis were gone. She would tour the regions of Hell and prove to the common souls that she was queen.

"Nora?" Aegis called from the balcony.

"You can come in," she replied.

Aegis glanced at the tub before turning away. He was always so chivalrous. He'd seen her naked before, but that was just how he was. Here she had taken lovers and ruled a world, but he still didn't see her for the woman she was.

"Where is your friend?" he asked.

"I sent her on her way."

Aegis's eyes went wide with surprise. "I thought—"

She played with the bubbles in her bath. "What? That I'm in love?"

His lips pressed together as he frowned. He wanted to say something more, but he couldn't. She imagined if she were a boy, he'd lecture her on not mistreating women, but how could he tell her such things? He was out of his element when it came to instructing girls on how to treat their lovers.

"We need to talk about yesterday," Aegis said.

"And today as well."

"What's happening today?" he asked as he sat on the bed, facing away from her.

"We will go to the fifth region to confront the rumors. I want Minerva to stay and help Peter with ruling in my stead."

"She will serve you well," he agreed.

Her toes were beginning to prune, but she returned them to the water. "After that, we will tour the rest of the regions—save the seventh, of course. What is it you want to talk about?"

Aegis smoothed his hands against one another as he struggled to find the right words. "Yesterday, the mirror …"

So, it wasn't a dream after all. Aegis continued to talk, but she no longer listened to what he said explicitly. It was more like she was receiving the emotions of his words. Undercurrents of the conversation between what he was saying and what he meant. The ebbs and flows of what people said and what they wanted to relay were often different. His was one of genuine concern and fear. Did he fear her? The idea aroused and saddened her under the stagnant waves of her bathwater.

"I just worry for you, and so does Peter."

What he was honestly saying was that he questioned her health, her stability, her abilities, and most of all, he questioned her. She said nothing as he confessed his concerns. Peter had gotten to him, no doubt. It was a bitter tea to drink. She trusted him above all others. At night, his subconscious only showed her love and devotion, but where was that now?

Nora stood up from her bath and stepped out before wrapping herself in her towel, unaware that he was still talking.

"We are looking for answers—"

"Excellent, Aegis. You may leave now."

He appeared wounded, as though she'd told him to piss off. No doubt, the nuance of their conversation went both ways. What she said was not what he wanted to hear. She was never one to be open about her feelings before, why would she change now?

"I'll wait for you with the litter then," Aegis said before he jumped off the balcony.

She waited until a thud rumbled from outside before she sank to the floor sobbing.

***

"She wants me to stay with Peter?" Minerva asked. Her eyes were wide with confusion. For someone given such an honor, she certainly didn't appreciate it. Nora trusted her, wasn't that a good thing?

"To rule in her stead," Aegis asserted.

Peter and Minerva both stared at him in disbelief. He presumed they would be happy to hear this news, but Minerva stood with her arms crossed, and Peter just shook his head. He wasn't exactly thrilled with Nora's decisions and attitude of late either, but he thought this was a wise choice.

"She freed me from a cell only yesterday, and now I'm to rule on her behalf?" Peter scoffed.

"What of the military?" Minerva asked.

He didn't know. Nora hadn't told him as much.

"She didn't think about them. Not when she has you," Peter said.

"What is so wrong with that?" he challenged. "I've protected the King's Soul since the beginning."

"Yes, it's nice to know all of that now," she said with a raised brow. "I think we should look into that irrigation system you mentioned. Imagine the fifth and sixth regions having access to more water."

He acknowledged the snub, but he wouldn't let it get to him. Minerva had every right to be upset with him. Would disclosing the pact with the King's Soul sooner have made a difference for them now? He suspected not. They'd had worse fights than this, and they would move past it.

He gave Peter a knowing nod and walked out of the room—slowly, as not to frighten the man. He walked through the court as the souls watched him curiously and had to suppress his laughter when he noted more than one courtgoer had a necklace made of garlic.

No doubt, they too believed the silly superstitions about drinking blood and garlic. Where did they get such ideas in the first place? Had he ever drunk blood? He reached into the past and only one incident involving blood drinking came to mind. It was when he and Tom had traveled to the second region to meet the witch on the mountain.

"I'm going to build a fire," Tom had said.

Aegis was not the best at making fire. It was evident right away that the boy would need to make his own fire, but he assisted where he could. The vampire was able to teach the boy other things, like navigation and hunting. Tom wasn't the best at killing rabbits, but he took direction well. He didn't know what souls could or could not eat, but Tom got tips from the locals as they went. Those early days with Tom reminded him of his travels with Nora.

Returning to the boy with an armful of wood, he saw that Tom had started a fire and had a few rabbits on a skewer. He didn't even pick up the scent when Tom skinned and gutted the hares.

"Good," Aegis said. "If you can go undetected by one of my kind, a titan doesn't stand a chance."

"I have a good teacher."

They spoke little as the fire climbed higher. Tom fell asleep against the tree, but he kept the fire going for the boy. They were a week or so away from the mountains. If Tom would just let Aegis carry him, they would have been there already, but Tom had pride and refused to be carried.

The scent of souls carried along the wind, like salt and earth covered in smoke. It would only be a matter of time before they came to investigate, but right now, his focus was on Tom. He said little, but when he did, it was with a wisdom that no young man should have.

"Why do it?" Aegis asked. "Why risk your life to end the titans?"

"I'll serve a thousand lifetimes if that's what it takes to make this world safe for souls."

It was the next morning when a group of wandering souls came to their fire. They were poor and ragged from travel. They held pots and other supplies tied to their backs with rags, and they smelled of body odor. Tom's nose wrinkled when he woke.

"Could we share your fire with you?" a brown man with white shorn hair asked.

"Please, join us." Tom motioned to the fire. "Aegis, you think your traps caught anything?"

"Perhaps," Aegis said. Without thinking, he stood and sped off through the grass to check his traps. In the distance, he could hear alarmed shouts and gasps. He returned shortly with two good size rabbits. It was enough to feed the boy, but not the other eleven.

The people brought out their bowls, and a woman fetched water to set on the fire. Another returned with rooted vegetables indigenous to the area. Tom worked at the rabbit and had the things peeled in minute. He beamed with pride.

"The potatoes are ready," someone announced.

The stew simmered on the fire while plain bowls were passed around. The white-haired man was the leader. He asked Tom what everyone wanted to know. "What brings you out here, young man? And how did you encounter such an unusual friend?"

"Titans killed my mother," Tom said. "Along with everyone in my village."

The people whispered in heartbreak. He had no idea that was Tom's reasoning. The boy had never mentioned it. It was no wonder he was so determined. Mothers were important to souls. It was an obvious detail about mortals, yet it wasn't until he experienced the sorrow Nora felt that he understood their impact on children.

"We've all lost people as well," the man said. "That is why we travel as nomads. There's no point in building a city when a titan can show up and tear everything down."

"I've been searching the world, looking for a way to kill the titans, but it's never that simple. To kill them, I must learn each one of their fatal flaws. I am not strong enough yet, but I will be soon. I must find the witch on the mountain."

There was a stunned silence. What shocked the people more—Tom's almost prophetic demeanor or his search for a witch? Aegis was constantly at awe with the boy, so it was gratifying to not be the only one for once.

"And this … this being?" the white-haired man asked.

"His name is Aegis, and he is going to help me," Tom said.

His eyes grew wet, but it took him a moment to figure out why. The boy had named him. It was a profound feeling to have a name. It was like being real in someone else's mind for the first time.

"I can see why." The white-haired man smiled a broad, kind smile full of healthy teeth.

"We've heard stories of the witch. She is not one to be trifled with, but she is not evil," a woman said.

"I figured as much. I'm not sure any soul is truly evil—" Tom let out a scream, and everyone jumped away.

He leapt over the fire and picked Tom up to search for what had made him scream. There was nothing, but Tom was holding a spot on his back. The boy trembled and gasped in pain. Aegis lifted his shirt to discover two small puncture wounds on Tom's side. There was a rattling noise as the grass parted for a small serpent.

"A death-rattle snake," one of the travelers said.

"He must have been leaning against the snake's burrow," another reasoned.

"Such a shame."

He wasn't ready to lose Tom yet. Rolling him onto his side, he put his lips to the wound. The vampire sucked the poisonous blood from the boy's body until the wound closed. Tom was unconscious, and his skin was pale white. The alkaline venom coated his teeth. He had drawn some of it out, but was it enough?

"We need a healer," Aegis said, searching the crowd for help.

The woman with the scarfed head came forward. "Prop him up. He will either live, or he won't. I'll do what I can."

Aegis paced around the boy most of the day and well into the night. Occasionally, the woman would tell him she needed a specific herb or water. He would retrieve the supplies as quickly as he could, but Tom remained unchanged. The others of her tribe were spread out, hunting and setting up camp.

"He's still breathing. That's a good sign," she told him on the third day.

"Good."

"What were you doing earlier?" she asked.

"I don't know," he admitted. "I thought I could draw the poison out."

The healer laughed. "Well, that won't work; all you succeeded in doing was frightening the tribe."

He gave an embarrassed laugh as a tribe member approached them with a reeking white bulb.

"Oh, garlic, thanks," the healer reached for it and began pulling it apart, only making the smell worse. She noted his expression and laughed. "You don't care for garlic."

He did not care for garlic. Especially not when souls wore it in ropes around their necks all around him.

The scent broke him from his memories and into the present, where a fat little man with a pert nose stood clutching his bulb necklace.

"I like your necklace," he said.

The arched wooden doors opened to the front of the castle where he was greeted by six white horses. Where was the carriage? He examined each of the horses before deciding on a golden mare with white spots, leaving the strong black stallion for Nora.

Alfie arrived. Two trackers and another hawk hunter accompanied him. Alfie greeted Aegis with an overconfident smirk, but that was just how Alfie presented himself. The other hawk hunter had a much smaller hawk than Alfie's. He had an identical chainmail vest and black linen pants, but he didn't wear the badge or the swagger that Alfie had.

The two trackers wore plain white tunics with brown pants—dressed for the road. One was bronze-skinned with brown hair, and the other was pale with black hair. Both were young girls, but older than Nora. He was beginning to worry that the kingdom was overflowing with young people. That was every old man's fear.

The queen stepped out dressed in leather riding boots and a similar tunic as the trackers. Her hair was tied back plainly, and she looked as though she were ready for a fight.

He smiled at the image. It reminded him of before she became queen—before he'd left when it was just the two of them. Only he had left a girl and came back to find a woman had taken her place. She smiled back at him and mounted the black stallion. "Feels like the old days," Nora teased.

"Yes, but I was the horse for most of that journey."

Nora grinned and turned back to her companions. "Aegis, this is Charlie, one of Alfie's."

Charlie's face had a hardened, worn look about him, like he'd experienced more than he'd bargained for in his lifetime. Shaggy brown hair surrounded his long face. His bird liked him well enough. It shifted around on his shoulder and would occasionally nibble at his ear, affectionately.

"The trackers are Bailey and Heather," Nora added.

He raised his hand in salute, and the girls gave the nod. He wasn't sure which was which, but he imagined he would learn somewhere along the trail.

Nora started her horse southward, and the troop followed, leaving him sputtering in the dust.

Spurring his horse, he caught up to the queen for an explanation.

She smirked as if she'd been waiting for him to ask. "We're going the wrong way."

"It's not the wrong way; it's just not the way to the fifth region."

He continued to stare at her, waiting for further explanation. The rest of the group knew where they were going; why didn't he?

Alfie's leer lingered on the back of his neck. Did she want him to appear like a fool in front of everyone?

"I wanted Minerva and Peter to think we were heading to the fifth region," Nora explained. "I even sent the royal carriage in that direction as a decoy."

"Why would you do that?"

"For my safety," she answered.

He wanted to tell her she had nothing to fear, try to shake it into her thick skull. "You're not in danger from them or anyone else."

"A girl is always in danger."

Nora spurred her horse ahead and continued to increase the distance between them. Aegis fell behind to the back of the group, allowing the others to move up.

Alfie nodded at Charlie, and soon, the riders flanked the queen. It seemed to Aegis that Nora didn't fear for her safety; she feared questions.

***

Peter pushed open the arched wooden double-doors of the royal library. He loved the dusty paper aroma of old books. So many scrolls and books called his name on this day. He was reluctant to leave the books he found, but Minerva was by far a faster reader and could glean information at a far superior rate.

He was old and his eyes watered if he read too much, so it was his job to find more books with possible leads and bring them back to his rooms. The daylight streamed through the windows brightly and exposed another eyewatering menace: dust. The particles floated all around, threatening to make his day a difficult one.

"What do I need, what do I need?" he mumbled to himself as he searched through the books. Anything of promise he stacked in a pile on a long pine table. Peter ransacked the shared library before entering the restricted area and searching there. Being an advisor for the queen wasn't a great job, but at least it had its perks. His fingers fluttered through crumbling texts and scrolls as if he could feel the right tome calling to him.

"Can I help you?"

Peter whirled around to find a man older than himself. He wore thick lenses and dressed smartly. Peter looked him up and down. He needed a double-button vest like this man. Peter liked the brown tweed pant that matched. The man's facial hair was immaculately groomed; he wished he could grow facial hair like that. The most Peter could manage was a sad, patchy little beard, an utterly useless thing.

"Ah, yes, I need texts regarding past kings and their ailments," Peter said.

The librarian frowned. "Well, there are several about the kings written by the stewards."

"I need something more specific," Peter explained. "About dysfunctional kings."

"Hm…" The man unlocked a glass-faced cabinet and produced a thin, flat book. It had lost several pages as the spine was far too large for the contents.

"Is there more to this?" Peter asked, examining the book.

"There was," the librarian said. "The king saw the records made by his steward, and in a fit of rage, he ripped parts of the book out. This was all that could be salvaged."

Peter took the nameless book in his hands and hoped it would provide the answers he sought. "Thank you."

"That king was a short-lived one. They called him the 'fractured' king."

Peter left the library as politely and calmly as he could manage before rushing straight to his room. What a sight he must have appeared! Servants and strangers alike watched the madman dash to his chambers before bolting the door.

Minerva acknowledged him from the desk. In the short time he had been gone, she had finished five books. "What is it?" she asked.

"I think we've found that we're looking for," Peter said as he handed her the book.

# Chapter Six

The rain fell in warm splatters across the lush green grasses of the first region. The dirt path widened from sudden use by the six riders. He smiled at the six mud-caked horses. The stench of muddied animals and wet humans was breaking through the rain. This was what he lived for, and judging by Nora's determined expression, she felt the same.

"Shouldn't we make camp?" Alfie asked.

The hawk hunter general had asked him, but it wasn't his decision. Nora was a seasoned traveler and had a better grasp of the road than the general who'd grown comfortable in castle life.

"Where exactly would we stop?" she asked Alfie.

The hawk hunter ignored the wet blond curls that dripped over his brow and into his eyes. "I brought a canopy," he offered.

"Enough for all six horses and six people?" she asked. "We'll arrive at the foot of the temples within the next hour."

"I don't think they're that close—" Alfie began.

"No, she's right," Aegis interrupted. No one belittled his queen, who knew Hell better than any soul alive. "We may come upon them sooner, even. I can smell fire up ahead."

"You forget I know this land," Nora told Alfie. "My soul has walked this world countless times. It was my soul that carved up the regions and forged the borders."

Her voice was distant and her tone softer. She wasn't bragging. It was more as if she were lamenting the fact. The only one in all of Hell who could shoulder more burden than him was Nora. She was not a child. She had told him as much time and time again, but he never listened.

He couldn't look at her then. It was like watching a hungry child and being unable to feed it, or watching an old soul riddled with arthritis continue to work. Things that reduced the arguably strongest being in Hell to utter helplessness.

A winged rooftop emerged from the clouded horizon. The rain distorted their vision, but one of the temples was a monumental sight. It had three tiers of roof and was nearly as large as the castle itself. What did she want with the monks? She had set up a diversion by sending a royal carriage and guards to the fifth region. Perhaps this was just a short visit to give the wagon a head start.

Outside the castle, no one in the first region cared about castle politics. The monks, caretakers, and the purest of souls lived in the first region. They were gifted with the rarest of blooms and jungles full of exotic animals. It was also one of the only places where melodies could be created. The last time they were here, he had been shot full of arrows, but he didn't hold any grudges.

"You've hardly spoken to me since this morning," Nora said to Aegis.

"I didn't think you wanted me to."

A rigid smile plastered on Nora's face suggested she was uncomfortable. Why mortals smiled when they were uncomfortable always confused him.

"You don't like that I sent the girl away, that I sent Peter to the cell, how I separated you and Minerva … how I've withheld information from you."

She was right. He disliked all these things. Not that the actions themselves bothered him. If she ordered him to slaughter the entire contents of the castle, he would do it. It was the fact that these actions bothered her, and yet she still did them. "I don't know why you sent the girl away, so I can't be angry about it."

Nora wasn't grinning anymore. "Then you're jealous."

He gave a silent laugh. "You should know better by now."

"No, of course not. You don't want me as your lover. You're

beyond such things." She posed airs to mock him.

"You know better than that even still."

"She wasn't my first, you know."

This surprised him, but he refused to show it. She was trying to prove to him that she was a grown woman, and he didn't want her to associate physical intimacy was adulthood. Being an adult wasn't about proving one's self with adult actions, but telling the queen as much would have little impact.

"But have you loved any of them?" he asked.

"No."

"All these things you think I'm angry with you for—they're not things I'm angry about. They are things you're not proud of and don't know how to reconcile. I'm not your moral superior, Nora. I have had my hand at all sorts of mistakes. There's nothing you can do that would make me hate you."

Nora's brow bowed down as she gasped. She struggled not to cry, but even if she did, it wouldn't matter. The rain was heavy enough to separate them from the riders several feet away. It was what made her feel safe enough to talk about such things.

"I know I'm losing control of my powers, but I don't know why. I'm not dying."

There was a relief in her voice. To finally say what they all already knew. He had been waiting for her to tell him her truth. Choosing his next words carefully was of the utmost importance. "Peter is trying to find a reason behind it. Whatever it is, we can figure it out," he promised.

Nora chewed her lip and turned away. There was more she wanted to say, but the rain had lessened and the temple was at hand. Alfie and the rest of the group closed in on them, anxious to get dried off.

"These people operate on a different level," Nora warned them. "No one will serve you here. Whatever you use must be returned to whence it came. Don't interrupt them."

He couldn't help but grin when Nora issued her orders. Dismounting their horses, they followed as she led her horse into a stable attached to the back side of the temple. Several other horses surrounded the trough sitting in the middle of the barn. There were no pens, and the horses could roam as they please.

Nora was already up to the porch steps and sliding the paper screen door open. Aegis sped to her side while the others scrambled up the steps. It was quiet inside. Aegis peered up to the second story and saw shadows. He went up the centered stairwell first to find people in various colored robes going about their day. Some swept while others waxed the floors by hand with rags. More than once, a member of the party had to dodge a person cleaning the floor with a cloth as they sped along the floor in a crouched position.

"Stay here," the queen ordered as she went up the stairs another level.

He assumed she didn't mean him and proceeded to follow. "I meant you, too," she whispered.

"Stop pushing me away," he said more sharply than he intended.

Nora's hand went to the small dagger at her belt as if she would strike him, but her eyes suddenly widened with recognition, as if she'd remembered just then that he was her friend.

He wanted to shake her. Nora had briefly contemplated stabbing him. It stung with betrayal, but it also gave him a sort of excitement he hadn't experienced since he first met Minerva.

She didn't apologize but instead nodded in agreement, and that was good enough for him. She could stab him if she wanted just so long as he could stay by her side.

The third story of the pagoda held a few people on mats. They were sleeping or meditating. Indoor plants climbed the corners of the room, and their blooms filled the air with honeysuckle. There was one more level to rise. The stairs narrowed, and they reached the top where one woman was staring out the window.

She wore a brown robe with a red arrow pattern on it. Her hair was brown and pulled back tightly in a braid. Just who was this woman, and who was she to Nora?

"You've come for help," the woman said.

He recognized the woman's voice. He couldn't place it, but it called to him through the centuries as though he should know it. The woman turned around, and her tanned skin, thick burgundy lips, and yellow eyes answered his question.

"You're the mountain witch," he said.

The witch smiled. "I am a descendant of the one you met ages ago."

Nora took in a deep breath as she stood motionless. "I need to ask you some questions," she said.

The woman bade them sit on the cushions on the balcony. The rain had yet to let up, but the rainfall soothed his frazzled nerves. He imagined he would feel more secure with Nora beside him, but it only heightened his urges to protect her and the sense of danger he got from her. Not that she could hurt him, but the bite of a blade made things more exciting.

He could hear the rest of the group shifting around downstairs, the whinnying of the horses as they nuzzled one another. The water from the tracker boots was soaking into the worn old wood at the base of the stairs where they had left them. It would no doubt cause the wood to develop a squeak. All the while, the witch watched him with a knowing smile.

"I'm not dying, but I struggle to control my powers," Nora said.

"How do you know you're not dying? How do any of us know we're not dying?"

"I'm not sick. Lately, I've seen things, losing control of … myself."

At this, the witch frowned. "How so?"

Nora told the witch of the mirror episode and confirmed Peter's suspicion that she couldn't wear the crown properly, things he didn't know about, but she glanced at Aegis occasionally as if she were gauging his reaction. He took hold of her hand to reassure her as her voice wavered.

"Sometimes, when I try to use my power, it doesn't work. Other times, it's like it goes into overdrive. Before Aegis came back, I almost boiled myself alive trying to reheat my bathwater. It happened so fast that I barely had time to get out before it was too late. I had blisters everywhere."

"Nora!" he gasped. To know she'd been in real danger while he frolicked the Starry Wood sent him reeling.

"I didn't tell anyone. I made some disappear even though my powers didn't work half the time. I was able to hide the rest while I worked on them throughout the rest of the day. You came back shortly after. You must have sensed I was in danger."

He had indeed. Minerva did as well. When they were in the Starry Wood, things began snapping inside him, like cords pulled to their breaking point. It reminded him of discovering her for the first time in the Starry Wood—only at that time, she was not hurt, merely in danger; and the pulling of the King's Soul; and the pact he'd made. But some instances were stronger than others.

"And the borders?" the witch asked.

Nora shrugged. "They're not deteriorating anymore, but they are not where they should be."

"That will take time," he argued. "You can't undo centuries of damage within a year."

"That is true," the witch agreed. "Your presence is ever working on the borders. It will take many lifetimes to undo the damage the stewards inflicted on Hell."

Her heavy shoulders slumped. She didn't appear as defeated as she had when describing the tub incident. He gave her hand a little squeeze.

"The matter of your powers," the witch said. "I'm afraid I do not have those answers. My ancestors have retold the story of the King Soul's rise to power, but if anyone has answered, it would be the stewards."

Nora's head snapped so quickly on her neck he thought it would break. There was a hatred in her eyes he had never beheld before. "I don't see what information Vinicio could provide. Besides, he's dead."

"Is he now?" The witch laughed. "There is no manual on a spell cast hundreds of thousands of years ago. There are, however, people who made it their life's work to study all the kings to understand their abilities better."

The witch was clear in this. If they wanted answers, they would have to find Vinicio in the seventh region of Hell. The idea was beyond dangerous. Even if they did find the last steward, there was no guarantee he would know about Nora's situation. That and the idea of bringing that infanticidal villain to the castle for any reason was something he couldn't stand.

"Aegis," Nora said, shaking free of his grasp.

"Sorry."

"The seraph does not like this," the witch said.

"What did you just call him?" Nora asked.

"You have many questions to unravel; this is not one that is of importance. You should find the steward and kill him. Sooner rather than later." The witch stood and gave a bow before descending the staircase.

Ignoring the tension in his jaw, he moved to stop her. The queen had not dismissed her, and she hadn't answered any of Nora's questions. She'd only given them more.

"Aegis, stop."

"She is getting away," he argued.

"These people do things their way. Even the queen has no

power over the first region's people."

She was right, but it pissed him off all the same. "What are we going to do about Vinicio?"

"Nothing for now. The seventh region is difficult to survive, even for the slimiest of monsters. The highest priority is the rebellions. We do our tour, squash the rumors of my demise, and go back to the castle for answers."

At this, he went to one knee. Nora was right, and she was far wiser than he gave her credit for. He bowed his head, and Nora nodded as she stood. In the light of the overcast sky, Nora was the queen Hell needed. Even when her powers betrayed her, he never would.

"If your powers are that unpredictable, there's no way you can use them," he said. "I won't allow it. It's too dangerous."

"Everything will be fine," she said. "I will figure this out."

"You're brilliant," Aegis whispered. "You know that?"

She smiled at him then, a genuine smile that lingered between them even when they rejoined the group and set out for the fifth region. He sent a note to Peter using Charlie's hawk. He wanted to know if there were updates. Threats loomed everywhere, and he couldn't determine the enemy. At first he'd thought it was Peter, but the advisor was on their side. Someone or something was working against Nora. He needed to figure it out and soon.

# Chapter Seven

The group rode in a V formation across the first region. The tall, green grass got shorter and greener the closer they got to the castle, and patches of clover and dandelions spattered the landscape. Nora rode at the front of the pack with the blackest horse from the castle's stall.

She made it a point to keep a harder pace than the others—mainly Aegis. There was nothing he could say that would make her feel better, but that didn't stop him from trying.

The witch's words were still running through her mind. Vinicio was still alive and the only person who could provide a solution to her problem. The prospect of finding the former steward in the seventh region was bad. Bringing him to the castle while rebellions raged in the regions was worse.

The last thing she needed was another enemy while she grappled with her powers. Aegis wanted to give her assurances against the problems they couldn't foresee. She didn't need promises or consolation. She wanted a resolution.

Daylight wavered and a sense of dread plagued her. She had hoped they would make it closer to the Starry Wood by now, but they were just a few miles from the castle. She didn't want Aegis running back to tell Peter what they'd learned—or what they hadn't learned. He probably had questions of his own. The witch had called him a seraph. It sounded familiar, but she couldn't recall what it meant.

"We should either make camp now or head back to the castle," Aegis yelled.

It was good that no one could see her disappointment. "We will camp here tonight," she said at last. "Everyone stays here. No returning to the castle."

The trackers set up camp while Aegis perched in a tree for a lookout. Not that it was necessary. She suspected he just wanted somewhere to brood. Usually she would've teased him about it, but she wasn't much better these days.

Was there a correlation between her mother's rebellion and Vinicio being alive? Perhaps they had found a way to keep in contact, despite the distance, and were plotting against her. She didn't think her mother was the plotting type. Bella wasn't bad, she just made bad choices and loved the wrong people. Nora hoped that her mother loved the child. More than anything, she wanted Bella to love the child.

Charlie approached the tree Aegis was sitting in and gave him a note. Her skin flushed with heat. He wanted them to stop close to the castle to communicate with Peter. When did he send a message? Aegis didn't so much as bother to mention it. She pressed her lips together, determined to let it go. It wasn't worth giving a reaction. A queen did not fuss over such trifles.

Aegis read the note and rolled it back up before pocketing it. He wasn't even going to mention it to her!

She stomped up to the tree before giving Charlie a dismissive nod. The tracker left without a word. She waited until Charlie was out of earshot, glaring Aegis with her arms crossed all the while. "From the palace?" she asked.

"I'm checking on things."

"And?"

Aegis frowned. "Nothing worth noting."

*He's lying.*

Shut up, she told the King's Soul. Still, it had a point. Why hadn't Aegis told her he was sending hawks? It wasn't his job to relay information. It was his job to protect her. How was he defending her by selling her out to Peter and Minerva?

Something in her broke. Aegis had dismissed her fears of Peter and insisted on keeping contact with him.

"Liar!" she shouted.

Before Nora could stop it, she imagined backhanding Aegis in the face as she had once seen Hacia do to a tracker for insubordination. He was knocked from the tree and onto the ground. She gasped in horror. It happened before she could put it out of her mind.

"I'm sorry," she said, with hands clamped over her mouth.

Aegis shook his head. "It's all right."

"It just flashed into my mind—I couldn't stop it."

He extended a hand to gesture that it was okay, but the slap must have hit hard because the vampire was still on his knees. She held herself as she rubbed the skin of her arms with consolation. Her eyes welled up with tears, and she cursed under her breath. Of all the times for her magic to decide to work, it worked when she really did not want it to.

Aegis held out the note for her to reach. It didn't matter what it said. She didn't need to see it, but a part of her still wanted to. A nagging, insecure voice—her own voice and not the King's Soul—needed to read the contents of the note.

"All is good here. One of the cooks burned her forearm, but it doesn't appear to be serious. P"

Her heart sank into the depths of her stomach. She had no reason to mistrust him. Aegis had already slunk to the shadows somewhere.

She ignored the stares from the trackers at the firepit a few feet away. She searched for Aegis as well as she could without rousing suspicion. He was close but out of her line of vision. She wanted to reverse time and take it back, but even her power had limits, and some things just couldn't be undone.

Sleep didn't come that night either. She spent the evening staring at the ceiling of her tent. Her eyelids were more cumbersome with each passing dawn, but even on those rare nights when she did sleep, there was still no rest. Her mind was churning with things that she needed to do, people that she needed to see, and a gruff old voice railing at her for every single flaw.

Sometimes she regretted the day she took the throne, but Peter said that good rulers hated ruling. It wasn't being the queen that she hated; it was the stares, the questions, the criticism. She made decisions, yet people who didn't have answers were always the first to complain. They didn't want to produce solutions, only fight her on hers.

That was what had created a rift between her and Peter. He was her worst critic. She couldn't make the most basic decision without his scowling face judging her. At first, she told herself that he was only doing it to make her a better queen, but there was no satisfying him. She couldn't control the King's Soul, but she could put Peter in his place.

The canvas of her tent glowed with early morning light. The dew was clean and chilled the outside of her tent and the birds chirped from their nests. She remained unmoving until she heard the trackers waking. They shuffled around the camp, rebuilding the fire, preparing breakfast. They spoke in hushed whispers about the weather. The rain was a concern.

She emerged from her tent to find Bailey or Heather working on the fire.

"Have you seen Aegis?" she asked.

The tracker shook her head. "Charlie, Bailey, and Alfie will be back soon, though."

This one was Heather. Her hair was longer than Bailey's, and she was much thinner. She made it a point to remember that.

The queen sat beside the fire and attempted to have a normal conversation with her. "How long have you been a tracker?" she asked.

"Since I was a child."

She cringed. Trackers and hawk hunters were recruited as children. Orphans didn't exist in Hell. Heather was likely found as a child and brought to the palace to train as a guard—a fate she could have easily found if something had happened to her mother, but she rather fancied the idea. Hacia cared for her trainees the way a good mother cared for her children. If only she had been so lucky.

"Hacia is …" She struggled to find the word.

"Amazing," Heather finished.

Her eyes lit. "Yes!"

"I once watched her slice an apple mid-air with her daggers."

"She and Alfie are getting serious."

Heather cast her eyes down at the fire as if she didn't feel comfortable speaking about it. "Tina said she overheard them talking about having a baby."

She was speechless. She hadn't thought about having children since she watched a woman give birth in the second region. It was awful, the whole thing. She couldn't imagine why anyone wanted to do that. If anyone should, it would be Hacia. She was beautiful, protective and, above all, strong.

"You ladies look like you could do with some breakfast," Charlie said.

He dropped the firewood on the ground before sitting beside it with his legs crossed. He was sort of good looking. His skin had a waxen quality that made it appear like wet paper laid against a skull. He was blond, not pale blond, but the sort of ashen color that fair-haired people had if they stayed all the time indoors.

"What's the plan, my queen?" he asked.

"We will cut through the Starry Wood to the fifth region."

Heather frowned, but it was brief, and she kept her opinions to herself. If only more people were like her.

"I suppose that's a much safer adventure with a vampire," he said.

"We can't go through the wood," a voice behind her said.

She turned to find Aegis with a deer corpse slung over his shoulder.

"Why not?" she asked.

"I told you about the new creatures that took residence when the giants all died. If it were just us, it would be fine, but with a party, it's too risky."

Aegis sat beside her and put the animal on the spit. She couldn't tell if he'd shrugged off the night before or not. She wanted him to look her in the eye, but he found an excuse not to with Alfie and Bailey joining the party.

"You were far more successful than we were," Alfie said, laughing.

"I've been following this one's scent since last night," Aegis explained.

He still wouldn't look at her, and it was beginning to infuriate her.

"Alfie," she said. "Aegis says we shouldn't go through the Starry Wood. What are your thoughts?"

Alfie gave a cocked grin. "If a vampire says it's too dangerous, it's probably too dangerous, my queen."

The tracker was being polite, but she knew he liked to compete with Aegis. She was surprised he wasn't agreeing with her just to spite the vampire.

"I've always wanted to see it," Bailey piped up from behind Alfie. Her strong body carried even more wood than Charlie.

"Let's all die because Bailey wants to see the Starry Wood," Heather muttered.

Discussions erupted in pairs across the campsite. Bailey argued with Heather on what appeared to be a more personal vendetta while Charlie and Alfie exchanged a few words while watching Heather and Bailey's dispute escalate. Aegis stared incredulously at her while the scene played out.

"I had to get you to look at me somehow," she teased.

Aegis's expression remained unmoved.

"I'm so sorry about last night. I lost control."

"I know."

"You'll come back to me?" she asked.

Aegis smiled. "Always."

She was relieved but grew flustered when his stare endured. There was a spark in his eyes, as though he were staring at someone else. Someone new. It wasn't until the trackers began outright yelling that Aegis turned to address them.

"We're not going through the wood," his voice boomed across the empty landscape.

Silence blanketed the entire region, perhaps all of Hell.

***

Peter had found only a few notes regarding what this steward called the fractured king. All through the night in a sort of fever, he cross-referenced everything he could find in the library. He suspected the fractured king was King Reginald. His reign was not very long and was eclipsed by his successor, Peter the Great.

Reginald was brought to the castle at an early age, like most kings. By all accounts, he had an uneventful reign until he was struck by lightning in his forties. The fact that he survived at all was a miracle, but the lightning was suspected as the culprit behind a drastic personality change.

The king would often become confused and wander the castle late at night. Much to the cook's chagrin, his food preferences changed often. One day he would proclaim to love beef and noodles, only to become irate the next time it was served to him. It was even noted that his shoe size changed from time to time.

*Then, there was the matter of the crown. The king refused to wear the crown, though he would refuse to say why…*

He struggled just as Nora did now, but there was no cure. Not that Peter could find. Reginald died in his fifties. There was no mention of how or why, though Peter suspected the king succumbed to foul play.

He leaned over the sprawl of books on the table and stared into the distance to release the tension from his eyes. He was old. Age ached in his eyelids, his temples, and in his bones. Nora hadn't been struck by lightning, and he didn't think she would come bursting into the court naked like the fractured king, so there was a plus side. Nora had self-awareness and was not mad, but what would become of her?

If only the vampire were present then. He found no records of Aegis who was off duty during that time. Another vampire had stepped in while he was off doing who knows what. Peter would have to ask him about it. It would have been much more convenient if Aegis had been the attending vampire, but he often traded with others of his kind until the stewards ruled.

"Have you told him?" Minerva's voice broke through his thoughts like the wind in a closed room.

He turned to find her only a foot or so away. It startled him, but he tried his best not to show it. Vampires were so silent. He had never so much as imagined that he'd see one in his life, let alone two!

She was frightening up close. Aegis had a more natural appearance and was more relaxed around souls. Minerva struggled to move at a soul's pace, and she had a feral look in her eyes.

He knew vampires didn't eat, but Minerva had a hungry expression at all times. Her eyes were constantly bloodshot. Nora said the whites of their eyes would burst red when they sensed danger, but hers were always that way.

In the time he spent in the king's dungeon—the first time — she'd lain on the top bunk and remained unmoved. Her skin was so pale that it reflected what little light they had from the cell window.

She was like marble when he touched her cheek, smooth and cold. He only tried because he had grown bored after several weeks in that cell. Testing fate with a vampire was better than staring out the same window for another moment. He figured that if he were going to die, it might as well be by the hand of a beautiful woman.

Her skin was cold to the touch, but when it sensed the heat from his fingers on her cheek, the flesh warmed to his. Peter surmised that vampires had cold-blooded qualities. Heat or cold did not dictate their activity level like a reptile, but their bodies imitated the climate and made them impervious to unlivable conditions.

"No, no," he stuttered, shaking off the memory. "I didn't want to risk Nora receiving the message."

Minerva nodded. "Perhaps, I should go and tell him myself."

"We don't have any answers."

Minerva's lips formed a thin smile. "We know that Nora shares the same qualities as this fractured king. What more do we need to know?"

He detected a threat in her words and bit back the urge to tell her to piss off. "We haven't found a solution. We don't know why this is happening. All we know is that the fractured king was a normal king until he was struck by lightning."

"We know of a solution. The next king turned out fine."

"Do you want to run that by Aegis?"

Minerva's eyes fell to the floor. He had won the argument with one question. Minerva loved Aegis enough to know how devastating it would be to lose Nora. He wondered if her solution wasn't in some way conceived from jealousy. Nora came before her in her mate's mind. They'd mated after the stewards took succession.

What she said was treason. If anyone had heard it aside from Peter, it would be Aegis himself that would be killing her or throwing her in a cell. An unbearable predicament for both, not to mention painful for Nora being forced into making that decision.

"Give me more time," Peter offered.

Minerva nodded. "Time is something I have in abundance."

# Chapter Eight

The Starry Wood was a dense, green forest that Aegis often called home when he wasn't in the service of kings or a queen. The vast supply of water from the caverns below fed it. Boulders were positioned in odd and seemingly random formations by the giants that once lived there. The trees had branches as wide as sidewalks, and moss draped and hung from the trees like lace.

Closing his eyes, he listened intently to the forest around him. Birds and some ground-dwelling animals went about their business. He wasn't worried about that; it was the other things that he feared. It was imperative that he formulate a plan for when they were attacked. Nora insisted against all reason to go this way, so all he could do was get them out as soon as possible.

"Stop fretting, Aegis," the queen commanded.

He shot her a side glance. She was smiling, and a chill sliced up his spine. How could she be so happy when she was unnecessarily risking lives? Where did the brave woman in the pagoda go? He turned his head for an instant and she had become someone else.

"What are you trying to prove?" he asked quietly.

Nora took a moment to consider the question before replying, "Because I can."

The breath fell from Aegis's lips. Nora was making them do this because he'd challenged her. Of all the arrogant, foolish bullshit. He had half a mind to lose them in the woods to give her a dose of reality. If it were anyone else, the vampire would have left her, but it was Nora. Somewhere in there, it was Nora.

She dismounted her horse and the others followed her lead. He reluctantly followed.

"It's all right, old man," Alfie teased. "We're skilled fighters."

The hawks were masked and remained perched on the horse saddles. They would have to guide the horses through the forest. There would be no riding them due to the difficult terrain. The horses shook their heads and voiced their displeasure. The hawks were just as spooked. They cocked their heads, and their feathers were fluffed up. They could hear the same things he could.

"They know we're here," he muttered before spitting on the ground. Nora didn't appear to be the least bit concerned, and in his heart, disappointment bloomed. Who would be the first to die?

The group traveled at a sluggish pace. Between the soft, muddy earth and fallen branches, the horses were frightened and reluctant to walk on the uneven terrain. Nora pulled at the horse's harness by the bit, and he reared up in protest. Charlie almost lost his horse in confusion. Bailey and Heather's horses were steadier in the center. Aegis followed slowly behind, keeping an eye on the flanks of the group.

Alfie was cooing to his hawk alongside Nora. At a glance, most would think him distracted, but that was far from the truth. The noises that he determined to be a squirrel or a cautious deer could sound like an approaching panther to a soul. Alfie's eyes would flicker at any broken branch or forest movement. Patient and alert, the way a killer should be. Charlie and the two tracker girls jerked their heads at every noise. Alfie had skill beyond the average soul. Maybe he should get to know the man a bit better.

The forest was already dark, with overgrown trees fighting for daylight as it was, but they would soon see the light. This was not the place to set up a camp, but they couldn't push horses through the dark. At the pace they held, it would take over a week to get through the forest to the fifth region.

There was still time to go back. He considered saying as much, but Nora was unpredictable, and he feared what that would mean for their companions. He hoped that Peter and Minerva had learned of what could be ailing her. He no longer suspected growing pains. Nora's worst traits were getting the best of her, and a more sinister version of herself was surfacing.

"We'll camp here," Nora announced.

She tied off her horse, and it began grazing on the grassy patches. The others followed her lead. He tied off his mount and started scavenging for dry wood. There wasn't much of that in this forest.

Nora already knew what he was about to say. "It doesn't matter if it's wet. Just stack it."

She closed her eyes, and the stack of wet firewood burnt as if it were dry grass. The warmth lightened everyone's mood except for his. Then again, he was always wet blanket. Maybe the queen had reasons to dispose of this group. Alfie did have a strong following. If he was a traitor spreading false information, it would make sense that Nora needed him dead. Charlie and the trackers may have been brought along to confirm his demise was an accident. The last thing anyone needed was Hacia's ire.

He clung to the hope that Nora had bigger reasons for entering the Starry Wood with six horses. Even if there was a reason, it stung that she wouldn't tell him what it was. If that were the case, he would have to wait. All he could do was patrol the perimeter all night while the rest of them took turns pandering to the girl-queen.

The fire kept most of the creatures away. He had yet to encounter anything all that dangerous nearby. He saw a big cat, but it already had game in its maw. It slinked off into the distance, unwilling to investigate the outsiders in his domain. For a long time, he sat perched in a tree, brooding, as Nora would say.

He didn't brood. There was just little for him to say. The former kings never said he brooded, though one called him mopey. He tried to remember which king said that, but it was too long ago. His memory was as strong about the beginning with Tom as it was now. It was just the middle that got fuzzy.

In the event of an attack, he could grab Nora and let the rest fend for themselves. If she commanded him to go back, it would be too late. They were not his responsibility, they were hers. It was a difficult lesson, losing those you're responsible for. He suspected Nora was beyond learning lessons. She flip-flopped between a wise and noble ruler and a budding tyrant.

"What kind of king will you be?"

Aegis found himself not looking at Nora, but at Tom. His mind often wandered these days. He wasn't certain if it was the turmoil with Nora or just the fact that he finally had memories to look back on. In the heat of the fire against his face, he saw a different pair of dark eyes on him. A pair of eyes from long, long ago.

Tom only smiled. He was still recovering from the snake bite. He had worked his way up to walking several hours a day before he would collapse in a sweaty heap. He caught Tom every time, but it frustrated him to no end. He wished the young man would take a break before that point.

He carried Tom to the shade of a pomegranate tree. They were still in the second region, but they were nearing the mountain. The foothills were steadily climbing the horizon, and the grass was growing thicker and greener. The breeze was gentle and the heat was mild, but Tom was still too weak to be in prolonged sunlight.

"What kind should I be?" Tom asked.

"I suppose the good and fair kind."

"Fairness is a farce," Tom said bitterly. "Was it fair that my whole family was ravaged for amusement?"

He shook his head.

"Was it fair that I killed a different titan out of revenge?"

"All the titans have sinned beyond redemption," he said.

Tom frowned. "Sin?"

"It's an evil act. Like murder, rape, torture, theft …"

Maybe it wasn't a word that souls used. Come to think of it, he couldn't recall a single soul using the word even to this day. Where did he learn the word?

"Is it fair to murder someone for the act of another?"

"No, but I'm sure the titan you killed had done so to others," he reasoned.

"And should I punish someone for stealing bread?"

"I think that's where fairness comes in."

"It will never be that simple, though," Tom said. He picked a pomegranate off the ground and peeled it open. The white rind was being stained red from the juice. "The man who stole the bread raped a girl but is kind to the blind homeless man who abandoned his children to starve while he gambled away his last silver." Tom plucked red seeds from the fruit and crunched the grain and all between his teeth.

"Perhaps we are all evil in one way or another and have been sent here as punishment," Aegis mused.

"When I'm king, I'll divide the world accordingly to a person's worst deed. Maybe then the rapist will be raped, the murderer be murdered, the gambler will only starve those who intend on growing up for the same fate."

"What if they are without sin?" he asked.

Tom raked the fruit with his red-stained lips. The red juice was rolling along the corners of his mouth and onto his neck. "We have all *sinned*."

In many ways, Nora reminded him of Tom the most. He was a peculiar king. Vulnerable yet strong, volatile yet enduring. Unnaturally wise and yet somehow naïve. It was as if Tom were somewhere else half the time.

The first king grew stronger each day, and he liked to take credit for some of that. The boy was always better at starting fires, but that was probably a soul trait. He became an excellent hunter and swordfighter over the years. Once he became king, he was skilled in so many things. Perhaps that was what Nora needed—life skills to give her more independence.

He fell to the ground with a thud loud enough to startle the group. Nora had already withdrawn to her tent for the evening. Alfie and Charlie were feeding their hawks dried pieces of meat while the trackers, Bailey and Heather, were having a close discussion about another tracker named Tina.

"Nora? Are you asleep?" he asked outside the tent.

"You can come in," she said.

The tent was small. It was only intended for one, maybe two people. It was light and easy to pack away, but he was forced to crawl alongside Nora to speak with her. "I wanted to talk to you about something."

"So I gathered." Nora laughed as he shimmied into the small tent.

"I was thinking of Tom, the first king."

Nora turned on her side to face him. She was genuinely interested.

"He had many hobbies. He was always learning something. When we're done with this tour, how would you like to learn how to swordfight?"

Nora's eyes lit. "I've always wanted to learn how, but I don't have the time."

"You must make time," he urged. "I think part of the reason you've been struggling with your powers is that you don't take enough time for yourself."

He struggled to read her expression. If he didn't know better, he'd say she was at war with herself. Part of her agreed with him, but another part was angry that he was so honest. "I care for you very much. You know that, don't you?"

"You mean you love me," Nora corrected.

"Yes."

She stifled an amused smile. "You're afraid to say it."

He struggled to answer, and Nora laughed at him. He'd never said it before, and that alone gave him the reason to pause. To throw that word lightly would be to throw a rock in a house full of mirrors. How many reflections of himself would he lose each time he said it? Aegis had already given his existence to a promise. How many more promises could he make on top of that?

He mourned for Nora while she was right before his eyes. Even in the prime of her youth, he saw her withering away. Her long hair reminded him of how much time had passed since he first found her. Her adolescence brought about feminine changes that she proudly boasted but to him only brought new uncertainties.

"Why did you send that girl away? Back at the castle?" he asked.

Her eyes fell to the blankets on the ground. "At night, when I sleep beside my lovers, I can sense their dreams and desires."

Never had a king managed such things. Her power was beyond any of those before her. It was amazing but concerning since she couldn't control it. "And she had ill intent?"

Nora shrugged. "Not exactly, but there is always motive beyond me. Everyone sees the crown as a bonus. All but you."

"Nora, that's natural," Aegis explained. "If someone is—"

"In love?" Nora finished.

"Yes. If they feel that way, anything that is positive is going to be at the forefront of their mind, even superficial things."

"I guess it's easier to keep myself safe this way."

That was the heart of the matter. Nora pushed people away to protect herself. She wasn't all that different from him. "What a pair we make."

"What?" she asked, propped up on one elbow.

"I'm afraid to say it, and you're afraid to feel it."

Nora giggled. "I'm going to sleep now. Will you stay?"

He wanted to, but he didn't want to leave the camp unpatrolled.

Just then, a bush nearby began to rustle. They both froze momentarily. It was Charlie, collecting more wood. Bailey and Heather were far quieter than the young hawk hunter, but they were preoccupied in their tent.

"I think it will be safer for everyone if I remain outside."

She nodded and nestled into her blankets.

***

Nora dragged her steed through the torrential downpour. She refused to look back at her miserable companions' faces—not that she could see them through the rain anyhow. She stretched out a hand and couldn't see it through the deluge. This was a stupid idea.

Aegis was right, of course. She didn't even know why she'd insisted on going through the Starry Wood in the first place. The words came from her mouth before she could stop them, and a sense of triumph bubbled to the surface with them. It was frightening, and it was far beyond the need for a hobby like Aegis suggested.

Part of her wanted to spite him and punish him for always being right, and now they were all held hostage to this need. Last night, after Aegis left her tent, she believed she was sleeping, but while her mind was resting, her body wasn't. She had lain there as she always did, fading in and out of the twilight of sleep, only to realize she was awake in a squatted, knee-hugging position, eyes open and everything.

It was more like a memory lapse than sleep, as if someone else inhabited her body for a short while. She "woke" like that several times. The last time, she had twisted into a position so unnatural, she had to stifle her cry her help. Lying on her side, she was bent backward, arms and legs twisted and contorted so severely she couldn't move them back without pain.

Her heart raced, and she fought to control her breathing. She closed her eyes and imagined herself going lax. It took a few attempts, but her limbs eventually released from their locked pose. She spent the rest of the early morning wide awake, too afraid to close her eyes again.

"There's a cavern to the left," Aegis called from the back of the group.

What was happening to her? She frightened herself and needed to find a way to hide what was happening. Deep down, she was afraid that she wasn't the true queen. That it had all been a weird mistake or that the King's Soul was trying to escape. Would Aegis still love her if she wasn't the queen?

"Hey," Aegis said as he took her hand. "Are you all right?"

His shoulder-length hair was black and plastered to his head when wet. Aegis's blue eyes were a beacon in the pouring rain. Was he doing this for her or the King's Soul? Did he even know the difference anymore?

Like a child, she began to cry. He wrapped her in his arms and held her close. She told him everything that had happened the previous night. Taking care to speak quietly, she was uncertain he could hear muffled voice against his chest while the rain poured.

"The scariest part of it all is that I think the reason I can't sleep is that when I do, I become someone else."

Aegis kissed the top of her head. Whatever was happing to her was beyond reassurances and solutions. She was going mad.

"I didn't want to come to the Starry Wood. I wanted to do as you said, but I couldn't stop myself—"

"Nora," he said.

"Someone else was talking through my mouth—"

"Nora!"

She stopped all at once.

"We need to get out of the rain," he said.

It dawned on her then that Aegis didn't care if she was crazy. If she was someone else when she slept, if her powers didn't work, or if the crown didn't fit. He didn't care if she was the queen. She could still be a little runaway and he would always love her. At the moment, he was more concerned about her getting sick.

Her mood improved greatly once she got to the cave. Heather and Bailey were nowhere to be seen, but Alfie and Charlie greeted them with a warm fire and some bread. "I managed to salvage most of our bread," Charlie explained. "Tonight, we feast!"

Alfie bit off a chunk defiantly. "A little rain won't stop us."

She stripped down to her undergarments and laid her clothes on a rock to dry as she rummaged in her saddle. Unfortunately, everything she had was wet. After laying all her clothes out, she joined the men by the fire. Charlie's face was the same color as the flames.

"Where are Heather and Bailey?" she asked.

"Scouting the mines," Alfie said, motioning to the void that descended.

She couldn't help but be curious. "Aegis, you've said the reason the trees grow so large here is from caverns … Does this lead to them?"

Aegis moved to take Nora's side. "Yes. This is also where I think the old monsters came from once they discovered the giants were gone."

Alfie was teasing Charlie in the distance, half-laughing at his subordinate's bashfulness. "Behave yourself, Charlie," Alfie warned. "You don't want to upset the vampire."

Charlie muttered something in reply that she couldn't hear but made Aegis grin. She was far too interested in the caverns to care, though Charlie was handsome.

Aegis led her through the dark. The earthy dampness was all around her, but it wasn't cold at all. Her feet met wet stone or ossified ground of some sort, but the water was lukewarm.

"Aegis, it smells like …"

"I know," he said. "I don't even do it, but I know what it smells like."

"Farts?" Poor Aegis, spending all of eternity with nothing but flatulent beings as company. No wonder he preferred to live in the Starry Wood.

"It's the mineral content in the water. It's drinkable, just stagnant and a little odorous."

"Does it always smell this strongly?" She was familiar with hot springs. This scent went beyond that.

"No, not usually," he admitted. "Something is different."

"We should find the trackers."

Aegis led her a bit quicker before she scraped the top of her toenail on the stone. She let out a gasp and, in his urgency, he scooped her up in his arms and moved deeper into the caverns. Once they got to the belly of the cave, her eyes adjusted thanks to small bits of light from above. The water pooled at the bottom of the unknown murky depths.

Enormous roots grew down from the ceiling and wrapped around the large stones and stalactites as they sought the water. Daylight peeked through in little patches with the roots, and the rain fell through these small openings, collecting more water for another day. Aegis held her with one arm and used his free arm to grasp root clusters to move from stone to boulder.

"How did they get this far already?" she asked.

"They didn't."

His eyes went bloodshot. Something was wrong, and he was on the scent of something dangerous. They came around a bend and into a cavern like the one they had left, only much shallower. There were echoes of a fight in the distance.

"Go to them. I'll be fine."

Aegis ignored her and brought her right along. She hadn't cared about it until now, but a breeze drifted along her mostly exposed chest. She resisted the urge to cover her body with her hands. If someone attacked Heather and Bailey, the last thing she wanted was to be standing there in her underwear. Aegis often forgot about such things.

They came upon Heather skewering a great wolf-beast that walked on two legs. It had bloody claws and roared at the tracker with defiance. Bailey was injured, but she managed to slice the heels of the creature with her blade. Aegis remained with her as they watched the two trackers kill something twice their size.

Once the creature fell, it slowly began to morph into a soul. It was a man, aA naked man with his legs badly sliced and a spear through his chest. His vacant eyes stared at the ground.

"Was he a wolf or a man?" Heather asked.

"Both and neither," Aegis mused.

"What happened to you guys?" she asked.

Heather shrugged. "It grabbed Bailey, and I chased after it. Told you we could defend ourselves."

"I'm going to take Bailey back first. I'll come back for you," Aegis promised.

"Hang on," she interjected. "Where are we?"

Aegis got her meaning and wandered outside the cavern to have a look before announcing, "We are closer to the fifth region. That little shortcut saved us at least two days, but what about the horses?"

"And Bailey," Heather added. "She needs medical attention."

"We're too far into the wood to send a single tracker with the wounded and all the horses," Aegis pointed out.

"No," she agreed. "We need to go back to the others. We will stay in the cave while Aegis takes Bailey back."

Nora could tell Aegis didn't like the idea. He clenched his jaw and turned his head away. It was the only way. He could get to and from the castle in less than a day without the rest of them slowing him down. "I'll be plenty safe with Heather, Alfie, and Charlie. This guy is proof of that," she said, motioning to the dead man on the floor.

Aegis relented in his gloomy sort of way, like a dog that didn't want to be put outside for the night. She wanted to say as much, but dogs only existed in the third region. No one would know what she was talking about.

Charlie and Alfie were examining Bailey's wounds when she arrived. The tracker was alert and, for the most part, okay except the bright red slashes around her arms. They were deep enough in areas that she would need stitches.

"I don't think it was trying to hurt me," Bailey explained. "I got most of these from trying to escape it."

"It was a wolf, and then a man?" Charlie asked.

Bailey nodded.

Rather than drag her and the horses back, Aegis picked Bailey up and disappeared into the tree line. Alfie and Charlie fell all over themselves trying to determine just what was going on. Nora snorted with laughter when she realized no one had told them what the plan was.

"We are to stay here until he returns. Probably just after nightfall. We will resume once Aegis returns."

"Oh, good," Alfie agreed with only a slight degree of indignation. "That's a good plan."

Some of her clothes were finally dry enough to wear. Charlie could once again look at her without turning red. His eyes would fall to the ground while no one else seemed bothered. The barracks for both military factions was co-ed, so she didn't anticipate any discomfort at her body. She supposed it had more to do with *who* was in her underwear than anything else.

"Well, since we have nothing better to do tonight," Alfie said as he pulled a flask out from his saddle pack. "If her majesty approves."

She took the flask from Alfie's outstretched hand and took the first sip. It was sharply acidic and burned down her throat, but she relished in the taste. She handed it to Heather, who did the same. They passed the alcohol around and shared stories until the fire burned low. Heather was long asleep, and Alfie's eyes had closed as well. It was just her and Charlie awake now.

"You're not tired?" Nora asked.

"I'm going to stay awake and keep an eye on things."

He was a sweet man. Like many of the trackers and hawk hunters, Charlie was an orphan brought to the barracks and trained for service. He had a younger brother that was also in training, but he didn't show a lot of promise, so he would likely go into an apprenticeship of some sort. Charlie blushed when her eyes met his, she knew, and it was adorable. He was a virgin.

She moved to kiss him, and he turned in shyness, but she didn't give up. Instead, she kissed his cheek and nudged at his face with her nose gently before pulling his face to hers.

"You're the queen …"

"I am," Nora agreed. "That means I can be with whomever I want."

With that, Charlie returned her kiss. She stood and led him by the hand into her tent. They giggled as they awkwardly undressed in the confined space. She knocked him in the face with her elbow and he fought with his pants.

The rain continued to fall outside the cave entrance and was echoing throughout the otherwise silent cavern. Charlie's shaky hands found their way to her as she helped him with his pants.

"I've never …" he started.

"I know."

He smiled, but in that instant, fear crept into his eyes while his lips froze. Before he could explain, a wet thud accompanied by a cracking noise made her ears prick. The horses whined, and she could hear their hooves beating on the floor.

"Charlie!" Alfie roared. "We have company!"

"Stay here," he told her.

The Hell she was. Charlie's exit from the tent gave her a glimpse of what was there—large, slimy appendages with discs attached to the underside. She emerged from the tent just as more tentacles emerged from the cavern. One of the things was wrapped around Heather's broken body, dragging it into the darkness.

Alfie opted for a machete instead of his usual daggers and was hacking at a tentacle wrapped around his hips. The skin was rubbery, and the blade bounced off harmlessly. Most of the horses had bolted save the unfortunate one Aegis had ridden. It, too, was being dragged back into the cavern.

She closed her eyes and imagined the tentacles turning to stone. In the moment of her visualization, images of Charlie's stone statue came to mind. No, not that. Her eyes flung open just as his feet went to stone. A slate stone worked its way from Charlie's feet up to is waist. He screamed in agony, and she screamed in horror as the rock made it up to his chest.

The pressure of all the blood in his body forced into a third of flesh turned his skin a ghastly purple. Their stares were locked before his eyes burst from their sockets. Blood erupted from his mouth, nose, eyes, and ears before he finally went limp and succumbed to the stone. Her knees went weak. The world around her was distant and surreal. Did her baby brother still have blue eyes?

She was falling but had no intention of fighting it. Nora never hit the ground. A pair of strong arms caught her, and before she faded into darkness, she was safe.

# Chapter Nine

Aegis caught Nora just as she fainted. He could understand why. Battlegrounds didn't stink this bad. The cave funneled every nasty scent into the open cavern. Blood and ink were everywhere. The remaining tracker, along with all the horses, was gone. With the amount of blood on the walls, it was clear that the creature had taken some, if not all of them.

Of all the horrors he had beheld in his long life, Charlie may have been one of the worst. The poor hawk hunter was three-quarters of the way turned to stone and the remaining quarter had exploded from its flesh casing.

Alfie was being pulled into the cavern. The creature's limbs were also partially turned to stone, and it had slowed its attempt on Alfie's life. Setting Nora aside, he walked into the cavern, passing Alfie's panic-stricken face along the way.

"Am I happy to see you!" Alfie joked.

He wasn't in the joking mood. Once fully submerged in the water, he could see the true nature of the beast, a bulbous form that had many appendages and a single eye. The eye watched him emotionlessly as it shoved the lifeless body of his horse into its toothy maw. With the utmost calm, he grabbed the mouth with each hand and began ripping the creature apart.

When he finished, the water was black, tainted by the beast's blood and the ink it released. He emerged from the cavern, soaked and stained an indigo color. Alfie was still trapped in the now prone tentacle. Aegis stomped hard on the limb and squished it underfoot before prying it off the hawk hunter general.

"We're going back," Aegis said. "Can you run?"

"To the castle? Absolutely," Alfie replied.

The rain had slowed enough that Alfie could send the frightened hawks to the castle by air. Aegis picked up the indisposed queen and ran at Alfie's pace. He was grateful for Alfie's agility and stamina. No doubt he was determined to leave the forest. He couldn't blame him. What he'd found in the cave was a nightmare, even by Hell's standards.

What happened to Charlie was not the creature's doing. It was clear that Nora had attempted to use her powers and it went horribly wrong. The kings sometimes struggled to control their abilities in the end, but this couldn't be the end for her. It was almost as if her powers were trying to sabotage her in some way.

The things she told him frightened him, but it was a fear he must burden for her sake. She would blame herself for what happened to Charlie. He didn't know how he could persuade her otherwise. Aegis couldn't think about that now; he had to get her home. He would talk to Peter and Minerva. Whatever they did now wasn't just in Nora's best interest, but for the safety of all Hell.

It was early morning when they arrived at the castle.

Alfie made it as far as the edge of the wood before collapsing. "I'll be fine here, just go," the man said. "I'm going to lay down and try not to die."

Aegis did not want anyone to see the queen indisposed. Instead, he jumped up to the royal balcony. He lay her gently on the bed and rang for a maid.

Bosh hurried in only to cry out in horror. No doubt the servant was overwhelmed with the mess he had left—an unconscious queen and vampire smearing black ink everywhere.

He didn't have time to explain. Instead, he rushed past the servant.

"Peter! Minerva!"

Minerva came around the corner and her eyes went wide when she saw the mess. Peter dropped his toast as he came around the corner. Aegis told them everything while Minerva stared out the window as she listened. Peter began pacing the room, frantic with nervous energy.

"We can't allow this to go on," Minerva said.

Peter was watching him, carefully gauging his response. Only Minerva would have the audacity to suggest such a thing. Peter was smart and aware of his mortality enough to know better.

"What are you saying?" Aegis said through clenched teeth.

"I don't think she means *that*," Peter interjected, waving his hands in front of him.

"It is exactly what I mean."

The blood vessels in his eyes burst and he lunged at his mate. She danced away just in time. Minerva crouched in a defensive position, hissing and fully aware of what she had said. What it meant.

"If you ever mention such a thing again, I will destroy you," he promised.

"Your mate?" she spat. "You'd choose her over me?"

"Always."

Minerva shook her head slowly. She didn't take his threat seriously. Despite his bloodshot eyes and the raw edge of his voice, she pressed on. "You'd have her kill the ones she loves?"

He roared and smashed against her, breaking stone and furniture with his mate's body. She threw him back and jumped to another corner of the room. Aegis wasn't listening. Red flushed his vision and his only desire was to kill the woman in front of him.

He chased and swiped at her, destroying everything in his path. The mortal in the room was grabbing books and attempting to flee but couldn't make a safe exit. Each time he tried to get out of the way, the fight crashed near him and forced him into another direction.

"Think, Aegis. Whatever is happening to Nora will be resolved when she's reborn anew. She can't die."

"But your betrayal remains," Aegis replied.

Minerva's eyes softened. She realized her error in all of this. It didn't matter what the King's Soul could or could not do. It wasn't about what was best for Nora. It was the fact that Minerva wanted to kill his queen, the one he swore on his blood to protect.

"I'm sorry, Aegis. I'd rather it come from me than anyone else."

"Leave before I kill you."

Minerva was defeated. She went to the balcony and gave him one last glance. "I shall leave for both our sakes."

With that, his mate fell from the window and his sight. He relaxed only slightly. Peter was on the floor, clutching his books. "I'm so sorry," Peter said. "She doesn't love Nora the way we do. She doesn't understand."

"Her blood is sworn the same as mine," Aegis explained. "She betrays me just as much as she betrays our promise to the king of souls."

"I see," Peter agreed. "For her to kill the queen would not only be killing your queen and loved one, but she'd break your binding contract to the King's Soul."

Aegis nodded. "If a vampire killed Nora, it would break the bond I have with the King's Soul. I don't know what would happen if she did that. It might kill all vampire-kind—well, the two that remain."

Peter nodded. "I think we've lost enough species in Hell. Let's figure something else out."

***

The pounding in Nora's head came on slowly as she became more conscious. Charlie's gruesome death refused to go away. It was all her fault. And not in a self-pitying sort of way—it *was* her fault. She envisioned him turning to stone and was unable to stop it.

Why did the image of him turning to stone come unbidden the

way it had? She wanted the tentacles to turn to stone. Maybe it was because he was on her mind? Was she so morbid that she'd envision lovers turning to rock rather than get close to them?

A new dread came to mind. She couldn't risk using her powers. She needed to quell the uprisings in her name, but how could she prove to the masses she was the queen without her powers? While she lay about in bed, the souls of the seven regions believed she was dead or in danger. She'd need Aegis now more than ever. Aegis would be proof enough without her taking any risks.

Once the fifth region's suspicions were resolved, the castle's border would be safe. She at least needed to regain control of the fifth and fourth. The first and second regions were not interested in much outside their borders. The sixth region could hang for all she cared. They were gamblers and thieves that would need to get past the fifth region. Rebellion or not, souls of the third region couldn't rebel for long. There were crops to harvest and animals to tend to.

She jumped out of bed and rang the bell. Black ink smeared the tongue of the bell. Inspecting her shaky hands, she had black ink smeared all over. Reluctantly, she gave the back of her hand a sniff. It was salty and pungent like fish. Charlie had exploded, and it was all her fault.

*Murderer.*

The King's Soul was right, she was a murderer. It made her staggeringly nauseous, but that could have been the intense fish smell. Her face was still scrunched when Bosh rushed in, his hair fluffed and his cheeks red.

"Boshy, you look like you've had a terrible day," she told him.

"Beg your pardon, my queen, but so do you."

She started to laugh, only she couldn't stop. Her high-pitched giggle was frightening, but she couldn't stop herself.

Bosh stared at her like the maniac she was. "I'll start a bath for you, ma'am."

She didn't stop laughing even when he left. Her laughter went to a loud cackle as she fell to her knees and struggled for air. *Help me, someone, help me,* she thought.

*You're not right.*

The King's Soul always came at her weakest. She had a strict policy of not speaking to what should have been a part of her, but she needed answers. The hyperventilation came on in large, heaving wheezes.

At that point, she resorted to a well-practiced maneuver. She held her breath whenever she could and for as long as she could. After several minutes, her efforts prevailed, and she was able to breathe normally.

"You did it," she said. "You killed Charlie."

*No, I'm afraid that was you.*

"I wasn't trying to do that. I was trying to save him."

*You're not right.*

"What does that mean? I can't make it better if you don't tell me how," she bellowed.

The voice went silent. Bracing the leg of her bed, she pulled herself to her feet before catching a glimpse of herself in the mirror. The bags under her eyes and the thinness of her hair only gave her a haggard appearance. She was not right.

Aegis was as still as a prop in the mirror's gaze. He was leaning against the wall casually, but his face was sullen and his eyes watery.

"I suppose you saw that." She was doomed by the reproaching presence of the vampire.

Aegis said nothing, but she could tell it frightened him. He was chewing on his lip and couldn't look her in the eye.

"Well?" she asked. "Did Peter discover anything? What's wrong with me?"

He shook his head, unable to utter the bad news. It was the King's Soul. It was making her do things she couldn't control, but why?

Bosh and three other attendants ran into the room carrying pails of hot water. They moved as if she and Aegis were not in the bedroom.

"I could smell the blood from the edges of the forest," he started. The servants pretended not to listen, but their ears pricked with interest. Who would miss such juicy gossip?

"Do you blame me for their deaths?" she asked.

"No more than the creature that killed them."

It was a gut punch. While the help did not understand what that meant, she did. Aegis blamed her for their deaths, too. There was nothing to be done now other than live with it, but for how much longer could she carry the burden of the dead?

She stripped out of her ink-stained garb and got into the tub. "We should plan a memorial for them," she said. "Their families should be properly compensated."

"I'll let Peter know," Aegis said as he straightened and moved towards the door.

"We leave for the fifth region after my bath."

That stopped Aegis in his tracks. "Are you sure that's a good idea?"

She waited until the attendants were out of sight before speaking. "I don't know how much longer …"

He walked off before she could finish. It was cruel to say such things to Aegis. He couldn't accept the idea of her demise.

She sank deeper into the tub while another round of pails was poured into the bath. It was a truth she had to face. The King's Soul was trying to tell her something. It could mean that she was indeed dying even though she appeared well. She didn't want to die, but more importantly, she didn't want to hurt Aegis.

Once, the voice in her head was a guiding light, an instinct of sorts that kept her alive. She trusted it because she believed it to be her own. Maybe the King's Soul did not have her best interests at heart, but rather had its own agenda. If she wanted to survive, she needed to recognize her own power.

There was a decision to be made here. Either she let the King's Soul continue to sabotage her reign and continue to disappoint Aegis, or she could rely on her own powers. She could no longer pander and cling to the idea that she was worthy of the King's Soul. It was a parasite that had attached to her and was trying to control her—but no more.

She let the gravity of the water take hold as she closed her eyes. Sinking to the bottom of the copper tub, weightless and silent, Nora made a promise to Hell and to herself that she would be the only person inside her head. She imagined the black crown dissolving in her hands—gems and all—while her eyes glittered black.

*I renounce you, King's Soul, and will make my pact not with witches, but with Hell itself.*

The copper tub reverberated as she clutched the railing so hard the copper yielded to her fingers. Emerging from the tub, she let out a roar that quaked the castle's very foundation. Something crawled from the pit of her stomach and grasped with spindly legs, pulling on every nerve and fiber of her being before taking hold. She could feel it, a power greater than the King's Soul took its place, and she laughed.

The King's Soul would become her hostage, not the other way around. If it wouldn't become part of her, she would rule Hell without it.

She opened her eyes, and a wicked little smile spread across her cheeks. There would be sleep on this night.

# Chapter Ten

Aegis stood by the throne as he had through so many regimes. It was the spot where he'd stood for Tom, for Percy, Felibert, Peter, Glen, and so many others. He drifted in and out of sleepy boredom while familiar voices echoed decrees in the court.

The stained glass that portrayed Tom's heroic deeds and the extinction of the titans made him smile. He didn't regret taking leaves of absence until the situation with Nora arose. She made him feel so laughably helpless. Here he was, an immortal that lived in the most dangerous part of Hell, but fell all over himself when a teenage girl laced her corsets too tight. She didn't even need to wear corsets. He was certain she wore them just to watch him fret over her oxygen supply.

The entire castle suddenly rumbled and shook beneath his feet, and he went on high alert. It was only for a few moments, but what was it? The windows shook, and the frames rattled against the walls. Perhaps he was having a dream. He relaxed once more and continued thinking about Nora.

This madness that she fought, it would only be a matter of time before she surrendered to it. She would need him to restrain her, to control her, and he wasn't certain he could. He'd never defied the order of the King's Soul, but he would do anything to keep her safe.

Footsteps from the great hallway paused before the steps of the court. Aegis beheld Nora, freshly bathed and wearing a low-cut black lace gown. It reminded him of thorns wrapped around her shoulders and wrists. It was corseted and far more mature than anything he'd ever seen her wear.

Her breasts were partially exposed, and she was wearing charcoal around her brown eyes. Her lips were stained a crimson red, and she was wearing the black crown without issues on this day. Her dark hair was plaited in a low bun. In the time of her bath, her skin recovered its dark olive complexion, and the skin under her eyes had restored.

"You look amazing," Aegis breathed.

She came down the stairs and gave him a coy smile. "We should go before it gets too late."

"I'll get the horses ready," he said.

"No need," she pulled him close. "Close your eyes."

Her body pressed against his. She wore no perfume, but there was a distinctly new scent about her. The coy smile she wore before he closed his eyes had his mind spinning. Aegis did as he was told. He kept them closed until she let go and said, "Open."

Nora had transported them instantly. They were in the center of a town. He made several turns, reeling from the speed at which they'd traveled. It was incredible. The bustle ground to a halt. Everyone was staring at Nora as they stood on the platform the fifth region people used to burn their perceived witches. The scent of the remains from the last unfortunate soul were still encrusted on the stake.

It was the way of the zealots of the fifth region. They all strongly believed in something—law, god, a cause—it didn't matter what *it* was just so as long as they were willing to do anything to protect it. This often resulted in village persecutions. The entire town would decide someone was a heretic to one thing or another before taking them to the town center for a good murder.

This region was between the sixth and the first for good reason. If outlanders managed to escape the seventh region, they could get by in the sixth, but just as the fourth region, these people would never suffer those beneath them. It was the law, and they would uphold it.

Whispers and murmurs grew as the people surrounded them. It

made the hair on his neck stand. Nora, on the other hand, smiled without teeth and posed for her adoring crowd. He didn't understand. What had changed in the matter of a few hours? Nora had gone from a hysterical, grieving girl—exhausted from everything she'd endured—to this? A vixen had taken the place of his lonesome young queen.

He was certain her powers would not fail or go awry. At any moment things could go terribly wrong, but why was she so confident? Nora appeared unburdened by the events of the cave. He could only stare at her, but no semblance of that girl remained. If it did, she was the most brilliant of actresses. She would need to be, he supposed. It was like she was someone else entirely.

Shouts of "The queen!" rose from the windows of barren wooden houses and from the dirt streets. "Show us!" they cried. "Show us!"

Nora raised her arms dramatically, and giant black wings emerged from her back. She beat them hard, sending wind and dust back at the crowd. They only cheered despite their faces growing dirty. Aegis had never seen her use magic without a few moment's delay. She usually closed her eyes and visualized her powers as the kings had before. Some were much quicker about it, but they all did the same thing.

Something was different with Nora. Something had happened. The scar on his hand burned the way it did when Tom first gave it to him.

"Where is my mother?" Nora said in a low, sultry voice.

It wasn't long until Bella came running from one of the thin wooden establishments. Her hair was longer than when they last saw her. She carried a baby in her arms. "I'm here, my darling girl. I'm here."

Nora smiled and her eyes grew wet. A prospect that once gave her dread and anxiety was now met with gladness. Nora smiled menacingly with stark white teeth against blood-red lips. "Is this my baby brother?"

Something was dreadfully wrong. Aegis fought the urge to tell Bella to run. Nora would never have harmed the baby, but this wasn't Nora. The woman who stood before him had a darkness behind her eyes that made him weary, and yet she excited him in a way he didn't understand.

Nora extended her hands to the babe offered before her. Her long, black-polished nails created shadowy daggers over the small bundle.

Aegis scooped up the baby before answering to Nora. "Perfectly safe," he lied. Bella was oblivious to anything.

Nora's eyes glittered in an unreadable way. She climbed up on the platform and hugged Nora. This put her off –balance. Her eyes were wide and blank. She patted the back of her mother awkwardly while Aegis held the baby.

"You've become a woman in the last year," Bella beamed. "I'm so proud of you."

The real Nora had returned if only for a moment. Her face returned to its pensive, moody expression. She examined the babe with a sulky expression. Her wings fell away in the wind, and she took the bundle from Aegis.

"He has your hair," Nora said. "Your eyes."

Bella agreed, "There's nothing of the bastard that fathered him. I'm going to make sure of it."

The admission that Vinicio was a bastard was exactly what the queen wanted to hear. It was all Nora ever wanted to hear. She wanted her mother to choose her for once, and Bella finally had. Vinicio's baby no longer belonged to Vinicio. It exclusively belonged to Bella.

"Let's get you inside. I've made a few treats for your arrival," Bella said.

The crowds parted for them without the use of Nora's power. People stared, and children struggled from between the adult's legs to get a better look at the queen. Two smudged little ones, a boy and a girl, came up to Aegis with mouths dropped.

"Hello," he said awkwardly.

"You're a vampire?" the boy asked.

"I am."

"You can eat my gran," the boy offered.

Aegis frowned and tried his best not to laugh. Children were never a strong suit for him. He just didn't know the right thing to say to them. They didn't make sense, and they were easy to frighten. He kneeled to their level to look them in their little faces. "I'm sorry, I can't eat your gran," he said.

"What about Kevin?" the little girl asked.

Aegis tilted his head. "Kevin?"

"He lives down the street," the boy explained.

"He's mean to me," the girl whispered.

"You tell Kevin that I am Aegis, the vampire, and if he's ever mean to you again, I will eat him," Aegis promised in a voice so threatening that the children's parents pulled them away from him. He gave the parents a wink and they returned nervous laughs. Nora would have chastised him for such things before, but he had a feeling she wouldn't mind it now.

He followed his queen and her mother to what Aegis presumed to be Bella's home. It was small and sparsely decorated. She had few furnishings, such as an old round wooden table with matching chairs besides her kitchen. Instead of couches or a coffee table, the main room was filled with toys and stuffed animals.

Aegis took the measure of Nora's expression as she took in the living room. What was going on in her mind? She was conflicted, no doubt. Bella had attempted to abandon Nora to her grandparents and largely ignored her for most of her life, yet here she was, making her small space a child's dream. The queen's brow was steady and her face impartial to what should have been a most conflicting moment.

At the same time, it was Nora's hope that the baby would be the subject of Bella's obsessive love. She wanted her brother to be loved even if her mother had been unable to love her. Even so, there had to be a level of envy. Nora was still a young woman who needed a mother, but hers was too busy loving another child.

Bella took the baby from Nora's arms and gently rocked him. "I'll put him upstairs to sleep. Make yourselves at home."

"Nora—" Aegis started.

"I'm fine," she said, stepping around at all the toys. "Really, I am. The child is no threat to me. Bella is sided to me."

Aegis didn't know what to say. That was not his concern at all. Why was it hers? Before he could ask her, Nora's mother was coming down the steps. She led them to the dining table while she went into her kitchen and put the kettle on the iron stove.

"You live in town?" Nora asked.

"Yes. When I came back, I was given the role of a law administrator. Living close to the office seemed right."

"What is it you do?" Aegis asked.

"Oh, when people come to propose a law, I look over the proposal before giving it to the lawmakers. Mostly I make sure there are no errors or that there are not similar or conflicting laws."

"That's a high-status job," Nora commented.

"Given my experience in the castle, it was natural to give me such a promotion."

Nora rolled her eyes and turned to Aegis. "The fifth region can't get enough laws. Most of its economy relies on the law-making process."

"They make up their own rules?" Aegis raised an eyebrow.

Nora gave a nod. "Hell has no rules, for the most part, unless you live here. Everything requires a permit, a notary, or a law. My grandparents had to put in a request to plant an apple tree in their yard when I was a child."

"They keep themselves busy. People run for offices and raise money from people who want them to make their laws. People submit proposals for laws, and she gets paid to look them over. I imagine she gets paid a bit more if she hands the bill off to the right person. This region lives off petty fines and bureaucracy."

Bella rounded the corner with a plain iron kettle and little white teacups. She made several trips to retrieve cookies, sugar, and cream before joining them on the plain brown sofas. "Now, I want you to tell me everything," she said.

Nora was slow at first, reluctant to share any information with her mother. Eventually she relaxed and told her mother of her lovers, her tea set, of happy things, the things she could say without causing worry. Bella was enthralled. She hung on every word her daughter had to say. Granted, he knew little of the woman, but she appeared much changed since he last saw her.

Nora's face softened from her former animosity. His mind kept going back to that moment where he questioned if she would hurt the baby. Was it jealousy or revenge that had made Nora appear so menacing in that moment? Or was it her sudden change in appearance playing tricks on his mind?

"What of these rebels?" Nora asked.

Bella gave a pouty frown. "There were those who thought that you were killed and replaced by an imposter. Naturally, I wanted to know my daughter was safe. Of course you are, look at you. It would take an extraordinary man to kill you."

"They'd have to get through me first," Aegis grumbled.

Bella gave him a smile so warm it would've made him blush if he could.

"Who created these rumors? Where are they now?" Nora asked,

leaning in as she spoke.

"Gone. For all the trouble they caused, they vanished this morning before you arrived."

He and Nora exchanged an alarmed glance.

"You didn't know these people?" Nora asked.

Bella shook her blonde head. "A month ago, a woman came to me asking about you. There was nothing unusual in that; people often ask about you, what you're like, and so on. Only this one proceeded to tell me about you. She gave me details about you from your childhood, things a stranger couldn't know. She told me you had died."

The tinges of a looming threat worked their way up his neck. Bella played with the teacup as she spoke, and Nora watched her mother's lips as she recounted the story.

"It upset me, but I shook it off. It wasn't long until a pair of men were speaking to the town mayor about an incident rumored about at the castle. One that involved you, and that no one had seen you since, but an old man was making decrees on your behalf.

"It became a regular occurrence after that. Rumors were coming from strangers of all sorts about strange happenings at the castle. I didn't mean to cause a panic, Nora, I really didn't, but after everything that happened…" Tears streaked Bella's cheeks. "I had to do something this time."

Nora said nothing, but her eyes were brimming with tears. They understood now why Bella raised the alarm, and it was not out of ulterior motive. She was attempting to compensate for her behavior during Nora's childhood.

They left before the baby could stir and demand his mother's breast. Nora and Bella exchanged goodbyes and promises to keep in touch. Aegis imagined this was a normal departing for souls. He thought back to Minerva and there was a twinge of regret, but he still couldn't bring himself to forgive her.

Minerva didn't understand how important his oath to the King's Soul was. There could be potential consequences to treason that they were not aware of. Much of what had happened was his fault. He'd told Minera little of his regained memories—the oath—and glossed over his feelings for Nora to protect his mate. If she understood that what she suggested could jeopardized their very existence, Minerva might have acted differently.

From the day Minerva pulled him from the ground, she was his superior. He had little memory other than his name, and he deferred to her in every way. He now understood that he was the leader of the vampires, or whatever was left of them after the war with the giants.

Especially now that there were only two of them. Minerva was just doing what she had always done. She was giving Aegis the answer to their problems. It wasn't her fault that things had changed without her knowing. At the same time, he couldn't forgive it. She wanted to kill Nora.

He restrained the urge to confess the failed plot, but it would only endanger everyone. Even if Nora were the same little girl from a year ago, she wouldn't have been able to forgive something like that. He understood that now. Her pain and resentment ran too deep. She had been changed, for better or for worse. His eyes lingered on the swell of her chest while he debated which way that pendulum swung.

"Why are you looking at me like that?" Nora asked as they walked through the town. Brown silt tinted the edges of her black gown only to return to black once more.

He blinked and she laughed. "Like you're worried."

"I'm always worried."

"That is true," she admitted. "You're thinking of the people who rabble-roused the region?"

"It's concerning," he said, though that wasn't what was on his mind.

The crowds of fifth region dwellers began to grow. They kept their distance, but they all wanted a glimpse of their queen. He hoped they wouldn't stay much longer. Chalking it up how tense he was over the queen's sudden transformation, he ignored the jealousy that took root in his heart. This must have been what she felt when he was galivanting around with Minerva, pretending that his world hadn't stopped at Nora's feet.

"It's a small region," he said.

"For no one to recognize them means they were likely from a different region."

Aegis followed her meaning. "Someone from the palace sent them here."

"Or the sixth region," Nora agreed.

"Either have access, but Bella said they had details … No one in the sixth region would know anything about you."

"But someone from the seventh would."

Vinicio. Nora's former stepfather and steward of Hell. He would know about her childhood. "He must be sending messages to people in the sixth region, promising them wealth. Gamblers and thieves hate the fifth region, but for the chance at being rich …"

Nora smiled a thin smile. "Only he would go to Bella with those details."

"But the mention of the palace…" His eyes were lingering on the swell of her newly exposed cleavage. Aegis tore his gaze from the queen, but her knowing smile prickled up the back of his neck.

"You're distracted," she said. "Why would Vinicio want us to think these rumors came from the palace?"

They would be far more legitimate from the palace than from the seventh region. There was also a chance that Vinicio was trying to frame someone within the palace as the conspirator. He fumbled over the most basic questions in her presence lately.

Her hand was on his, pulling him around to face her and she

wrapped her arms around his neck. It was intimate, and that moment she intended to kiss him. He closed his eyes. In the place of a kiss was anticipation and a breeze. There was a mocking giggle, and he opened his eyes to find they were somewhere else.

They stood in the center of a garden beside a three tiered fountain. The plush green grass was carefully manicured and surrounded by beds of wildflowers. Nora released him and walked away slowly. They must have been in the fourth region because no one else in Hell cared that much about their gardens.

Something indeed had changed in his queen, and it changed how he felt about her. There was no doubt in his mind that she had come fully unhinged. She was dangerous and volatile. There would be no reasoning with this version of Nora.

There would also be no disputing the fact that he was falling head over heels for her.

# Chapter Eleven

Of all the better parts of Hell, Aegis hated this one the most. He preferred the dustbowl of the sixth region to this pretentious, overcrowded region any day. It was only aesthetically pleasing to those who'd never know nature in its true form. Every shrub, every patch of grass perfect. A single weed was met with scorn.

The towns in the fourth were the only ones with actual sidewalks because everyone was afraid of getting their clothes dirty. He couldn't imagine how painstaking it was to remain pristine while building their ornate homes or mucking out sewage trenches, but these people went to great lengths to maintain appearances.

Nora would have blended in if it weren't for the black crown. Few did not know what that crown meant. No one dared to speak directly to her, but they moved to let her pass. Gentlemen even risked mudding their boots be stepping off the sidewalk entirely. They were unsure of the proper greeting. Some gave curt little bows and averted their eyes while others kneeled.

"What are we doing here?" he asked.

"Don't be so cranky," she teased. "I have my reasons."

"It's near the seventh?" The vampire only glared at the overdressed crowd. Nora strutted down the street full of purpose. She wasn't searching for something; the queen had already found it.

"Yes. The areas of concern were the fifth and fourth. Who is more easily upset than my mother and the social climbers of Hell? If Vinicio has any supporters left, they would be here."

Nora was cunning in this form. She was always clever and wary, but now she walked with purpose. Nothing was accidental anymore. How would he keep up?

"You had a little falling out with Minerva," Nora said as they strolled the streets of the town.

Ladies with parasols moved to the side, and the queen gently took a white lace umbrella from a woman also wearing a black gown and gloved hands. She smiled at the woman, rested it easily on her shoulder, and waited for Aegis to answer. He didn't know how. Nora hadn't been in the castle long enough to learn about the spat.

"It's my fault," he said. "I didn't explain to her my oath once I regained my memory—among many other things."

"Your love for me," Nora said with a lifted chin.

"Yes," he said breathlessly. She could say such things so easily.

"Is it over then?"

He couldn't say for certain. They had fallen out many times before. Sometimes they just lived separately for long periods for no reason at all. This time it was different. His purpose in life had changed and he didn't know if there was a place for Minerva in his life anymore. If they did reconnect, it would be well after Nora was gone.

"Yes."

She didn't answer, but she was happy. He could tell in the ways she didn't respond—her swagger and the tightness of her jaw as she tried not to smile. Nora had won. Perhaps in the past that would have made him angry, but since Nora descended the stairs earlier that day, he had all but forgotten about his mate. Deep down, he was just as cruel as this version of Nora was, and it felt as though a long suppressed part of him had reemerged, like a wild animal released from a cage.

They stopped outside a large grey brick building with a domed top. There were several dozen steps to the top. People coming and going down the steps almost didn't notice the queen. Her heels clicked against the stones and people paused to look only to continue their way once she passed. Each stone she stepped on glimmered in the sunlight. Perhaps it was just his imagination.

"What is this place?"

"Social services office of the fifth region," Nora said.

Aegis stood before the building and shook his head. "More regions with their own laws?"

"Not laws per se, more like guidelines," the queen said as she walked into the building. "They determine who has clearance to visit the court of the first region, keep track of who gets married, where the wealth goes when a soul passes on."

The region of status went hand in hand with wealth and greed. They needed laws and protocols in dealing with it. This made sense, but the concept of wealth was exclusively a soul concept. If he required silver for survival, he would have groveled for it, too. As of now, the concept disgusted him as much as the fourth region, if not more.

Nora spun her parasol, and a luminescent light flickered through the holes in the lace as it rained down on the shadowed stone. It wasn't just his imagination. Nora radiated magic seamlessly and was enjoying it. He was in awe of the magic that happened all around her as if her very presence made little miracles wherever they went.

The shaded pavilion of the building was much cooler. Nora handed Aegis her parasol and pushed the revolving door to go inside. He gave the parasol in his hand an indignant squeeze. "I'm an immortal man with the strength and speed of a thousand men," he complained. "I've lived to see the titans fall. I've lived throughout the ages of Hell—"

"Then you'll know to close it before going inside," Nora said absently.

She was reading a plaque with various names, scanning the plain halls and corridors. The queen was searching for someone, but how would she know who? He supposed Nora was aware of the various leaders in the regions, but he'd never seen her work with them in any way. The closest she associated with anyone from the fourth region was the courtgoers.

Nora abruptly stopped reading and proceeded down the hallway to the left. The black and white marble floors were littered with souls eager to catch a glimpse from a safe distance. The marble floor turned a black onyx, reaching outward as if at war with the white of the marble with each of the queen's steps. Gasps and even weeping resonated through the hallways. The people at the large wooden desks made no move to stop her, too stunned by the visit. He trailed behind as she swung open a pair of double doors, secretly enjoying the spectacle.

She rounded the corner before he could follow but heard a stuttered greeting. He turned the corner to find Nora seated on the opposite side of an older white gentleman with grey hair and a pale suit. The plaque on his desk read Court Diplomat, Kevin Bannister.

He was fat as most men are by this age, wide around the belly. His puffy skin was flushed around the face, no doubt by the surprise visit. Nora, however, did not seem nervous. Her face was unreadable as she sprawled gracefully in the chair. Vines broke through the molding in the room and fingered along the walls. Did no one notice but him?

"Aegis," she said, and he shut the door behind them. He could pick up traces of violence in the air, and he licked his lips with the excitement of what his queen would do next.

"I don't believe we've ever formally met, Mr. Bannister."

"No, I don't think we have."

"You oversee who attends court in the castle. Am I correct?" Nora said with a tilt of her head.

"Yes."

The man was scared. Perspiration glistened across his sparse hairline and Aegis was brimming with anticipation. "My queen," he reminded the man of the proper way to address her.

"Of course."

It was deliberate, and Aegis was unsatisfied. His hands were clenched, and he struggled not to snarl. He moved towards the man with the intent of making him say it, but Nora stopped him with a lift of her hand. With a grim nod, it was clear that his queen would provide satisfaction.

"It's not an easy task," she started. "Getting correspondence to and from the seventh region."

"Not with the right leadership," Mr. Bannister replied.

The admission enraged him. His eyes went bloodshot and once again, he moved to lunge at the man, but she stopped him.

"Aegis, stay," Nora ordered. "I hope you're not intentionally trying to bate my vampire. He doesn't like you."

"I don't imagine he does." Sweat was now rolling down the man's face.

Nora remained cool. If he weren't so angry, he would've admired her composure.

Bannister's office wasn't too large, but on its walls hung many plaques and framed awards. His desk was also adorned with framed pictures—all facing him. Despite his disdain for the queen, he was an otherwise loved person.

"You've been doing Vinicio's bidding," Nora said.

How did she come to this conclusion? Perhaps she already had that information and just hadn't told him. She'd been keeping many things from him as of late, so it wouldn't surprise him.

Mr. Bannister had the same question. "Who told you this?"

"You did." Nora pursed her lips in a knowing smile. "You're the communication director of the fourth region. Any member of the royal court that hails from this region would write to you with any and all gossip. I came here for that reason alone. It was your reaction to me that told me everything."

Mr. Bannister was scared and now angry. His face was red and twisted with anger and tears. "I didn't get to where I am now just to be bossed around by a girl," he told her. "I didn't do anything wrong."

Nora opened her mouth to speak, but Mr. Bannister cut her off. "I don't deserve to be interrogated by you or your wretch. Hell has always been ruled by men. Why would the king suddenly return a girl?"

"Why, indeed?" Nora replied.

"You're not the real king and I know it," he rebuffed. "You can fool everyone else with your witchcraft, but not me."

"So, you think I am a witch and that I don't have the King's Soul," Nora said, "because I am a woman?"

"You come from the region of witches," Mr. Bannister added. "Where else could you learn such things?"

Of all the deluded ideas, this was by far the most ridiculous of theories. His misogyny simply wouldn't allow him to comprehend the truth. It didn't matter what evidence countered his theory; it was a lie or some elaborate conspiracy to trick him into thinking otherwise.

Aegis could only shake his head in response. Nora had lost her interest in this man. "I want all letters from the former steward," she demanded.

"I don't keep letters," he replied smugly. For probably once in his life, his paranoia had paid off.

That was not what Nora wanted to hear. She straightened, and Mr. Bannister went pale and loose in his overstuffed chair before he began to quietly convulse.

"What are you doing to him?"

"Searching his mind," she replied.

No king had such capacity before. It was fascinating to watch. The veins in the man's forehead swelled and his eyes rolled back in his head. Despite her abilities, the queen's face was bored, if not annoyed.

"It wouldn't be so painful if he would just stop fighting me."

Nora wasn't intentionally torturing him, but he was in pain. Aegis licked his lips and relished the moment. She was being practical, but he was darker still. Warm ammonia trickled on the floor as foam and blood trickled from the soul's lips. Mr. Bannister was not fit enough to endure the queen's attempt to search his memories.

"You're killing him," he warned.

"And what if I did?"

Aegis shrugged. He didn't care, but it would be good to warn her before it was too late. Then again, what if this was not Nora? What if this wasn't what she wanted? Doubt entered his mind, and he couldn't push it out.

"I've killed countless in my lifetime," he said. "It starts with one, and then it never stops."

"How altruistic," she sneered. "I've already killed a man, or have you forgotten?"

The man deserved to die for his treason, but the way she spoke of Charlie startled him. Had she truly made amends with his death? The bitterness in her voice suggested otherwise. She was not totally changed after all. This was his queen, just with a sharpened edge.

The man's face grew a pale shade of purple before going white. His body went limp, and he stopped breathing. Nora frowned and the man's body jolted a few more times. The queen remained seated while she stared at the body. She clicked her tongue against her teeth and drummed her fingers against the arm of the chair. She was not pleased, and he wished he could remedy that.

Nora stood up and exited the room. "Come, Aegis."

***

That night, they stayed in the most renowned hotel in town. It was a far cry from Abigail's inn, the place they'd stayed in nearly a year ago. This place was an immaculate estate with a tall, stately house surrounded by gardens and a hedge maze. There was not a stick of furniture that wasn't overstuffed, hand-painted, polished, or gilded. It made his stomach churn.

They were greeted at the door by the owner—a large, proud woman stuffed into a corset and a burgundy couture gown—and given a grand tour. He could have done without the grand tour, but Nora enjoyed the pomp and circumstance. Souls were falling all over themselves to impress her. Before it would make her awkward and self-conscious. Now, Nora was elegant and gracious towards her subjects. Better her than him. He hated all this and would have rather found a nice tree to sit in.

The lavish hotel was much like the hostess, stuffed with finery in a way that could only be described as tacky. Overdressed windows smothered what natural light the windows could provide. The furniture was of the softest leathers and decadent upholstery, and there was so much of it, the hostess's dress was getting caught on every corner. Not a single space went to waste. There was a painted vase or a nude sculpture stuffed into every corner.

"It was only a matter of time before the queen accepted my invitation," the woman huffed. "My letters and prayers have finally been answered."

He doubted that Nora had seen any such invitations. "Yes, it is a beautiful establishment," she agreed. "We wish to stay in your best room."

The word *room* echoed in his mind repeatedly. They had stayed in close quarters many times, but that was before Nora's unusual and radical transformation. He found himself painfully aware of how low cut Nora's dress was. How tightly it wrapped around her form. Part of him did indeed want this, but he had so many questions that needed answers. For the first time in her short life, Nora was unafraid and fierce. It was attractive, but was he the best thing for her? She would change with each passing day when he never would.

The royal blue damask wallpaper and crown molding lined the walls towards the royal suite. The owner paused her jabber for a moment to open the room and allow them the moment of awe. "Even the rooms of the palace fail to compare," the woman gloated.

He had to stifle a laugh. It was unlikely she had ever seen the castle. Most never left their regions. She must have garnered such praise from people who stayed in her hotel.

Nora nodded approvingly as she indulged the stuffy woman. "It's lovely," she said before feigning a yawn. "I am quite tired."

"Of course." The owner gave a deep bow as she closed the door. "The bell is right here; we will answer all hours of the day and night."

He sat on a carved and cushioned chair and regarded his queen. Maybe now she would tell him. "What's happened to you?"

Nora's eyes shifted. They were alone. She couldn't avoid the question.

"You've changed overnight," he said. "It's not that I dislike it. Some of the changes are rather nice …"

Nora gave him a sideways glance that suggested she was annoyed. She instead sat on the four-poster bed and removed her pointy black heels. "Why don't you scout the perimeter or something."

"The room's not big enough to ignore me," he said. "I just want to know what's going on in that head of yours."

"No," she snapped. Her brown eyes burned with anger. Startled, he straightened, not certain of what he said that offended her so much.

"No one else is going to be in my head ever again. Now get out!"

He'd pushed her too hard. Reaching out, he tried to console her, but before he could, she ran to the bathroom and slammed the door. "I said go away!"

She only hid away like that when she was crying. He had said something that upset her. She hated crying and linked it to weakness.

He leaned against the door and closed his eyes. "You know, when you hurt, I feel it, too."

"Then you can burn in it just as I do," she growled from the other side of the door.

"I can take it," he said. "Whatever you're going through. Whatever hurts you, I can handle it if you just tell me what you need."

"But can you accept it?"

"I accept you," he promised.

She was quiet for a long while after that. He waited on the other side of the door, hoping she would come out and tell him just what she had been dealing with. He was beyond the idea that he could make her better. It was a mistake to think that she needed to be fixed.

"Scan the perimeter," she said.

He straightened and stared into the door as if he could make it collapse between them. "I'm not leaving you."

"Now!" she ordered.

He refused to obey. He planted his feet firmly onto the glossy pine floor and set his jaw. It wasn't long until a searing pain ripped up his arm. It started as a tingling sensation from the scar. The longer he stood, the more it burned. She said he could burn just as she did. Was this what she meant?

He fought the urge to scream as the pain surged up his arm and into his chest and head. He was burning from the inside out. His jaw locked so hard he couldn't cry out. Forced to his knees, he wrapped his arms around his chest.

In fleeting moments, he considered ripping off the scarred hand, but it was the scar Tom had given him an eternity ago. As his vision went, Aegis succumbed to the memories.

***

The mountain between the first and second regions was a beast.

The top of it lived within the clouds and the feet were just as tall as the trees in the Starry Wood. Aegis marveled at the expanse. Tom's eyes had gazed the extent of the mountain with a slack jaw. "They said the witch lives here," he said. "And we have to climb up the rocks and find her."

"Where should we start?" Aegis had asked, overwhelmed by the task before them.

Tom's eyes narrowed as he scanned the base of the mountain. "I suppose the nearest foothold."

The first night in the mountains, he found a goat. He was surprised by how much wildlife lived at such heights. There were hares and wildcats, goats and birds. Tall patches of grass, wild weeds, and berries, even mushrooms grew. He was starting to understand why a witch would want to live up here. Most of these plants could be medicinal.

The evening's fire crackled, and the heat moved within the circle of rocks and cliffside they called home for the night. Tom skinned the animal before putting parts of it on a rock halfway into the fire. "I can see why someone would want to live here," he said, looking up to the sky. "It's perfect."

The smoke of their campfire entwined with the clouds. The occasional break would reveal a black sky just out of reach.

"But it's not practical for someone who deals in trading potions," he commented.

"Perhaps she only deals with the truly desperate like me," Tom chided.

"At least you have a cause," he said. "I feel like me and my kind were destined to wander without purpose."

"Is that why you're helping me?"

He stared into the fire as it charred the goat flesh and thought about the question while Tom's eyes were fixated on the sky.

"I've seen mortals defend themselves and others," he explained.

"I've seen them win. I've seen them lose. I've seen your kind do so much despite its limitations, but I've never seen one stand up on behalf of all the way you are. I suppose I want to see what happens."

Bats squeaked overhead, and a cool breeze made its way through the crags. Tom closed his eyes before returning a thoughtful gaze into the night air.

"I imagine somewhere, the night sky is filled with lights."

It was improbable, but it made for a beautiful idea.

Not all their nights on the mountain were as lovely. The higher they got, the harder it was for Tom to breathe. The height weighed heavily on his lungs. It was also colder, much colder, the higher they climbed. When the freezing rain relented, pounding winds took its place. As Tom's strength deteriorated, Aegis was worried that the rumors were wrong. Maybe there was no witch in this place and they were on some fool's errand.

After four days of strife, Aegis couldn't stand it any longer. "We have to go back down," he said. "I will scale this whole mountainside on my own and come back to tell you about it if you like, but you can't survive up here."

By this point, Tom couldn't argue. Between trying to keep up with Aegis and the lack of air, speaking was not a luxury the soul could indulge. Aegis grabbed Tom, slung the paper-light man over his shoulder, and made his way down. He moved quickly, jumping from rock to rock, but every few hours, they would stop and rest.

"I'm feeling better now," Tom promised. "I can make the rest of the way without you carrying me."

He would have preferred his method, but Tom insisted. "Just remember, the way down can be more dangerous than the way up. You're more likely to misjudge a step or take more risks because you're eager to get down."

Tom nodded absently while searching for a good footing. For a moment, Tom smiled at hi before suddenly plummeting from the side of the cliff.

He lunged for Tom, but it was too late. The boy didn't even have time to scream. Tom had fallen off the side of a massive mountain, and he was powerless to stop him. The one soul that could change all of Hell, and he was now dead.

Aegis kneeled and looked over the edge to find Tom only a few feet down. He choked out a laugh at the sight. Tom was prone, but unharmed. He merely stared up at Aegis in a daze. As much as he wanted to lecture him, he figured the soul had probably learned his lesson.

He paused at what sounded like the scraping of sandals against stone. Tom's eyes went wide as an ancient woman in grey rags and chunks of red hair approached him.

"So, you've come," the woman said.

He jumped down to Tom's side. The woman was blind. Both eyes were white, and her skin was wrinkled and scarred far beyond her years. She did not appear like any soul he had ever met before. She was likely an imposter; perhaps she was a titan in disguise.

"You've seen him in visions?" he asked.

The witch stared at Aegis hard for a moment. "Word spreads fast about titan killers."

"How do you speak to people up in these mountains?" Tom asked, still prone on the ground.

The woman sneered half-laughing and her crippled fingers gave a dramatic wave. "From beyond!"

She was mocking them. The hunched woman waddled back into the depths of her den. Aegis turned to Tom, who could only shrug. He had never met a witch before, but he'd imagined someone more exotic with lots of piercings and tattoos, or perhaps someone with a long beard and a pointy hat. If anyone had made mention to Tom about who the witch was, he'd never shared it.

"Come on," the woman's patchy voice echoed along the stone.

He trailed behind Tom along the hollowed part of the mountain to find a home that exceeded his expectations. He had imagined something more rudimentary, with stone tools and boulder seats. What they came into was a large room with soft rugs and wooden furniture. White linens hung along the walls, giving the den a more open appearance.

The opening continued straight through the other side of the mountain, giving the room an airy, natural feeling. It didn't feel like a retired old bear den like he'd imagined. They followed the woman through her home and out the other end where a great cast iron kettle hung over a fireplace by a thick iron chain.

The old witch had created a sort of lever and pulley system. Attached overhead was a pulley that the chain rolled on. When the witch had her kettle at the desired distance from the fire, she slipped the chain link over the nail she had fixed into the side of the mountain.

"Well, now that's clever," he muttered.

Tom's eye shifted as he stepped forward. He swallowed and stuttered over his words. "I'm here so that—"

"I know what you're here for." The witch waved him off with a hand full of crooked fingers. "You want to kill the titans and rule this world."

"At any price," Tom answered.

The old woman lowered the kettle until it smashed the fire and sparks wisped into the now sunset sky.

"Price," the woman repeated. "It's not so much a price as it is a consequence." The witch began to drop various things into the kettle—herbs, and roots mostly. She extended a wrinkled arm holding a pail. "Here, run down there and fetch me some water."

He peered over the side of the cliff, and the witch only stared at him. "Take the stairs this time," she said, pointing to the side of the cave.

Beside a few bushes were a flight of stairs. No wonder she thought them stupid. They had climbed this mountain twice over when there were stairs just outside her home.

Aegis did as the old woman asked. He flew down the stairs and found a stream at the bottom. Wasting no time, he filled the pail and ran back up. She thanked him and poured the water into the kettle before raising it back up a few feet above the smashed fire.

"If I give you the power you seek, your soul will never again be able to leave this place," the old woman explained. "I won't give you life eternal—I'm sure your friend can confirm that that would indeed be a price, but to give you the power to kill the titans, you'll need to ground your soul to Hell forever."

Aegis frowned, not knowing what to think of that. Tom either understood on some level, or he didn't care what it meant if it made him stronger. Tom nodded. "I understand."

"As souls, we travel from this world to the next and back again. We are reborn into new lives and new bodies each time. Your soul will be forever tethered to this one. You'll die, but instead of going to the other world, your soul will remain here to be reborn again."

"So, there is no afterlife for me," Tom nodded.

"No beforelife either," the witch joked.

All this made the vampire feel uneasy. He didn't doubt the witch's intent or dispute Tom's resolve, but he'd never heard of anything like this, nor had he ever encountered anyone who could give such power. "What do you want in exchange?" Aegis asked, hoping to find a motive.

The woman squatted on a three-legged stool beside the fire. "I want a safer world for my daughter and granddaughter. They refuse to live in the mountains with me, and I don't want to live down there with those ignorant plebeians. This world needs to change. My only condition is that you always stand by your king."

He nodded. "I will stand by him no matter what shape he takes."

"Can you swear it?" she asked.

Aegis gave a sullen nod before looking at Tom, who masked his excitement terribly. Tom twiddled his thumbs behind his back and had to shift from one hip to the other, either because he needed to relieve himself or because he wanted to sit down. Aegis never could determine these things with souls. Despite her age, the witch had no problem lifting logs off her stack of firewood near the cave opening and throwing them under the kettle.

She held her hair back as she inhaled deeply the aroma of what was in the kettle. It did indeed smell pleasant—like a bean soup, he supposed.

Tom frowned as he peered over the kettle, less impressed by the contents. "Is that the potion that will change me?" he asked.

The witch glanced in the pot and grinned. "This? Oh no, this is dinner. You'll need all the strength you can muster."

She went back into her home within the mountain and returned carrying an ornate blade with a carved wooden handle. Taking Tom by the hand, she led him to the edge of the cliff.

"Each time you die, you will be reborn into this world as someone different, yet the same. You will be the king of this world, but also its prisoner, as you'll never be able to leave with the rest of us. You will have all the powers of Hell until Ragnarök. Are you sure you want to do this?"

Tom nodded. Aegis moved to stand between the witch and Tom in case of foul play. The witch caught his hand despite his speed and said, "Do you swear to protect and obey the king regardless of the manifestation he takes?"

"Myself, as well as my kin, we swear this to you."

The witch smirked. "Don't see that blowing up in our face at all, do we?"

In his stubbornness, he refused to relent, and the witch agreed. "Very well."

The old woman closed her eyes and began to chant. The winds of the mountain carried her voice into the air as it channeled all around them. Her echoes bled into one another until the voice resonated a new language all its own. Tom gulped and clenched his eyelids shut, too afraid of what was happening around him.

A cold, piercing pain slipped down his palm when the witch cut his hand. She dug into it and carved a C shape. "Open your mouth, boy. Stick out your tongue."

Tom did as she said, and she wiped the bloodied blade along his tongue, careful not to cut him. Once the blade was clean, she gently closed his mouth. Aegis's wound healed straightaway as it usually did, except a scar remained. He traced the ridges of the scar with his thumb and prided himself on his first and only scar.

"The dagger of monsters," she told Tom as she handed him the knife. "It will kill most of the creatures in this world, including your friend here," she motioned to him. "It won't kill your titans, but your powers should help you determine their fatal flaws."

Tom frowned. "It's done then?"

The witch smiled and nodded. "Yes, it is done."

He and Tom exchanged looks. "Nothing has changed—"

But something had changed. The witch was older than she had been when they'd first met. The bags under her eyes drooped lower, and her skin was chalky. She appeared dried out and her rags hung even heavier. A clump of red hair fell to the ground where a pile of hair had already accumulated.

"The price was yours to pay," he said. "You put what life you had left into that spell."

The old woman nodded with a serene expression. A gust of wind whipped around the side of the mountain and blew straight into her. Tom reached out to grab the woman, but he caught nothing but a handful of old rags.

# Chapter Twelve

Aegis woke on the waxed wooden floor. The scar on his hand still burned as he traced it with his index finger. He bolted upright to search for Nora. The bathroom door was wide open, and no one else was in the room. He was furious that she had run off without him, but he denied the residual hurt. She didn't even stick around to make sure he was okay. Nothing like that had ever happened to him before, and vulnerability wasn't a pleasant feeling.

He opened a window and the night air hit him. It was dark, and by the cool breeze, the night was in full swing. Most of the buildings crammed along the main street were dark. He noted there was some laughter, and the scent of bodies and alcohol mingled in the night air.

A small string of lights was stung along the boardwalk of a pier. Aegis leaped from the window and strode in the general direction. It wasn't long until he found a party barge tied along the dock. This barge was not for passengers. Rather, it was a place that hosted parties.

The souls of the fourth region held celebrations so debauched that no one wanted to host them in their homes. Rather, they would host them in an older boat and allow it to be trashed by the guests until they either burned it down or sold it to a less wealthy person.

This boat was large—larger than the royal boat. He wasn't certain it could sail most of the river of Styx. The waters were probably too shallow as the vessel was bigger than a boat. He wasn't sure what to call it. The party was raging on all levels of the barge, and he could hear laughter and vomiting, among other things.

Everyone was dressed in large, elaborate gowns. Even the men wore long tails and curled wigs. Some had canes and top hats. The women wore masks and wide hoop skirts and fanned themselves with silk fans. He stood in awe of the spectacle for a moment. What it would be like to not give two shits about anything in the world besides the next party?

No one questioned him when he boarded despite being woefully underdressed. They were all too busy being self-absorbed. He could make out Nora's voice somewhere in the boat. It rang like a bell and pulled at him from all directions. She was here, and he would find her. If she weren't the queen, he wouldn't be hunting her down at a party. If he hadn't sworn a blood oath to protect her life, he'd leave her be. He told himself these things as he searched the lower decks, but in his heart, he was lying.

The further he waded into the party, the less clothing people wore. A woman in her underclothes with a three-foot wig was pouring alcohol into reclining man's mouth while a gaggle of half-dressed women laughed on an oversized settee.

Some were snorting powder off a glass table, and around the corner, there was a mostly dressed woman vomiting while a man pissed over the balcony. It was laughable to watch them play Go Fish as though they were staking their lives on it, but since they had absolutely no concept of gambling, their stunted version ended in applause and lines of powder to celebrate.

The carpets that lined the hallways were probably nice at one point, but now they were soiled from footprints and wine stains. The lighting fixtures that lined the walls were nice little wall-mounted lanterns except for the one that someone broke. Glass shards decorated that patch of carpet. It protested as he stepped on pieces with his boot.

Opening the cabin door, he found Nora in one of the getups that the other women were wearing, only hers was a shiny black gown that ruffled and bowed at every corner. Her crown now also supported a black veil that was folded back, revealing black lips and a garnet choker with black lace.

She was being entertained by several men in tights and wigs. He debated throwing them out the stupidly small round windows of the cabin. Nora had been drinking. He could tell by the cup that sloshed around in her hand and the stink of the room. Her boys ignored his presence, but Nora waved them off.

He dismissed their stares as they lurked away. He relished it, and Nora gave an approving smile.

"You're the jealous type after all."

He didn't know where to start with her. She had him confounded on so many levels. Maybe he did want her as a lover, but she was so young, and it wasn't his place to make such a decision. At the same time, he feared for her mental state and what it meant for Hell. His lack of words wasn't uncommon, but his intense stare was still enough to make her pause.

"You didn't want me before." Nora crossed her legs and leaned back into the giant leather chair beside the bed.

"What's changed in you?" he asked.

Her eyes shifted before motioning for him to sit on the love seat beside her own. She waited until he settled before slowly nodding her head. "You're right. I have changed. I don't have all the answers. I don't know why or how, but I was at odds with my own soul. I can now say that I've made peace with myself and embraced the aspects that I tried so hard to constrain."

He was oddly satisfied with the answer. Admittedly, he wanted to accept her answer because he wanted her, but he couldn't be with her unless she was of sound mind. It also pained him to know she'd been unable to be herself wholly.

"You were repressing parts of your personality you assumed people wouldn't like?"

Nora's eyes shined in the dim light. She eyed him before she answered carefully, "Yes. I let the voices of others dictate who I was and what I wanted. I've since locked them out."

There was more she wasn't telling him. It was in the pauses between her words and in her right hand that drummed the arm of the chair with her fingers. He didn't suspect she was lying to him, merely withholding information, but if he remained open-hearted, she would come to tell him more in time.

Nora was a fiercely untrusting creature—no doubt a result of her upbringing. He couldn't blame her for trying to protect herself. Though there was still something that troubled him. "What happened in the hotel room …" He didn't finish the sentence.

He could tell by the way her eyes narrowed and her head tilted that she didn't know what had happened. "You didn't do that?" he asked.

Nora appeared alarmed for a moment but recovered quickly. "When I came out and you were asleep on the floor. I figured you would wake when you were ready, so I let you be."

She hadn't caused the pain directly, and she wasn't aware of what had happened. If she saw what had happened, would she have stayed with him? It must have been the result of the oath. He'd never disobeyed a direct order before, so he never knew, but there was indeed a consequence. He didn't have time to contemplate the implications. Nora was standing up. She wobbled to one side before tripping on her pointy shoes and falling the other way.

It might have been the dress that threw her off balance, but as she disrobed, it became clear that she was drunk. It was a complicated dress to remove, but in Nora's state, it was as though she were at war with the garment. At the end of the battle, the dress remained standing, and Nora collapsed on the bed.

Her eyes softened as she motioned for him to come over. Nora took his hand and tried to pull him on top of her. Aegis snorted in laughter. "I think it's time to sleep."

He tucked her in bed before reseating himself on the loveseat to contemplate the newfound meaning of his scar and the blood oath he'd made eons ago.

***

Peter sat in his usual spot at the table. His eyes flickered to the vacancy where Nora usually sat. In her absence he and the two military leaders, Alfie and Hacia, were making decisions in the queen's stead. He wasn't worried at all about that—there were hardly any decisions to be made. The soul safe might get a little crowded, but that was not something he was able or willing to deal with.

He was worried about other things. For one, the story Alfie gave him of what happened in the caves was terrifying. Nora had lost control and accidentally killed a boy. Before Peter could determine Alfie's loyalties after the incident, Peter was receiving reports about Nora's behavior in the fifth region.

If what he read was true, the queen had sprouted wings and vanished in thin air, taking Aegis with her. His most recent report was that she was in the fourth region and that one of the diplomats had been found dead after she paid him a visit. Peter had no idea what to make of all this, and he needed to know where the military stood.

"Good morning," he greeted.

"Any news on our queen's whereabouts?" Alfie asked.

"Not since yesterday."

"No more suspicious deaths, I gather."

"We don't know that was her," Hacia interjected.

Alfie stretched out his arms in frustration. It seemed they had had this argument several times before. "She walked into a diplomat's office, and he was no longer alive when she left."

"We don't know the full situation!" Hacia said.

"You're both right," Peter interjected. "It's safe to assume that she, and not Aegis, killed the man. There would be evidence if it were

Aegis's doing. What we don't know is why. It may have been an accident like with that boy of yours."

"Charlie," Alfie corrected. "His name was Charlie."

"She didn't do that intentionally," Peter said.

Alfie leaned in. "No, she certainly did not. I'll never forget the look on her face."

Hacia gave Alfie a sympathetic nod and rubbed his arm. "We are loyal to our own first, the crown second," she explained. "It has always been this way."

Peter understood this. Both military branches were considered their own entities. They were at the castle's disposal, but only if they supported the cause. This was the primary cause of the tensions between the hawk hunters and the trackers. When the generals couldn't come to an agreement on whether to support a cause, conflict arose. Even now, when Hacia and Alfie were a couple, it was clear they had different feelings on what to do about their queen's problematic behavior.

Peter stood up and walked around the table. Pacing helped him think. "She went to the fifth region and put on a show. She was effective in quelling any doubt that she was dead. Less than an hour later, she was at the coordinator's door. I would surmise that she learned from her mother that he was conspiring against her. She went to confront him and killed him."

"If it were an accident, she would've come home like she did when she murdered Charlie," Alfie said.

Hacia glowered at Alfie. As much as Peter hated to see the couple quarrel, he needed them to be divided on the subject. If Alfie sided with Hacia, Peter would have all the armies of Hell to defeat. The very idea made him go weak in the knees. No, he had one army pitted against the other, which served him better for the time being.

"We need to find out why," Peter said. "Alfie, I need your troops' eyes to report her every move. Hacia, have your trackers come up with anything on the rabble-rousers?"

Unlike her partner, Hacia was relaxed in her chair. Her black coiled hair swayed as she nodded. "The rumors are coming from the palace."

That was not what he wanted to hear. The last thing they needed was increased paranoia of a traitor. Trust was the only thing that could save Hell this time. "And that's where the information ends?" Peter asked.

Hacia nodded again and chewed on her bottom lip. She wanted better results, and Peter couldn't blame her. Information was precious right now, and everyone in this room was starving for it. He clapped his hands together. "Let's do our best to figure out what's going on."

Hacia rose to leave as Peter made his way for the door.

"To what end?" Alfie asked, still seated. Both Peter and Hacia turned to look at the hawk hunter general.

"What?" Peter asked.

"Are you going to put her in a time out? She's the queen, she can do whatever she wants."

This made the hair on the nape of his neck stand. Alfie cared about his subordinates, but Peter misjudged the man. He didn't care in the slightest why Nora had killed the man in the fourth region. Alfie wasn't searching for answers; he was awaiting his next order. Much like Aegis, he was probably more upset that he didn't get to kill the man on her behalf.

"We must do everything we can to help our queen," Peter said.

Alfie nodded slowly, appeased by this answer. Hacia gazed at Alfie in renewed admiration before she took his hand in hers.

Once Peter was alone in his room, he found it hard to study on the past kings. His mind kept finding its way to Alfie's nonchalant attitude towards killing at a whim. He would need to be more careful, indeed.

# Chapter Thirteen

Aegis watched as Nora's eyes opened in the early afternoon. It was hot in the cabin. He tried to open the port window, but it was not designed to be opened. Instead, he scavenged the upstairs areas for food and drink for his queen. Nora would wake up thirsty and possibly hungover. It appeared she wouldn't be the only one.

Aegis stepped over the bodies of partygoers as he made his way to the bar and searched among the unlabeled bottles on silver and gold trays. There he found a tall pitcher of orange juice. All the ice had melted, so it would be warm, but it would be better than nothing. He also found olives in vinegar. Perhaps she would want that as well.

He set the items down on the table surrounded by sofas and returned to his spot on the loveseat. Nora had tried to seduce him last night. She wasn't a child anymore, and it was wrong to treat her as such. Still, the ramifications of being with a mortal were unchanged. She would still grow old. She would still die.

The idea of her demise made him feral with anger as Minerva had experienced. As much as he wanted to feel ashamed about attacking his mate, he didn't. It was more than just an oath to him. Nora was more than just a queen. Sex couldn't possibly make him feel anymore attached than he already was. At least that's what he told himself.

"Come back to me, Aeg," Nora said. She was sitting on the loveseat beside him, and the juice was gone. The olives were not.

"How long have you been awake?" he asked.

"Only a half hour or so." She was wearing the same lavender dress as the one she'd got in the fourth region the last time they were there, only this version was more fitted. The lace and pearl embellishments were of a quality unknown to any region. The lace was impossibly delicate, and the pearls shimmered in the light.

It was then that the truth struck him. While he had decided he had romantic feelings for her, Nora had outgrown him. She tried to tell him in the hotel room, in a way, and she only invited him to her bed last night because she was heavily intoxicated. She assumed he was more than willing to accommodate her but she was far too drunk.

This dress was nostalgia, designed to please him, but its utopic quality was not of this world, and neither was she. Whatever Nora had gone through in the last few days proved that she had transcended the King's Soul and had become something much more—and he was forever bound to Hell.

She took lovers and pushed them away in mistrust. Would she do the same to him? She said she could feel their intentions while they slept by her side, and that she wanted him because he had no ulterior motives, but that was before she changed.

"Thank you for the drink," she said. "The juice was a little too citrusy, but I feel much better after drinking it."

Nora loved orange juice. They didn't have it in the fifth region where she grew up. "You don't like olives either, I take it."

She giggled. "Those are garnishes. Most souls don't eat them."

Tears came unbidden to him then. The Nora he'd found in the Starry Wood would've eaten anything because her grandparents only fed her the plainest crumbs, believing it would make her a better person. They once withheld bread because it was too fresh in fear that it would spoil her. Orange juice was her favorite.

"You're not the same person anymore, are you?" he asked. Her face was one of pity. Nora pitied him.

"The irony," he muttered.

"I am me. I'm just more of me now," she explained.

He cocked his head. "What does that even mean?"

"Remember how the voices told me things, and then we

merged?" Nora reminded him.

"I do."

"The voices started coming back," she explained. "Around the same time I started losing control of my powers."

Aegis thought back to the hawk hunter boy, whatever his name was, and the episode with the mirror. "So, how did you make it stop?"

"I imagined a cell, and that's where it is. I locked the soul away."

The simplicity of Nora's explanation sent prickles up his spine. Her voice was so soft and innocent. Despite Peter's and his best efforts, Nora was not a queen who wanted to be questioned, not even by her own conscience.

"So, the King's Soul is locked away somewhere in your mind as you use its power."

To be fair, no other king had struggled with this issue as Nora did. They were born as the undisputed king and had no one to tell them otherwise. There were no past selves to contend with. No advisors. No voices. Just one king stumbling through one life after another. Nora had a purpose. She was attempting to remake Hell's placement process, to make the world a better place. Why should those who squabbled their lives get to interfere with hers?

Nora shook her head. "I tried to do that," she said. "I tried to draw the power from the King's Soul while locking it away. It was what made my power so inconsistent. The soul kept escaping and causing mischief."

"Then whose power are you using?" Aegis asked.

Nora pursed her red lips together in a soft smile. "Mine."

He couldn't stop his mouth from falling. The girl he knew was Nora in partial restraint by the King's Soul—held in check and afraid of what she was. The Nora before him was free and unbridled in her own powers. Perhaps that was why he became so profoundly attracted to her. What in Hell could have greater power than the King's Soul?

Her smile glittered in the dim light of the room. His queen smiled, pleased with his shock.

"Come," she said, standing. "We've got more visits to make."

He followed behind Nora, still numb from the revelations. They exited the party barge, which was now a ghost ship. There were still bodies here and there. Some of them were breathing, and some were not. Nora wasn't offended by this. She merely stepped over the inconveniences and walked across the ramp onto the pier.

"Where are we going now?" he asked.

"There's another traitor in this region."

So she intended to kill the traitor just as she had the last one. They were in correspondence with Vinicio. "The witch was right," Aegis said. "We need to deal with Vinicio sooner than later."

"First, we cut off his intel and his supporters."

Nora slinked along the stone pathways and overly pruned gardens until they reached a great, big cabin on the outskirts of the fourth region. The underkept garden with all its wildflowers and thorn roses made the place look abandoned, except even abandoned homes in the fourth region were maintained.

This place was intentionally chaotic. It would have driven the neighbors insane if there had been any. He was certain there were committees dedicated to this property alone. He spotted a wild hare in the green grass. It stood its ground and its nose twitched as large round eyes observed from a safe distance, unaware of the danger that had just entered the property.

Nora didn't knock. She walked right in to find an older woman with grey eyes and dark hair, waiting with a pipe in her mouth. She was sitting at a great square table made of the same wood as her pipe. She eased back in her chair as though she were relaxed, but Aegis noted her eyes were squinted with tenacity. "So, you've come," the woman grunted.

"Yes."

"Took you long enough," the woman said. "Vinicio said you were weak and that you'd never bother with me. I guess he was wrong."

"He is wrong about many things," Nora agreed. "You're helping him spread rumors about me. To lead an uprising."

The woman laughed, and a plume of smoke erupted from her mouth. "I've kept correspondence with the former steward, but spreading rumors, child, no. I've better things to do with my life."

"Like break region four's lawn code?" Aegis jabbed.

The inside reminded him much of the outside. Beautiful furniture and décor, but there lacked a pride that most held in their belongings. These were generally materialistic people, but the madam didn't share the same sentiment.

The woman cackled. "Oh, yes, there will be no questioning my death, to be sure. They can't wait to pull out my wildflowers and trim the grass to the precise length. Everything must be in its place."

Nora laughed and enjoyed the woman's rebelliousness. But just when his mind began to release every horrible outcome Nora might have in store for the woman, his queen smiled her wicked smile. The old woman was not going to survive the encounter.

"Why are you speaking to him?"

"You're an only child. Well, until recently, I suppose." The woman puffed on her pipe. "You can't understand the bond between siblings. We are the same, yet totally different."

"Vinicio has a sister," Nora scoffed. "He never mentioned you."

"I'm not made for palace life. I was the terror of maids and servants. Old Rebus would get so flustered by me that he'd go and cry to my father."

Nora tilted her head and smiled. "They sent you here?"

"I belong here," Vinicio's sister claimed. "While wealth is not my interest my vanity, perhaps my pride, brought my soul to this region. I have regular correspondence with my brothers. Hawk hunters are easily bribed. There's nothing you can do to stop that."

Nora's smile remained unchanged, but something behind it shifted. He was growing uncomfortable but pushed it aside for the time being.

"I'm going to kill you," the queen said.

He stared at Nora but found himself utterly speechless. The woman straightened. She suddenly forgot about the pipe that she gripped in her hand as she uncrossed her legs and sat up. "How?"

It was a curious question. What did it matter when she was dead? He supposed some deaths were worse than others, but there was a concern here that went beyond death—but what?

Nora's smile had distorted into something more sinister.

***

It made sense. Nora was a matriarch whose reign had come under question. She couldn't allow the sister of the steward to live. The woman openly challenged the queen. He had many reasons and justifications as to why Nora *had* to do it. Yet he was grateful that she didn't ask him to take part in it.

A crowd of people was accumulating outside the property. He wanted to shout that he did not strip the woman bare and hang her on an upside-down cross. He did not write the word *traitor* in blood on the cross Nora created from pieces ripped from the beautiful rustic cabin. He did not nail the old woman—alive—to the cross, leaving her screaming in agony.

But he didn't stop it either, which made him just as guilty as Nora. Though they were without judge and jury, he wanted nothing more than to flee the scene. The strongest being on Hell was torturing an old woman. He hid his face away from the crowdthough his shame was nothing in comparison to the humiliation that woman was experiencing. The cruelty of it was unfathomable. He found himself turning away, ashamed of his queen for the first time.

He couldn't tell if the people of the fourth region were gawking at what their queen had done or how unshapely the woman was as she hung there bleeding out. The way she'd pulled nails and logs apart to reconfigure them into this form in mid-air was astonishing and unlike anything he had ever beheld. If only Nora were putting these abilities into something other than maiming an old lady.

The woman writhed in pain as gravity pulled at the nails embedded in her wrists and feet. He had killed for kings and his queen, but never in this way. There was a purpose to this. Nora wanted to make sure that the people of the fourth understood their queen was alive and well and that she'd suffer no traitors—but it was horrid to watch.

Nora wasn't the least bit upset by this. She licked her lips and beamed at her handiwork. The back of his throat grew tight, and his upper lip threatened to curl upward. For the first time since he had known her, Aegis was disgusted with Nora.

"She's not going to die," he said. "She's injured, but this won't kill her."

"You'd know all about that, wouldn't you?"

He flinched at the comment as much as he did the woman's animalistic noises. "I'm just saying, it will take a long time, if at all."

"Good. Let's go then."

Nora snaked away, and he reluctantly followed. He could hear the woman scream as the nail tore through her foot another inch. Queen or no queen, he could not abide this any longer. He kicked up a stick with his boot. It wasn't all that sharp, but it was straight and strong.

In an act of defiance, Aegis turned and hurled the spear at the woman. The spear went through her ribs and she died moments after.

Nora turned and appraised his work. "She died after all."

"You knew I'd do it."

Nora wrapped her arms around him and smiled. "Of course."

In an instant, they were back at the castle. No matter how many times she did that, he never got used to it. It was as if everything changed the moment he blinked his eyes. Change was hard for the immortal, and he was at his wits' end with all the changes Nora was going through.

"You look tired," she told him as she stroked his cheek. "Go to sleep. I'll wake you when I need you. The soul safe is a bit crowded. I must tend to it," she explained.

"I love watching you do that, remember?"

The impenetrable darkness in her eyes subsided and gave way to recognition. She blinked back the wetness in her eyes and gave a stiff nod. "Right, of course. If you feel up to it, you may join me."

They said nothing as they walked the halls of the castle. Many maids and servants gasped as they were caught unprepared for the queen's return. No doubt Rebus scuttled nearby, seeking to pander to someone. She moved deftly to the room across from her own and unlocked its metal door.

As if all her cruelty had dissipated, Nora gently harbored the souls from the safe to their homes. The door spun open, and the images of the upside-down woman faded. Orbs of glowing light filtered into the room, and Nora pushed and pulled them with the sway of her hands until they passed through the sections of the map etched on the inside of the safe door.

Did her lapse in humanity cause her to forget her decree about the seventh region's souls? They scarcely saw the black souls that hovered along the floor, weighted by all their misdeeds. There had been enough time between soul sorting that a black soul did indeed emerge from the safe. This one wasn't as black as others. It was black on the outside but in the center, a faint, grey light glowed.

Nora scooped up the soul, careful not to dirty the lace on her dress, and peered into its center. She could see its whole life. "This one had no choice," she explained. "It was kidnapped as a child and forced into war. If it hadn't become one of them, it would've been killed itself."

"There's always a choice," he said, his arms crossed while he leaned against the wall.

For a minute, he was afraid she would shout at him. Her face swelled with rage, but she forced it down and continued. "It will do well in the fifth region. It needs guidance and discipline."

The safe door swung closed, and the bars spun into the locked position. He stood to join his queen as she strode from the room. Like a dog, he chased his master, but then again, what was he without her? The tables had indeed turned in their relationship. He fought against the ironic laughter that bounced in his ribcage.

He wanted to ask her what she would do next, but he feared what she would do next. More than anything, he wanted to confer with Peter, but doing so would put them both at great risk. Nora was now using her powers to seek out treason as she saw it.

He stood beside the queen as she sat on her throne, black crown resting on her head, and obeyed. Nora smiled the smile of a victor.

# Chapter Fourteen

"There have been sightings of Minerva in the Starry Wood," Alfie said over breakfast.

He said nothing and remained by his queen, who was eating a croissant with almond paste. She finished her bite and nodded, dotting the corners of her mouth with a napkin before she spoke. "We don't need to track her movements. She's not a threat. Not for now, at least."

Over the past few weeks, things had settled down somewhat. Once she was back in the castle, Nora's behavior leveled. With threats no longer imminent, she was more like her old self. It was everyone else who was acting differently now. Word of her actions with the traitors had spread. It was now known that the queen was ruthless towards traitors. He had to stop from shuddering in revulsion. It was a rather effective campaign.

"Very good," Peter said as he checked off a list on his scroll. "And what's to be done with the river situation?"

Nora smiled. "I'll handle that myself." She took a sip of her juice and nearly spat it out in disgust "What is that?"

Everyone stood in alarm, and Alfie unquestioningly grabbed the cup and took a drink himself. He swished it around in his mouth before swallowing. After several moments he concluded, "It's just grapefruit juice."

Nora wiped her face and scowled. "Peter, let the kitchen staff know the next time they give me that I will see them hanged. Everyone knows I prefer orange juice."

Peter's eyes darted to Aegis for only a moment, but the advisor didn't dare look longer.

"Yes, ma'am. I'll see to it myself." Peter rushed to the kitchen to deal with the ever-changing request for juice. Aegis had an idea and followed Peter to the kitchen. Nora eyed him skeptically as he made his way out.

The kitchen was a large room where at least fifteen souls were working. The center island was dedicated to meal preparation where the left counter was for cleaning and the right workbench was for setting up the meals to go out. The network of workers made him chuckle at how impressive it was.

Peter wove deftly in and out of the lines of workers. He was making his way to a great, big oven where a pair of plump souls bickered. The woman was wearing a pale blue dress with an apron and her hair was covered by a wrap. She was middle-aged with an unyielding scowl. She was dark, but not as dark as Hacia, and she had freckles.

The man wore a large apron as well as a tall white hat. He had a waxed mustache that curled out at the ends. His lips puckered as he engaged the woman in a stare-down. They were locked into a heated battle. Peter, oblivious to the exchange, ran right into the middle of it and began to chatter about juice.

"What?" The woman sighed. "Again?"

"Last week she said she hated orange juice and wanted something sour," the man argued.

They were not wrong. Nora's tastes were constantly changing. It wasn't a matter of growing tired of a food. It was more polar than that.

One day last week, she had demanded hot peppers in her soup, just as she had the day before, only to scream and throw the bowl at the wall in a panic. She cried and mucus ran from her nose as she began to vomit. He didn't know what to do. When water didn't help, someone from the kitchen returned with milk. She drank the milk down and gasped for air. He held her in his arms and wiped her face. Once the burning had subsided, every one of her limbs collapsed in a heap of helplessness and self-pity.

"I don't understand." The queen had shaken her head. "It tasted just fine yesterday."

He opened his mouth to speak, but before he could, she pushed him away and straightened herself. Her back became rigid and straight and her hair recoiled to its coif on its own. When she turned to him again, her face was perfect as if the pepper incident had never happened.

Today's dilemma was only a small reminder that things were still not right with the queen of Hell. Peter had his hands raised as he attempted to calm the two chefs, but Aegis had a better solution. He wove in and out of the traffic between him and Peter, but he grew so frustrated with running into staff with bowls and plates of food that he finally jumped over the table to where Peter was standing. It caught Peter's attention, as it did everyone in the room. They all stared at him.

Peter waved everyone back to work and they did resume, if more slowly.

"I have a suggestion," he announced.

After a great deal more discussion that he enjoyed, he and Peter emerged from the kitchens. Peter appeared more disheveled and battle-worn than ever. The more Peter kept in, the more fatigued he became. The new Nora scared him greatly. He no longer challenged or asked questions. He simply obeyed and watched her from the shadows. She frightened everyone, and he didn't enjoy being lumped with everyone.

Nora sat on her throne, and even the crown bent to her will. She smiled warmly at the court jester as he fooled around while the next round of entertainment was being set up. He could smell the soft hide of a beast and expected the performance would entail a large animal doing tricks.

He had no notion of ruining the surprise. Nora was enjoying

herself. The least he could do was let her be surprised. When the great doors swung open, a trainer walked into the court with a male lion on a chain. The crowds gasped as the majestic beast padded along submissively.

The lion leaped onto a small pedestal and the act began. The master would whip the air and make snapping noises, and the lion would follow the cue. He jumped from his platform through hoops of various sizes before running along the perimeter of the show for everyone to get a good look at him.

Did the animal enjoy the attention or was it just well-trained? The lion was treated well, his fur soft and shiny, but the lion had a sort of vacant look in its eyes. Nora's expression remained somber as she watched the act. She was staring with interest, but something was rippling beneath the surface.

When the master belted his whip and raised his arms in the air for applause, the crowd reciprocated—at least until it caught on that the queen was not clapping. There was a flash of fear on the master's face, but he hid it with a smile.

"How did you get this beast?" Nora asked.

He glanced at the lion who was sitting on his platform, watching the encounter without interest.

"He was abandoned by his mother in the Starry Wood," the master explained. "He would have died if I hadn't raised him by hand."

"And this is what you do with him? Force him to do tricks at the snap of the whip?" Nora's words were biting.

The master took off his top hat and bowed. "My queen, I needed to make a living. Meat for a cat this size is not cheap."

Nora snapped her fingers, and Peter came running from whatever corner he waited in.

"Yes, my queen …"

That night at dinner, a great lion laid beside Nora's chair while she picked through an assortment of dishes. Out of the five plates, she selected the rare beef and a salad with vinegar and red wine. Her new companion was fed a sheep's leg. His great claws ripped into the leg and he licked and savored the meat.

The dinner was occasionally interrupted by the crunching of bones. Peter poked the food on his plate while the animal gnawed his bone, occasionally giving the beast a look of contempt. Alfie and Hacia were unbothered since they both ate just as loudly.

"Have you named him yet?" Alfie asked.

Nora savored a sip of her wine. "Hamish, I think."

He couldn't help but smile. The beast looked like a Hamish.

"I want animal sporting banned in the court," Nora announced. "Regions may have their own laws, but in this castle, we do not use animals for amusement."

"It shouldn't have been permitted at all," Peter agreed. "I shall speak to Rebus about his taste in court activity."

When Peter truly agreed with Nora, Aegis could tell. He may not have approved the new addition to the household, but the idea of being cruel to animals was a strong dislike among everyone in the room. This gave him hope that they could bridge the gap that had opened and mend their bond.

That night, Nora sat on her balcony in her white robe. The tea ritual was something she no longer did alone now that he was here. The queen had lost all romantic inclinations toward him, but she still enjoyed his companionship, and he could live with that. She stretched out in her seat to look at the night sky while he stood at the edge.

"Peter is settling in these days," Nora said. "He's no longer pushing me to do things. I tell him what's to be done, and he does it. Though I've noticed if he's not keen on the idea, he goes about it slower than others, but I think we're on the same page now." Nora sipped her tea. "She's in the second region," she said.

Aegis didn't respond. It didn't matter where the traitor was, especially not to him.

"I know our relationship has been strange, but I think we've come to a lasting conclusion. You have my blessing."

"I can't leave you," he said. While she may had figured out her feelings, it didn't mean he had. He still wanted to be with her even though he had no control over who she was or what she did. If her reign came crashing down, he would be the one to hold it up long enough to help her escape.

"Go to her. You need to settle some things," she said. "Come back when you're done."

The familiar pull of his scar beckoned. This was an order. There was no declining this offer. He gave her a nod before stepping off the balcony. He touched down with an earth-quaking rumble before setting off into a run towards the second region. Nora was right. He needed to resolve things with Minerva, but to what end?

Grass plains blurred past him. The shadows waxed and waned with whatever light the souls illuminated. He came to a full stop when he realized the light was coming from the sky. He looked up in awe as hundreds of twinkling lights hung against the black sky.

The pagodas were unlit. It took him a moment, but the souls were standing outside. They were also staring at the night sky. A couple of children were surrounding a paper box on the ground. One child with long brown, scraggly hair lit a candle. She placed it into the lantern and picked it up. Her eyes met his when she held it. She smiled at him before letting the lantern float slowly into the air.

He had his suspicions as to Minerva's whereabouts, and he was correct. He found her at the base of the mountains, also staring at the distant lights in the sky. Minerva was just as mesmerized by them as he was.

"It's as if it calls to me somehow," she said when he came into the clearing.

"Do you think they've been doing that for a long time?"

"I think it's to celebrate the return of the King's Soul."

They both stared up at the sky for a long while before she said, "She's not the same girl."

He didn't break his gaze from the sky. He shook his head. "No, she's not that girl anymore, but she's still my queen."

"Do you love her?"

"More than ever."

He was surprised when Minerva charged at him then, her eyes crimson red against the white skin and grey hair. She shoved him hard enough to make him fall several feet away and crash into the hard, rocky ground.

"I deserve that," he said, sitting up on his elbows.

"You and your disgusting queen," she spat. "I heard about what the two of you did to that woman."

He didn't disagree. He grimaced and pulled at his tunic. He assumed she was attacking him for leaving her. Minerva was angry at the way he was when he was with *her,* and she had a point. His edge was always a bit sharper. He was always a little more willing to shed blood and now, so was Nora.

"I'm not proud," he said, "but I'm not sorry either."

Minerva rested a hand on her hip and shook her head, unable to look at him. "I knew she had a hold on you. From the moment we left the castle, I knew we were over, but watching you now, I understand."

He was scowling at her but didn't get up from off the ground. "Understand what?"

Minerva walked away, but before she did, she said, "You're just her dog."

He didn't deny it.

# Chapter Fifteen

Peter waited patiently for Nora to come downstairs for over half an hour after Hacia and Alfie left the breakfast table. He was served several cups of tea while the servants eyed at him sadly. He imagined he appeared quite pathetic at the table waiting for a girl.

When he knocked at her door, Bosh opened the door and gasped. "Thank Hell, you're here!"

"What happened?" Peter asked.

He pushed the door open and walked into the room. Nora was still in bed. Another servant, the blonde girl he employed to spy on the queen, was sitting on the bed holding a mirror to Nora's face. He stared at Bosh, waiting for an explanation.

The lad shook his head and big, fat lips jiggled. "I don't know, sir. We've been trying to wake her for hours."

"She's breathing, she's just not waking up," the girl said.

Peter touched Nora's head with the back of his hand. She was feverish. Her breathing was strong, but she was using up all her strength to fight the illness and needed to sleep. He threw back the covers, exposing the queen in her white nightgown. The maid stared up at him wide-eyed.

"Don't just stare at me. Make a cold bath," he barked.

He carried Nora into the bathroom and put her in the tub, nightgown and all. She let out a gasp as she sank into the water. He stayed by her side and when she opened her eyes wide, and he was the first one she saw. "Nora," he said.

She opened her mouth to speak, but her jaw trembled so badly that nothing came out.

"Call a doctor," he ordered.

The maid scurried out of the bathroom and out the door. Bosh was trying in vain to be useful in the background. From the other room, Peter could hear the servant tripping over a rug while trying to make the bed. He must have given up on the bed because there came a crashing noise—a vase or something priceless, no doubt.

He closed his eyes and raised his brows to extend his weary eyelids. "Bosh, please just go to the kitchens before you hurt yourself."

Despite her fever, Nora laughed through chattering teeth. She loved Bosh, and he couldn't blame her. "I know. He is a good lad," he said and gave her a gentle smile. "You sent Aegis off, didn't you?"

Nora nodded.

He shrugged. "Not that a vampire would know how to help a human with a fever anyhow. It's a good sign, the fever. I know it doesn't feel like it, but it means your body is fighting off whatever infection you've got."

Nora's brown eyes were full of apprehension, and he pitied her. She no longer resembled the vicious queen of Hell and had returned to the girl he'd raised.

He pulled the drain and rummaged around the bathroom for a towel. As the water was sucked out, his search became more frantic. He wanted to cool the queen down, not induce hypothermia! He could not for the life of him find a bloody towel. Meanwhile, the queen shook violently in the tub. He gave up on the towel and leaped into the bedroom to fetch Nora's robe. It was fluffy like a towel and she loved wearing it.

He helped her up and wrapped her in the robe before carrying her back to a half-made bed. He realized why Bosh was falling all over himself. There were several spots of bright red blood staining the pillow she slept on.

Without a word, he tugged the pillow off the bed with his free hand. He propped a new pillow in place and set her on the bed. He pressed his hand against her forehead again. She was still warm but no longer scalding to the touch. He waited until she fell back asleep before he took the bloodied pillow into the bathroom.

The stain came out of the casing easily enough, but there remained a little pink blotch on the pillow itself. No one else would know it was there except Peter and perhaps the laundry service. It would remain as a constant reminder that there, beneath the surface, something was wrong.

***

Aegis stood as Minerva stalked the clearing they inhabited. She knew where things stood, and he didn't see the point of toiling anymore. "Have you said your peace?" he asked.

Had he given her the closer she needed? She was still pacing, hands on her hips as her thin, waiflike body relented to the weight on her shoulders. He was sorry he'd put her through all that he had, but he couldn't be the person he was before Nora. He couldn't be the vampire who forgot everything.

"With you? Yes." She acknowledged him with a nod.

Once again, he found himself confused as to Minerva's feelings and movements. He was often at a loss when it came to women, but Minerva wavered between the grand scheme of things and the cracks in their relationship so deftly he couldn't keep up.

"Why are you here?" he asked.

She seldom left the Starry Wood. Minerva was like a wild animal herself and didn't adjust well to living among the souls. If she was near the mountain where he and the first king encountered the witch, it probably meant that she was looking for clues about Nora.

"I was reading up on the King's Soul mythology."

"She's no longer in the mountains," he said. "Nora and I paid the witch's ancestors a visit over a month ago."

Her eyes were narrow and pensive. "It really happened, then."

He shrugged. "I was there."

"I want to ask the witch a few things," Minerva said.

He brushed his hair away from his face and turned to lead the way back to the pagodas. Minerva's head jerked between his back and the mountains that loomed over them. "The books said …"

He rolled his eyes and kept walking. She couldn't reconcile with the fact that he knew things she didn't. "She died creating the pact," he yelled as he waded through the jungles. "Her family didn't live in the mountains."

It was late at night now. The noises of birds and lizards filled the forest. There was no point speeding off to the pagoda because they would all be asleep. Instead, he forced Minerva into a slow pace that she did not appreciate.

He pretended not to notice as she stumbled around the forest, tripping as a soul would if they walked the forest in the dark. Minerva couldn't see his smile, and he was grateful for that. The dark allowed a line of questioning that she wouldn't have normally asked.

"Are the two of you intimate then?" she asked. "I've gathered souls find that sort of thing important."

"They do, but we are not shagging."

"She's never … asked you to?"

"We've never been together. Not before. Not now."

It seemed to him that Minerva was more concerned about it than Nora ever had been. Sure, she wanted him to love her, and she craved intimacy, but she grew out of it. She'd grown out of him just as he found himself wanting her.

"She doesn't want me like that. Not anymore," he admitted.

"She lost interest after she—changed," Minerva said.

He walked ahead until the forest thinned into plains of green grass, and the streams twisted across the landscape. The sun moved along the horizon and he found himself staring into a small pond filled with lily pads. He watched the sun come up in the surface of the pond and wondered what she was doing now. Probably lying in her bed staring at the canopy. She couldn't sleep when he wasn't by her side.

Minerva's long legs reflected in the pond. Her hands were in her back pockets. She preferred to look directly at the sunrise.

He sat at the edge of the pond and relied on reflection in the water. "The witch's ancestors are in that one," he said, pointing at the smaller of the three pagodas ahead.

"Aren't you coming?"

He had gone back and forth on the merits of seeing the witch again. He'd spent most of the night debating it with himself, to the point where Minerva would stand and stare at him until he realized he had led them in circles in the forest.

"You go ahead," he said.

"This is goodbye, then?"

What could he say? There was no telling if this was goodbye or not. It was a small world.

Minerva let out a sigh of frustration. "Honestly, you're moodier than the teenage girl you pine after."

He didn't have any sort of retort. He watched her march towards the pagoda where the witch ancestor lived. Maybe she would find her answers, but he didn't think there was much the witch would tell them. The funny thing about witches and prophets, you never understand their divinations until well after the fact.

He assumed Minerva was wise enough to know that, but she seemed less wise to him these days now that he had all his memories. He clambered up off the ground and gave his reflection one last hard stare before making his way back to the castle. His queen needed him, or so he told himself.

He set off into a run and found himself pushing open the large wooden doors and walking into the courtroom shortly after. The mid-morning sun softly illuminated the stained glass that told the stories of the kings of the past as if it were a warning.

The court was quiet on this day. No jugglers or entertainers, just a few overly dressed court ambassadors and Rebus shuffling around nervously beside an empty throne. The souls were fearful of him, but he didn't care.

He sped to Rebus. The ancient soul fidgeted violently in surprise. "Where is she?" he growled.

Rebus couldn't stutter out the words. Aegis rolled his eyes and walked away before the man could finish his sentence. The servants were in a rush about the halls. None of them noticed his presence. The palace smelled of illness. Something was wrong.

The advisor's room was as empty as it was plain. Most souls had trinkets or sentimental items they clung to. Peter's space was void of all personal belongings except for books. On a round table, a stack of books on the history of kings rested beside a much smaller stack of medical and anatomy books.

The closer he got to Nora's chamber, the smaller the hallway became. His throat closed. A swarm of jittery maids streamed in and out of the queen's private space. His feet went numb and his gait mortal as he made his way among the maids—and nurses—and into the bedroom.

Nora lay propped up on her pillows in bed. She was ghastly pale except her red-stained lips.

Peter regarded the vampire slowly. Everything was written on his drawn, worn face. The man hadn't slept in days. The bags under his eyes were puffy and bluish.

He approached the bed. Nora's face had a sheen of moisture on it, and she was staring through him. He sat beside her and took her hand. She was burning up. Peter didn't need to explain, but he did anyway.

"It started shortly after you left," Peter whispered. "I have doctors coming from all over, but I'm afraid …"

Aegis hissed, and Peter stopped talking. He instantly regretted the reaction. Peter wasn't at fault. The advisor was merely giving him the truth. He understood nothing of soul illness, only that when a king was dying, the King's Soul would leave the body and return to the soul safe. Seeing Nora like this brought back a surge of memories he wished she hadn't restored.

When Tom died, it was like this. The first king was much older, but he didn't go peacefully in his sleep like many after him. Tom had an illness that ripped through him in the same manner as what was happening to Nora. Tom lay in that ghastly bed, pale, as he, too, vomited blood while fever racked his body. Tom didn't last the night.

Nora being in the same position needed no explanation, but he denied it all the same. She was stronger than Tom. She was younger and more powerful by tenfold. He had been gone for three days and she was still fighting.

"Nora, come back to me," he said.

The queen was delirious. Her eyes rolled around in her head, the whites murky and watery. Her dazed eyes searched the room for him.

"I'm right here, holding your hand. You need to fight it."

She gave a nod as if she understood before closing her eyes. Her breathing became shallow but steady. Both men took a breath before a fussy man came in and pushed Peter aside. He was wearing a suit with a long, tailored coat. He gathered that this was the doctor.

The soul made a step toward the queen but paused. He eyed Aegis cautiously as if he were some feral beast. The doctor was close in that approximation.

"I need to examine her," the doctor told him.

He didn't want to get up. He stared the doctor down until the pompous man took a step back.

Peter let out a noise of interruption. "Aegis, this is the best doctor in all of Hell. Please ..."

He had no choice but to relent, but if he returned to find Nora worse off than she was, he would renew those blood-sucking rumors.

He followed Peter into the adjoining room, the green room, and the man's composure nearly collapsed before him. Peter fell into a chair and rested his tired brow on his hand. "She was fine, and then she wasn't …"

Aegis nodded. "It was the same for the first king."

"I'm not a doctor. I know little about the body. Nothing beyond personal experience and books. I've seen this happen to many. It doesn't seem contagious—not that you'd care."

He couldn't remember if Tom had been the only one sick with the disease or not. It was too long ago. Even still, he didn't care about anyone else. He needed Nora to be okay. More than Tom, more than any of them. He needed her to recover.

Peter was watching him. The advisor's eyes were on him as he paced the room.

The ostentatious little doctor, who wore thick glasses and a grave expression, stepped into the room before Aegis paced a groove in the floor. Peter stood as if standing could help him hear the news better, but he already knew what the man was going to say; he could hear it in his well-rehearsed voice.

"I suspect it's an acute food poisoning or an infection. I can give her herbs to keep the fever down, but she will either survive or she won't."

Peter didn't cry, though he half expected the advisor to burst into tears at any moment.

"How long until we know?" Peter asked.

"In our line of business, we prefer to give the worst-case scenario. It's better to be proved wrong than to give false hope, but—"

"What!" Peter snapped.

"She's a young and otherwise spirited girl. Her odds are better than most. If anyone can come out, it's her. But she will be weakened by it forever—if she survives."

The doctor gave a soft nod to Peter and to him before backing out of the room and closing the door behind him.

"We're in for a long couple of days," Peter groaned.

# Chapter Sixteen

Aegis caught Nora as she lurched upright in the middle of the night. She cried for a few moments before vomiting blood down the front of his tunic. He grabbed the glass of water and fed it to her. It had been several days since the doctor left, and Nora's condition remained the same.

Peter was beyond exhausted. He finally got the soul to sleep, but it took far too much effort. The man was jittery from coffee and stress, and it was only when he was certain that Peter was going to fall over where he stood if it weren't for his constant movement that the man relented.

"Are you sure?" Peter asked for the fifth time as he fidgeted with the cup of tea beside the bed. He had been making it for Nora personally with her favorite set.

"Yes."

"Because I know you don't understand human functions."

"I understand enough."

Peter headed for the door, only to turn around and say, "If you need anything, I'm just in my room. Send a servant …"

"Yes!" he shouted.

That sent the old man out in a hurry, but he wasn't annoyed. He'd be amused with the nervous man under different circumstances. If she were better, she'd laugh with him. Instead, she was dying in his arms, and he was helpless against it.

"Hey, hey, hey …" he whispered down her neck.

Nora wheezed. Sometimes it felt as though she knew he was there, and it was one of those nights. She was lost in the haze of her own mind. Rendered speechless most of the time. He tried to pour some tea into her mouth, but she pushed it away suddenly and made a throaty noise.

She knocked the teacup out of his hand and onto the ground. He winced as it rolled onto the carpet. It didn't break, thankfully. It belonged to the tea set the monks of the first region had given her. Their tea was the finest, but she didn't want it tonight.

He tried with the water. Nora pushed her face against the glass and tried to grab it with her hands, but she gave up as if her hands were numb from weakness. She wanted water.

"Bosh, more water."

Bosh went out, leaving them alone together for the first time in months. He ignored the new surge of sweat breaking from Nora's body as he kissed her forehead.

"Please, Nora, stay with me."

She was no longer scalding hot, but wet. He didn't know what to make of it, but Nora was aware of him. She was really looking at him now. His whole body eased with the sigh of relief. Her fever must have broken.

Nora had opened her dry peeling lips to speak when Bosh ran back into the room with a silver pitcher of water.

He wanted to curse the boy, but the servant was only doing as he'd instructed. "Set it there, then get out."

Nora drank nearly the whole pitcher of water before falling back asleep, cradled in his arms until the sun rose in shades of peach and lavender as they illuminated the room. The bedroom door opened, and Peter stepped in with a cup of tea in his hand.

"Purple skies," the man murmured. "I woke up and took it as a sign she's on the mend."

Peter set the cup beside the empty pitcher. He peered into the empty pitcher before taking it to Bosh, who was standing ever attentive outside the door. "Keep these coming," he said, and shut the door.

***

Nora slept for most of the day. She only woke to drink water or broth. The fever had broken at some point in the night while Peter slept an exhausted sleep. The queen was stronger with her vampire by her side. With the queen indisposed, Aegis had grown ill-tempered and outright scary. He sent everyone fleeing, which probably spread rumors of the queen's demise.

Peter didn't want to face the morning council, but he had no choice. Alfie and Hacia's couriers waited silently for him outside his bedroom door when he got up. Their leathers and light chainmail vests had a different ring than the whooshing of servant skirts and trousers. The army generals wanted answers, and rightly so. They served as advisors for the queen yet were entirely shut out when the queen fell ill.

He stepped into the dining room, and the generals rose. Hacia was fuller around the middle, if he weren't mistaken—and what a terrible mistake that would be to make. Her breasts pressed against her leather vest, and her stomach peeked out from the bottom. She frowned at him noticing, and he reigned in his wandering eyes. Rebus sat expectantly and easily ignorable in the corner.

"Are you going to tell us what's going on?" Alfie said with gritted teeth.

Peter gave an apologetic nod. "We've scarcely had time to breathe ourselves." He fell into his chair beside the empty queen's chair, and a servant came with a mug of coffee. He sipped the bitter drink and relished its splendor. "A week ago, the queen suddenly fell ill with a fever. Doctors think it could be a food poisoning, but most likely an infection of sorts. She's been battling this thing ever since. Her fever breaks off and on, but she had a solid breakthrough last night. We think she will recover."

The generals took in the news as if they were inhaling fresh air. Rebus's head bobbed, and then he spoke. "She won't be able to fulfill her duties for a long time, if ever."

Peter toyed with the fork on the napkin. "We don't know that."

"Don't we?" Rebus countered. "I've seen children go dumb from prolonged fever. Old men are driven crazy from it. She will be unable to walk and be sickly for years, if not indefinably."

"We don't know that," he insisted.

It was Alfie and Hacia's turn to speak on the matter, but they had news of their own. Alfie eyed at Hacia expectantly. She slammed both hands on the table, "I can't now. Things are different."

"We talked about this," Alfie said. "It's not a good time."

"It's never going to be a good time!" Hacia's voice had reached new heights and Alfie's head fell back as he pressed his fingers against the bridge of his nose.

He had an inkling as to what was going on. "You're expecting, I take it."

Hacia was sulking and Alfie's concern was written all over his face. He didn't want his pregnant partner taking any sort of risk. Peter had a solution that he hoped would make them both happy. "Hacia, we still need you as an advisor, but perhaps you could abdicate from your role as general."

Alfie agreed. "I think Tina is ready to become general."

Hacia's stare lingered. She was not entirely convinced, but she gave a nod of consent. The last thing he needed was any of the current advisors taking flight. Peter needed everything to remain consistent and as close to normal as he could manage. If word got out …

"You should know," Rebus said, "that rumors have once again taken root within the regions."

*Well, there goes that lid.* With a deep sigh, Peter folded his fingers together and set his hands on the table, "Give me the report, I'll handle it."

After the less than stellar meeting, he made tea for the queen and brought it up to her room. To his surprise, she was awake, sitting up unassisted, and chatting with Aegis. Her voice was dry and shaky, but she was alive. He tried to push away what Rebus and the doctor had warned him about. Look how far she'd come in a few hours. They didn't know her, and they didn't know how strong she was.

Her eyes fell on him, and she gave him a weak smile. Aegis was a bit more relaxed now that his queen was on the mend. He no longer stomped around the castle ready for a fight.

"It's good to have you back," Peter said, smiling wistfully.

"She was just telling me about all the strange things she dreamt over the last week," Aegis said. His gaze was intense and scrutinizing. It made him frown, but he said nothing of whatever Aegis was or was not trying to imply.

"We need you to recover as soon as possible," Peter told her. "Hacia is with child. I asked that she remain as an advisor. I assumed you would want that."

Nora's thick brows furrowed. "Yes, please make sure she stays on."

He set the cup of tea on the serving table and approached the bed. "Tina will be taking her place. Rebels are threatening once again. I've sent Alfie out to handle the situation."

"Which region?" Nora asked.

His eyes fell to his shoes. He hated saying it. "The fifth again, my queen."

Nora shook her head. "I don't understand, we were just there—"

He raised his hand to motion for her to stop. "These are not rioters demanding to see their queen. These are rebels."

The room grew cold and silent. Even Bosh's clumsiness was stilled by the news. Aegis's blue eyes widened like a cornered animal. He was still clutching the queen's hand.

She pulled loose from his grip before patting his hand. "It's Vinicio, isn't it?" she said.

"It seems that way, though I have no proof of it yet."

"She said I would have to deal with him sooner or later."

"Normally I would suggest this be a mission for Aegis, but considering the circumstance, perhaps we should just wait this one out."

Nora's eyes were watery, and her face was pale. The few hours she'd been awake had taken their toll. There was no way Aegis would leave her this way.

Aegis gently laid her back down against the pillows, and they whispered a conversation so soft that he couldn't overhear.

Soon the queen fell to sleep, and Aegis approached Peter. "We need to talk."

***

Aegis led the advisor into his room adjacent to the queen's. The servants didn't go in this room, therefore it was much more secure than any other. It also didn't have lingering scents of Minerva like Peter's rooms. At this point, he regretted not accompanying his ex-lover to the witch. She had warned them about Vinicio. They were not done with him yet.

"How bad is it?" he asked.

Peter hemmed and hawed for a few moments. "We're only getting preliminary reports right now. It's as though people are rebelling over the decree Nora made several months ago regarding the black souls."

Was it truly that long ago? He wasn't the best with keeping track of time. "Of course the fifth region would be upset."

Peter chuckled. "They're not alone. No one is thrilled about the prospect."

He didn't understand what the problem was. He'd seen her work the soul safe. Maybe two or three black souls had been placed since she made the decision. It didn't seem right to allow people to be born in that region. Nora was probably the first to behold the depravity of the seventh region. He didn't blame her for wanting to make the change.

"It doesn't matter what they want," he argued. "She's experienced the seventh region firsthand, unlike most, and lived to tell the tale. She is their queen."

"I agree with it," Peter consoled. "Giving evil souls no choice but to be evil has only one outcome."

He paced the room as he had so many times over the last few months. "So, what do we do?"

"You need to stay with the queen. Ensure her health," Peter said. "Let's see what the hawks find."

After his meeting with Peter, Aegis sat beside Nora while she slept. Bosh bustled in with a book from Peter, *A History of Kings: Volume Fifty-Two.* Reading wasn't his favorite pastime, but it was better than brooding, as Nora called it.

He read on the balcony with a small lantern. Most of these kings were guarded by other vampires—vampires that were now long gone. Killed by giants or titans in the war. Where in Hell was Minerva during this time? She was one of them, but he didn't meet her until after the vampires rose in what was the third age, according to this book.

When Nora restored his memory, he remembered the twelve others, yet Minerva remained elusive to him. She knew why he had no former knowledge of her, why she was bonded as the rest of the vampires, but unaware of the pact? Minerva had her secrets. Even more now that she had spoken with the witch.

"Aegis," Nora called faintly from her bed.

He flipped the book page down on the table and went to Nora's side. He helped her drink water. Once she gulped two full glasses, she gasped and uttered the word, "Toilet."

He carried her to the bathroom to do what she needed. Along the way back, Nora eyed the cup of tea still sitting where Peter had left it. "I'd like that tea."

"I can have Bosh make you a fresh cup."

She shook her head. "It's fine. I'll just drink it. I don't want anyone else looking at me the way they do."

He frowned, and Nora clarified, "Like I'm dying."

Peter explained that she would likely keep odd hours due to the amount of sleep she needed while recovering. Her face had lost all its warmth and was sallow and drawn. He hated seeing her this way. Nora drank the tea in a few sips before laying back down, pulling him down with her.

They laid together, wrapped in each other's arms. Nora's lips brushed against his tunic as he held her. She went in and out of sleep, and he worried that her arms might have fallen asleep pressed against him. He understood that if the blood didn't circulate well enough, it could cause pain and even loss of limb after prolonged periods.

He released his embrace, and Nora's body went slack against the space he had inhabited. Her arm fell outward, but her sleep remained undisturbed. He returned to the book on the balcony and read until the sun rose over the tree line.

He was quite lost in reading a story about a king who attempted to tax Hell's most wealthy. The book depicted in great detail how that king was assassinated. A faction within the army itself had been bought by these wealthy souls who did not wish to pay higher taxes. The trackers cornered the king in the gardens and stabbed him before hanging his dying body on a tree.

With the king's sudden death, his wife and the children left the castle and settled somewhere in the third region. Aegis mused that no matter what the kings did, the children and wives were always spared. If kingship were maintained the way the stewards ruled, from parent to child, the child would be at risk during a rebellion.

Vinicio was attempting to protect his family in a premeditative manner as his father had before him. If the souls rebelled, he would die, but so would his children. Even if he abdicated in favor of Nora, there would be no safe avenue for his family. It painted the former steward in a light that he didn't care to view.

"Sir," a young man's voice whispered. Bosh was standing at the balcony door. "I wondered if the queen wouldn't mind something to eat."

He didn't know if she was ready to eat solid food or not. She had been drinking broth without trouble. He figured at the very least when she woke up, she could decide herself. "Maybe a few things for her to snack on. Light, easy to digest things."

When she woke, Nora nibbled on a few crackers and sat up all by herself. She asked for a chair with wheels. Bosh said he would look for something like she described though no one had any idea what she was talking about. In the meantime, Aegis offered to carry her wherever she needed to go.

"The soul safe," she told him.

Aegis was reluctant to take her there. He half expected a glowing gold orb within the safe. More than anything, he didn't want Nora to see the King's Soul. It would mean her time was at an end. It was one of the cruelest aspects of the gift the witch on the mountaintop gave the Ling's Soul. They didn't always see their own end, but it made them all more aware of their mortality, of their impending demise.

# Chapter Seventeen

"This can wait," Aegis protested.

He held her the way a groom carried his bride over the threshold, only there's wasn't the threshold of a happy little cottage somewhere. He carried her into the room that held the safe of souls. It was the portal between Hell and the other life and, despite Nora's illness, she insisted on ferrying the souls home.

"Just set me on the chair."

He did as he was told. From the chair, Nora used her power to unlock the safe with ease. Her magic was not weakened, even if her body was. Her fingers worked and turned the bars on the safe, spinning it open. Glowing wisps of light came spilling out, and she used her magic to push them through the map of Hell pinned inside the door of the safe.

She didn't need a map; Nora could will the souls where they needed to go. It was the stewards who had used the map. They relied on the soul safe's magic to harbor souls when the King's Soul didn't return. Nora just liked the visual, he supposed.

A pair of black souls bounced along the castle floor. Aegis couldn't help but feel disdain for the things. Not only were they evil beings, but they were the cause of the looming rebellion against his queen. He didn't doubt there would be consequences for the people in those regions they were born into, but Nora was right about this.

"Those little bastards are the cause of so much trouble," he said.

Nora lifted them into her lap with an elegant swoosh of her arms. She peered into them for a time before saying, "This one to the sixth region, but this one …"

"What is it?"

Nora frowned. "It's beyond any evil I've ever seen. I …"

Her eyes darted around the orb in distress. She was so engrossed in what she saw that she was totally unaware of the water flowing freely from her eyes.

"Nora," Aegis said.

She tore her eyes away from the orb. "I don't want to send it to the sixth, but I don't want to send it to the seventh, either."

He kneeled and regarded her tear-stricken face. "You do as you must."

Nora bit back her tears and nodded. The soul was lifted by an invisible current and sent to the seventh region. "It can try to redeem itself in the other life."

Soul placement must have taken a great toll on her. Before he could lift her up, Nora fainted and slumped into him. Muttering a curse, he carried her back to her room. He had to move slowly. She got motion sickness if he moved as a vampire did.

Peter was waiting in the newly placed chair beside the bed. He stood at their arrival, his eyes on Nora. "I feared it would be too much for her."

Aegis told him about how her powers remained unhindered. She was fine until she had to make a difficult decision. Peter's eyes danced wildly as he told him this. He always looked sort of madcap, but there was more that Peter had to say. "Any news about the rebels?"

"Yes," Peter said slowly.

***

"Are you sure you want to do this?" Peter asked, running alongside Aegis as he walked towards the castle's front door. He normally would take the window, but he wanted to be seen by the court as he left. He wanted them to know that he wouldn't stand for the bullshit they spread around the kingdom.

"I'm going to settle this. The queen gave me orders to handle any rebels as I see fit," he said loud enough for most of the court to hear.

Aegis pushed the great doors open so hard they slammed against the castle stone. One of the doors shattered and fell loose from a hinge. He walked out far enough to allow the crowd to gather before he leaped dramatically and hit the ground running.

Even a vampire's speed was reduced in the depths of the Starry Wood. He slowed to dodge the man-sized roots erupting from the ground and swung from the low hanging branches of the ancient trees that even he seldom climbed to the tops of. It brought back memories of him and Minerva during the time they made this place their home. It was strange being back there alone. How a massive forest full of creatures could feel so lonely, he couldn't say.

A rush of air and noise swiped him from the right. He turned to his side just barely in time, but the blur of leathery winged hide scrapped his hip and ripped his pants, exposing his thigh to the cool forest air. He tucked and rolled along the branch before pausing. What had hit him? Whatever it was, it was now silent and unmoving in the greenery.

An almost soul-like screech came from the forest. Whatever attacked him wanted him to know he was still out there. It would be best to outrun the thing.

He sped along the branch as fast as he could before leaping onto the next tree. He cleared several miles from where the monster attacked, but he could still sense its presence and trace the air circulating beneath the creature's wings.

It must have antenna. The creature couldn't follow him by sight. He was too fast. There were subtle clicking noises. It must have some sort of echo capacity. It would continue to pursue him until it either grew tired, picked up on easier prey, or died.

Skidding to a stop, he held his feet firmly on the branch and awaited the beast. It came at him from an angle, but he saw it despite the attempt to make itself look smaller. Its wingspan was impressive, somewhere around sixteen feet across. It had round, glowing red eyes that enabled it to see in the dark. It was a strange creature, but the Starry Wood was full of them lately.

It made no noise as it swooped closer, but its face became more visible. It was furry and did indeed have feelers around its maw. It reminded him of an insect, but its body was the size of a man and it had the wings of a bat. He struck it with his fist, connecting with the thing's face. It split in two against his arm and green ooze splattered on each side of him. The smell was acidic, like the scent of a crushed ant.

He flicked his arm out to shake off the guts and looked himself over—mostly clean, though offended by the smell. There was no avoiding this monster, whatever it was. He had yet to find anything that could kill him, but it didn't mean he welcomed the challenge or the mess.

Then there was the tear in his pants. He didn't have the means to fix them, and he didn't carry money. At the same time, he couldn't walk around with damn near his whole flank exposed. He found the edge of the fifth region and stood before a familiar cottage, only this time things were different.

This was once Gerta's home, a widow with far too many children. The little home was quiet and dark. The clothesline was empty, and the windows were dark. Gerta had moved again. It was probably better that way. With the emergence of new creatures in the Starry Wood, she'd probably moved her brood to town for safety.

He opened the door and found the place half empty. Some things, like furniture and other heavy items, remained. Scattered belongings and other abandoned things were strewn about. He imagined the place had been ransacked a few times, but he was relieved to find that many items were gone and there were no bodies to be found.

It took some time, but he eventually found a small sewing kit in one of the bedrooms. It held a set of thick, dull needles with large eyes and rough string. It probably belonged to one of the girls who'd just begun to sew. Taking off his pants, he sat down on the squeaky bed that sank low in the middle and got to work on mending.

He wasn't the best with these sorts of things, but he'd sewn up a few wounds in his time. He held up his pants and examined them. It wasn't pretty. The lines were uneven, and the light blue thread was obvious against the tanned leather, but it was better than nearly exposing himself. He had dealt with worse.

Aegis left the house and set a course for the town. While he wasn't exactly sure of who these people were, supposedly they were preaching at the town square. He'd find them, murder them, and then return to the castle as quickly as he could to be with Nora.

It was late at night when he hopped from wooden rooftop to rooftop. Torches were lit, and people were still active. A man stood on the town platform where they burned heretics. He wore a long linen, unadorned robe. His brown hair was shorn close against his square face.

On a more positive note, there was no sign of any recent witch burnings. He suspected this was due to the rebels using the platform to spew their propaganda, but the region smelled nice for a change.

"This queen—what has she done for us?" the agitator shouted at the small crowd. "She's going to empty the outlands with her law. Even now, they could be living among us. I say we kill every newborn until she comes to her senses!"

The crowd gasped at the statement. Women turned away, and the men sneered and began to heckle the man. He wasn't as popular as the hawk hunter's feared. This wasn't something he needed to leave Nora for. This was something the military could handle.

Peter had made it seem like such an ordeal, but the crowd was throwing rocks at the man. He laughed and welcomed the town's hatred. He folded his arms and watched as the man was struck until he fell to his knees. That was when another, a woman this time, came forward. Her brown hair was tied back in a severe bun that only stretched the age along her face.

The crowd stopped, and two other men in similar garb came and rescued the injured man. The woman raised her arms, and everyone grew silent. "You must forgive our youngest. He is merely seeking paths for an otherwise dreary road.

"Our lands were promised to us. The worshipers with the worshipers, the gamblers with the gamblers, the pure with the pure, the nomads with the nomads …"

The woman's eyes caught his own, and she smiled knowingly. "The farmers with the farmers, the socialites with the socialites. The evil with the evil. This is the way it has always been, and this is the way the king has always ruled. This new law, this decree, we do not accept it, and we do not believe that a real king would ever deem this necessary.

"For, what's more, she sends her vampire to do her dirty work. We all know of the woman in the fourth region, what the queen is capable of. Even now, she seeks to silence us by taking our lives." The woman pointed at Aegis and the crowd gasped at the sight of him. "Do you deny your orders, vampire?" she called to him.

Nora did indeed want the rebels dead, but he doubted she wanted a martyr. "Have you been to the outlands?" he called.

The woman smiled and held her hands in front of her. "No."

"I have. The queen has. For all of history, the kings sent evil souls to a place they never had the balls to go themselves. If it weren't for her, we would never have escaped. She has seen the horrors that transpire there, things you couldn't imagine. Things that no child should ever endure."

The crowd was listening to him, particularly a woman holding a newborn in her hands. He jumped off the roof and walked among the people. "Evil begets evil. If the black souls do not improve themselves with love and guidance, they will be sent to the outlands without a second chance. But I've watched the queen at work. She does not do this carelessly."

The woman on the stage bowed her head and took a step back. It was clear that she had lost. SThe crowd surrounded him and began to ask him questions. He couldn't very well ignore them, and the woman smiled with triumph. She used the mob as an escape while he tried to leave before he said the wrong thing.

"Where is she sending them?" one voice asked.

"How many have come here?" another wanted to know.

The questions bubbled around him but were the same. He raised his hands, and the people went silent on cue. "You'd be surprised by how few black souls there truly are. Out of the number I could count on one hand, most of them have gone to the sixth region where the strongest military presence is."

It was important to reassure these people, but he needed to pursue the woman and her followers. "Please excuse me," he finally said, and left the square.

The night had claimed the sky, but that made no difference for him. The rebel's sweat and body odor followed along the currents of the wind as he hurtled towards them. The tang of fear in their scents made it easier to track them. He smiled as he ran upon the shack there they hid. Maybe he would keep the woman alive and bring her before the queen. A prize for his now-notorious mistress. Nora was too sick for dramatics, but the woman could rot in a cell while Nora recovered.

Without hesitation, he ran through the door and into the shack. Smoke enveloped him, rendering him blind and without a sense of smell. It was anti-vampire equipment. Somehow these rebels had gotten hold of some and filled this shack with it. He tried to back out, but the wooden door shut and the groaning of wooden bolstering came from the other side. He smashed his hands against his eyes to stop the burn, but the only way he could breathe would be to escape the shack.

He jumped, fully intending on tearing a hole in the roof and escape into the cool night air, but instead found himself entangled in a net. Not just any net. It was the kind developed to catch his kind in the event they rebelled against the steward. He was blind and choking on the smoke when the net was pulled down and around him.

He swiped viciously with his hands whenever he sensed one near, but he never landed a hit. They managed to get cuffs around his ankles so he could no longer kick out. He fumed with rage. Maybe he wouldn't leave any of them alive after all.

"This is the place where the queen was conceived," the woman said.

Her voice was muffled. They must have had masks, too. It was safe to assume they had all the anti-vampire arsenal. A cuff found one hand, but when they tried too hastily to get his other arm, he caught whoever it was and threw them. The body whacked against the shack wall before sliding down in a heap.

"I know her lineage, the daughter of an escaped outlander and whore mother."

He flailed with his free arm at the direction of the woman's voice, but he found it cuffed instead. He was chained to the net and being pulled now. Another coughing fit took hold of him as the souls grunted and pulled him into a dark bag.

"Where? How?" he asked.

"The rebels are everywhere," the woman said.

He was pulled out of the shack and into the open air, hacking as the smoke sifted through the bag. They rolled him along the ground until gravity suddenly took hold. He was rolled into a hole with a thud. He felt clumps of dirt being thrown on him, little bits at first, followed by more and more. The pressure of the soil was upon him. He had been buried alive.

Whatever happened, no matter how long he waited there, he vowed that he would not go back to sleep.

# Chapter Eighteen

"He should be back by now," Nora said from her bed.

Peter was worried, too, but for different reasons. He needed to keep a brave face for her. There were reports that Aegis had made it to the fifth region and that he encountered the rebels. But what became of them after that? "I'm trying everything I can," he promised.

Nora had taken another turn for the worse when Aegis left. Right after he left, really. The fever was taking hold of her once again. The salves the doctor prescribed were not working and they were all at their wit's end. She needed a bedpan now because she was unable to control her bodily functions. He tried to stay with her when he could, but the kingdom still needed to be managed.

He sat beside the queen and offered her more tea. She drank it steadily. He followed it up with some broth from which she turned. "Now listen here," he said. "We need you to eat."

She tried to smile at him, but her eyes went suddenly wide, and she coughed up handfuls of blood. Nora's gasps were coming in shrieks now and he muttered curses at Aegis for taking so long.

Bosh came into the room and went pale at the sight of Peter's jacket covered in congealed blood. The servant's knees shook. He left and there was a loud thud outside the door. The poor lad fainted.

Peter shook his head. Nora was unconscious now. He hated seeing her in pain and wished it didn't have to be this way. He sighed and stepped out of the room.

Stepping outside the room, he found the boy lying prone. He thought of all the things he could have said to the boy but realized they would either end in gossip, a hysterical servant, or a fatal accident due to the boy's clumsiness. He squatted down and shook the servant until he groaned and rolled over. "Bosh, I need you to get Hacia and Alfie to meet me in the council room."

"Yes, sir."

"I'll be here until then."

"Yes, sir."

He shook his head, fell heavily into the seat, and stared at her. The closest thing he had to a daughter was dying. He had hoped it would be quick and mostly painless, but it dragged on and on. Just when everyone believed she was getting better, she was being ripped from their clutches again.

This would destroy the vampire. Aegis was not only losing the person he loved, but also the renewed purpose in his life. He would see to it that they found the King's Soul and brought it back to the palace. They would raise the child right. Bella and Vinicio wouldn't be here to muck it all up for them.

A soft knock at the door told Peter that the council was ready.

No one was seated at this meeting when he entered the council room. All three advisors were waiting for him at the edge of the table. The look in his eyes must have told them everything. "She's dead?" Alfie asked.

Peter shook his head and steadied the swallow in his throat. "No, no, not yet. But …she's in so much pain. Aegis is nowhere to be found. I …"

He looked down and realized he hadn't cleaned the blood off his jacket. No wonder they all assumed she was dead. At least they didn't think he murdered her. The thought made him laugh. A small chuckle at first, but he couldn't stop himself from laughing at the irony of it.

Rebus ignored him. They all ignored what they suspected to be grief. "I have substances that could ease the pain."

He was aware of what Rebus was talking about. The old man had opium stashed away for medicinal reasons. If they gave enough to the queen, she would fall into a peaceful sleep. The most serene sleep. The ending he wanted for her in the first place.

Alfie and Hacia looked at each other as if they were having a discussion solely with their eyes before looking back at Peter's jacket with concern.

"She will not improve. You are certain?" Hacia asked.

"There is no doubt," he confirmed.

Alfie embraced Hacia, and she leaned into him, nodding her head. "We must check the safe first."

***

The scar on Aegis's palm burned like the time he'd disobeyed Nora's direct order. Something was wrong, very wrong. He needed to get back to her. He struggled futilely and screamed with rage. He cursed and vowed to end every soul in sight if he couldn't get to Nora in time.

He screamed until his throat went hoarse and his tears matted his hair. It was useless. He was trapped and there was no getting out unless someone found him.

The scar throbbed and burned as if to remind him that he was failing her. Nora was in danger, and his arrogance had gotten him trapped.

The rebels had anti-vampire weapons. That meant they had people within the castle. Nora had had those things dumped in the cell with the broken door. Even Alfie and Hacia didn't have access to the private dungeon, and Rebus was barred from it as a precautionary measure. The locks had been changed once Nora ascended the throne.

The only people who had access to it were himself, Nora, and Peter. It was possible that Minerva had somehow gotten in there, but why would she give souls the very things that caused her own capture and incarceration? His stomach dropped and he realized this must be what souls felt like before they got sick.

Peter knew where the anti-vampire gear was. He knew Nora's history enough to incite rebels. The books on his table were medical books and histories of kings. He knew Aegis would go insane with grief because what was happening to Nora had once happened to Tom. Was the first king poisoned as well? He couldn't imagine anyone wanted him dead, but regardless, the symptoms were the same.

Nora's symptoms got worse when he left and better when he returned. Peter was giving her tea. He was the only one to serve her tea, and he didn't have servants do it, he made it himself. No one suspected it because Nora drank tea every night. Peter manipulated the rebels and probably the other riots as well, an excuse to get people out so he could work behind the scenes.

New resonance came to his voice, and Aegis let out a roar that shook all of Hell. A short time later, he heard thumps coming from above where he was buried.

***

"Have you ever done this before?" Alfie asked in a whispered voice.

"No," Peter admitted. "She told me how Vinicio did it just in case."

It took several tries, but the safe door swung open, and a few souls rolled out. "She must have been here recently," Rebus said.

He picked up the little balls awkwardly as he pushed them into the map on the inside of the safe. To his surprise, they met no resistance, but his fingers only touched cold steel. He gave a chuckle of delight.

"I don't think any of those were the King's Soul," Hacia said.

"Does that mean she's not dying?" Alfie asked.

Rebus pipped in, "Not tonight at least. The body can live without the soul for several days."

He eyed Rebus suspiciously. It made him wonder just how much the old man was aware of the steward's deeds. Just when he was about to shut the safe door, a glowing gold orb came from the void.

Alfie stifled a cry as Hacia squeezed his hand, and Rebus gave a sullen, knowing nod. A funny thing happened when Peter saw the soul. He denied it. "No, that's not it. It can't be."

But there was no mistaking it.—a soul as gold as the sunset and as the purest metal. The King's Soul waded towards the council, and no one dared touch it.

Peter shook his head and moved to close the safe door but was caught by Alfie and Hacia. "I'm sorry, man," Alfie said as he struggled against the hawk hunter.

"I'm sorry," Peter said as he sobbed. "I'm so sorry."

The orb floated up to eye level, where it hovered for a moment. It was as if it were listening to him. He shoved Alfie off when his grasp loosened by the shock. With shaky hands, he touched the wisp and it showed him everything. It showed him the past and the inside of Nora's chaotic mind. It also showed him glimmers of the future. It was beautiful, and it was what she deserved all along.

The orb broke free of Peter's mind and floated through the center of the map. For a long while, no one spoke. Hacia closed the safe door. The weight mechanisms thumped closed and yet they continued to stand there in disbelief.

"I will administer the opium," Rebus said before leaving the room.

Hands pulled at Peter, but he shrugged them away. "I'm fine. I'm fine." He followed everyone out eventually. He took his seat beside Nora's bed and watched as Rebus poured white milk into her mouth. There was only one thing left to do now.

"Bosh, give me a pen and paper. Rebus, leave me that bottle of opium just in case she needs more."

Rebus frowned, but he did not question Peter. It was only the worst day of his life, after all.

***

The ground above him grew lighter, slowly at first, then all at once. He could breathe without a struggle. The fighting of several young voices hinted at his rescuers.

"You're a lazy bitch, you know that!" charged a small voice.

"*You're* the lazy bitch," another voice retorted.

"Boys! Shut up!"

It was Gerta and her children! They were living in town and they must have figured out where he was. He was saved at the hands of countless unruly children. Several pairs of feet landed in the hole. One pair landed on him before hopping off his back. They untied the bag and the webbing.

"Can you free yourself from the cuffs?" Gerta asked.

He pulled at the cuffs attached to his feet and snapped them free. He couldn't budge the handcuffs because they were too thick for removing with just one hand. Instead, he broke his thumb to pull a hand free before doing the same to the other.

He rolled over and came face to face with several little scrunched faces staring down at him. "That's nasty," a taller boy said.

Aegis gave a nod at Gerta. "Good to see you're all doing well," he said as he pushed his thumbs back into place with fleshy clicks. Some of the children groaned. Jesse, who was now much older, was leaning against the dirt wall. "You've been better," Gerta retorted.

"Nora …"

"Go, go," Gerta told him. "Come back and we'll have a chat then."

He thanked her as he climbed out of his grave and rushed to the castle with all his might. His scar was throbbing in a consistent somber pattern. One that was a continuous *buh dum, buh dum, buh dum* …

It was Nora's heartbeat, and it was slowing.

***

Peter finished writing his letter and left it on the table. It was addressed to Aegis. The orb had given him glances into the future, and Peter understood that he was not going to be a part of that future. He readily accepted that fate. The King's Soul was freed and there was nothing left here for him now that Nora was dying.

Nora was awake, but she was still drowsy. Droopy lids threatened to close again at any moment. This was her last waking moment. He looked her in the eye. It was the least he could do.

"You did it."

"I did it," he said with a gentle nod.

His betrayal was easy to hide from her because he truly didn't want to do it. He wanted her to be safe and he wanted the world for her, but she had become a monster, drunk on power. Someone he knew all too well and the opposite of what he taught her. This couldn't be his legacy.

He coughed into a sob. That was Vinicio's concern, too—his legacy. What was it about old men and their progenies? So she didn't turn out the way he expected, but this wasn't what he wanted either. Never this. In truth, he feared her, and it broke his heart when she didn't care.

She didn't cry or appear even remotely upset. It could have been the opium, but she relaxed against her pillow with a serene expression. Nora was at peace now that the King's Soul was no longer using her body as a fighting cage. Every night the servant girl came with a report more disturbing than the last. So many sleepless nights he spent racking his brain, trying to find a way to save her, but there was none. This was the only solution he and Minerva could find.

"Where's Aegis?"

"I gave rebels anti-vampire weapons. They must have worked," Peter said.

"He's going to kill you when he finds out," she wheezed.

Peter picked up the ceramic bottle and shook it before popping the cork off. "Already taking care of that." He drank the contents of the bottle. It would be enough to kill him soon. "You're not going to ask me why?"

She rolled her eyes like the pretentious woman she was. "I know why. I was a bad ruler."

"It was destroying you, and there was no other way..." Peter's body was growing heavy. He could feel the opium course though this body and euphoria washed over him partly because of the drug, but the confession was lethargic. The only way his plan could succeed was to purge all the plans and ideas from his mind in the event she picked up on it. He truly had not wanted it to come to this because he loved her, and that was the only intent she could perceive.

His head became incredibly heavy. There was no choice but to rely entirely on the back of the chair. He didn't know if Vinicio was alive when he began to spread secrets from the castle. Nothing detrimental, of course, just sort of casual conversations overheard by maids. When reported opportunities came, he exploited them. Nora took care of the rest.

She laughed, a sort of strangled chuckle. "You were afraid I'd corrupt the King's Soul?"

Peter shook his head, "No, Nora, it was the King's Soul that corrupted you, not the other way around. You were perfect."

Tears fell down her cheeks. She knew the truth at last, his brilliant queen. He wanted Aegis to be out of the castle when Nora passed on. At least he'd thought he wanted that, but now he wasn't so sure. He hadn't expected his fate to be sealed with Nora's, which is why he loaded the rebels with equipment … but Hell, he was high.

Peter's eyes closed against his will. He wanted to outlive Nora, to see the thing through, but there was no point in that. The soul had left her body and it could not be undone. If Nora was still awake, she said nothing. He really did hope Aegis returned in time.

# Chapter Nineteen

The sun was high over his head when Aegis landed on the balcony. The scent was earthy and slow like there was no air. The senses that told him the tales from miles away had abandoned him in this moment. The stained glass figures on the balcony doors silently watched as he entered the room. Its white drapes and linen canopies hung elegantly as ever. The black crown glimmered menacingly in the ray of light that hit it directly.

Peter was in his chair facing Nora. Aegis could see the top of his grey head and an unmoving hand. He'd deal with Peter in a moment. His eyes were on Nora, who was no longer sweating profusely, but was still and her breathing faint. The reek of stale urine and feces in the bedpan confirmed things had taken a turn for the worse while he was gone.

His face went stony, cold and bitter, but he gasped when he touched her hand. Nora was warm and still breathing. He would wait until she was gone before allowing himself to feel sorrow. Instead, he laid in bed beside Nora, his queen, and gently stroked her hair until her eyes pulled open.

"You made it," she managed.

"Peter—"

"I know," she told him. "I know everything. It's too late, Aegis. The soul departed."

What could he say? He gave her a nod. In his heart, he already knew it was too late.

"You were the best thing to ever happen to me." Nora's voice cracked.

At that, his tears joined hers. Only Nora's tears were warm as they streamed down her face. He lifted her hand and put it to his own. Her fingertips played in the tear drops.

"Why are your tears cold?"

He didn't know why; they just were. He scarcely ever cried before Nora. Now it seemed he couldn't stop.

He broke his gaze from her to check on the coward in the chair. The man was still and his skin was slightly blue, but he was still alive.

Nora's hands pulled his face back to her weakly.

"You're not in any pain?" he asked.

She smiled and shook her head. "No, Peter gave me opium before taking the rest of the bottle himself."

That explained it. It was a highly coveted product in the sixth region, o rare that those who had it didn't dare keep it in their own homes. Safe breaking had become a highly lucrative yet deadly profession.

He kissed her then, allowing himself to feel her loss and the softness of her lips. This would be the last kiss they'd share. She returned his kiss and he sunk into the bed beside her. No matter how much she changed, she still loved him.

"I love you," he muttered before kissing her more deeply. Nora opened her mouth and allowed him. "I love you," he said again. Her mouth went lax, and he said it again in a whisper.

The queen was dead, and yet the world had the audacity to keep going.

Peter was shitting himself, and his stomach bile foamed at his mouth. Aegis ignored the smells behind him and let the man seize while he pawed at Nora's corpse.

"Come back to me, Nora …"

Bosh came into the room. His pudgy lips trembled, and he, too, was crying. Poor fool. They were all fools.

He untangled himself from Nora's cooling body and stood on the balcony watching the lavender sunset that she'd probably used the last of her magic to conjure. She was somewhere out there again, only as someone different. He would need to find her once again. It wasn't fate; it was a promise.

"Come back to me."

# PART TWO

# Chapter Twenty

A woman screamed as she tore into the world. Hands took hold of her and pulled her from the woman's body. Yet even in this form, she was more aware and sentient than any normal baby. But it was bright and cold. One day she would rule the world, but today all she could do was cry. Picked up and wiped down, wrapped in a soft cloth, she was returned to the woman who bore her. She opened her eyes and came face to face with two, blotchy-faced souls.

They named her Freya, and she was fed at her mother's breast. Her father would come in to hold her while her mother slept. He smelled of earth and sweat. She was their firstborn. They fussed at every sniffle and slept with her between them. They bathed her in the kitchen sink with warm water and a soft cloth. She enjoyed their affection.

As her body continued to develop, the world became larger. Her ever adjusting eyes began to see a full spectrum of colors. The walls of the bedroom were blue. The bedsheets were an off-white. Freya was usually dressed in pink or white. Her parents cooed at her when she was awake. Her eyes followed the movement of their lips.

While she had no real way to confirm it, Freya suspected they watched her sleep as well. They were almost always there. Sometimes she needed to cry to wake them, but one of them was always there. There was security and comfort. Love and affection. The more she grew, the better in control she was of her faculties.

Hands were a great point of interest. She could bring them together, pull them apart. Her mother and father were overjoyed with her every development. It made her feel proud of her accomplishments. It made her smile, and her parents cried. While she enjoyed infancy, the unconditional love and joy, Freya still understood things that most infants did not.

She understood her parents when they fretted about the harvest. Her father was going to kill a sick horse, but they didn't have enough money to buy another workhorse. Her mother sometimes paced back and forth in the early hours of the morning, shaking and crying.

Sometimes Freya made it a point of remaining quiet despite the pangs of hunger, prompting her to cry out. It was the least she could do during the times of stress. And while she had the knowledge of her former lives, it didn't make growing up any easier. In fact, it made things harder.

At six months old, little Freya struggled to sit up when her peers were able to. Knowhow and experience meant little when the body simply wasn't ready. She missed real food. Her parents were slow to provide mashed foods, and her frustration often boiled over into a rage at the dinner table.

Mashed potatoes, that was all she wanted. They had it in abundance since her father got a large discount for them being too old to sell. They ate potatoes in every sort of fashion and then some new ones Freya was unfamiliar with. Her mother regularly experimented with new ways to cook the vegetable.

Her mother's body was lean. Her brown, frizzy hair fell to the middle of her back and was usually tied back. Her name was Jess. Her father, a tall, tan-skinned man with brown hair and brown eyes. His name was Mike. The other addition to the family was a dog named Pete. He had two different colored eyes and boundless energy. They were poor, but a perfectly normal family in the third region.

At one point, she had longed for this life, but now she was someone different. Not that she had any reason to complain. This was an ideal upbringing, but growing up took time and effort. Whenever she grew too frustrated, she would cry, and her mother would pacify her. She found ways to entertain herself—mainly with her feet. They tasted like fingers but were more fun. Freya wanted her body to match her mind. Couldn't these people understand? Somewhere a black crown called to her.

After dinner, Freya was laid on a blanket on her belly to exercise her neck while her father played the guitar. Her mother read and the dog, Pete, rolled around on the floor beside her blanket as if he was encouraging her development. His ears perked and he tilted his head as he regarded her with curiosity. She wanted to touch his fur. It tufted out in patches of brown, black, and white. Long, straggly grey hairs grew randomly, making him look unkempt.

Freya swung a leg out and rolled over on her back—something she'd mastered months ago. As she continued to roll around on the floor, Freya considered the last decree she made as queen. She wondered if it was causing problems.

Pete was now lowering his head to the floor with his rear end in the air, beckoning her to play. She swiped at him with her hand but only grazed his soft fur.

Did the castle still implement the rule in her stead? She also worried about Aegis. Poor Aegis was probably heartbroken. The dog growled at her playfully as Freya managed to grab a fist full of chest hair. Only when she did, to both her and Pete's alarm, she couldn't let go.

"Oh, Freya, you did it!" her mother squealed.

The elation in her mother's voice shocked her into unclasping her fist, releasing the dog with fewer chunks of hair. Freya regarded her mother and then her father before looking down.

Freya had sat up, but she found that she was unable to remember the law she'd put in place or the name of the sad man with the scar on his palm. Alarmed, Freya began to cry, and her father's strong arms swooped in for her. They reminded her of someone else's arms. His eyes were also kind, but his face and name escaped her.

***

At times like these Aegis almost wished Peter still lived, almost. He preferred to lay on the balcony and stare into oblivion. Rain, sun, night, it didn't matter. His queen was gone. Nora had died because he hadn't figured it out sooner. He should have known. Peter loved Nora, and that was what had made him do it.

A long-robed person came shuffling into the bedroom. Rebus made a throat-clearing noise as if he hadn't heard him coming a half-hour ago, The old bastard walked so slow. "Aegis, sir, how should we proceed with the funeral arrangements?"

He didn't say anything.

Rebus didn't get the hint. "The preservation process is limited. We only have a few days … the last thing we want is to present the queen half decomposed."

Images of her unmoving body staring at him on the bed flashed into his mind, and he winced. "Piss off."

Rebus understood what that meant. The old man huffed and left the bedroom, leaving him to his thoughts. How much of the rebellions were real, or were they exaggerated by the traitor? The woman and her minions were real enough, but they were incited and heavily aided. No doubt, their sense of purpose was heightened by Peter's confidence. Radicals would do nearly anything to prove themselves to their superiors.

"You don't care what they do with the body?" Hacia asked.

"Not unless she's in it," he said. Hacia didn't give him condolences, tell him she would be there if he needed to talk or some other bullshit. That it was meant to be or that everything works out. She just got right to the point, and he appreciated that. He detected the swell of her belly.

She stepped forward. "It will arrive in about six months. After that, you must help me lead."

He scoffed at that notion. Why would souls want an immortal to lead them? What good would that do? He couldn't keep one soul alive; how he could keep a whole world of them going?

Nora's body had been moved from the bed and the room was in the process of being dismantled. The servants were cleaning out her closets, all the décor, the pillow she slept on. They threw away her perfumes and toiletries. The carcass of the traitor was dragged out, chair and all. He would have offered to help throw that piece of shit into the outlands if he weren't so busy feeling sorry for himself.

"Where did the soul go?" he asked Hacia, who lingered just barely in the shadows.

"We're not sure. It was as though it went into the Starry Wood."

He frowned at the notion. The baby wouldn't be born in the Starry Wood. There were no souls there to give birth to it. It took him a moment, but the reasoning hit him. "She doesn't want us to find her."

Did that mean that Nora suspected a traitor all along? Kicking the railing of the balcony, he sent clumps of stone cascading into the black sky. He had never hated himself more than he did now. Nora walked with a target on her back, and he'd left her. His mind paced the events of Nora's death so many times that he began to wonder if he was inventing more conspiracies than there actually were.

He wanted to go after her, to find her, but he doubted there would be any signs this early. That, and Hacia—the steward—would need his help and guardianship as well. Before too long, Hacia would become huge with pregnancy and need assistance. As much as it wounded him, he needed to stand by and wait for the King's Soul to give him a sign.

***

It was a beautiful day. The green fields were lush with weeds and wildflowers, and the sun was gentle overhead. Mama took her to have a little picnic on the hill that overlooked their neighborhood. The land that surrounded them was farmed into patches with various crops and made it look like the blanket Freya now sat on.

She was growing teeth and having a difficult time with it. A white tooth emerged from her bottom gum. It was the third one she had grown, but her mother still withheld certain foods. Mama took items out of the basket—glass jars filled with brightly colored foods and juices. Her eyes were drawn to the bright reds, greens, and yellow colors. After some struggle with prying her tiny hands from the jars, her mother handed her a spoon. She was delighted with this spoon and waved it around.

The jars were opened, and her mother took out a small spoon and dipped it into the jar before offering it to her. She understood that this was food processed on her behalf and that she was to eat it, but her baby urges got the best of her. Instead of leaning her head into the spoon, she grabbed hold of the utensil and managed to wrestle it from her mother before flinging the red goo everywhere.

"Freya!"

She didn't mean to do that. Her hands formed tense little balls and her lips quivered, but her mother refused to give up. Now that she had a spoon in each hand, she couldn't possibly botch up the second attempt. Mama prepared another spoonful of the red goo and delivered it to her mouth.

The inside of her mouth exploded with sour yet sugary flavor. It was overwhelming and sent her tongue into activity. It explored the textures, and the berry ripe filled her sinuses. Her tongue also pushed half of the paste back out in the process. This would take more time to figure out than she anticipated. In the meantime, she was determined to take the socks off her feet.

When the picnic was over, Pete the dog greeted them as they approached the fences of their property. He bounced around happily as Mama put away the blanket and jars of food. Mama had set her down on the kitchen floor to play with cups and wooden spoons while she did chores about the house.

Papa's loud footsteps stopped at the entryway. He was looking at Mama with fear in his eyes. Something was wrong and it made her tummy hurt. She uttered a single wail and Mama turned around. Her face fell when she saw Papa's sullen expression.

"Mike, what's wrong?"

He took his hat off and wrung it between his hands. "No one can lend me a workhorse. When I went to the store, they told me that we couldn't take any more credit out. Jess, I don't know what we're going to do."

"Maybe we can ask my dad." Mama went up to Papa, and they hugged.

Papa's face pressed onto the top of mama's head. "If it were just me, I'd sooner starve than ask him for help, but for baby Freya …"

Mama nodded in agreement. "For Freya."

That night, when Papa was taking a bath, Mama cried while she nursed her. She didn't understand entirely, but her parents did not want to ask her grandfather for money that they desperately needed. It was a matter of pride. She disliked her parents being so upset.

She fell asleep, still attached to her mother's breast. Visions of large, sturdy horses filled her head until one final image came to mind: a large, cow-like thing. It was twice the size of a horse and had horns. It wore a great leather harness and pulled a new, sharp, and steely plow three times the size of the sickly old workhorse.

In the night, Pete began to bark and refused to stop. It woke her against her bidding, so she cried in frustration, which then aggravated her father. "Better not be coyotes," he said as he grabbed his shotgun and made his way down the stairs.

"Jess! Jess, come down here," Papa shouted from downstairs.

Mama picked her up and wrapped her in a blanket before carrying her out. Her brow was creased with worry. Mama and Papa couldn't handle another blow. They went down the stairs and out the front door to find Papa standing on the porch with his hands on his hips.

The three of them came upon a pair of cattle sitting beside a plow machine. The ox was huge and strong with black hair, and the cow was brown. The ox posed as if he realized his importance. The savior of their family without the sacrifice of her parent's pride. "Look at these two!" Papa shouted.

"Is it a bull or an ox?" Mama asked.

Papa walked around to the back side of the ox. "He's docile so…yup, he's an ox."

"He is big enough to pull that thing?"

"It's designed for two, but we have such a small patch of land I think he could handle it." Papa patted the ox's back and the sable cow nudged her papa, demanding pets as well. "And this plow," he said. "It's unlike anything I've ever seen."

"It's a gift, for sure. But from who?" Mama asked.

Her father stepped up to the steer and stroked his neck and head, "He's trained and she's ready to have calves. I bet another rancher would be willing to mate her. This equipment—no one has anything like this. Have you spoken to your parents?" he asked. "I don't think even they could afford it."

Mama shook her head. "I haven't spoken with my father since before the wedding. He'd never give us anything like that."

"Your mama, then?"

She shrugged and shifted her weight to adjust for her ever-growing body. The baby now rested on her mother's hip. "I sent her a letter awhile back, letting her know I was pregnant, but she never responded."

Papa shook his head and patted the cattle. "I'll get them and this equipment in the barn. Tomorrow I'll ask around and see if I can't get an idea. The least we can do is thank whoever gave us this. It's …" Papa began to cry. "It's just incredible. We could breed our own cattle. We can do this."

Mama was crying happily as well. She walked around the front gate with Freya in her arms in search of the gift giver. She occasionally wiped at her eyes with her free hand. There was no one there, and Freya was once again growing sleepy. Pete was so excited by the intrusion that he began to run circles in the front yard.

The animals were led into the barn by their soft leather harnesses. The ox dragged the plow with the teeth mechanism pulled up so the device could be wheeled away. Papa didn't have enough room in the small decrepit barn for the plow as well, so he pulled the machine around the backside of the barn before they went inside.

The stairs creaked as they made their way up and back into the bedroom. She fell asleep to her parents chatting excitedly about the cattle and the machine and what it would mean to their family. Her little body eased in the bed and she fell into a content slumber.

The next morning, Mama took her to the tree beside the house to play on a swing that hung from a branch. There, she kicked her bare legs in the open air and watched her parents marvel at the new machine.

Papa was so excited that he never went back to sleep that night. Instead, he waited until the first signs of light before running outside to build a makeshift fence for the cattle. She and her mother slept on as her father attached the new plowing gear to the ox, who he named Sampson, and had their tiny plot of land plowed and ready for seed before they got out of bed.

"Check this out, Jess." He led his wife around the freshly tilled field. "Once Delilah has a few calves, we can trade some to keep breeding them."

The neighbors came by to inspect the new machine and cattle as well. Papa conversed with other people about the miracle. She kicked her feet and bounced wildly, and not the slightest bit disturbed by drool coming from her mouth. She didn't know where the pair of cattle or the machine—unlike any her father had ever seen—had come from, but everyone was so happy, and it made her happy to be a part of it.

# Chapter Twenty-One

It didn't take the family long to learn that Delilah was already pregnant. They had no idea how, but it was received as a blessing nonetheless. Mike interviewed every cattle- owning family within miles, but no one had a pair of cattle to spare, nor would they have been able to provide such an extravagant machine.

"I'm going to plow Reed's lot," Papa announced while they ate breakfast one morning. "I could probably plow half the town's fields with that machine and still be back in time for supper."

"They need all the help they can get," Mama said while spoon-feeding Freya something savory from a jar. It was green and mushy, but sweet and earthy. She struggled to maintain control of her mouth, but Mama was patiently scooping the food off her face and returning it.

"They're worse off than we are. It's only right we help them. She's got all those kids and no way to care for them."

Mama played with her feet. She let out giggles as her mama blew on her feet and pretended to eat them. It was absurdly funny that Mama would eat baby toes. She would put them in her mouth, and the toes would vanish momentarily. The shock of the missing appendages and the delight of their return would never lose its hilarity no matter how many times Mama performed the trick.

The days grew longer for her. She was awake more and more. She learned to crawl and chased the dog around the house. One day Pete leaped over the baby gate that barred her from the stairs. Pete considered her with one brown eye and one blue eye before he cocked his head as if he expected her to do the same. The dog was somewhere she couldn't be, and her arms shook her balled fists.

Gripping the wooden bars, she pulled herself up and gave the dog a piece of her mind. The dog responded by jumping back over the gate. His claws skittered against the wood floors as he ran outside the open front door. She, too, questioned why the front door was open. Detaching from the gate, she made a few steps towards the door.

A crying scream came from the kitchen and startled her. Freya turned to find her mother covering her mouth. Her eyes were filled with tears. It alarmed the baby so much that she, too, began to cry. In a confusing turn of events, her mama began to laugh. Freya didn't know what to make of the ordeal and laughed a near-toothless laugh.

She looked down and realized she was standing, and not only that, but she had taken her first few steps. That was why Mama was acting so strangely. She fell back on her butt and stared at the open door before her. Soon, there was nowhere she couldn't go.

***

Aegis sat where Nora once sat for the morning council. It had been six months since Nora had died, and he waited for news of a baby with each passing day. If it was anything like Nora, he would be waiting a long time, a dreadful and anxiety-inducing prospect that came to him often.

His chin rested on his fist and he was filled with contempt and misery. He did not want to be here in this chair. He wanted to stand beside his queen, but she was gone. Only temporarily, he reminded himself. But was it temporary? What if the new king or queen wasn't anything like Nora?

His grief was unending. He had lost many kings in between Tom and Nora, but they were similar in many ways. They were both so strong, so unaware. They died in a similar manner, which made him wonder if Tom hadn't been poisoned all those years ago and if that was how Peter got the idea in the first place. Not that knowing such things now wouldn't do him any good. More than anything, he just wanted this to all be over.

Until the King's Soul made itself known, he would wait here. Hacia was very pregnant and ready to burst at any moment. He found he couldn't deny her requests in her current state not because she was pregnant, but because he regretted placing such a burden on her in her current state. The amount that woman could endure was astonishing.

Poor Hacia couldn't push her chair up to the table anymore; her belly wouldn't allow it. Her leather vest had been abandoned months ago in favor of flowy linen gowns that tied above the belly. Her black locks were braided away from her face and down her back. She should have been resting, not running a world, but he had been too eager to kill rebels that he'd left his queen. This was the least he could do for Hacia and for Nora. He didn't give a damn about Hell which had gone quiet since the passing of the queen. Either they understood what they had lost, or they had lost the only one inciting rebellion. He wasn't certain.

Of all people, Rebus was rather cheerful. His stride had more spring to it. "How is our mother-to-be today?" Rebus asked as he shuffled in.

"The steward feels fine," Hacia said, the whites of her eyes exposed as she rolled them. Her size had her constantly adjusting and readjusting, and she would fan herself in normal weather conditions.

Rebus ignored the warning as he had for the last several months. He admitted it was rather funny. The old man risked life and limb to dote on a lethal killer simply because she was reproducing. Rebus had feared Hacia until she began to show.

"But not for much longer," Alfie said. The father-to-be was fussing over his partner as well.

Poor Hacia sighed. "Yes, Alfie, as we agreed."

"That is precisely why I'm sitting in her chair," Aegis said.

Everyone went quiet. His emphasis on *her* was painful for all of them. They were all still carrying the weight of their dead queen. He carried the weight of many dead, but her death was profound. It echoed in his mind every evening as he lay on the balcony staring up at the blank sky.

"So, what's on the agenda today?" Alfie asked.

Discussions bubbled around the room. He tried his best to remain attentive, but he found himself wishing she were there. He wanted her to be in the chair. He wanted to watch her drink her favorite tea, and he wanted to watch her make the decisions. He wanted to watch her grow older and surer of herself even if it frightened all of Hell in the process.

The rooms had been stripped clean. Not just hers, but the one next to it—the green room, Nora called it. Peter's rooms were remade into simple guest rooms, as was the white room. All her decorations had been removed and put away.

A new ruler would emerge and want their own décor. He told himself that it was just stuff and that it didn't matter, but more than once he had to suppress the urge to chase the servants out of the bedroom as they removed her presence bit by bit.

The lavender dress was a special case. He saw Bosh carrying it out and stopped him. His fists balled, and the boy stuttered. He was at war with himself on what to do, but he ultimately decided to tear a strip of lace off the dress and he braided it into his necklace. It would be his only keepsake of her.

"… Aegis," Hacia said.

They were all staring at him. He must have missed part of the conversation. "Whatever you think is best, Hacia."

She was giving him a look of pity. He hated that, but he supposed he was rather pitiful at the moment. "I had an artist render a portrait of Nora as well as a stained glass window. We're trying to decide where to put it."

Hacia decided that since all the portraits of the stewards had been removed, it was only right that the wall of faces begin with Nora's. He liked the idea but said, "It depends on how good the portrait is."

"Traditionally, an artist unveils the portrait where it is hung," Rebus explained.

Soul traditions were naturally lost on him. Had the artist even seen the late queen before? Was he a good artist? What if they made her look horrid? The last thing he wanted was to walk by a demented rendering of the love of his life. Everyone in the room bowed their heads.

"I had the best artist in Hell paint the likeness," Hacia assured him. "It's going to be a party to celebrate her achievements."

He leaned back in the chair and crossed his arms over his chest, flexing his rigid hands. "Fine, but if it's a shit painting, I will murder the artist in the middle of your fancy ball."

There was no further discussion on commemorating Nora's queenship.

***

It had been several weeks since Freya took her first steps. She had since improved walking, though she relied on any nearby furniture or wall for assistance. Pulling herself upright with a chair or table, she walked with one hand, always supported by something.

Her parents would stand behind her and lean down, extending their fingers for her to grab hold of and use for walking. This pleased her enormously, as it gave her more agency over the direction in which she wished to go. It was especially fun when her father lent his support while they took expeditions outside.

"Weee!" Papa cried as she sped through the barn giggling. The cow, Delilah, watched from her stall while chewing blankly. Papa had been making repairs on the barn to make it more suitable for the animals. Though the repairs were made with scraps of wood and leftovers he salvaged from town, the ox and cow were well fed and quite healthy.

She overheard her father and mother speaking about the barn while she was in her crib, supposedly napping. "It's not pretty, but it's warm. It was only made for a horse and a few small livestock. If we're going to have cattle, we'll need a bigger barn."

"We can't afford that," Mama argued.

"No. I think we should sell the calf once it's big enough and use that to buy some smaller animals, like chickens and goats. We can sell milk from Delilah, and Sampson can plow the fields. Once we save up a bit of money, we can build a bigger barn. Then we can keep the calves."

Her mother said something, but she couldn't make out what it was since she was in the other room. It was her father's voice that carried into her room. "Yeah, that, too. The horse probably got sick from how drafty that barn was. I know we did the right thing, but it just kills me to put an animal down."

The conversation continued downstairs in the kitchen. She could no longer hear her parents apart from the muffled speaking through the uninsulated farmhouse. She didn't understand entirely what they were talking about, but from what she could gather, her parents were going to sell the impending calf for fear that the barn was not a suitable place for it to live.

She liked the cow. It was big and stared at her with a wet snout and big, black eyes. It had large teeth and a huge tongue. She wasn't allowed near Sampson. Though he was docile, her parents did not want to risk her safety near such a giant.

Sampson had his own pen that he occupied in an untilled portion of the field. Papa would put blankets on both animals to keep them warm as a precautionary measure. The makeshift pen he'd created for Sampson did little to keep the ox from wandering. Many times, her father woke to find Sampson standing outside the barn or in his outdoor pen with the door wide open as if he understood his place.

What's more, the family was evidently becoming the talk of the town. There were many occasions where people would knock on the door with pie and other foods to offer. Mama would invite them in, and they would talk over coffee about the mystery of the cattle and the odd machine.

Mostly, it was the same sort of conversation. Mama was most rehearsed as to what to say before the company grew bored and left. Sometimes they brought toys and clothes from their children as gifts for Freya. She received a rattle and a painted rocking horse. She liked the rattle but was still not big enough for the horse.

Every day, her steps became more certain. As the crops of corn and wheat grew taller, their family's security became certain in the eyes of her parents. Mama slept more easily, and Papa smiled with a sense of pride.

She dreamt often. Sometimes it was about applesauce and Mama. Other times she was being carried, jumping from branch to branch of great big trees by a man with brown hair longer than Papa's. Mama playing with her feet and Papa showing her the cows. The leaves glittering on the hill near her house—and her mind was often occupied with lavender sunsets.

***

On the eve of the portrait unveiling, the council convened to go over the final details—mostly the catering, which had turned into a fiasco under Aegis's management. Evidently, no one approved of his food selections. When the servants gave him a list with various foods, he simply circled random items and that was that.

"Raw oysters, brown beans, and turnips," Rebus read off. "For drinks, we have rum, water, and cranberry juice."

Alfie snorted out a laugh, and Hacia's lips quivered as she tried not to snicker. Rebus had a twinkle in his eye to suggest he found the choices funny, but he feared the vampire too much to make any real jest at his expense. He shrugged and flippantly reminded them, "You asked a vampire to select food for souls."

At this, they all had a good laugh, except for the two head chefs. The man with his curled mustache shifted restlessly outside of his kitchen. The woman was cross, with her hands on her hips, glowering at how casually the council took the situation.

"Chefs." Aegis turned and said, "You are the experts. Please do whatever you wish."

At this, they began throwing out words to one another as if they had their own language. He had only ever witnessed them fight, but at the prospect of creating something of their choosing, the pair became partners, throwing ideas at one another in a symphony of collaboration.

He turned back around in his chair and grinned. "I think they can resolve my mistake."

With the rest of the preparation for the event set in place and the chefs pacified, the council concluded. Everyone stood, and Alfie helped Hacia from her seat. As he pulled her up, she lurched over and had to steady herself on the table with both hands.

He smelled it before he heard it. Warm, metallic-smelling liquid rained on the cobblestones of the castle. Hacia's water had finally broken. Rebus moved faster than he thought possible. He was sprinting to the door, shouting at the servants to call the doctor. The baby's time had come. The old man was at Hacia's side coaching her over breathing while Alfie turned paler and paler.

"We need to get her to the bed," Alfie said.

"She's in the midst of a contraction," Rebus explained. "It's difficult to move, and she won't be able to speak when she does this."

That did nothing to warm Alfie's pale expression. He was now gazing around the room blankly. Aegis went to pick Hacia up to carry her, but she pushed him back with a free hand. "I'm fine," she panted after several minutes. "It's not that many steps."

Rebus did not accept that answer. "It's four flights of stairs to the barracks," he scoffed. "If you had just taken a room in the palace we could have—"

Hacia had had enough of men fussing over her. She stepped over the puddle of fluid between her feet and walked out of the room and down the staircase. Rebus was stupefied by her independence. He shot Aegis an incredulous look as if he expected the vampire to reprimand her.

"She's fine," he said.

A slap of chainmail and flesh hit the stone steps. Aegis turned to find Alfie on the steps in a daze and sighed. "It seems I'll be carrying someone," he said.

The scene was astonishing. In all his lifetimes, nothing could have prepared him for this moment. Last year, Alfie and Hacia were sent to kill him. Now, he was a part of this strange motley crew that consisted of a pregnant tracker, an unconscious hawk hunter, and a very old man. The group descended the stairs after the laboring woman and he mused she was running from them.

They followed the trail of fluid on the steps and eventually caught up with Hacia. She had paused on the steps and was bracing the stone wall.

"It's been approximately six minutes since the last one," Rebus said, waddling after Hacia whose eyes were now filled with contempt. "Labor is moving quickly, but you still have plenty of time."

He was familiar with childbirth. Many kings had wives, and those wives gave birth to many children. He was never in the room with a woman in labor, however. Usually, he was introduced to a newborn baby by the king when it was all over. He understood how it worked, but he never anticipated being in this situation.

He thought about Nora then. Would she have had him in the

room with her if she gave birth? Though the father probably wouldn't have liked that. He honestly couldn't see Nora becoming a mother. That notion didn't make him feel sad. It didn't make him feel anything.

"Almost there," Rebus coached.

By this time, Hacia finally allowed Rebus to hold her hand as she made her way down rest of the steps. It took the better part of an hour to get across the pavilion to the barracks. She must have been in great pain because she sucked in air between gritted teeth. Rebus coached her on how to breathe though he suspected she hadn't forgotten.

A blessing of three women dressed in white aprons and folded hats emerged from the far side of the pavilion and surrounded Hacia. They asked questions about when her water broke, how close the contractions were, and other such things before surrounding Hacia and escorting her to the barracks.

The women paid no mind to him or the man he carried in his arms who was now moaning, "Is she okay?"

It seemed to him that the generals were prepared for a great deal. They were taught to fight, hunt, and track. They were taught to be cunning and decode letters and military strategy. They learned the basics of poisons and were equipped with essential medical training, but they were never taught how to live past their utility.

Neither Hacia nor Alfie expected to live long enough to have children, to know the fear of a loved one dying. Alfie had witnessed many atrocities but was unable to shut out the fear of this day because he had so much more at risk. He pitied them then. Alfie and Hacia's certainty in life was now lost to a baby they had not met.

He set Alfie on the stone bench beside the entrance of the tracker barracks. The man leaned his head back as he returned to conciseness. "How long have I been out?" he asked.

Aegis stood in the center of the pavilion, glancing up at the castle. "Not long. She's inside with three midwives and Rebus. You should go to her."

Alfie shook his head and wiped his hair from his forehead. "Some man I am," he muttered.

"You've never done this before. Nora nearly puked when she saw a woman give birth in the second region."

"Nearly made a naive teenage girl feel ill."

He realized that his comparison wasn't what Alfie wanted to hear. He tied his masculinity to his ability to withstand things he had no experience dealing with. To compare the deceased queen to his current state wasn't going to help the man regain his confidence.

"Nora had a panic attack in a corset once," Aegis said. "I didn't know what was happening. I thought she was dying. I've never felt so stupid. We don't realize how little control we truly have until the ones we cherish the most are suffering and there's nothing we can do to fix it," he added, though he was no longer thinking of the corset, but rather the dimming hours that he last shared with Nora.

Alfie embraced him then. It was a fast, abrupt hug that he didn't see coming. It made Aegis laugh with surprise. Alfie turned to go into the barracks, but before he walked through the door, Aegis called, "Good luck."

Hacia's labor was not an easy one. Despite how quickly her contractions came, her progress stalled, and it was well into the next day when baby's cries finally broke through the barracks. Rebus burst from the building with all the zeal gone from his face. "Hacia has given birth to a boy," he announced. "Now, if you don't mind, I'm going to sleep for several days."

He laughed at the old man. Rebus would no doubt miss his own party, but he didn't expect anyone cared anymore. Since he was not a new parent or an old man past his bedtime, it would no doubt fall to the vampire steward to pretend to care about a party. He imagined it would go horribly.

# Chapter Twenty-Two

All in all, the party went better than Aegis had expected. He was surprised to find Rebus in attendance after all, though he was much more reserved after the excitement of the previous night. There were very few attendees—mostly merchants, monks, and people from the court. He wasn't surprised to find Nora's mother Bella in attendance.

She was not dressed in finery, just a simple black empire waist gown, and her hair was pinned back with uncharacteristic sophistication. She played the part of the grieving mother well. He approached her, fully expecting her to unleash a mother's anger on him.

"Hello, Bella."

Her lips made a thin smile. "Hello, vampire."

He walked with Bella up to the bedroom that she once shared with Vinicio, the bedroom that Nora claimed as her own when she ascended the throne. It was bare now. Not a single stick of furniture in it. Their footsteps echoed on the crème marble floors.

"Oh, you haven't had it decorated."

He shook his head. Bella walked around the empty room and stared at it. The clicks of her heels echoed in the room—Nora's room— as she opened the balcony doors and stepped out to the patio. Bella stood there clutching her shawl overlooking the first region. "I—I have so many regrets."

He stood beside her and regarded same landscape. "As do I."

"But you loved her. You still love her. That was all she wanted. That's all any of us want, I suppose."

"She died because of me." His throat bobbed.

Bella turned to him and placed a delicate hand on his shoulder. "No, Aegis. She died because people were afraid of her, of what she would become. There was always a darkness in her. Even as a young child. The way she looked at my parents. Oh, she hated them. They died shortly after she became queen."

"At the same time?"

If Bella believed it curious, she didn't let on. "Yes, the doctor said it was as though they starved to death, but that couldn't be; they had plenty of food. I was left with their estate. Fortunately, it was substantial enough to cover anything Malachi and I could need."

He swallowed and shook away the possibilities. Nora never mentioned her grandparents once she ascended the throne. He assumed they had gone about their lives as they all did.

"They were so proud of her. They gushed about her at every chance they had. I'll always be proud of her."

He was certain Nora interpreted her grandparent's pride in her as gloating and using her status to further their wealth in the fifth region. Bella wouldn't know how they treated Nora because she wasn't there to watch it.

"I miss her," he redirected the conversation.

"It must be terrible for you." Bella was openly weeping now. "I know we had a strained relationship, but I'd give anything to get her back."

Bella turned and leaned into his arms. He embraced her awkwardly and tried to console her, but he wasn't comfortable with the proximity. He still resented Bella for abandoning Nora as a child and for choosing Vinicio over her, but that was in the past. He reminded himself they had made amends.

Her blue eyes dripped with tears. She was beautiful, even when she cried. Her bottom lip trembled when she looked at his. She closed her eyes and parted her lips, tilting her head toward his and he couldn't help but stare at her. He wanted to ask her what the Hell she was thinking, but then he realized exactly what she was thinking.

Whether it was intentionally or subconsciously, Bella was trying to fall in love with him. Everyone in the fifth region had an obsession. For some, it was religion; others it was law or a political stance. For Bella, it was love. She was obsessed with love. She would do anything for it, and it would be all the more convenient if she fell in love with an immortal man who shared her grief over the loss of her daughter. Especially the heartbroken steward who needed a good woman's love to save him from himself.

"They will be unveiling the portrait soon," he said.

Bella's eyes snapped open, and she gauged the look on his face and understood she had made an error. He was not desperate for anything to fill that void, not as she was. His misery would only end once Nora came back. He didn't know what form she'd return in, but she would come back.

She broke from him and hurriedly went towards the door. "We wouldn't want to miss it."

They came downstairs to find that Alfie had joined the party. He was telling everyone about his newborn baby boy. To see him like this, no one would ever know Alfie could murder an entire brothel full of people without anyone noticing. To be fair, he had only heard that story secondhand, but that was another life for the hawk hunter general.

Rebus stood beside a large cloth next to the hallway. A tall, strong-looking woman with short, blonde hair and a wide forehead stood beside him. He made a noise to request silence and was mostly ignored. It wasn't until Alfie hit a fork against his glass that everyone went quiet.

"Hello," Rebus rattled with his old man's voice. "Thank you for coming. The loss of our queen was sudden and devastating, but she is not lost to us. The King's Soul is in Hell and will make itself known to us when it is time. We have commissioned a portrait of our late queen, and this hallway will be dedicated to her and will forever be known as the hall of royalty."

Applause came from around the room, and the blonde woman stepped forward and spoke. "I only met her a few times, but I will be forever grateful that I met the first queen of Hell. I thought long and hard about how I wanted to present her. Without further ado, I give you the queen of Hell," the woman said before pulling the red silk from the portrait on the wall.

Everyone held their breath, including him, as the curtain came down. He found himself staring face to face with Nora. Not as she was towards the end, but as she was before the change. She was wearing the lavender dress and walking along a dirt path with a dark shadowed man not far behind.

The artist had captured the uncertainty on Nora's face. No doubt, this was a depiction of her and Aegis traveling together before her powers fully manifested. Nora's violet dress contrasted with the earthy background that his image blended into—just the way he wanted it.

He wiped the tears from his eyes and returned to her old bedroom. He would wait until the party was over before returning to gaze upon the portrait.

***

Squeals of delight echoed throughout the house as Mama gave pursuit. She was emerging from infancy and running fully into toddlerhood. Though her first birthday was several months away, her mother and father spoke of it a great deal.

"I can't believe she's going to be a year old soon," Mama would say.

Papa would shake his head. "Every day she reminds me of how little time we have with her."

Their conversations would go about in that sort of fashion. From there, it would be a conversation about what kind of cake to make for her party and what to give her for her birthday. Freya was still uncertain about gifts, especially if there were many of them at once. She found it overwhelming and would have preferred one gift at a time so that she had time to fully master it.

"Your parents are coming?" her mother asked one day out of the blue.

Papa grinned at her, and his eyebrows wiggled on his face as if he wanted to say something but wished to proceed with caution. "You want to invite your parents," he said.

Mama was conflicted with the prospect. Freya had long understood that a conflict had arisen between her parents and maternal grandparents, but she didn't know why. Her mother eyed her then. "You ever notice how she sort of stares at us when we're talking?"

"Like she can understand what we're saying?"

Well, that was because she *could* understand what they were saying. She frowned at the notion that she was too stupid not to. She was a child, not an idiot. She uttered several syllables to express her displeasure, but her parents thought nothing of it. "She's just copying our tones and expressions," Papa said, though Mama continued to stare as if she wasn't convinced.

"I think you should invite them," Papa said. "If they turn it down, that's on them."

He picked up his plate and her mother's plate and carried them to the sink where he began to wash the dishes.

Mama picked her up. "Come on, girl, let's get you in the tub."

Oh, she loved tub time! She clapped her hands and squealed, and Mama mimicked the cry.

"We got to get this harvest in before we can talk anymore about her birthday anyhow," Papa said. "I'm thinking of hiring the Reed boys to help me."

Mama filled the tub with water she had warming on the stove. She tested before adding some more cold water to make sure it wasn't too hot before plunking Freya into the shallow water. "I think that's a great idea. They need new clothes. Poor Miss Reed has damn near darned the darning on their socks, and the patches are near threadbare, too."

She splashed in the warm bubbly bath while Mama washed her with an old rag. She could feel new teeth coming in and couldn't help but chew on the end of the rattle. Mama talked loudly to her Papa so he could hear her, but she disliked that Mama was not giving her direct attention.

She yelled and splashed at Mama, and even threw the rag at her, but her mother was too caught up in telling Papa about how neighbors had a surplus of chickens that she was rather put out. Finally, she decided enough was enough.

Freya stood up in the tub and shouted, "Mama!"

That got her attention.

***

As the birthday drew near, there was another discussion that came up frequently. It was becoming a point of contention in the household. Freya was playing in the grass while her parents picked and pulled the crops. The Reed children, two boys and a girl, were on the other end of the field picking as well.

"I just think it's time," Mama started.

Papa snapped another corn cob from the stalk. "You know what that will lead to, and I want to be in a better financial position before we have more children."

She pulled grass from the earth and picked blades of it out of her hand one by one, sampling it for good measure. The flavor of grass could only be described as green, but not in a good way. Mama wanted to put her in her own bedroom. A terrifying prospect. She slept through the night and nursed at her mother's breast less now that she ate solid foods, but being separated from her parents at night was unsafe and cruel. She frowned and slapped at the grass, punishing it for tasting awful.

Mama pushed past the corn leaves and embraced Papa. "I know, but I miss just having time for us. We can take precautions."

At this, Papa relented. "Maybe we can give it a try, maybe work into it. Have her take naps in her room and eventually stay some of the night in her bedroom."

Mama beamed at Papa, and Freya scowled at her mother. If Mama thought she could be rid of her that easy, she had another thing coming!

Over the next several weeks, her wails echoed clear to the Reed farm. Her parents tried baby steps by putting her in her room for naps to which she fully rebelled, even to her own detriment. She would cry until her parents gave up and released her from her bedroom, only to fall asleep in her highchair or on a blanket at a later point in time.

So, her parents developed a new strategy. They would remain in her room until she fell asleep to which they would sneak out. When she woke from her nap, she would become aware of the deception and scream a wail so fearful that it would take Mama nearly an hour to soothe her.

This daily situation prevented her parents from attempting to place her in her own room at night, but as she relented the nap situation, the discussion of bedtime crept back into her parent's interest. "She needs her own space," her father would say.

"Most parents agree," Mama add.

She didn't give a damn what other parents said. She was the child of Jess and Mike, and she had no intention of sleeping in an empty room to fend for herself just because her parents wanted to see how long they could "take precautions" before becoming pregnant once more.

As the baby fell into a fitful sleep, her mother snuck out of the room. Her mother's callused feet scrape along the wood, but she was too tired to fight it. Mama had won this night. Her frustrations eased as she slumbered, and she dreamed of being the only baby.

The war over bedtime became an enduring battle over the next several months. She usually surrendered the evenings that followed busy days for her. Now that she was walking and even running, the world opened just a little bit wider. Mama took her on play dates where she played within proximity of other children. She observed the children and their behaviors and often took notes on things they did differently. She wasn't the only one who noted the difference in behaviors.

"Freya is so aware for a baby," Freya overheard her mother's friend say. "It's like she's a grown-up trapped in a baby body."

The child came up to her and demanded the toy she held in her hand. She resisted the urge to deny the child. From what she had learned on these play dates, the child would lose interest in the toy after several minutes and she could then retrieve it. She handed the toy over and the white-haired baby gleefully played with the little wooden boat.

"Good share, Freya," Mama coached. She squinted at her mother in broad daylight and resumed playing with the dirt clump she had acquired. This dirt clump she would not hand over so easily.

"I know, Mike and I swear sometimes it's like she's listening to us," her mother said.

A cloud blocked the sun momentarily, and Mama's face grew dark with concern as she watched her play. "Before the queen passed, she made that decree …"

"I know, I was scared too," her friend admitted as she anxiously straightened out her dress. "But I don't think that's Freya. She's too sweet and thoughtful."

Her mother softened. "You're right. She is a sweet little girl. I can't imagine anyone being inherently evil who loves animals so much."

"And who shares her toys," the friend added with a smile. "She's the most popular little girl to have a play date with," the woman teased and nudged Mama. "I had to book this weeks in advance."

"She's just an old soul," the woman added.

She smiled at the two women then, none of them knowing of just how old her soul truly was.

# Chapter Twenty-Three

Aegis was lying on his usual spot on the balcony, resisting the urge to sleep. For one of his kind to sleep meant centuries could pass before they woke again. He told himself she was out there, waiting for him to find her. He couldn't sleep. Not now. He needed to be patient and move past his grief.

"Did anyone ever tell you that you're a sour old bastard?" a male voice said from within the bedroom.

"In more or less those words," he replied.

There was only one person who could slip into a room without him hearing it. Alfie made his footsteps audible now as he stepped onto the patio. He breathed in the fresh air as if it were the morning after a victorious battle. "Smells better up here. Hacia never wants to leave the barracks these days."

"A few dozen highly trained assassins surrounding her baby—I can't say I blame her."

The blue of the sky was patched with white, fluffy clouds. Another perfect afternoon in the first region, as always. It was nauseating.

He longed to return to the Starry Wood, but he would wait in the castle for signs of her. She would eventually make herself known. Maybe she blamed him for her death and was trying to punish him. He couldn't imagine her motives would be so cruel, but she was cruel in the end sometimes.

"There's been no sign of rebellion since she died," Alfie said. "But you should know, a spy returned from the seventh region. Vinicio is indeed alive. The mean prick."

At this, he sat up and turned his full attention to Alfie. "Did he have anything to do with it?"

Alfie nodded. "The correspondence with the sister and the fourth region diplomat that Nora executed was indeed real, but it's isolated from the rebels Peter incited. Our former steward has made himself the lord of the seventh region."

That was an unsettling notion. Alfie's grimace suggested he shared the feeling. "I did things I'm not proud of under his command. Nora was my chance to make amends for that."

"We've all done things we're not proud of."

Alfie shook off his dark past and smiled. "You should come and meet the baby. He's a fat little thing. Poor Hacia eats her weight in food and still struggles to keep up with his demands."

He considered the proud father. "What's his name?"

"Sebastian."

He had no idea if that was a good name or not for a soul, but it seemed as good as any. "It's a nice name," he said.

"Oh, and the stained glass arrived. It's been fitted to the window you requested."

Aegis stepped into the garden and looked up at the mural. It was a dark-skinned, brown-haired girl with thick eyebrows looking down into the garden from her bedroom window. A crowd of servants was gathering in the garden to have a look as well.

"It's like she's still here," a servant whispered.

His heart ached at the statement because of how untrue it was. She wasn't here, and the growing collection of depictions of her didn't make him feel any better. The myths of who she was and what she could do only grew and spread throughout the court and servants as if they didn't remember who she truly was.

She was right here most of her life, he wanted to scream at them. Their queen ran around the palace right under their noses for sixteen years. They ignored her and shooed her away from the kitchen like she was just any child. When she returned as the rightful queen, it was as if she wasn't the same girl that grew up before their eyes.

Still, he supposed it served a purpose. Nora had surpassed queenship and gone on to become a legend in their minds. It was the only consolation he could take out of the loss. Her faults were diminished, and even the troublesome concerns of the black soul decree were remote and small in the face of her legacy.

In a way, she became more successful in death than she had been in life. Nora signified the beginning of an era, one where myths and legends returned to Hell. Magic was real once again. Beasts and vampires dwelled in the forest, and somewhere there was a king or queen among the souls of Hell, just waiting to take the crown.

For him, this mattered little. It was best for Hell, but he would have traded Nora for the betterment of Hell any day. She'd still be alive if she'd taken his advice. They could have forgotten all about the palace and lived a life in the third region. She loved it there. He would have gotten her one of those pet dogs and they could've lived on a little patch of land.

It was a deluded dream. Vinicio would have never permitted her to live. There was no safe place for Nora as long as Vinicio ruled. He didn't think there was safety for anyone with the King's Soul as long as the steward lived—something he would need to resolve sooner than later.

Rebus made his way to his side and regarded the glass. "It's quite lovely. She often stared like that into the garden from her room." He handed Aegis a hawk hunter scroll. "This came in just now."

"The lava is returning to the canyon." He read the paper in disbelief.

"The King's Soul is alive and well. The borders are not only holding, but they are returning to their former glory."

He returned his gaze to the stained glass. She was out there somewhere. Not just somewhere. There was only one region she would have gone.

Aegis found himself struggling to contain his excitement. She was in the third region where he once suggested they stay. Of course she was.

At that moment, it would be most prudent to keep her secret. It would be safest if it remained a secret. If he went looking for her, word would spread that she had returned. It was too soon, and Vinicio was gaining power. As much as he hated it, he would need to wait and run this shithole while she lived the life of an ordinary child.

He told himself these things, but as days went by, he realized he did not have the patience to sit by and wait. Unable to leave the palace and alert anyone, it killed him to know she was out there and he didn't know where.

Almost a week after the epiphany, he sent for Alfie and asked if his hawk would send a message for him. Alfie was happy to comply, but naturally, the general wanted to know who the message was for. "I'm trying to get in touch with Minerva," he said honestly.

Alfie gave a knowing nod. He probably assumed Aegis was lonely in the way that mortal men grew lonely and was requesting her presence for companionship. He had no intention of resuming that relationship, but he needed her help.

Alfie fed Gwen morsels before sending her from his leatherbound arm. The magnificent bird flew into the horizon and disappeared in the distance. "She'll find her," Alfie promised.

He had no doubt that the hawk would find Minerva, but would she answer was the bigger question on his mind. While he was the leader of the vampires at one point, Minerva wasn't around then for whatever reason. She had no reason to comply with his request. He only hoped the love they once shared would bring her forth.

One night, several days after the hawk had taken flight, rocks ricochet down the side of the turret. There was only one other being that could scale the walls so easily. He stood up to greet her. He didn't want her to know what a total loss he had become since Nora died.

She was wearing dark pants and a flowy blouse that draped across her slim frame. Also, her grey hair was braided back in a fashion similar to how Hacia wore hers. He wasn't sure what to make of the outfit. It was so different from her usual clothing choices.

"Hi," he said stupidly.

She smiled. "How have you been holding up?"

"The room looks so much bigger now that all the furniture and things have been removed. I don't suppose you asked me here to look at an empty bedroom."

Minerva standing in the empty room only reminded him that she was the one who first spoke of assassinating Nora. He was still angry with her, but he needed answers as well as a favor.

"Did you know that Peter planned to kill her?"

Minerva's brow creased, but she did not look away and shook her head. "Before I left, his intention was to find a cure. To find a cure, we needed to find the cause."

"Is that why you spoke to the witch as well?"

Minerva shrugged. "I needed a better explanation of the pact you made and what it meant. You're not exactly the most articulate fellow."

He couldn't deny that. It was ironic that his name suggested otherwise. "You got it all figured out then."

Minerva nodded and gently paced the empty room. "Your pact with the King's Soul is much more involved than I realized. You can't disobey an order without consequence. You're forever tied to it. Wherever it goes, whatever it does, you will follow. You wanted a purpose, but it became a curse."

"I don't think it's a curse," he said.

"Now that I understand, I pity you." Minerva took a deep breath. "Why you became as angry as you did. I was trying to reason you out of your very nature. Not just because of some ancient pact, but who you are as a person."

"You mean loyal," he spat.

"Before I left, Peter had uncovered the history of a king known as the fractured king. Another vampire served as his guard. Israfil was his name."

He recalled other vampires. There were six, including himself; Minerva came later. He remembered riding with them. Two of them died at the hands of titans. Two more died in the war with the giants. Israfil was one of them.

He nodded at the mention. "I helped patrol the Starry Wood at that time."

"You were never really one for palace life," Minera teased.

"Israfil most certainly was!" He chuckled at his joke only to find that he was the only one laughing in an empty room. Israfil was a rather prissy vampire who loved luxury. He supposed no one would have known that but him now.

"Nora showed similarities to the fractured king. He was struck by lightning and began behaving oddly," Minerva explained. "The constant change in taste, the inability to control their powers, all of it."

"And you think it was the same problem?" The edge in his voice was sharper than he intended.

"The witch said that Nora had two souls. One was her own, the one she was born with. The other was the King's Soul that remained dormant until she found you. It caused her personality to fracture. It appeared she was at war with herself—because she was."

He thought back to what Nora had told him about controlling the King's Soul. Minerva and Peter's theory matched. It didn't make him feel any better about what had happened. It didn't make her loss sting any less. It wasn't Peter's job to take her from him, even if she was broken. And what she became after the so-called fracture was unlike anything he had ever seen.

Minerva approached him and stroked his jaw. "Do you still hate me even when you know the truth?"

She was inviting him back into her embrace. She saw his wounds just as Bella had, only Minerva had reason to believe that she could put him back together because, at one point, she had. Things were different now. He wasn't the same lost vampire he was all those ages ago, and Nora was out there somewhere.

"I need you to do something for me," he said.

"Anything."

***

The crowd surrounded her as she sat in her highchair at the dinner table. She'd been dressed in a pastel pink dress with ruffles, but that was removed before she was seated. Everyone began to sing, "Happy birthday to you…" in a droning, off-pitch melody that she decidedly did not enjoy. At the same time, it suggested something special to come, which she was most happy to enjoy.

Her mother and father walked out of the kitchen with a small cake lit with a single candle as everyone sang, "Happy birthday, dear Freya …"

It had white frosting with rainbow sprinkles, and she was most interested in touching it, tasting it. She had learned a great deal over the last year by taste alone. Sometimes things tasted bad, bumpy, or bitter. Sometimes things left a tangy aftertaste, and sometimes they tasted good despite her mother shouting, "Yucky!" She was quite certain this would be tasty.

They removed the candle before presenting it to her. The faces of her friends and family were staring at her expectantly. They gave her an entire child-size cake but no utensils—not that she could properly wield them, but all the same, they clearly expected her to use her hands.

The baby took a single finger and gently poked the cake, and the faces got more excited, happier. She tasted the frosting. It was sweet and sugary, like happiness in her mouth. She took several samples of the frosting before moving to the yellow sponge underneath. She made a small break in the cake with her fingers before taking a bite, and it was one of the best things she had ever tasted. It was light and buttery with sweet notes that ran along the sponge.

Everybody cheered and encouraged her to eat more, and she readily complied. Grabbing handfuls of the cake, she tasted and savored each bite. Naturally, she dropped some frosted crumbs on her lap and some frosting smeared across her face.

"She's so lady-like," someone commented.

"So dainty," another agreed.

She gauged her parents' expressions, and they made happy noises. Her mother was smiling, and Papa was pretending to rub his face with his hands. Did he want her to wipe her face? The baby wiped her face with her frosted hands and in doing so, only smeared cake and frosting all over her hair. Everyone cheered and laughed, and she began to understand. She was entertaining them with a mess. Maybe messes were only encouraged on one's birthday. Any other time she made them, Mama told her no.

That night after her bath, she stood in front of the full-length mirror in her mother's bedroom. Mama picked up clothes and brushed her hair. In the reflection, she observed her own face and compared herself to her mother. Mama's skin was pale and freckled. Her father was tan from the long days in the sun. Her skin was peachy, and her hair golden. Neither of her parents had such warmth to their skin or hair.

For what was more, her eyes were a vivid green. Papa had green eyes, but not quite like this. Many commented on her beauty, but no one pointed out that she bore no resemblance to her parents. Growing distracted, she toddled off to chase after Pete. Paws were scraping for traction on the hardwood floor and she wanted to know why.

The baby gate barred her from getting downstairs. She rattled the gate and yelled in protest. She yelled, "Down!" but she wasn't certain if it came out right. There were some giggles and a pause of silence before her mother removed the lower gate and retrieved her from the top of the stairs.

After being set on her mother's hip, she was brought downstairs to find Papa standing with something hiding in his coat. Whatever it was, Pete found it most exciting. "Freya, you have to be nice and gentle," her father cooed.

He produced a kitten with orange and white fur. It was fluffy and had golden eyes. She gasped at the little thing. It mewed back at her fearfully. "The Reed's barn cat gave birth to some kittens a few weeks ago. I figured we needed a housecat to keep the mice out."

She demanded that the kitty sleep in her room. She screamed and pleaded with outstretched arms, but her parents were steadfast. Her screeches and wails went unheeded until the noises escalated to a point where they no longer seemed human. She couldn't help it. Somewhere in the house, there was a tiny, fluffy that was hers, but they withheld it from her.

Mama sat in the room with her until she fell asleep as if it were an ordinary day, and not a day she was given a kitten. She threw her blankets out of her crib in protest. If she could not have the kitty, there will be no rest. Her mother grimaced while she made all sorts of protests, but Mama would not yield.

That night, she dreamed of Kitty. It was soft and warm, and it purred so loudly that its tiny little body rattled. She would always be kind to Kitty. Even if she did want to play with its toes or stick her finger in its mouth, she wouldn't. She would be as gentle as an adult with a small creature.

The next morning, her parents woke to find the kitten gone. In a panic, they searched the bedroom and the hallway. Her door was still shut, so there was no way the kitten could have made its way into her room. The baby gates were still in place, but the kitten was so small they feared it had wiggled through the bars and made its way downstairs with Pete.

The dog had been around adult cats and knew well enough that felines were not to be trifled with, but this one was so young the couple feared the dog might hurt it with its exuberance. Papa didn't bother taking the gates down. He stepped over them, his legs too long to be hindered by such a device.

Pete showed no indication that a tiny little ball of fluff had entered his domain, so they returned to their bedroom to look further. Mama called for the kitten, and after a moment, a muffled mew came from Freya's room. The parents exchanged an incredulous glance before opening the bedroom door.

The kitten was sitting in the crib with the sleeping baby.

# Chapter Twenty-Four

Minerva stayed within the tree line of the Starry Wood, just on the edge of the third region. Aegis wanted her to find the King's Soul and report back to him. She would have preferred not. She'd had quite enough of kings and their souls, but this was important to Aegis. She was partially responsible for his miserable predicament.

She would find the child, tell Aegis of it, and that would be all. He just wanted to know the baby was safe and secure. It didn't occur to Aegis that she wouldn't be up to the job, however. He could blend in with the souls if he wished, but she didn't have that skill.

It was so obvious she was not mortal. They could sense it in her bloodshot eyes and grey hair. The way she darted around in a freakishly quick manner despite her best effort to slow down. Everything about her was unnatural. If one of these families spotted her, they would know something was amiss. The last thing she wanted was to frighten a whole region of souls that thought vampires drank blood. The absurdity of the notion made her nose wrinkle. As if she, Minerva, required blood for sustenance.

When the starless night fell, she stalked the region, searching for babies in windows of homes, an act beneath her. Her patience waned as she found no sign of a magical mortal baby. There were many, many babies in the third region, and many light sleeping farmers as well. More than once, she was nearly caught. She couldn't begin to imagine what these people would think if they found a vampire peering over their sleeping baby.

She did have it narrowed down slightly. The estimated age of the child gave her an idea of what to look for. He or she should be walking and capable of a few words. That only left oh, thousands of babies or so. She wanted to be angry at Aegis for asking this of her, but he was broken with grief and desperation. He needed to know where the King's Soul was. His soul needed something to cling to.

Minerva set out across the region the next night in search for the baby. The green landscape was partitioned by fences, and the rolling hills gave vantage points for her to perch and admire the landscape before investigating another series of homes. It really was a beautiful region.

Standing before a circular driveway sat a shabby grey barn she could knock over with the swipe of her hand. To her right was a whitewashed two-story farmhouse with a long patio and a windchime that remained still in the airless night.

This home was one with a baby around the correct age. It also was one of the many homes that owned a dog. A rather energetic one, if she remembered correctly. As silently as she could, Minerva landed on the roofed patio and investigated the child's bedroom.

The crib was the closest thing to the window, and the drapes were cracked just enough that she could see the baby sleeping. Inside the room, there was a rocking chair, a horse toy, and a dresser. It was sparse with furniture, but toys were strewn across the floor. An orange kitten slept dutifully beside the baby.

This family had humble means, but they no doubt loved their child very much. The child slept with her face down on the mattress, and her diapered rump was high in the air. Though children made her uncomfortable, she couldn't help but grin at the baby's preferred sleeping position.

The dog began to bark in his doghouse on the side of the house. When her sights returned to the window after the distracting dog settled down, her breath caught in her chest. The baby was standing up and looking at her. Too afraid to move, she didn't want to risk frightening the child. She didn't mind scaring old men, but the baby didn't deserve it.

The child braced her little hands on the railing of her crib and observed her curiously. After several moments, it was clear that the baby was not afraid. The child was now smiling and touching the glass that separated them. She placed her hand on the window to meet the baby.

"Well, aren't you a brilliant little thing," Minerva said.

This was hardly proof that this was the future queen of Hell. The baby had been awakened by the dog barking and was too innocent of perceiving the woman in the window as a threat, but her heart told her otherwise. The baby's green eyes were so intense, it was as if she understood she had a greater purpose in life.

The dog's barking intensified, and the farmer stumbled off the patio, grumbling about foxes. She crouched down to minimize her presence and watched the farmer check out his farm. He wasn't the least bit afraid. If anything, the tall working man was ducking his head under the barn door and peering into the empty field expectantly.

"No miracles tonight?" a woman's voice asked from the patio.

"Just Pete barking at nothing. I suppose a miracle can only happen once in a lifetime," the man answered.

The dog was brought into the house, which freed her movements. She stood to look into the window again, only to find that the baby was fast asleep in the same high rump position. They were talking about miracles.

She left the window and went to the barn. Inside, she found a cow and an ox. More than just that, she noted the harness for the ox was perfectly fitted and of superb quality.

The leather was soft and the bit was still shiny. There was no way this family could afford such items. She walked around the back of the barn and found a device that was beyond the abilities of third region farmers. Her hands felt the mechanical wonder, gathering information on the machinery.

There was no doubt that this machine was not of any design

known to Hell. Her recent search of the third region only confirmed this, as no one had anything like this device. It was indeed a miracle. A gift from someone who had a vast knowledge of a world beyond their own.

A gift from a queen.

***

Freya dreamt of a woman with white hair and red eyes watched her through the bedroom window. It didn't scare her because the woman's smile was kind. She sensed the woman's motivations were pure. She hoped she would see the woman again.

The next morning it was business as usual for the baby. Her parents were normally awake before she was. Freya would shake the crib railing and howl until Mama came to retrieve her. Then she would eat scrambled eggs fresh from the neighbor's hens.

Papa came in from the front door, taking off his hat and wiping his forehead before repositioning the hat. "Honey," he greeted Mama with a kiss. She had to stretch up on her tippy toes to reach him.

"How did it go?"

Papa's wide face spread into a smile. "Enough to pay off our debt at the store, buy more seeds for the next planting, and we still have some money left over."

Freya couldn't see Mama's face, but it was clear she was happy. Her happiness reflected in Papa's eyes. He hugged her, picking her up and spinning around with her. Freya laughed with delight at how happy her parents were, and Pete also grew excited and began to jump around the couple.

"This changes everything!" she said, her eyes filled with tears.

Papa's arms went wide. "It's just the beginning. A few more seasons like this, and we can rebuild the barn."

"And maybe buy another heifer."

"Delilah should be ready for milking after the calf is born and weened."

Kitty mewed to announce its arrival to the downstairs, and her eyes went instantly to the feline. She wanted to play outside with Kitty following beside her. They were brave explorers, she and Kitty. They would venture the wilds of the backyard and the vast, unending plains of the fields. The toddler fully intended to resume her expeditions, but her parents had other plans.

"You need to wash up before we head out," her mother said to her husband.

"Why? I'm just going to get all dirty again."

Mama pressed her lips together to suppress a smile. "You stink to high Hell."

Papa relented and went into the washroom. She was picked up from her highchair and taken into her bedroom to be changed as well. Kitty yawned, dejected, as it had traveled such a great distance only to return from whence it came.

"Mama," she said, hoping her mother would tell her where they were going. Her mother responded by making noises and funny faces, but no explanation. It was hard not to be amused by her mother's faces; they were truly hilarious. However, she had learned the secret of her disappearing face. It never disappeared at all. Her face was behind her hands the entire time!

Papa briskly washed up enough to be considered presentable by Mama, and they set off down the dirt and gravel path. Pete was instructed to stay home on this day. Sampson was in his field already, grazing on the lush pasture. The grass was greenest in the third region, though she did not know what to do with that information.

Her parents walked along the worn dirt road and dreamt of their future. Papa carried her in his big arms while her mother carried a wicker basket filled with tasty snacks. They talked about what animals they should get next, about their own barn raising, even as far as building a new house. A conversation grew about their plow and how underutilized it was.

"I wish we had more land," her father said. "We have this incredible plow and only a small patch to work."

"The Reeds are certainly grateful for you plowing their fields."

The neighbors had been showering them with pies and other tasty treats since the harvests came in. Several times a week, a neighbor child would come and bring something that made her mouth water.

"Yeah, those boys are getting older now. They'll be able to manage things a bit better now. I was thinking maybe we can buy some of their land and plant some apple trees or something."

"They really have more than they can handle," her mother agreed.

She had grown bored with the conversation. Her attention turned to the sky with its white, fluffy clouds. She tried to make out shapes of things in the clouds. She saw Kitty, and then a rabbit. After a long while, she saw Pete. After plodding along that road for long hours, they came across a crowd of people all circling one area.

She was at a high enough vantage thanks to Papa's towering height that she could see it was a platform, and there was timber stacked neatly beside pots of nails and ropes. Ladders of various sizes were upright and waiting. She didn't know what to make of the mess.

"Here you are, darling," Papa said as he set her shoed feet on the ground.

Mama guided her to a picnic table with other women and their baskets. They were greeted, and there were discussions about pickled and preserved things. A beautiful woman in a pair of overalls and braided brown hair approached them. "Thanks for coming, Jess."

Mama stood up and hugged the woman. "Happy to help," she said. "Where's Amy?"

The woman grinned and nodded to the men and women who

were gathered around a stern-looking woman with a straw hat and a matching pair of overalls. "She's bossing folk around."

"Well, someone's got to," another woman chimed in.

The woman called Amy climbed a few steps up a ladder and gave a loud whistle with her fingers in her mouth. The crowd went silent. How did she do that?

"Thanks, everyone for coming. I'm going to divide people into four different groups. Each group will take a side of the barn," Amy explained. "The music will be your cue to start. The group that gets their side done first wins the contents of the box over there."

Amy pointed to a large wooden box. Inside were half a dozen chicks. They were fuzzy and shuffled around in their little box eagerly. In Mama's eyes there was a deep desire for the chicks. They didn't have a house built for the chicks, which meant the babies would need to stay in the house temporarily. That would mean she could have access to the little yellow fuzzies, and excitement grew in her belly. Unsure of what to do with the sensation, she let out a squeal and clapped.

Hoots and cheers went out, and it was clear this was a most sought-after prize. Papa gave Mama a knowing nod. He had an advantage as he stood nearly head and shoulders over most of the farmers. Freya wanted him to win. She wanted him to be happy, and she wanted Mama to be happy. Most of all, she wanted to pet the chicks.

The volunteers were divvied up into four groups. Dad got the group to work on the front of the barn. A trio of men began to play a lively tune on their violins, and the barn-raising started. From the beginning, it was clear that Amy was an effective leader. She stood in the center of the barn and orchestrated the workers.

The excitement filled her, so she stood on top of the picnic table to watch and jump up and down. There were jokes at her expense, but she didn't care. She was so fascinated with the symphony that was being conducted before her. Tall pine beams were raised and nailed into place, and people worked as teams to make it happen.

Her father's team was on pace with all other sides. It was too soon to tell who was in the lead. People cheered for their partners from the sidelines and she bounced up and down and made bubbles with her spit.

The beams were up and standing free from their support. Men were now using ladders to scale the top of the barn to create the roof. This is where Papa had the advantage. He climbed the ladder and reached heights that others struggled with. Some needed to trade ladders with other teams, and others braved climbing along the beams to reach certain spots they could not otherwise nail.

"Keep it safe, folks," Amy shouted upward. "No prize is worth dying for."

Mama stood up and cheered as Papa pounded in the last of the roof frame before climbing back down while the rest of his team was working on the siding. Different groups had different approaches to this. Some focused the entire team on the top then the siding while others broke off into subgroups like Papa's team.

The siding did progress much faster once the whole group was working on it, but neither strategy was superior. It really came down to who was faster at nailing, and to this, Papa was rather efficient either due to his size or experience. Their barn was nailed in every spot imaginable due to its poor condition.

Despite her Papa's efforts, his team's siding was not the first to come up. Her father's forehead creased, and he urged his team to move faster. She noted that his team had a few older men that did not wish to pull their weight. The women on his team outpaced the men, but there were not enough women to counter the few lazy men.

There was also the condition of their clothing. It was newer. Those men had no holes in their clothing, and they were a few shades paler than the rest. They were too wealthy to care about the prize that Papa most certainly desired, needed even.

Mama frowned as she noted it as well but said nothing. It was another woman who spoke up. "Why even enter the barn raising if you're not going to try?"

"Old Jennings doesn't need the chicks. He's got plenty of money," another added.

"They are only here to maintain their pillar of the community status," a man chimed in.

Now two sides were up, and the third was nearly ready. Defeat was in Papa's eyes, but it didn't stop him from doing his best. His team was the last to get their side of the barn up. Papa was on top of the roof nailing in shingles for his side as well as another side that got stuck with a short ladder. At the end of the day, her Papa helped the other teams finish their sides even when he couldn't win.

Papa approached the table, covered in sweat and defeat, and Mama offered him a glass of cold tea. He gulped it down and gave her an apologetic look. Mama hugged him.

"Papa, Papa, Papa!" She was proud of him even if he did come in last. Her Papa smile was warm even though he was sad.

The group that won divided the chicks between them, and everyone applauded. Papa clapped the loudest. As everyone started to leave, one of the winners approached her family. He was a thin, bald-headed man with a face wrinkled like her fingers after too much bath time. "I wanted to thank you for helping us out up there, Mike."

Papa shook his hand and told him he was more than happy to help. A plump woman came behind the man and opened her basket. Three little chicks began to tweet. "We got plenty of chickens. The last thing we need is more. Why don't you take these?"

Papa thanked the man, and she squealed and danced in place. The plump woman was pleased with her excitement and gave her candy on a stick. It was a brown, sticky sweet clump that had a warm flavor.

The family returned home in success. The walk back was shorter. Perhaps it was because she closed her eyes for a few moments while resting her head on Papa's broad shoulders.

# Twenty-Five

"Are you certain?" Aegis asked. He practically trembled over the news.

"It could be no one else."

It had been nearly six months since he'd asked Minerva to find the future queen of Hell. He spent most of that six months fretting and pacing the halls of the castle waiting for her return. She told him of the plow device and the appearance of the cow and ox.

"She has seen me many times in the night," Minerva added. "She isn't afraid of me."

He was still skeptical. The child may have just been exceedingly friendly. Then again, to mortal eyes, Minerva was rather alarming. He often speculated as to why, but mortals sensed things just as vampires did, he supposed. Like animals hiding from a storm, mortals interpreted Minerva as a threat.

The first time Nora saw his eyes go bloodshot, she was frightened. She had never seen him in such a feral state. This girl might be who Minerva thought she was. The fact that she chose to be a girl again made Aegis's heart drum louder. It was Nora. He would get a second chance.

"Show me," he said.

Minerva took him to a small farm under the dark of night. It was a shabby little place, but he noted where things were improving. He'd had the hawk hunters investigate the couple. Their names were Mike and Jessica, young couple who married despite her family's strong disapproval. Mike had been a hired hand for the family since he was a boy, then went and ran off with the boss's daughter.

Her parents hoped she would marry into another farmer's family so they could combine their wealth, but instead, she eloped with the farmhand and they were paying on the property they currently owned. The cattle that Minerva had mentioned did appear misplaced on such a dusty little farm. Both were in their prime and healthy but resided in a sad little barn patched together with scrap wood. Beside it was a newly built chicken coop.

The device Minerva spoke of was beside the barn. His fingers traced the complex piece of machinery. It was compact but vicious, with sharp talons that could rip through the earth like claws in flesh. This was indeed something no one on Hell could create. It reminded him of the electricity in the royal dungeon. Technology that didn't normally occur in Hell. Hope sparked in the vampire's tired heart.

"Show me the girl."

Minerva pointed to the window, and he was there in a moment. He peeked through the glass to find a baby sleeping with her orange kitten, waited for a sign. A tingling on his scar, a golden glow around the baby, anything. The kitten woke for a moment and observed him with sleepy eyes. It yawned and went back to sleep.

He stayed there long after Minerva left. The sun was starting to rise, and the farmer was readying himself for work. The bedroom door opened, and he had to duck from sight as the man walked in. He came into the bedroom and watched the child sleep for a few minutes before kissing her on the head. They were parents Nora would have wanted. Even if this wasn't the queen, the family warmed him.

Once the farmer left, he jumped off the roof and moved off the property. With Hacia's return to stewardship, he was free to remain. She and Alfie both knew this day would happen, so it was no surprise when Gwen, Alfie's hawk, circled the sky. He extended his arm, and the bird landed on it. He took the note from the foot of the bird and sent her back to her master.

If this note doesn't return, we will assume you found her. ~ A&H

The note released him from his obligations at the castle. Hacia was more than qualified to handle stewardship, even with a baby. On more than one occasion, she had issued orders from the throne with the baby at her breast. The things he struggled with and had no idea of how to even address, Hacia regally delegated and maneuvered.

She continued Nora's decree. The black souls were sent to varying regions for a second chance. It was still too early to tell, but there had yet to be any problem with the decree. There were currently twelve black souls roaming Hell. All would be young, near the baby's age. Nora's reign would go down as one of mercy. Redemption would be given to all because evil wasn't born, it was made. Peter had made sure of it in his own way.

He walked the perimeter of the property for several hours, about to make another loop when he stopped short. A several inch groove in the dirt circled the small farm. He was exasperated by his own stupid behavior. This was the first time he had been happy or excited in a long time. He could only laugh at himself. Okay, what's the plan?

"You lost, stranger?" a baritone voice asked. Mike leaned on his fence while watching the vampire wearily.

He wasn't certain of what to say, but it would be best to remain truthful. "It feels that way."

Mike's thick brows knitted. He noted the size of the man. He was tall, taller than Aegis, which was uncommon. Beneath the sweat and the dirt, he was an attractive fellow. It was no wonder the mother went for him.

"You a farmhand?" Mike asked.

He thought back to his brief stay with Lacey's family and saw an opportunity. They would no doubt vouch for him without giving away his identity. "I worked for Lacey, but she's got enough help, and I'm looking for work."

Mike leaned with his forearms on the fence. "Lacey's farm is a pretty big operation. That's a cattle ranch. Did she fire you, or did you move on?"

He realized his error. If he wasn't careful, it would appear to Mike that he'd parted on bad terms with his former employer. "I had to move on," he said. "My former lover is still working there and I couldn't stand to see her every day."

Mike gave a gentle nod. "I could use an extra hand, but I honestly can't pay you all that much."

Aegis gratefully accepted the offer and introduced himself. Mike gave him a tour of the farm he was already well acquainted with. He feigned awe over the plow and the cattle. The dog named Pete was a little weary of the newcomer. The dog scampered away and gave a little whine from his doghouse. He hoped the dog wouldn't give him away.

Mike brought him into the house and called for his wife. "Honey, I'd like you to meet our new farmhand, Aegis. Aegis, this is my wife, Jess."

She smiled politely, but he could tell she was unhappy. So could Mike. Evidently, she didn't enjoy the idea of him springing new people on her. He couldn't blame her caution, especially with a young child in the house.

"Aegis, why don't you have a seat at the table. I'm going to make some coffee."

Coffee must have been code for *beg my wife's forgiveness* in mortal language. He pretended not to hear the argument transpire. Mike explained that Aegis was willing to work for nearly nothing. That he had been previously employed by Lacey and that he was going to ask for Lacey's reference. This pacified Jess a little bit, but she was still unhappy.

Mike came out of the kitchen with a look of remorse on his face. "Well, we got a young baby, you see. Jess just isn't comfortable with strangers around the baby."

He nodded sagely. "I fully understand," he said, standing up.

"A few other farms are looking for help …"

"I'll go back to Lacey and ask her to send me somewhere. It's what I should've done in the first place. I guess I just needed some air."

He left the house, disappointed but relieved at the same time. Her parents were protective—which was good—but he wanted to meet the baby. He had no choice but to come back at night. Still, it seemed a little shameful to lurk around a sleeping child, even if she was his queen. Or rather, the future queen.

That night, Minerva found him along the edge of the Starry Wood before he returned to the house. She shook her head and said, "You know it's her. Just leave her be."

"I can't leave her be anymore than you can leave me be."

That was harsh, but he was annoyed with her judging him and telling him what to do. Minerva crossed her arms over her chest and stood her ground. "She's safe. She needs to grow up. You hovering over her will only raise questions. People are already asking why you've left the palace. It's not hard to put things together."

"What do I do then?"

"Go back to the palace. I will keep an eye on her," she promised.

She was right. It was only a matter of time before people figured out who he was, what the baby was. If he remained, even in secret, it would only raise more questions. He didn't want to leave, but it was her only shot at having a childhood this time. A normal, healthy childhood.

"I just need to see her first, then I'll go."

He gently padded along the roof to her window once more, hoping she would be awake. He just needed a sign, anything. Before he could peer in, a small hand pressed against the window. He shuddered as he tried to stifle a sob. The child regarded him, watching with expectant eyes.

There was a moment of hesitation. He wasn't sure he could do this all again. There was no choice. This was his queen. He pressed his hand against the window where hers was waiting, and the scar on his palm began to hum. It was her. She was smiling at him with green eyes and a droopy smile, but it was her. His ribs released as if this were the first full breath he'd drawn in months. He laughed at the absurdity of it all.

She remained with him for a long while before she slapped her little hand against the window, as if she was telling him to go away, before she curled back into a sleeping ball. The kitten got up, stretched, and sat beside the baby's head.

It took several minutes for him to recollect himself as he sat on the roof. Dawn was creeping along the horizon when Mike emerged from the house with a cup of coffee in his hand. He dodged off the roof and out of sight before the sleepy farmer could notice him. When he returned to the woods, Minerva was waiting.

"It's her," he said, no longer trying to hide his relief. She was back. His queen was returned to him.

"Go back to the palace, Aegis. Wait for her."

"Thank you, Minerva," he said, embracing her. It was a hug of friendship and she received it as such.

"It's the least I can do after everything that's happened. If I'd had any idea of what Peter was up to, I would have told you."

He shook his head. "It wasn't you're fault. He somehow managed to hide it from even her."

Minerva gave a hard look. "How do you think he managed that?"

"There's no way to be certain," he said. "She once told me she could sense people's intent if they slept near her. My guess is that his intentions were always to help her, even though his solution was a bad one."

He turned and left without saying goodbye, too caught up in his memories of Nora. Like he could still pick out her scent or expected to hear her voice at any moment. But it was only a matter of time until the baby grew up and she would be back in his life once more. A few years would go by with the turn of his head, and Nora would be there again.

"When she's ready, I'll have her call for you," Minerva called as he dashed through the forest with elation. He needed to run and leap. He swung from branches and flew. She was alive and growing. She would be under Minerva's protection, and this time, things would be different for her. Nora was alive.

When he landed on the balcony, he found Hacia waiting for him. "You're back."

He told her everything. As she listened, her face grew more serious, but she said nothing. "What is it? This is good news," he said.

"Sit down," she told him. He sat on the edge of the balcony, where he'd spent so much time staring at the sky above, wishing that Nora would return. "I am happy you found the King's Soul, but I feel like you've forgotten something important here."

He nodded but said nothing. He didn't want to know what he had forgotten, and he really didn't want her to say it.

"Nora is gone, Aegis. That child will not grow up to be her. She may not have anything in common with Nora."

What Hacia said made sense. It was true, but it didn't change the way he felt. He locked his jaw and tried not to show it.

"You are still grieving Nora's loss. You cannot replace her—"

"You should leave."

Hacia didn't say another word. She stood up and left Aegis alone on the balcony. He was fuming, but it wasn't because of what Hacia had said. She was right. He was struggling with grief. It was something he should have been used to by now, but it never got easier. His rage was only quelled by the waves of sadness that pulled him under. The quiet, heavy undertow that pulled at his tired heart.

He couldn't resist any longer. Nora was never coming back. He laid down and stared at the dawning sky before he did the thing he swore he would not do. Aegis fell asleep.

# Twenty-Six

The third region had its own unique weather system. While buds blossomed and animals were born in the spring, and the summers were dry and warm, the cool air of autumn transitioned into what the farmers called "the raining season." Freya disliked the raining season. It was the most boring one of all.

It rained almost daily for months. Any rooted plants would rot if left in the ground during these months. Livestock had to remain indoors. While it was a lucrative time for rice crops, it was a miserable time for a child.

Two pudgy little hands propped up the head of a little girl looking through the window. It had rained nine days in a row, and the three year old was desperate to go outside. Kitty sat in the windowsill beside her, also peering out. Kitty was also unimpressed with the wetness that turned their front yard into a giant puddle that only Papa could stomp in.

"Come on, Freya, let's do some laundry," Mama said.

She was not interested in doing laundry, so she ignored her mother and continued to watch for the rain to slow. A loud groan followed by a thundering crash sent her mother running to the front. She couldn't see what had happened, but she took the opportunity to escape, even if it was just for a moment.

"Mike?" Mama called. The rain muted her voice.

"I'm fine," he said as he came around the side of the house. "I was at the rice crops. It came from the barn."

Papa ran to the barn while she and Mama waited for some time before he came back.

"Part of the roof has collapsed in the barn."

"The cattle—"

"They're fine," Papa assured her. "Sampson is pretty mad, but it was just a chunk of roofing. The support beams are still there."

"We can't let them get wet. They will get sick." Mama's voice was high.

Papa held her. "Hey, hey, it's going to be all right. I can patch it up for now. Come spring we will talk about building a new barn."

"We won't be able to afford that."

She stood on the porch beside her parents. Papa was desperately trying to console her mother who was in a state of panic she hadn't seen since they'd had to put the horse down. Mama relaxed in Papa's arms. He was strong enough to take any blow dealt to the both of them.

"Why don't you get the baby inside. I'm going to fix up the barn the best I can for now."

Mama said nothing but did as Papa asked. Mama played dolls with her as the uneasiness grounded them more than the rain ever could. They ate some sandwiches for lunch. Mama was sullen but tried her best to maintain a cheerful face. Papa came in to join them. He sat down opposite of her and wiggled the caterpillars on his face to make her laugh while they ate.

"How's the barn?" her mother asked.

"Well …" Papa was committed to his sandwich.

"It's that bad?"

"I'm going to ask the Reeds if our cattle can stay in their barn for the season. Once it dries up, we will have a barn-raising of our own."

Mama was mad. She could tell because she didn't sit down to eat with them. Instead, she stayed in the kitchen, not wanting to show how worried she was. Mama didn't say anything, but she could tell from Papa's expression that Mama was unhappy.

"We'll get through it, Jess," he said. "We've gotten through worse. We're just building a barn sooner than we planned."

"I know, I just … things would be easier if we just asked for help."

Papa sighed as he set down his sandwich and shook his head. "We've gone over this. I don't want to ask your parents for money. You're just now barely on speaking terms."

"We could pay for half, and they could pay for half and we'd still have money in our savings."

Papa leaned back in his chair and raised his voice. "Dammit, I'm not going to go begging your father for money."

This startled Freya, who wasn't accustomed to hearing her father raise his voice. She tried to be a big girl, but her eyes watered, and her sobs betrayed her.

"Oh, hey, darling, it's okay." He got up and went to her. He picked her up and rocked her. "*Shh*."

Safe in her father's arms, she stopped crying, but Mama was furious now. She stood outside the kitchen with her hand on her hip. "Now you're making the baby cry!"

She couldn't see the look on Papa's face, but he said something that made Mama stop speaking. "You promised me," he said. Her mother responded by going upstairs and slamming the door and she started crying all over again. Papa danced around the room with her slowly as he sang her a lullaby.

The low rumble of his voice vibrated along his shoulder, where she rested her head. In a matter of minutes, the toddler was asleep. Her father carried her up to bed for her nap. "Come on, Kitty," he called to the ginger cat who slinked along the hallway a few feet away.

Papa laid her down and mumbled something about Kitty. "Sleep awhile, darling. I need to go and make up with your mother."

She slept and dreamt of the barn-raising they had been to last year. The freshly treated pine was a soft shade of orange. The scent of timber went for miles. It reminded her of a forest and a man. His name was Aegis. Her father said that name before, but what did it mean?

Frantic shouts woke her. Eyes fluttered open despite the fatigue.

She sat up and rattled her crib to indicate she was awake, but no one answered. Both of her parents were outside. They couldn't hear her. She went to her window and saw what they were shouting about. There stood an enormous new barn—the old one had disappeared.

It took her parents far too long before they came up to get her. Papa carried her around the barn, giving her the tour. There were six roomy stalls already full of fresh hay and Delilah was chewing in one of them. In one corner was a chicken mansion surrounded by a mesh-wire fence with a door large enough that Papa did not have to duck when he walked in.

Passersby would stop on the road and stare at the new barn before knocking on the door to ask about it. Papa gave everyone the tour of the amazing new barn, even into the evening. She sat at the window and watched with her arms folded. Glaring at Papa wasn't enough to get his attention. Determined to get her Papa's attention, she stepped onto the porch with her hands on her hips—the way Mama did when she wanted him to come in—and shouted at him.

The group of men donning overalls and big straw hats laughed and teased Papa. "I think your little lady wants you to come inside."

She did indeed, and it was no laughing matter.

The next few days were spent theorizing how such a thing could possibly happen. Her parent's conversations would always return to the miracle. Especially over supper—which was supposed to be her time with Papa.

"No one has anything like it this side of the region," Papa said.

Mama absently dabbed her face with a napkin and said, "That timber is unlike anything I've ever seen."

"It smells … strange," Papa agreed. "The water just rolls right off of it."

"And that roof!"

She was growing rather annoyed with all this chatter. She could talk a great deal more now, but seldom did because she disliked the noise of her own childish voice, but today, she would tell them to the best of her ability.

"Talk to me!" she cried over dinner one night.

Both parents stared at their toddler in shock. "I'm sorry, darling," Papa said. "We're just so surprised by the new barn. Barns don't just spring up over naptime."

"I know!" she said. "But stop talking about it."

"Okay, okay," her mother said with a smirk. "We won't talk about it in front of you."

It only irritated her more that her mother found it amusing. She had been neglected for days over that silly barn, and instead of thanking and praising her, they laughed at her. The toddler crossed her arms and declared, "I'm never making you a barn again."

It finally dawned on them. It registered slowly across their faces and Mama dropped the spoon. Yes, it was time they understood. She was the source of the unexplainable things that happened around the property.

***

Minerva landed on the balcony to discover Aegis in the same position he'd been in half a year ago. For one of their kind, this was effectively death. The guard standing on duty left the empty bedroom and it wasn't long before Hacia came to greet her.

"Do you know how to wake him?"

Minerva shook her head. "No, once we get that way, we wake up on our own. It could be minutes. It could be centuries. Some are still sleeping to this day."

"Do you think the queen can?"

She nodded. "If anyone can, it would be her. She's still a young child. I think he will sleep until she summons him."

"How does our queen fair?" Hacia stepped into the light. From what Minerva could tell, the steward was pregnant again.

Hell had grown quite fond of Hacia. The court had been thinned over the last year as many of the socialites felt the steward did not appreciate their fineries and talents. Nowadays, the court resembled a place of the people. Souls that had something to say to the steward could bring it forward, provided they were thoroughly investigated by Alfie first.

"She's okay," Minerva said. "She has a good family. They are kind people. I can see why she chose them."

"Do they know?"

Minerva wiped her hair away from her face. "I think they do. Her father is in denial, but her mother is fully aware, and frightened."

Hacia frowned. "Do you think we need to intervene?"

Minerva honestly didn't know. She couldn't stand the idea of letting Aegis down. If something were to happen to the child, he would be devastated. At the same time, a healthy upbringing would lead to a more stable queen. Hacia emerged onto the balcony and regarded the sleeping man.

"He was heartbroken," she said. "In his heart, he wanted this new queen to be Nora."

Minerva shook her head. "This girl isn't like Nora at all. She is, well, you would have to meet her to understand."

It was difficult to explain kings and queens even on the best of days, but this girl, Freya, was nothing like her previous incarnation. She was delicate yet strong. Wise but childish. Minerva would sit and listen to her play with her dolls on the lawn, and she bounced between nurturing them and commanding them.

"She is intelligent?" Hacia asked.

Minerva nodded. "I suspect she can read. Her eyes follow words as if she can. Her name is Freya. She seldom speaks, but when she does, she uses words a child her age could not know. Her parents fear enrolling her in school, but it has finally been done."

"Let's hope she doesn't gather too much suspicion," Hacia said.

Their fears were aligned. The people of the third region could grow afraid of the child. So far, it had yet to happen, but people feared what they didn't understand. "Has there been any issue with the black souls?" Minerva asked.

Hacia shook her head. "A few of them have gotten into mischief in the sixth region, but nothing dangerous. Nothing vindictive."

"Were any placed in the third region?"

"No. Mostly the sixth."

The third region feared the prospect of hosting black souls more than any other region. They were lambs fearing that a wolf was among them. Little did they know the queen of Hell resided in a co-op singing the alphabet song. The King's Soul had unwittingly put its subjects to a test at its own expense.

"Keep a close eye on her," Hacia said. "The moment something goes wrong, intervene."

"I'm afraid his life depends on it," Minerva said, stroking Aegis's cheek.

Both women observed the prone man in agreement. He may have forgotten at one point, but now that he remembered, he could never return to that ignorance.

Aegis needed to walk alongside the King's Soul always. They would come back to each other time and time again. It surpassed the pact they'd made. It was true love.

Despite their failed relationship, Minerva was going to help him any way she could. And right now, that meant watching and waiting.

# Chapter Twenty-Seven

She had become quite accustomed to visitors. At the age of five, her awareness developed to an extent she could no longer hide. She remembered things beyond her own existence and often startled others with her knowledge. While her body was immature and lacked the muscle memory of an adult, she had always possessed literacy.

The miracles, as her parents called them, were due to the lack of control of her own mind in her infancy. Her desire to please her parents was something all children possessed. She was very much a child in some ways, but as she developed, it became clear that she was much more.

She had stopped producing miracles for her parents since after the barn incident, but her maturity continued to raise questions. Her mother feared for her. Despite the welcoming faces of the kind people in the third region, Jess was reluctant to allow her to play with other children. Her many attempts to pull her from schooling were blocked by her father, who was in denial.

"She's fine just where she is," Papa said.

Their arguments often bubbled through the thin wooden walls of the upstairs. "She needs to play, be a kid," Papa argued. "Nothing is different about her." "You know she's just like me!" Mama said. "She's different."

"She's mature for her age, and she's an only child. She needs to be with kids her own age."

"People talk about her, Mike." Mama's voice was strained. "About us. The barn. The plow."

"Let them talk," Papa said. "She's perfect, and you're a wonderful mother…"

There was mumbling that she couldn't make out, followed by

kissing and other loving noises. She tuned the rest of their activities out and turned her attention to Kitty, who was now a lean orange cat constantly on the prowl for mice. He found them in abundance in this farmhouse.

Her crib had been replaced with a bed that Papa made. It was a simple structure, but it was sturdy and safe, much like him. It was still light out when they went to bed, as most farmers did, but she could never grow accustomed to that. At night she snuck out of her bed and wandered the farm to talk with the animals. She gave old Pete a scratch behind the ears before she left. He had grown accustomed to her nightly walks and watched her go by.

On this night, she took to the perimeter of the farm and walked the tilled earth and the sapling grove her father had planted last year. The farm had flourished since she was a baby. Delilah had given birth to a second calf. There was still an abundance of room inside the barn for more. She had heard her father discussing the purchase of a cow from another farm.

The chicken coop was now stuffed with pompous little hens guarded by their rooster. Their family sold many eggs, along with the milk Delilah produced. It would be many years before the trees produced fruit, but it was a good investment. Kitty had been prowling several feet behind her, but the cat was no longer there—yet she was not alone.

A flash of white sparked in the corner of her eye. She turned, but it was gone. She could still sense it, and she knew it to be inhuman. It did not belong on her farm. She reached out her small hand and played with the air in front of her. There was a tug of something moving in the opposite direction of the wind. Grasping it in her hand, she yanked, and a woman with grey hair and white clothes fell to her knees.

The woman's red eyes were wide with fear as she bowed before her. She did not give the woman any indication that she was satisfied with her success. She was not the gloating type. "Who are you?" she demanded.

"My name is Minerva." The woman tried to get up, but she deemed it prudent to keep her where she was.

"Why do you come here, night after night?"

"You knew?"

"Sampson and Delilah told me. You've been visiting every night since they arrived."

"I was sent here to watch over you."

"By whom?"

"By Aegis, and the steward of Hell."

At the mention of Aegis, she released her grip on the woman—the inhuman woman with her unnerving red eyes and quick movements. She couldn't come during the day and risk frightening the people of the third region, the child surmised. But still, Aegis. The mention made her heart hurt and she didn't know why.

"Aegis," she echoed. "Who is he to me?"

Together, Minerva and Freya walked the farm while Minerva spoke of the immortal named Aegis. People called their kind vampires, and they were loyal only to the king or queen of Hell. Aegis was the queen's personal guardian before she passed.

Minerva's summary of recent history came as no surprise to her but was still uncomfortable to hear. It was like someone telling her about her own lingering dreams from a previous night, and it made her little tummy swell with fear. Dreams that were real yet inexplicable if someone were to ask her about them.

"Well, where is this guard? Why are you here instead?" she asked.

"He fell asleep. He won't be able to wake on his own."

The amount of information she'd been given was too much and she grew frustrated with it all. After all, she was a small child, well past her self-imposed bedtime. This woman clearly expected her to do something, and she hadn't the slightest inclination as to what that was.

The things she had made happen were accidental and years ago. She hadn't attempted those things again because of the attention they got. Freya didn't like it. Her little fists balled at the memory of her parents not hearing her crying because they were too busy looking at the barn, or the hours of conversation that didn't involve her.

Yes, she had made those things happen, but she also understood that things had a way of working out without her abilities. When Delilah got sick, her Papa nursed the cow back to health. She did not simply wish it away. They made it happen. When the floor rotted in the bathroom, it was not resolved by her whim; her neighbors came and helped Papa replace the floor.

This woman wanted her to believe she was the queen of Hell—and maybe she was—but she was still a child and was not willing to make those sacrifices yet.

She stopped walking and turned to the woman. She huffed a deep breath before saying, "Go away!"

The woman opened her mouth to protest but said nothing. She stormed away with all the anger that a child could. She returned to the house and kicked off her shoes before creeping back into the house, avoiding each creaking floorboard as she tiptoed back upstairs. Rubbing her eyes, she crawled into bed with a yawn. Kitty was already waiting for her. He purred and kneaded the blanket at her arrival. She fell into a deep, dreamless sleep.

"Darling, come downstairs, we need to talk," Papa called the next morning.

"Come on, Kitty," Freya said to the cat as she rose to go to her father. The cat stretched along the bed with no intention of moving. She scowled at him. "Fine, but I won't give you any meat from my sandwich."

The little girl climbed down the steps, suspecting nothing. He came in the same time every day to eat and chat with her. As she came down the steps, it occurred to her that she had gotten into trouble. Her mother wore that expression only when something was very wrong—and her father's expression mirrored her mother's.

"What is it, Papa?"

"Sit down, Freya," Mama said.

She did as she was told, not wanting to anger them further.

"Darling, you were walking around outside last night," Papa said.

Her eyes went wide as she suddenly remembered last night's encounter. "I forgot. I thought it was a dream."

Neither parent appeared pacified by her statement, Papa continued his interrogation. "Who walked with you last night?"

Her feet did not reach the floor when she sat at the table. Her legs swung casually as she told her parents about the woman she'd met the previous night. She spared no detail of the encounter—of who the woman claimed to be and why she had come. At some point, she stopped talking because her parents had turned an unusual shade of green. She did not want them to worry but at the same time, it was wrong to lie.

"But you don't need to worry because I told the woman to go away," she concluded.

Her parents were speechless when she finished. With a child's perception, she struggled to grasp the enormity of what had happened the night before. She was too sleepy and irritable to consider it, but her parent's minds were swimming with it. She possessed the King's Soul and had bent a vampire to her will last night. That was all.

She did not know what a vampire was, but she supposed they were lonely creatures that lived in the woods when they were not doing the king's bidding. When they were sad, like Aegis, they slept. As for her being queen, she didn't understand why so much had to change. She was already a queen in her mind. It only meant that at some point in her life, everyone else would see it too.

It was her mother who finally spoke, "Well," she said with a level of calm. "This explains a lot."

Her father said the only thing a father could say in a predicament like this. "Well, this doesn't change anything. You don't get out of bed and wander around at night. There could be coyotes out there who would drag you off and eat you!"

Her mother choked on her own laughter, but when it was clear Papa was serious, she stopped. "A vampire couldn't touch her, Mike. What could a coyote do?"

Papa was at a loss for words, and Mama was teetering on the edge of a nervous breakdown. This information was something that would take time for all three of them to understand. He glowered at Mama and his eyes lit with anger.

"She's a child, Jess, our child. She's also the future queen of Hell!" he bellowed.

"Don't yell at her, Papa."

"Sorry." He softened immediately and turned his gaze back to Mama. "I'm sorry, Jess. I don't mean to get upset, but you heard what happened to the last one. I'm not ready to let my baby girl go live a life like that."

Mama nodded and stifled the tears before her face grew calm once more. "Here's what we need to do. Freya, I know you already know this, but no more miracles. We can't risk anyone discovering you. We need you to act like a little girl as much as possible. No more big words, no more outsmarting the parents at the co-op."

She was playing with her hands under the table. She disliked sitting still for so long. Papa nodded in agreement with Mama. "We need to keep this a secret, okay?"

"What happens if people find out?" she asked.

"Sweetie, I don't want to scare you, but if you are found out, they take you to the castle and you'll be forced to do grown up stuff."

That was exactly what she feared. There was far too much fun to be had, she wasn't going anywhere just yet. She nodded and agreed. "I don't want to do that. Not yet, at least."

***

Minerva didn't go back to the palace. Hacia would be desperate for an update, but she couldn't admit defeat. Her cover was blown and the child had practically banished her from her sight. What would Aegis say if he found out? He would probably laugh if he would ever wake the bloody Hell up.

She pouted in a ginormous tree a few feet from the beginning of the third region. Minerva was too far away from the farmhouse to pick out any scent or hear anything, but the child could call her if she wished, she supposed. The girl was strong, even at such a young age. Minerva cringed at being brought so low, even before a queen.

There was no point going back to the farm, She was certain the child would kill her. No point going back empty-handed to Hacia. Aegis would've told her to remain where she was and wait, but she was not one for stillness. She'd rather let Aegis sleep through several queens than wait for even a few days.

She wrapped her scarf over her hair, creating a low hood, and sought out the nearest town square. It was a way from the Starry Wood, even further from the farmhouse. It must have taken Freya's father hours to walk back and forth whenever he bought supplies.

The city was lined with lit lanterns and wooden stores. Each had its own stencil-painted sign. Minerva noted some were in better condition than others. The ones on the edges of the town were worn and a little deteriorated, whereas the ones in the center of the town was freshly polished and maintained.

It was evening, and most of the shops were closed. She followed the remaining bit of commotion and found herself outside a tavern. The smell was the first thing to hit her. The astringent smell of alcohol mingled with the scent of bodies.

Beside the tavern, another establishment was awake. It was a heavily decorated house with many rooms. Most of the windows had the blinds closed. The few that didn't had scantily clad women leaning out the windows.

One woman with cascades of brown ringlets waved to her. "Howdy, stranger. Looking for some company?" the woman asked.

"Perhaps," she said.

The woman smiled. "You just wait right there."

The front door opened a few minutes later, and the woman with long brown curls came out. She was quite attractive. She was young with blue eyes and a slightly upturned nose.

"My name is Gracie."

"Minerva."

"Come on in." She took Minerva's hand and pulled her into the house. Instantly, Minerva's eyes were assaulted with pink. Everything was pink. The floor was laden with pink rugs and the multitude of sofas were pink—pink wallpaper, pink lampshades with little pink fringes—everything.

She supposed this was a good thing. The house was dimly lit, which made her eyes less noticeable—not that anyone was interested in looking at her eyes. Everyone here wished to remain a stranger, her included.

"It's lovely," Minerva stammered.

Gracie laughed. "It's tacky, I know. The madame loves the color. Don't worry, my room is a little less bright."

Together they went up the stairs to Gracie's bedroom. The room had a dark floor with a blue, ornately designed rug. The woman's room was indeed easier on the eyes. Her bedding matched the blue of the carpet, as did her curtains. The rest of her belongings were a cream color.

"Take a seat, make yourself comfortable," Gracie said.

She sat at the small table to the side of the open window, and she listened to the conversations at the bar. Gracie was in her washroom. She said nothing, and that was how Minerva preferred it. In the bar she heard mostly drunken laughs and conversations, but nothing particularly relevant.

After some time, Gracie returned to the room. "You're just going to sit there all night?" she asked with a smile.

She tossed the prostitute a solid gold coin. "I'm not here for your services, just for information and your silence."

The girl snatched up the coin and sat on the bed to play with it. That gold coin was more than she probably made in a year. Minerva had a pocket full of them. She would gladly hand them to the girl if it meant she could glean information from that window.

In the tavern next door, old men were talking. It took some time before she picked out a relevant conversation.

"You better make up with her, Tavers, otherwise you'll never meet your grandbaby," a man said.

"Lorraine wants to see the child. She still hasn't forgiven me for that," the man known as Tavers said.

"We know," another chided. "You wouldn't be here with us otherwise."

"We all know about how stubborn old Tavers can be."

This was all well and good, but Minerva hoped for news outside the region. She sat and waited, seeding out the talk of harvests and livestock. Finally, when most of the voices went quiet, a man voiced up. "A hawk hunter was talking about the outlands the other day. Evidently, they're mobilizing."

"What?" Tavers said.

Minerva leaned toward the window. She feared this would come sooner or later. With a steward on the throne, it was only a matter of time until trouble started again. With Aegis asleep, and the queen being just a child, this was not a good time for war.

"I didn't get all of it. Those hawks have their own lingo, but it sounds like the outlanders are banding together, trying to escape the seventh region."

Mutters went around the room before everyone went silent. "Well, they won't get past those snobbish, soft-handed folks in the fourth region!" a man said. Roars of laughter went around the room.

A chill washed over her. There had been word that Vinicio was alive. Had he rallied the outlanders in revolt? There had been discussions on what to do about him. *What a stupid time to fall asleep, Aegis.* She would need to go to the seventh region and learn for herself.

Minerva jumped out the window and ran until the little city's lanterns were flickering in the distant horizon.

# Chapter Twenty-Eight

Freya woke and came down the stairs to the scent of fresh coffee and eggs. She was wearing her favorite yellow nightgown and wanted Papa to spin her around in it so she could pretend she was wearing a ballgown. Her parent's quiet yet urgent conversation made her forget all about ball gowns and dancing.

"It's up to you, Jess," Papa said. "They were always kind to me until—"

"Until my father forbade us from being together," Mama said.

Papa shrugged. His large hands nearly swallowed his coffee mug. "He was worried about his daughter. I can relate."

"It's been nearly six years, Mike. You don't miss out on your child and grandchild's life over a little worry. He's not doing it for Freya or for me. He's only trying to mend fences because Mama's finally had enough of his bullshit."

Papa's brows raised with delight and surprise. "She kicked him out?"

"Not quite …" Mama hesitated to tell him, but it only piqued his interest.

"Then what?"

"She moved out."

The wheels in Papa's mind turned as he stared at Mama, but before she could say anything, the front door opened and a woman who resembled Mama, only older and surer of herself, came bustling in wearing a pretty red dress. Mama smiled at Papa pleadingly, and Papa rolled with the punches.

"Lorraine! Welcome to our house," he said, standing to greet her.

"Michael!" The woman embraced him in a hug. "Thank you for

letting me stay. I promise I will be a guest and not the mother hen." The woman handed Papa her suitcase and hugged Mama. "I'm sorry it took me so long," she whispered in Mama's ear.

Mama winced. "It's hard to walk away, I know."

The woman spotted Freya standing in the stairway. It was silly to be afraid, but the butterflies in her tummy fluttered all the same. The woman smiled warmly at her. "This must be little Freya."

The woman kneeled, and Mama gave her an approving nod as she struggled to keep the tears at bay. Freya stepped forward and the woman took her hands. "Do you know who I am?"

"I suppose you are my grandmother."

The woman smiled, and tears streamed down her face. "Such an eloquent little lady!"

She smiled at the woman and decided she liked her very much. Papa set Grandmother's belongings in a room upstairs that was reserved for guests. It was a room she wasn't permitted to enter usually because it was to be kept clean for events such as this.

The door was opened, and she followed the adults into the bedroom where Grandmother would be staying. "Well, it needs a few homey touches. But first, I want to spend time with my granddaughter."

In the coming days, her parents were able to finish several things Papa had been meaning to do but didn't have the time, thanks to the extra set of hands. Grandmother and Freya baked cookies together, which was more fun than it was with Mama for some reason.

"You're rather good at this!" Grandmother exclaimed. Freya beamed with pride.

"Looks like we need a tablespoon of vanilla."

Freya handed her the tablespoon. Her grandmother eyed the spoon with curiosity, but took it and measured the liquid. "Three cups of flour …"

Grandmother smiled, reached for a quarter cup, and attempted to use the small scoop when the full cup was right beside her. "The one cup, Grandma, it's right there."

Her grandmother looked at her and asked, "Does your Mama bake with you often?"

"Sometimes, but I've never made these cookies before."

"That's because it's one of my very own recipes."

The ratio of baking soda was a little off, but Freya only smiled politely in response.

Grandmother made roasted chicken with greens and rolls. She helped by setting the table. When her parents came in, her mother was wearing big boots and overalls. Dirt was smudged on her face, and her hair was pulled into a bun. She wore gloves, and with her short sleeve shirt, she was rather formidable in her work wear.

Her parents washed up before sitting down. "Did you set the table?" Mama asked.

Freya nodded, and her mother gave a nod of approval.

Grandmother brought the food to the table before sitting herself. "Freya also helped me make my famous chocolate chip cookies. I must say she is quite capable for a small child. That must be some co-op."

Her parents exchanged a worried glance as if they were two mischievous children hiding a secret from their mother. Grandmother saw it but let it go in the way that only adults could. The sentiment lingered in the room, and she began to worry. Her childish mask had failed, and it was only a matter of time until Grandmother also knew the secret.

Mama and Papa still put her to bed every night. It was a sacred ritual that even Grandmother would not intrude upon. They no longer stayed in her room until she fell asleep, like when she was a toddler, but one would usually read while the other brushed her hair, got her dressed, and tucked her into bed.

"I won't be able to stay a secret for much longer."

"Freya—" her mother started.

"You know it to be true," she said. Kitty curled up beside her. "You can have other children now if you want."

"Siblings are not your replacement, Freya," her father said.

"I know, but it's because of me you've not conceived more, so I am undoing that miracle, if you can call it that."

Her parents both frowned. "You're still our baby, no matter who you are."

"Even if I were a black soul?"

Her mother's throat bobbed, but she nodded. "Even if you were evil. I'd still love you."

Freya wiggled her toes under the rough fabric of her handsewn blankets. "That's why I did it, you know. That's why I decreed that black souls are not to be born into the outlands. I wanted every child to be loved."

Papa's head fell into his large hands as he took in what his daughter had said. She had to prepare them for what was to come. They would need to let go of her far sooner than they planned. She would still be their daughter, but she would also be queen.

She fell asleep with her parents still in the room. She wouldn't be bothered by her future as a queen just yet. After all, her sixth birthday was fast approaching. Hell could wait just a little while longer, she hoped.

***

Minerva checked the balcony once more, hoping that Aegis would be awake. There was no such luck. He remained on the stone railing unmoved, like some handsome statue. His skin had developed a film of moisture from the early morning dew, but he was otherwise unchanged.

"Oh, Aegis," she said, sighing.

Steps scurried down the hall—no doubt a tracker gone to report to Hacia of her movements. She had rather hoped not to have this conversation, but with the rumors in the third region swirling, she needed answers.

It wasn't long until Hacia came into the room. She was groggy and trying to compose herself from what must have been a heavy sleep. She had birthed her second child, for her breasts were swollen and her stomach soft but smaller. "Minerva," she said hoarsely.

"Steward," she greeted.

She told the steward about everything that had happened. Hacia sat on the balcony beside Aegis and listened with heavy lids. She was worried that the steward would call her a failure, that she had left her post and broken a promise.

"You did well to leave," Hacia said at last.

Minerva frowned. "What?"

"She wants to be a child. Let her be one for as long as she can."

She had never been a child, so she supposed it was something she could never understand. "What of Vinicio?"

Hacia sighed. "He knows a steward sits on the throne. He also knows that the King's Soul is still alive and well. The borders have only increased and strengthened, especially the seventh region. Lava flows in the canyon that separates us from the horrors they wish to bring to our lands."

"Can he escape?" she asked.

Hacia deliberated for a moment, or maybe she fell asleep, but she finally answered, "If they found a way, even the combined efforts of our military would be hard pressed."

"Do you think Vinicio will find a way?"

Hacia regarded her darkly. "If anyone could find a way, it would be him."

Minerva flew from the castle balcony and landed solidly on the ground. She went west until she crossed the river moat that separated the castle from the soft green grass of the first region. She thought about what Hacia had told her. About how Vinicio had been testing the bridges and the depths of the canyon that separated the seventh region from the rest of Hell.

Hacia had trackers and hawk hunters on patrol. Quiet, discreet patrols designed not to frighten the populace. The sixth region souls disliked policing, so the military presence went incognito mostly. If a coordinated assault was made there, it would be nearly impossible to assemble a counterattack. Still, the sixth region had an absurdly large wall around its major city. The citizens would feel safe for the most part. Vinicio's goal would not be the city, but for the palace itself.

Dense forest air hit Minerva, and she inhaled deeply and closed her eyes for a moment. How she missed her home. She belonged here with the beasts and the rain, not in a palace, not among the souls.

Climbing the trees, she burst from the canopy and into the sky. Morning sun hit her full on and it was blinding. She wore a slight smile before falling back into the understory and onward.

The fourth region was another matter. With little to no defense, they relied entirely on hawk hunters and the trackers. It was a poor area to defend strategically. Vinicio knew this as well as Hacia. She had most of the patrols just outside the fourth region, observing movements from a distance.

It was midafternoon when she approached the dusted lands several miles away from the woods. She stepped softly, feeling as though she was being watched. Two rail lines connected the seventh region to the mainland. Beneath the rails was a canyon that deepened by the day thanks to the return of the King's Soul. She inhaled the sulfur and brimstone rising from below. Lava was indeed pooling at the bottom. When she investigated the canyon, she saw nothing but darkness. She couldn't see it, but she could feel the heat against her face.

The railing was unguarded, and she found that to be deeply troubling. She supposed the ferryman had to take breaks just like any other soul. It was hot out here. She couldn't imagine a soul surviving, standing beside the cart, waiting for no one to cross into the seventh region.

"You want to cross?" a young voice asked.

Minerva spun around to find a young black boy near the age of Freya. He had short, black hair and wore dark pants and a cotton shirt, and he wasn't the least bit alarmed by her.

"Do you know what I am?" she asked.

"Do you wish to cross?"

Minerva hesitated. She didn't know what she would do if she did cross. Would she kill Vinicio and do them all a favor just as Aegis once intended to do? What would she have to gain by that? She was immortal, but not indestructible. A crazed mob of souls could overwhelm her. A bomb could blow her up. The makeshift weapons they had in the seventh region could damage her greatly.

There had to be a line. Yes, she loved Aegis and wanted to help him, but he'd left her for duty as well as another woman. It was for the good of all Hell, but what did she owe to these souls? Her involvement was for Aegis, and while this was an extension of her promise to him, there had to be a line.

"Do you wish to cross?"

She shook her head. "No. No, I do not wish to cross."

The boy was gone, but she didn't bother to look for him. She had questions, and he couldn't answer them even if he wanted to. There was a reason he was the ferryman of this gate.

Instead, she walked along the ridge of the canyon and tried to peer into the seventh region. She walked for most of the day. Between the mirage and the dust blown in the distance, there was nothing to see but a blurred, tan distance that appeared to move in waves. More than once she saw figures standing on the other side of the canyon. Before she could focus better, they dissolved before her eyes like hallucinations.

It was on the second day that she became certain that outlanders were indeed standing guard on the other side. Frustrated by the inability to use her sense of smell to confirm it, she squinted all the harder at the distant figures who would vanish once more into the sea of sands. They were watching her.

On the third day, at the same time of day as she'd found herself encountering the first railway, she stood before the second rails. The ferryman of this track was an old black man in the same clothes as the child, only his were torn and ragged. His hair was cut the same way, but it was white, and he was balding.

He sat on a wooden stool and did not look at her when he said, "Do you wish to cross?"

"No," she replied and walked on.

His white, cataract-clouded eyes followed her as she walked along the canyon. While she would not cross into those dangerous lands, she would patrol the border herself and wait. If the outlanders made their move, she would be able to move the fastest to alert the military.

She pondered if anyone was aware that a ghost guarded the rails to the seventh region. Perhaps they knew at some point. Then again, maybe they just didn't care. Souls were funny that way. They craved the unusual but were blind to it when it stood before their very eyes.

***

It was Freya's sixth birthday when another family member entered her life. Grandma had lived with them for over a month now, and she had become a staple within the household. Grandma cooked the meals and tended to Freya, allowing her daughter and son-in-law to work on the farm.

The summer season was at a full roar. Her birthday fell at the end of the season, which made planning her birthday a difficult time. They usually didn't celebrate until the middle of the fall season, but with Grandma there to help, her party would be celebrated on the day of her birth.

Her entire co-op was invited to the party, and everyone intended to come—mostly to gander at the mysterious barn that had suddenly replaced the old one several years ago. It was as if visitors assumed something else would simply appear and if they lingered long enough, they would get a chance to witness it.

Her mother and grandmother bickered over the cake they wanted to make while she and Kitty escaped the house and ventured onto the farm. They stopped by the young cow and the calf. Sampson gave them a nod with his horned head before lumbering off. Delilah, ever undisturbed, paid them no mind even when Kitty brushed against her front hoof.

"Hey, darling," Papa said from outside the barn. "You come to get away from the baking?"

"They're still at it," she said, folding her arms tightly around her chest.

Papa kneeled and took her hands in his. "Aw, honey, they just want it to be a good day."

The skin between his brows ridged out when he squinted or frowned. It was from all the days he spent in the sun. She desperately wanted him to come with her when she became queen, but he belonged here.

"I love you, Papa."

"I love you too, darling," Papa said as he stood. "You want to check out the groves with me?"

"Yeah."

She wandered the fields with her father until the house bell rang, summoning her for a bath to get ready for her birthday party. Mama was waiting on the porch. After her bath, she was dressed in a frilly yellow dress.

She examined herself in the mirror. Mama loved the dress

enough to get teary-eyed, but she wasn't as taken with the frock. It was rather impractical. It stuck out in every direction and had far too many bows and white gatherings. There would be no playing in this dress. Mama was so happy, so she sighed and put on a smile. It was her party, after all.

So many people had come, and the yard was decorated with bright colored paper streamers Grandma bought from town. She played a game where she pinned a tail on a cow, which she could easily have won but refused to use her abilities for such things. The principle of the thing was to win fairly, and she did. Everyone screamed and cheered as her pin, with a yarned tail attached to it, was pinned on the canvas painting of a cow's behind.

They played race and tag, during which she took every opportunity to dirty the tacky yellow dress. She was not as agile as the other kids. She was also not particularly fast. But she had so much fun that she lost all track of time.

Soon it was time to blow out the candles on a cake with chocolate frosting. Mama and Grandma had finally come to terms with what kind of cake to make. She had no idea what it was, but it was most delicious.

"It's so good!" she said, thanking them.

"My recipe," Grandma agreed with a proud nod.

Mama rolled her eyes and laughed, allowing her mother the glory of the cake. She opened the biggest gift set before her. It was a toy box Papa made. He'd painted a red rose on the top of the lid. It was so beautiful.

"Papa, why is there a gap here?" she asked, sticking her fingers into the space between the lid and the box.

"Just in case you climb in and get stuck."

She gave him a weird smile. "I know better than that!"

The crowd laughed. Sitting along the picnic bench, she spotted Mama. She was all pale and was clutching her stomach. Before she could say anything, a second gift was pushed at her. It was a little soft paper box. When she opened it, something soft was inside. She moved the parchment paper aside and found a new nightgown. It was blue with white dots. The quality of the material was so soft. People gathered around and smoothed their hands over the fabric and gave little gasps. She took the gown out and held it up for everyone to behold. "Thank you, Grandma!"

But Grandma's eyes were now on Mama, who was leaning against the tree beside the picnic table. Someone was fanning her with their newspaper.

"She needs some air," a woman called.

"Honey?" Papa waded through the crowd around the table. Just as he reached her, Mama turned and vomited on the grass beside the tree. Grandma went running into the house. Freya dropped her expensive nightgown and ran screaming to her mama. Someone pulled a chair out, and Papa helped Mama sit down.

"Oh, I feel better now. I'm so sorry …" Mama began to apologize.

She clung to her mother's side in a panic. Grandma returned with a cup of water and a rag. Something terrible was happening to Mama. It had been years since she last made a miracle happen, but she closed her eyes and whispered, "Make her well," repeatedly.

Reassuring hands wrapped around Freya. "Hey, baby, it's okay. I'm okay."

Freya stopped chanting and opened her eyes. "You're sick," she said.

Mama smiled. "No, honey, I have morning sickness."

"But it's afternoon." Freya said. Why would she only be sick in the morning? She shouldn't be sick at all. The crowd began to sigh and laugh.

Papa turned her around to face him. "That means you're going to have a little brother or sister."

There was a strange smell then, like warm metal. Papa's mouth dropped and his eyes welled with tears. She turned back around to find Mama standing with a pool of blood between her feet. She'd wished for Mama not to be sick anymore. It was the baby that was making her sick.

"I didn't know!" she cried.

Everyone stared at her with confusion. She was surrounded by tall people staring down at her. She had murdered her sibling. "I wanted you to be better. I didn't know it was a baby that was making you sick."

Mama started to speak, but the crowd was already murmuring. Mothers were pulling their children close and staring at her as if she were some sort of monster. She shook her head and tried to explain. "I didn't mean to kill the baby, I didn't know."

Papa's eyes met Mama's, and a fierce look took over. He picked her up and said, "Party's over," in a rough voice before rushing her into the house. He set her down inside and went back out to help Grandma with Mama. She couldn't stop crying. Her parents would hate her forever for this.

"I'm sorry," she shrieked. "I'm sorry I killed the baby."

Grandma bustled Mama in and took her to the bathroom. Papa stood before her and she couldn't bear to look at him. She stared at his large, scuffed boots and sobbed. Maybe it would be better for everyone if she went away, but she didn't want to leave!

Papa kneeled and wrapped his arms around her, blanketing her in warmth and safety. "Hey, darling, it's all right. *Shh.*"

"You don't hate me?" she asked between wheezes.

"How could I ever hate you?"

"I killed the baby!" she wailed. "I just wanted Mama to not be sick. I didn't know—"

"It's not your fault, darling," he said, kissing her on the top of her head. "These things just happen."

There was a squeak from the door. Muffled voices carried through the uneven doorframe. She was frightened now. Why wouldn't they go home? "Papa, people are still here. They're listening."

Papa was afraid. He took quick breaths and stared at the door as if it were about to be broken down. "Freya, see to your mother."

She went to the bathroom to find her mother in the tub. Blood trailed from between her legs and into the drain. Her mother was pale, though smiling. But it was just a brave face for her, like the kind Freya made when she went to the doctor's.

"Mama," she whispered, "I ruined everything."

Her mother shook her head. "No, never. This sort of thing just happens. I never told you about how Papa and I married."

She sat by the tub and waited for the story.

"My parents own one of the biggest farms in the region. They have several dozen farmhands working the land all three seasons. My father is a strong-willed man, an ambitious man. He wanted me to marry into the family of another landholder. What he didn't know was that I was deeply in love with your father.

"I think my mother had an idea, but my father found us together one night and demanded that I break things off with your papa. He said I had no future with your father, that he couldn't take care of me in the fashion I was accustomed to living. He was right, of course, but what he didn't know was that I was already pregnant with a baby."

"Me?" she asked.

Mama rested her head against the lining of the tub. "No honey, not you. When I told Mike—Papa, that I was pregnant, he insisted that we get married and run away together. I loved the idea. We claimed union and ran off together. Papa and I both worked as farmhands at other people's farms. It wasn't long after that that I lost the baby.

"Doctor said it just happens sometimes. If it happened once, it's more likely to happen again. This may not have had anything to do with you. You only wished to make me well. It was just bad timing is all."

She silently disagreed. While she didn't understand her powers enough to know either way, deep down, she knew it was her fault. What was worse, gossip would spread about her like wildfire.

Papa's voice boomed from the other room, but she couldn't make out what he was saying, only that his patience was wearing thin. She was in danger, and she was putting her parents and Grandma in danger as well.

# Chapter Twenty-Nine

A clanking noise echoed along the canyon. Minerva assumed it to be a falling rock at first, but the noise happened again and again. Her sensitive ears told her it came from the northern railway, closer to the sixth region. She sped to the railway and found the boy looking out at the mirage the heat produced.

"Do you wish to cross?"

The ferryman didn't notice anything amiss, but she caught a whiff of sweat, blood, and infected flesh. A slight click came from under the cart, and the cart pulled away, exposing a vile man with wild eyes and rotted teeth hanging onto the rails from underneath. He grinned at her as the cart was pulled to the outlands.

She stomped on his hands, and the beast let go. He fell some way before jerking into suspension. The clever beast had tied himself to the rails with a bit of rope and now dangled just out of reach. She could either walk onto the railway to sever the rope, or she could run and alert the nearest hawk hunter to send word.

If Aegis were here, she would urge him to run and alert the others, but he was not. Wisdom only came to those in parting, not in the moment of action. If she held them off, stopped the onslaught at the source, perhaps the outlanders would lose their faith in Vinicio and his scheme would fall apart.

Agile and quick as a cat, she ran across the tracks to the spot where the man was dangling. Through the gaps in the rails, she spotted him and shook her head. "You should have known that your mission would only have one outcome."

Another noise in the distance made her jerk up. Metal screamed in protest as the cart was pulled off the rails. She froze, and a painful understanding came to her. They had no intention of crossing at this railway. They only wanted the cart. They wanted to trick her.

The man was laughing with unadulterated hatred for her—for everything. His insane eyes bulged as his fingers with their broken nails toyed with something in his hand.

She didn't wait to learn what the device did. She ran, cursing herself along the way for her rashness. A booming noise, followed by a wave of heat and debris, blasted behind her. The railway fell away. She was no longer running across the rails, but upward.

The edge of the canyon was within range. She leaped away from the falling railway to the ridge. Her hand landed on the cliff edge and into a sticky black tar. There was a box stuck to that Vinicio was indeed a force to be reckoned with. As the blast blew her back into the canyon, Minerva closed her eyes and accepted the loss.

It's all up to the queen now.

***

The next morning, Papa found a notice on their door. There was to be a town meeting and her family was expected to come. It was noted that if they did not attend, the meeting would be brought to them. Papa seethed at the threat. He ranted about it sporadically throughout the day.

"This isn't the fifth region," he grumped. "We don't persecute folk for being different."

"They only heard half the conversation," she reminded him. "They are scared. They have a right to be."

Papa bent low and shook his head. "No one needs to be afraid of you."

Mama had rested the whole night and into the day. She insisted that she was fine, but Papa and Grandma would push her back to bed. "It was an early miscarriage," she would argue. "A little more than a period."

"We talked about this," Papa stonewalled. "If you want to come with us to the town meeting, you need to rest until then."

Freya still struggled with it. Despite the constant assurance from her family, closure eluded her. Could using her powers to make someone feel better actually do harm? She had not wished for the sickness to cease to exist, but only for her mother's symptoms to stop. Then again, she had not been that specific. She was too young to comprehend the magnitude of all of this. She didn't want it!

The night after the party, when she lay in bed, she reached out to the ceiling and let gravity work against her arms. Her outstretched fingers tangled with a silk ribbon she could not see. The palm of her hand pulsed as she grasped the ribbon, not knowing what it was. She gave it a slight tug, but the ribbon did not give. Her hands fell through the ribbon and collapsed on the bed. Perhaps she had imagined it, but for a moment, it felt as though someone were on the other end of that ribbon, waiting for her.

They had spent the day in quiet anxiety. Papa's outrage was not quelled but he kept it to himself as much as possible for the sake of everyone else. Grandma said nothing about it. She took up cleaning the house in a desperate manner. Thinking her aware, Grandma and Papa made quiet exchanges.

The tension in the house was overwhelming. She found solace with the person she least expected—her mother. Kitty had spent the whole day snuggling with her mother in bed, taking advantage of the warm bed as a prime sleeping space. She suspected the cat was trying to comfort Mama, but cats would never admit to such things.

"They making you nervous?" Mama asked.

She nodded and sucked the tears back the best she could.

"Aww, come here."

She crawled into bed with her mama and they talked about little things. About Kitty's toes and funny stories about when she was a baby. About how much they loved her and what a blessing she was to them. It was as though Mama was trying to say goodbye, and she didn't like it.

Papa came into the room and said, "It's time."

They went downstairs together, Mama swatting at Papa's helping hands. "I'm fine, Mike."

In that instant, fear gripped her throat and she spun around and clung to her Papa. He picked her up and held her—and Mama held her, too. "I can't promise that nothing bad will ever happen to you. That's just life, but what I can promise you is that no one will hurt you here."

Mama nodded. "We won't let anything happen to you."

"Where's Grandma?"

"She went on ahead to get a coach so Mama wouldn't need to walk," Papa said. "She's outside waiting for us."

Her anxiety was momentarily abated by the promise of a coach. She had never ridden in one before. Many people rode horses or wagons, but a coach was something fancy.

The family went outside and were assisted into a wooden vehicle with red velvet interior. It was shabbier than she'd imagined. The velvet was worn and musty, and there were no trimmings or anything ornate about the coach. It appeared more like a new wagon.

Still, she got in and sat with her arms wrapped around her mother. Her father shifted around uncomfortably. It was too small for a man his size. He was forced to crane his neck slightly, and he had to be mindful of his long legs knocking into Mama. He was awkward when he was nervous, and he did not belong in that cramped space.

The ride was also more uncomfortable than she anticipated. She and her parents were bumped over every rock and pothole along the road to the point of nausea. Papa was focusing on a point outside as if it were the only thing that mattered in life. Mama struggled to keep from reacting, but she swallowed frequently and would look up as if she were trying to keep from vomiting.

As the roads became more worn and consistent, the ride did become smoother. They were approaching the town now. She never ceased to be amazed by it. It was the smallest town in the third region, but to her, it was a sprawling city. Buildings several houses tall were all lined up with light posts. People walked along the wooden sidewalks quickly as if they all had something important to do.

The coach lurched to a stop as the pale blue of night blanketed the sky. The door was opened, and Papa got out first to help the women out. He gave the coachman a knowing nod and they approached a building. It was a big brick house with big windows that had curtains. It was the nicest house she had ever seen.

"Does someone rich live here?" she asked.

"It's the town hall," her mother explained. "It's where decisions are made officially."

It had stone steps and lanterns along the steps to the front doors. There were pillars along the front of the house. Inside the place it appeared more like an office. There was a small desk off to the side where a woman with blonde hair was writing. She stopped what she was doing to consider the family before her. She supposed people didn't live here after all.

"Everyone is waiting in there," she said, using her pencil to point toward a second set of double doors.

The woman stood up and followed behind them as if she were making sure they went in. She didn't hear the doors shut behind them because she was so frightened by the whole town staring at her. Everyone she knew was standing in pews before a small platform where two men and two women stood.

She recognized three of them as the barber, the general store owner, the farm supplier, but she didn't know the short woman with brown hair cut just below her ears. She wanted to know who the woman was but was too intimidated to speak. She wished she had gone potty before they came in.

Her parents led her to the platform, and the barber smiled thinly. "Thanks for coming. You can all just have a seat right here," he said, pointing to a bench just off the side of the stage.

"Now," the store owner began. "We're all aware of the decree the late queen put into law before her passing. She put our communities in danger by allowing black souls to be born into our families. I don't fault any parent for trying to protect and care for their child, but we must decide what's best for our community, law or no law."

"She's not a black soul!" Papa interjected.

What was a black soul? Her head whirled around the room with confusion. The four town leaders turned to Papa with pity. "We heard everything she said in the house. I heard it with my own ears," the farm supplier said.

"Did you also hear how frightened and upset her was that her mother was sick? I wouldn't think a black soul would be so worried about the welfare of others."

At this, the farm supplier was taken back they shook their heads and muttered under their breaths. The woman with the short brown hair spoke. "Black souls are evil, but they also do not have the ability to make a woman lose her baby."

She didn't like the way Papa was pleading to them. It made her tummy hurt and she sucked in the tears. Was she evil? She didn't mean to be. It was an accident!

The crowd murmured, and someone shouted, "What about the barn?"

"What indeed?" Papa asked. "Black souls don't come with barns, plows, and cattle."

"Can you explain all this to us, Mike?" the general store owner asked.

Papa was at a loss for words. If she'd given him the word, he would have torn the whole place down for her. He was so strong, her Papa. She swallowed. It was time to tell everyone what she was.

She gave him a reassuring nod before standing up. Her feet went clumsy as she moved to the center of the stage. The town leaders flanked her, and the room went quiet as everyone waited for what she was about to say.

"I don't know if I am responsible for what happened to Mama or not," she started. Her tiny voice echoed around the room. "When I saw Mama sick, I wished for her to be better. I didn't know her sickness was a sign of pregnancy."

The faces stared back at her in pity as big wet tears fell down her warping expression. "I didn't mean for anything bad to happen to anyone, I swear. I didn't know."

Papa stood up to come to his daughter's aid but was stopped by the barber and the store owner. She stepped under the light and took a deep breath before saying it. "I am not a *black* soul, I am *the* soul. I am the queen of Hell."

In that moment, the invisible silk tie she'd gripped the other night was there, slipping through her hand. This time she grabbed hold of it and pulled hard. Her destiny was no longer her parents' but her own. The crowd gasped and people began to argue. They did not know whether to believe her or not.

People were standing and slowly approaching her now. The town leaders moved in front of her as if to protect her from the crowd. She turned back to look at her parents who were waving at Grandma and an older man at the emergency exit.

No individual had the intent of harming her, but as a group, people often acted irrational, and it could be dangerous for her and her parents. Papa pushed past the leaders and picked her up. "Any of those miracles up your sleeve, darling?"

"No more miracles," she said firmly.

"Oh, yeah?" Papa asked nervously as he made his way to the emergency exit. "Well, it's okay to change our minds ..."

She had been raised in an environment where people worked to make things happen with their sweat and blood. For her father to suggest she wish something to be otherwise was laughable. She trusted in her parents. The way Grandma was poised at the door suggested that they had a plan should things go wrong.

People were shouting demands at her now. They wanted their illnesses cured, their crops to be free from bugs, and other such wishes. Desperate faces were frightening faces as they allowed their needs and wants to contort their sense of self. Yes, Freya confirmed, miracles were a frightening thing indeed.

Papa backed out the door as the town leaders blocked the crowd and into the coach they went. A hard knock of Papa's fist on the outside of the vehicle told the driver they were ready. The horses pulled hard and they sped away from the frenzied crowd.

"Where do we take her?" the older man beside Grandma asked.

"The castle," Papa said. "She will be safe there."

***

The world came crashing back to Aegis. Pulled from his sleep and back to Hell. His scar pulsed as his eyes shot open. He was being summoned.

He bolted upright and stood on the balcony railing. Closing his eyes, he let the scar guide him. It was her heartbeat and his scar would guide him to her. Footsteps quickened behind him. The stationed guard would alert Hacia of his movements. He would not be alone if his queen needed aid.

He went south. The ground trembled beneath his steps, and the animals of the forest hid from the coming storm. She called for him. His queen had returned. He found himself wondering what she would be like. What would she want him to do? How would she rule? Nora was not forgotten, but at the prospect of the new queen, he was finally able to let go of the past.

Emerging from the forest, he found the third region in a strange state. The farmers who usually went to bed before the sunset were up and patrolling the roads with torches. They were in groups of three and four and stood waiting for something.

He wasn't about to wait to find out. It either had something to do with the queen or the foul smell rolling in from the west. Either way, it was time to get to work.

***

Freya stared at the old man that sat across from her for several minutes before the question burst from her. Who was this man, and why was he here? Everyone seemed to know who he was but her. She was annoyed with his presence at what was a rather frightening moment in her young life. "Who are you?" she asked coldly with her arms crossed.

The fear and ill-ease of the town hall meeting was broken. Giggles turned into full-on rolling laughter. She didn't get what was so funny. Her little nose scrunched as she glared at her mama with displeasure.

"I'm sorry, sweetie," Mama said. "This is your grandfather, Doug Tavers."

"May I shake your hand?" he asked, extending his hand across the aisle. He didn't look mean or overbearing as he'd been described. He had short, wispy grey hair and lots of lines on his face.

She turned to her mother, who nodded with permission before she obliged. The man's hands were soft and not at all like Papa's hands. "I'm pleased to finally meet you," he said with a sigh. "I'm just sorry it took me so long to do so. I'm a stubborn old coot."

"When your Mama ran off with your Papa, I was very sad." The man shifted from her to her Mama. "I waited and waited for them to come home, but when they didn't, I didn't want to admit I was wrong. By the time you were a baby in diapers, I was too ashamed to come see you. Too much time had passed. I didn't think any of you would want me around. If it were not for Lorraine, your Grandma, leaving me, I'd never be here. Isn't that silly?"

She did not know what to say. It was indeed silly. Mama beamed at the man.

Grandma took his hand and held it. "The moment I left he was already sending letters apologizing and promising to make it right. I told him about you and we both agreed that I needed to stay for a while."

"You knew all along!" Freya realized.

"Sweetheart, you look nothing like your parents. They probably didn't know what that meant, but I knew. Either my daughter had another fella around or my baby granddaughter, who knows more than I do, is not just an ordinary little girl."

The coach hit a bump, and everyone rocked within the carriage. "He's the one who sent the carriage. He knew about the town hall from hanging around the tavern."

That was the real reason Grandma went ahead of them. She wanted to meet with Grandpa and make sure the coachman was waiting outside. Freya was overwhelmed by the conspiracy, but there was a sense of validation. Her family did exactly what she expected them to do. They relied on each other, and a plan, not Freya's miracles.

The coach came to a stop. The coachman yelped and fell from his bench. Grandpa and Papa stepped outside first. She could hear the voices of her grandparents—and someone new. Mama was blocking her view. Grandma got out as well. She was so afraid her head was dizzy.

After several moments, Papa said, "Freya, you can come out now."

She stepped out of the coach behind her mama. The carriage was unstable and shifted a little when her mother stepped off. She peeked behind Mama's skirts to find a man with them. He was tall and had shoulder-length brown hair with eyes bluer than buckets of water. He wore a long, dusty jacket.

She was a bit wobbly, but his eyes were wide and full of anxiety. He swallowed hard and said, "Hello."

The man got down on one knee, and she slowly approached. His face was familiar to her, from one of her dreams perhaps, and she wasn't afraid of him.

She took his hand in hers and traced the scar on the palm before examining his face with her fingers.

She remembered something—a name. It called from inside her like a promise. "Come back to me, Aegis."

He choked a cry and nodded. "That's right. I'll always come back to you."

He was her Aegis. She embraced him then. He smelled of the forest and of citrus and he was her best friend—other than Kitty.

"We don't have much time," he told her. "Outlanders have escaped the seventh region."

The family let out stifled gasps.

"They're coming from the fourth region. I think they are coming for you."

"Who told them?" Papa demanded.

Aegis stood to face the family. "Vinicio has spies and connections. I should have killed him when I had the chance."

"No," she said. "It is my charge. Take me to the town square."

Aegis stepped away and shook his head before the objections from her parents and grandparents struck in chorus. She turned and faced her family and gave them the most commanding voice she could manage.

"I am the queen, and this is my job. Just as it's your job to plow the fields and rear the cattle, it is my job to ensure that the evil in this world does not run rampant. If you don't let me do this, I will never be safe, and neither will anyone else."

Mama was now sobbing in Papa's arms as if she had been given a death sentence. Papa only shook his head in disbelief. It was Grandpa who spoke. "Good to know I'm not the most stubborn one in the family."

Grandma eyed him before he got an elbow in the ribs. "But you're still the biggest ass."

Aegis appeared torn. His eyes pleaded with her family—either for forgiveness or intervention, she couldn't tell. This didn't mean her childhood had to be over, she just needed to finish something that was started before her time.

"I realize it must be difficult, taking orders from a child when her parents do not approve, but you have no choice. You understand that, right?"

This was enough to get his attention. His eyes fell to the palm of his hand before he nodded. Aegis picked her up and it was all too familiar, like finding a long-lost security blanket. Yes, wherever she went, he would follow, and that was how it should be.

"We won't make it in time unless she comes with me," Aegis said. "Meet us there."

# Chapter Thirty

The town square was the largest and the most central point of the town. It was the only part of the road that was cobbled with stone before it carried on all the way to the edge of the second region and onwards. If someone followed the road, it would ultimately lead to the palace itself. She would one day travel down that road—one day soon if this didn't go right.

Here, she stood on her own two feet. "Go stand over there," she told Aegis. "I don't want them to know who I am just yet."

The stench hit her first. The outlanders did indeed smell putrid. The infection and disease they brought with them was stifling the clean country air. They marched out of time but in a solid formation, singing a nasty song about what they wanted to do with the women in the towns as they carried a makeshift litter overhead. On the litter was a slight man with dark hair that greyed on the sides.

He smiled widely in amusement, and the march stopped. "Is this all the third region has to fight with? A little girl?"

She pretended as though she were scared and began to cry. It wasn't that hard to do; she was indeed frightened by the mob. Tears streamed down her cheeks while the hoard laughed. This was an army, poised at retaking the palace by sheer force and numbers. Every creature in the seventh region was in this shamble of an army, and the military the palace had was spread out too thin to take them on.

Though it appeared that hadn't stop anyone from trying. Many of the outlanders were wounded. Fresh blood stained their scarred and mutilated flesh. The berserkers, more monsters than men, had metal jutting from their flesh like armor. They stood on the outside while the slighter villains took center.

"March on!" Vinicio ordered. "Take the girl for whatever entertainment you'd like." He made sure to say it loud enough so that the people hiding indoors could hear them. Fear and propaganda were Vinicio's aim, to do what people feared the most.

"You look a little worse for wear, Vinicio," she said.

Vinicio's smile grew cold. He shook his head. "No, they said no one could find you. That Aegis was asleep—"

That was when Aegis stepped from his hiding spot, and the whole outlander army flinched. She smiled. Yes, they knew better than to tangle with Aegis. They didn't know she was here after all. They were counting on her being lost and Aegis asleep, leaving the palace mostly defenseless.

Vinicio probably intended to use one of the secret passages to get in and lower the bridge to allow the black souls to ransack the castle. The outlanders would be his personal army until they all killed each other and probably everyone else along with them.

It was preposterous that this man had once haunted her so profoundly in a former life. He was no more than a man to her now. A brilliant and resourceful man, but she did not fear him. His smile reminded her of the desperate faces pleading for miracles at the town hall meeting. She understood that, for Vinicio, this was his only chance at survival. He could not go back, and she respected him for that. She did not harbor the same resentments her last incarnation held. It was simply time to end all of this.

"You all carry so many memories," she told the ghastly crowd. "Memories of pain and wrongdoing, of abuse and trauma. But no more. Kneel, and I shall give you a fresh slate."

The rabble wavered, and the litter was lowered despite their leader's instruction.

"It's a trick, you fools!" Vinicio shouted as the litter disappeared in the crowd. There were so many of them. So much pain at the hands of a region for things they did not remember doing. The

Outlanders filled the plaza and surrounded her. Aegis stood beside her, ready to shield her against whatever.

"Come, I will release you from it all."

"You would really let us go? All of us?" a man missing an eye said. His empty socket glared at her.

They were evil, but what stood before her were lifetimes of hurt. She nodded. "Enough of this. None of you will be returning to the seventh region."

Even Vinicio's lips trembled. Countless numbers had kneeled before her. This had gone on long enough.

She tilted her head upward to better observe the sea of rotten people before her. She closed her eyes and gave a gentle nod. When she opened her eyes, there were countless bodies on the ground. She had given them all painless deaths, even Vinicio. She turned to Aegis who was scanning the battleground for signs of life.

"They will go to the other world and live out their lives. Their slates are clean," she said.

People were looking through their windows. Lights were being lit. "Are you going to leave all these bodies?" Aegis asked.

Freya hadn't honestly put much consideration into that part. She supposed it would be bad manners to leave the bodies everywhere.

With a wave of her tiny, trembling hand, the bodies dissipated into tiny purple flowers scattered along the winds. It was their souls that mattered to her. They would never again be allowed to accumulate into an army large enough to sweep through the regions of Hell.

"You going back to the castle now?" he asked.

"No," she said. "I still have some growing up to do."

"For the love of Hell, don't make me go back without you."

# Epilogue

It was decided that Hacia would remain the steward of Hell until Freya became a few years older. She and Alfie had several more children, four altogether. They ran rampant around the palace, eventually causing old Rebus to retire.

Freya remained on the farm with her parents. Initially, her parents struggled with just how to discipline an omnipotent child, but she never used her powers after the battle of the town square. Not when Delilah was put down, not when Kitty vanished one night, not when her grandfather had a heart attack and passed away. She insisted on being a normal child, or rather, as normal as she could be.

Aegis seldom got into the family squabbles as he nothing but a hired hand. The vampire lived in the extended broom closet under the stairs. Papa tried to give him the guest bedroom multiple times, and he refused. He secretly preferred the broom closet because he wouldn't be obligated to decorate it.

The Outlanders took Minerva's remains and made a grotesque statue. It was immediately taken down by local trackers. Hacia had a memorial set up in its place beside the broken railway. There was no reason to rebuild it since no one wanted to go into the seventh region. There was talk of decommissioning the second railway as well, but those conversations would wait until Freya took the throne.

Aegis visited the memorial often with flowers. He would sit with the statue of her likeness for hours and sometimes days. He mourned her loss, but not once did he try to fall asleep. Freya suspected he blamed himself for her death, but no one truly knew how she died, as the gatekeepers were no longer at their posts.

While the townpeople still regarded Freya with curiosity, they had grasped reality once more. She was still wary of big events like barn-raisings or socials, but there was very little discussion about miracles after the battle of town square.

Just before her ninth birthday, Freya snuck out of the house and went to speak with the animals. The barn was now full of them. Old Pete walked dutifully behind her because Kitty was long gone.

"Your parents will be mad if they find you out past bedtime," Aegis warned.

Freya smiled and petted Sampson. "I'm just talking to the animals."

"I thought you didn't use your powers at all."

"I don't," she argued. "Well, it's a latent power. It's just something I can do."

He strolled beside her in the barn. "Are they happy?"

Aegis wasn't talking about the animals. She smiled. "Very much."

"Good," he said. "Enjoy it while it lasts. Queenship is a bitch."

Freya rolled her eyes—a new thing she'd learned at school. She followed behind him like the prisoner she was. Back to bed before her parents found out.

"I know, I know …"